i

South on Pacific Coast Highway

A Novel

Gary Paul Corcoran

Also by Gary Paul Corcoran

The Trip Into Milky Way
The Last Love of Eleanor Sands
It's Always Christmastime In Cratchitville
The Tribe
Postmark Paris: Destination Unknown
The Twelfth Commandment
Afghan's Lipstick Warriors: First Chronicle
Afghan's Lipstick Warriors: Darkness Falls
Afghan's Lipstick Warriors: The Deadly Sins

A Michael Devlin Sequel

Love in a Dying World

Coauthored by Gary Paul Corcoran

The Slow Train to Rishikesh
Purgatory: Origins
Storm Cloud Rising

Stargazer Press
Charlestown, Rhode Island

Published by Stargazer Press
Charlestown, Rhode Island
garypaulcorcoran.com
© *2013 Gary Paul Corcoran. All rights reserved*

Printed in the United States of America
ISBN 978-0615935379

Learn more about the author at
garypaulcorcoran.com

For Trie, we knew eternity for that little while,
moments that live on in my heart.
Thank you for the laughter.
I will always remember our laughter…

Acknowledgements

Maria Tover, for being a patient editor and her many kind words, Michael for the cover and his help with countless other invaluable things, Mr. Staggs for loaning this book his character and smile, Carolyn, a kind friend to all and a saint to every struggling LA writer, Joe and Fran for being such troopers at the last minute, the city of Laguna Beach for providing such a lovely and irreplaceable backdrop, the many haunts and establishments around Southern California, both named and unnamed, without which this story would have lacked its character, enchantment and color, Vic, over in Parks & Maintenance, for setting me straight about those Hollywood twisted junipers, Chandler, Hammett, et al, who intrigued me with their hardboiled characters and stark settings as a boy growing up, Gretchen for loaning me her I-pad and last but not least, every kind soul who has shown their interest in my work over the years.

South on Pacific Coast Highway

South on Pacific Coast Highway

1

Dropkicked from a lousy dream, I bolted upright and stared into the darkened room, not knowing where I was, not knowing how I had gotten there. Just lost and confused and thinking oh god no, not again, Michael. What town have you landed yourself in this time?

I jumped, feeling the woman stir beside me. Stole a look and saw that she was sprawled face down the other way, the back of her head facing me, her wispy dark hair etched with white scalp lines. A blonde wig sat on her nightstand. A glass ashtray was parked next to the wig, spilling over with cigarette butts. A spent pack of Benson & Hedges completed the composition.

God help me.

I looked forward in the darkness, fishing among the ruins of my mind for answers. I vaguely remembered something about a bar but nothing precisely about her or how we had met. I racked my brain but could not recall a single detail.

I had started to look for my phone when the woman moaned and rolled over towards me. I froze, then watched her being chased around in her own lousy dream.

I looked forward again, unable remember a thing. About her. About the time and place. About any of it.

I was thinking of the phone again and how best to escape when another jolt of adrenalin shot through my brain. I was supposed to be tailing a client's wayward wife right then, not slumming around in a strange woman's bed.

Carefully, I slipped out from beneath the covers and poked around among the clothes on the floor. Disentangled my briefs from her bra and pulled them on with another wary look her way. Located my dress shirt next and buttoned it while feeling around on the carpet with my bare feet, still looking for the phone. I checked in my sportscoat and all around that side of the bed and then around on hers but nothing. And no sign of her phone either. It was probably in her purse there on the floor. I thought about looking inside but blew it off. She'd probably wake up and think I was trying to rob her.

Christ. If I just knew the time, I'd know a lot of things. A lot more than I did right now.

I found my slacks and took in the rest of the room while getting them on. The woman clearly had a thing for baubles and knickknacks. They lurked everywhere in the grainy darkness.

My vision froze on a herd of cat figurines, gathered together atop a shabby chic dresser, their long stylized necks and heads turned my way, as if sincerely wanting to tell me something.

Jesus, Michael. Get a grip.

I went looking for my socks and found one lodged in a dried floral arrangement. The entire arrangement was encrusted with a few decade's worth of dust and mold. The veneer paneling behind it was peeling away. A cobweb was doing lazy ballets up by the ceiling line. Oh god. This was just way too close to the wrong side of the tracks.

I found the other sock and stood up with a faded out Peter Max print staring me in the face. Oh yeah. Peter Max. I had almost forgotten how much I hated him. Max and his whole kitschy pop culture schtick. Some psychedelics, a flower in your hair and a joyous fairyland awaited you. Yeah right. There weren't any joyous fairylands out there awaiting me. I had taken a wrong turn back down the road somewhere. A thousand lifetimes of misplaced fortunes and bad luck were straight ahead.

I shook my head. Just ditch the rants and find your phone, Michael. You need to get out of here before this '70s wormhole completely swallows you.

I had turned to start looking again when the window curtains flapped in the breeze.

Wait. I went back and parted the curtains. The far horizon was etched with hues of burnt orange and pastel pink.

Now there was a clue.

I dropped the curtain and looked back into the darkened room. But was it dawn? Or that smoky hour just before nightfall?

I had no idea.

And then it all came flooding back, all the cringeworthy memories came flooding back. The cheering crowd. The man doing handstands on a barstool. Then more cheers as he hand-walked from one end of the bar to the other, a martini glass balanced on the bottom of each shoe.

I stood there, remembering it all now, ashamed.

Then the exact moment I had met this woman rushed back into my thoughts. There, opposite me at the bar, achingly voluptuous with her red lipstick and piles of lustrous blonde hair. I had sent her a drink and switched barstools and before long the two of us were dashing over here to her place, clothes flying as we backed into her bedroom. I recalled that much and a lot of smutty sex, but the rest of last night's drunken escapades remained a complete blank.

I pulled on my sportscoat, gathered up my shoes, had one last quick look for the phone, decided it must be back in the car, prayed that it was and headed for the door. My only other hope was to make a clean escape but the hinges creaked as the door opened and the woman's face came around.

Well, that much was a relief. The room had brightened ever so slightly and I could see her now. She had a touch of Monroe's cherubic beauty about her, however much forty years of cigarettes, heartaches and hard luck had taken their toll.

I smiled, as best I could under the circumstances.

"Hi…I uh…"

I gestured to let her know I was at a loss. She hid her face under the pillow.

"It's Rhonda."

The words came out muffled. I stared back, still scrambling for some kind of graceful exit.

Rhonda peeked out again. I gave her my best shot at another smile.

"So, hey…it was nice meeting you."

She disappeared back beneath the pillow. A demonstrative nod followed.

"Okay, well, look, I'm late for work, so…"

Nothing. No response.

Haunted by what I knew and didn't want to know, equally, but already busted, I returned to the bed with my shoes and socks.

Before leaving, I bent down and kissed the back of Rhonda's neck. Her hand came around and touched my face. It was a nice hand.

"Sorry," I said. "I saw you were dreaming and didn't want to wake you."

She gently squeezed and I squeezed back.

"Okay. I'll see you again."

Again, no response. I gave her hand a last kiss and went off to use the bathroom.

Outside in the growing light, the lies I had just told went on haunting me. Every morning there seemed to be another Rhonda, and every morning another round of BS.

"Hey, it was great meeting you…I'll see you again."

When I never would.

I climbed into my Impala, found the phone on the floorboard, got the car started and whipped around in the street, racing against the clock now. If I didn't catch Debbie before she headed out for the day, there went a paycheck, and I needed a paycheck.

Having no time to shave and shower, I stopped for an espresso at a drive thru joint on Coast Highway, threw in a banana nut muffin and hurried on to Debbie's apartment, relieved to find her car still parked at the curb. I got the Impala situated a safe distance down the block and settled in to wait.

Feeling like hell from all the late night boozing, I grabbed the metal flask out of my console and splashed a bit of bourbon into my coffee. The seconds ticked by and turned to minutes, the minutes to an hour, then two. Shame and regrets plagued my moments alone.

One prayer kept repeating. Please make your move, woman. I don't want to be sitting here all day.

Personally, I could not have cared less what Debbie did with her life but a thirty-something iron worker named Jake had hired me to put a tail on her. Decent enough guy, that Jake, but a fool in love, as most men were. His wife files for divorce and he springs for someone to shadow her.

That said, there were bigger fools in this world. Jake suspected Debbie of being strung out on meth and figured he wouldn't have to pay as much in alimony if we could prove that fact. I had been keeping an eye on Debbie for a little over a day now, doing Jake's dirty work for him. That was my job and I had a license to prove it.

I was off draining my bladder behind some azaleas when old Debs finally popped out the front door, sporting oversized tortoise-shell shades, bruises on her arms and looking in roughly the same shape I was. I hurried back to my Impala and followed her out the canyon away from the coast, and eventually onto the freeway, headed north.

Half an hour later, we were zigzagging through the rough streets of west Santa Ana. If you liked gangs, tattoos, pit bulls and chain link fences, this was your kind of place.

Debbie eventually parked in the driveway of a stucco house and disappeared inside. The house was a grim looking thing, the tan stucco bleached close to white by the sun and the front lawn more or less the color the house should have been. Clearly no one had bothered to water the grass for a number of years. There were iron bars over the windows and a Ciudad Juárez grade screen door in front. Every house on the block looked like it had been transported out of a warzone.

I parked several houses down and left the car idling with the air-conditioner on low. A maze of asphalt streets and power lines radiated out around me for fifty miles in every direction. The entire LA basin was wavering in the summer heat. I knew the San Gabriel Mts. were out there on the horizon somewhere but you would never have known it with all that smog.

Resigned to a long wait, I turned on some new age music and settled down lower in the seat.

I hadn't been there ten minutes when a car full of gangbangers cruised by. They turned around and came back in a crawl, trying to size me up through the tinted glass. On the third pass, I grabbed my .38 out of the glovebox and set it on the front seat, though what I hoped to prove with a pistol, I wasn't exactly sure. Those boys were probably sporting an assortment pack of Uzis, front and back.

When I wasn't otherwise distracted by the threat of a drive-by shooting, I had my eyes on the bleached stucco house. The seconds dragged by like a man waiting for the gallows.

Thankfully, Debbie popped back out the front door an hour later, hanging onto some biker looking trash. I grabbed my camera and started clicking off shots. They both looked abundantly stoned, and that was proof enough for me. As those two meth freaks climbed onto a Harley and motored off deeper into hell, I turned the other way and made a dash back down the interstate to Laurel Lagoon.

In need of a drink, I settled for a fresh dress shirt out of my trunk and a splash of cologne before heading down to the oceanfront bar at the Surf & Sand Hotel. There were lovelier places to hide away from the world, but not many. The shore was right there, all sailor-blue and bristling white. Balmy breezes rustled in through the open windows. Seashell dreams whispered all about the shady interior. If that place failed to comfort your heart, you probably didn't have a pulse.

I had that much going for me, offered the bartender a tally ho with the first drink and turned around to take in a summer day at the beach. What a relief. You could not get much farther from seashell dreams than the west side of Santa Ana and still be in Orange County.

I quickly polished off the first drink, ordered a second one and sat back with the bristling white surf soothing my jangled nerves.

The hours passed. The drinks added up and soon afternoon was tiptoeing into the mystery of dusk. Surrounded now by an overly chirpy happy hour crowd, and still a bit bruised from last night's debauchery, I offered my best Jean Gabin every time someone tried to get too chummy from the next barstool.

I wouldn't have minded one of the dolls saying hello. The rest of it you could keep.

In all of that, Rhonda returned to my thoughts. If not for the wig. I considered driving by her place but that idea came up hard against my conscience. If it wasn't going to be all the way, what was the point?

In the end, I decided to head downtown and check on things at my office. Pretend to be responsible for a spell before heading back home to my favorite bottle.

I caught a break when someone was backing out as I pulled up to the front of my office building. I grabbed his slot and jumped out. A wild summer night at the beach was in full swing, the sidewalk packed as thick as a small-town carnival. I slipped through the crowd and dashed upstairs. The door to my office opened with a blast of hot muggy air. Half a block up from the beach and there wasn't a breeze in the world.

Very much weary of the sultry heat, I began to question the wisdom of having abandoned my barstool at the Surf & Sand. There was a thought to head back. Have a few more drinks.

Maybe Rhonda would appear. The wig aside, she had looked a bit like Marilyn Monroe.

Instead, I leaned back at my desk and surrendered to what I could not seem to escape. I had been trying to kick a handful of dreams for the better part of five years now, without much luck. And it was long past time to get honest about where those dreams had landed me.

I had been seated there in the dark for a good long spell, watching the kaleidoscope of lights and shadows made by passing cars, when the phone rang. I glanced that way with the usual flicker of hope.

Was it her? But no, it never was. It never would be again.

The caller ID read the Laurel Lagoon Police Department. Detective Whalen, I assumed. I could not imagine anyone else calling me from the police station at that hour and had no interest in talking to him.

About the tenth ring, I gave in and answered on speakerphone.

"Devlin here."

"Michael, it's Steve…Steve McPherson?"

Steve McPherson? What in the world was he doing, calling me from the police station? I grabbed the receiver and turned off the speaker.

"Hey Steve. What's going on? I didn't recognize your voice. What are you doing down at the police station?"

"Connie's dead."

"What!?" I slumped back in my chair. "Oh god no. What on earth happened?"

"I don't know, man. I really don't know anything right now. The cops said she'd been strangled. They found her body out by Irvine Lake this afternoon and came by my house a few hours ago to question me."

"And what? Arrested you?"

"Yeah."

"For what?"

8

"Well I guess I kind of lost it there when they started to question me."

"They dragged you in for losing it?"

"Well, shit, Michael. They started grilling me like I was the one who had killed my own wife and I mean, I really lost it. Then next thing I know, I'm face down on the front porch with the cuffs on."

"Christ. So who was in charge? Detective Whalen?"

"Yeah, he was the lead cop. Do you know him?"

"Yeah, I know him. He's a decent enough guy, as far as cops go."

I sensed Steve cupping the phone.

"He was anything but decent with me. Someone murders my wife and he has to pull that shit on me? I was sitting around watching a ballgame in my boxers. Then I've got three cops in my face, giving me the third degree. Then all of a sudden, I'm out there on the front porch getting cuffed with the neighbors watching. I was waiting for somebody to order a pizza."

"God, Steve, I'm so sorry to hear this. Poor Connie. Jesus. This is just so hard to believe."

"I know. It's so totally fucked up. Anyway, I had one call and figured I'd better make it you. If they really think I did this, I'm going to need a criminal defense attorney and seem to remember you knowing one."

"Yeah, yeah, I know one. A good one."

"So? Suppose you can get in touch with him and get me out of here tonight?"

"Well, no problem with calling Jim. I'll do that as soon as we get off but I'm not so sure anyone can spring you tonight. Do you know if they actually charged you with something or are they just holding you on suspicion?"

I sensed Steve cupping the phone again.

"Whalen charged me with resisting arrest. I don't know what else he's thinking but I heard him talking about taking me up to county jail in a little while."

"All right, hang on. I'd better call Jim right away, but like I said, I don't know if anyone can get you out of there at this hour. We'll give it our best shot. That's all I can promise. If not, we'll get you out first thing in the morning."

"I didn't do it," Steve said.

I heard him break down.

"I don't care if she had filed for divorce and all that. I still loved her. I still do. I never would have hurt a hair on her head."

"I know, Steve. Hell, we've known each other since we were kids."

I let Steve have a good go at his emotions, relieved that he had proclaimed his innocence without me asking. Did you do it, Steve? Did you kill your soon to be ex-wife? Business was business but you hated to pop a question like that on a man, especially one in grief, and especially when he was one of your oldest friends.

"Okay, the cop's gesturing for me to get off. Get in touch with my parents, okay?"

"Sure. I'll call them as soon as I get off with Jim. And I'll walk up there to have a talk with Whalen. See what's on his mind. You hang in there in the meantime, all right?"

"Yeah. I'm trying."

"Okay, I'd better call Jim. I'll see you in a bit."

"All right."

"Oh, hey," I heard Steve saying before I could hang up.

I brought the phone back up to my ear.

"Yeah Steve, what?"

"Can you go by and do something about my dog?"

"Dog? When did you get a dog and what kind is it?"

I had visions of a giant Rottweiler and dreading the task.

"It's a miniature poodle. Connie had one and I thought, maybe if I got one too, I could win back her heart...I know. Stupid of me."

"Yeah, well, I'll see what I can do."

"Please. I don't want to leave him up there all alone. He'll at least need to be fed and let outside tonight."

10

"Yeah, all right. What's its name?"

"Butch."

Of course, I thought with a look to the heavens.

"All right. I'll deal with it."

"The house key's inside a fake rock by the front door."

"All right, and just hang in there. We'll get you out of this mess as soon as we can."

"Thanks, man. God, I can't even believe this is happening."

As soon as the phone went dead, I dialed my attorney Jim Harrison's number.

Miniature poodle, I thought while listening to the phone ring. I was picturing one of those Westminster Kennel Club numbers, fur balls on its tail and paws, nervous as a gerbil. What the hell was Steve thinking? What the hell was I going to do with the little monster?

Jim answered after several rings. His Mississippi roots came right through the phone; laidback, laconic, like a sultry summer breeze whispering through the bayou willows. Being a loner like me, I pictured Jim kicked back in his easy chair, a brief in his lap. I quickly explained the situation with Steve.

"You know this guy that well?"

"Yeah. I guess he kind of blew it there with the cops this afternoon but he wouldn't hurt a flea."

"They've said that about a lot of guys with dead bodies in their basements."

"Jim, you want to know if I'd go out on a limb for this guy? I would."

"All right. Because I don't want to be out there all alone."

"I'm walking up to the station right now to talk with Whalen."

"I'll call and make sure they don't haul your friend up north before we've had a chance to talk with him."

"Thanks, Jim. I'll see you there in a few."

I was about to call Steve's parents but decided to gather a bit more information first. My next impulse was to pour myself a shot of bourbon but I decided to hold off on that, too. I owed

11

Steve a clear mind. I owed myself a clear mind, but that was another story.

I went out into the hallway with the flaking plaster walls and the hundred year old floral carpets. The worn wooden stairs creaked and groaned as I hustled down to the street. The landlord rarely dropped a dime on the place but rarely raised the rent and never came around to bother anyone, and that was a good enough tradeoff for me.

2

As I waded back into the crowded sidewalk, a pair of twenty-something dolls strutted past me, heading down towards Coast Highway. I heard one of them whisper, "Obsessing."

They both stole a look over their shoulders and giggled. I stopped to stare, ready to sell my soul for a handful of kicks. Both of them were wearing Barbie Doll shoes and I was a sucker for Barbie Doll shoes. I was a sucker for any woman with nice feet and red toe nail polish. Plus-sized, pushing sixty, it didn't seem to matter all that much to me.

Remembering Steve, I reluctantly turned up the street the other way.

The minute I crossed Beach Lane, the street grew dark around me and the hubbub died away. Not a thing was stirring in the sultry heat, not even the Ficus trees.

I came to Third Street and hustled across the intersection. City hall was straight ahead, this bit of mission revival architecture with a red tile roof. A belfry right out of Cordoba accented the roofline. Two Hollywood twisted junipers adorned the fire station in front. One stately pepper tree and a handful of eucalyptus shrouded a grassy courtyard off to the left.

Over on my right, across a short alley from the police station, a nicely tiled fountain gurgled in front of the water department. In Southern California, water departments always smelled of money, lots and lots of money.

The police station occupied the backside of the fire station. I started around that way. A couple of news trucks were already parked up on the street behind it. The vultures had arrived. One of them, Bernie, was reaching for the wooden door of the station as I walked up. Bernie was the equivalent of a cop on the baseball stadium beat. He had secured a cushy gig down at the beach and there was no tearing him away from it.

"You here about the McPherson murder?" he asked me.

"Nope. Just feeling lonely tonight."

"Come on, Devlin. You know something?"

"I can't say a word right now, Bernie."

"Fine. See if I play ball with you next time you need help."

"Yeah, yeah."

Bernie opened the door for me and we stepped into a madhouse. Dirk Vanderhof, an online gambling mogul was being fêted for a $100,000 donation he had made to the Policemen's Association. He and the police chief were holding up a beach towel sized poster of the check for a gaggle of photographers. Vanderhof was all smiles, the chief not so much. Given Vanderhof's reputation, you had to figure the more temperate law and order types would have to hold their noses a bit over that one.

I hid well back among the crowd, having little use for Dirk Vanderhof and expecting he felt the same about me. Fortunately, he was too busy hamming it up for the press to notice my arrival. A few moments later, the festivities swept him out the back door. The photographers went the way of the party and things quickly quieted down.

I was left face to face with a petulant looking cadet at the front desk. I had seen this kid in years past, trolling for action outside the Boom Boom Room. Now he was apprenticing at the police station. Only in Laurel Lagoon.

"I'm here to see Whalen," I told him.

He stared petulantly, thinking to disappoint me. Whalen must have heard my voice and called out from his back office.

"Send him in!"

The young cadet hit the buzzer and the gate opened. I winked going by. Pat was sitting at his desk. I flopped down in the opposite chair.

Pat had been a lifeguard in town when he was a young man and still looked the part — his blonde hair cut in a butch, his once boyish face still tanned and taut, albeit with a few lines it had acquired over the years. Setting aside Pat's age and the way he had beefed himself up with the weights, you could easily picture him in a photo dated 1990, goofing off for the chicks with a lifeguard buoy strapped across his chest.

"What's going on?" I asked him.

"They're making a big to do over Vanderhof's hundred grand donation. Did I miss something?"

He hadn't bothered to look up from the file in his hands.

"I'm talking about Steve McPherson."

"Oh that," Pat said, still not looking up. "Well, don't worry yourself too much. Your bleeding-heart attorney just called in."

"Spill it, Pat. The guy gets a little upset when you accuse him of killing his own wife and you have to haul him in?"

"He got more than a little upset."

"What the hell kind of evidence is that?"

Pat finally glanced up from the file in his hands.

"Look, whatever I've got on him, it's none of your business."

"Come on, Pat. My bleeding-heart attorney is going to make it his business in a couple of minutes."

The squawk box crackled out front. Pat threw the file down on his desk.

"I'm holding him, that's all."

"Nice work, Pat."

"What?"

"Your bluff. Talking like you were ready to haul Steve up to county jail, and just loud enough for him to hear it. See if that would scare him into saying something you wanted to hear, since you didn't like what was coming out of his mouth up to that point."

Whalen scoffed.

15

"His wife was divorcing him and we've already heard from a half dozen witnesses that he was plenty pissed off about it."

"With that logic, I've got a couple hundred thousand murder cases you'll need to solve this year. In Orange County alone."

Pat stared.

"Come on, Pat. Admit it. People get divorced all day long without killing each other."

"Yeah? Well this is one case where somebody did get killed, didn't they?"

I heard voices out in front. It was Jim. Whalen shook his head with a look to the heavens.

"Send him in!" he called out to the petulant cadet.

Jim appeared a moment later, tall and lean, with shaggy hair and slumped shoulders. The detached look on Jim's face suggested he had just noticed the weight of the world was on his back and was deciding what to do about it.

Jim shook my hand, nodded at Whalen and took a seat. A notebook and pen came out.

"All right," Whalen said. "Let's get this straight right now. I've got nothing solid on the murder yet, but I've got all kinds of circumstantial evidence pointing in his direction and he started a scuffle with me and Fowler, so I'm holding him for twenty-four hours. If nothing pans out, I'll let him go. If it does?"

Whalen gestured.

"Let's start with whether or not you followed the law," Jim said.

"Oh, here we go." They stared at each other. "Yeah, yeah, I read him his rights. What do you think?"

"I think sometimes the police don't like to play by the rules."

Whalen had another look to the heavens.

"Have you established the cause of death?"

"Strangulation?"

Jim wrote in his notebook and looked up.

"Looks like it was some kind of thin rope or cord. I presume that's what you were wanting to hear. Would you like the name of the manufacturer?"

"The time of death?" Jim asked, ignoring Whalen's sarcasm.

"Sometime yesterday, late afternoon to early evening. Just when your friend back there has a gap in his story."

"We'll see about that," Jim said. "Any evidence that establishes Steve at the scene of the crime?"

Whalen drummed his fingers.

"This is going to be Giovanni's case over at the DA's office. Maybe you'd better direct the rest of your inquiry his way."

"All right," Jim said. "Get me a copy of the police report and I'll stop asking you questions."

"I'll have one for you in the morning."

"And just so we're on the same page here. No more questioning Steve without counsel present and I'll expect Giovanni to show probable cause within twenty-four hours or you let him go."

"Yeah, yeah," Pat said.

"And please don't go shipping him off to county jail unless you have probable cause."

"You done?"

"With you, yeah," Jim said, standing up. "But I'd like to have a word with my client."

Whalen stood up with a big sigh. Jim and I followed Pat back to the holding tanks. Steve stood up from the bench at seeing us, looking lost and scared. His dark hair was showing signs of gray. The once youthful face was looking haggard. Every cheerleader in high school had dreamed of winning Steve's heart but no one had dreams of winning it now.

Whalen unlocked the cell and we went in.

"Don't take all night," he said and locked the door behind us.

I introduced Steve and Jim and sat down. Steve joined me. Jim remained standing. I patted Steve on the knee

17

"I need to hear it from you right now," Jim said in a hushed voice. "Did you kill your wife?"

"No," Steve said without hesitation.

"All right. Have they questioned you?"

"They tried."

"What did you tell them?"

"I explained what I've been doing for the past few days."

"Which was?"

"Work, mostly. I had a beer with a buddy of mine on the way home last night."

"Where?"

"At Hennessey's. We caught part of a ballgame. I went home early today."

"What time did you leave work yesterday?"

"Around four."

"What time did you meet your buddy at Hennessey's?"

"Around seven."

"What did you do in between?"

"Nothing. I drove around a bit. Took a walk down at the beach."

"Anybody see you? Did you stop to buy something? Anything that might have left a record of your whereabouts?"

"No...At least not that I can think of."

Jim looked at me and back at Steve.

"What?" Steve said.

"They've pinned the time of your wife's death yesterday, late afternoon to early evening. Just when you seem to have a gap in your story."

"I didn't kill her."

Steve hung his head in his hands.

"I thought you were going to bring me a defense attorney, Michael. Not another cop."

"He's only trying to help you, Steve. If your story doesn't hold water with us, how do you think it's going to look up on a witness stand?"

Steve looked at me through his grief.

"Shit, I'm sorry. They've been questioning me for the last two hours like I killed my own wife and I had nothing to do with it."

"All right, let's get back to the facts," Jim said. "Have you had any kind of contact with your wife in recent weeks?"

"No. She won't even talk to me…I mean she wouldn't…"

Steve inhaled deeply and looked down.

"Anything I should know that you're not telling me?"

"No. Not that I can think of."

"Any idea who might have done this?"

Steve looked over at me and back at Jim.

"No, not really but a name came up in conversation with my friend Tim recently. The one I had a beer with. You ever heard of a guy named Dirk Vanderhof?"

Jim and I shared a glance.

"Yeah, I've heard of him," Jim said, looking back. "What do you know?"

"He was part of this crowd we hung out with after college. I haven't seen him for years but I was talking with Tim a few weeks back. His wife Lisa and Connie were close friends and I guess Tim overheard Vanderhof's name come up when the two of them were talking on the phone."

"And that's it?" Jim said.

"That's all I know. You can ask Tim but I'm pretty sure that's all he knows too. I'm guessing his wife would know more."

"What's your buddy's last name?"

"Durant."

"Phone number?"

Steve read it off to him.

"All right," Jim said. "I'll look into it. Now if Whalen and the DA don't have anything to charge you with within the next twenty-four hours, I'll file a writ of habeas corpus. But if they want to play rough, this could drag on until Monday. Either way, they have to come up with something or let you go. If they do charge you with murder, I'll see what I can do about getting the judge to grant bail. If we're lucky enough to get it, it's going

19

to be a lot. Maybe as high as a million. You'll need that much in collateral and ten per cent in cash. Any way you can come up with it?"

"With the help of my parents, yeah, probably."

"All right. I'll look into that too. In the meantime, if they try to question you again, you tell them you want to talk with your attorney."

Steve nodded. Jim was studying him.

"You know this is going to cost you some money."

"I know," Steve said.

"No need to discuss that now, but just so you're ready."

"I trust you."

Steve looked at me and back at Jim.

"If Michael recommends you, that's good enough for me."

"All right."

Jim reached out his hand and Steve shook it.

"Oh, have they fed you?"

"No."

"All right. I'll have them send something in. Hang in there. Hopefully we'll have you back out on the streets by tomorrow."

I stood up with Steve and gave him a hug.

"Sorry, old friend."

"I know," he said. "Poor Connie."

"I know, I know."

"Oh man," Steve said.

I gave him another hug.

"Thanks. Thanks for your help, Michael. You too, Jim."

Jim called for Whalen.

"Hey," Steve said. "Did you take care of Butch?"

"Not yet, but I'll drive up there. I promise."

"Okay, thanks."

Whalen appeared and let us out. He had a look for Steve, like he didn't trust the ground Steve walked on.

Jim and I followed Whalen back to his office. Whalen sat down. I did too. Jim remained standing.

"Please call me if you're going to charge him," Jim said.

"You'll be the first to know."

"And please get him some food. The man hasn't eaten since lunch."

"I'll see about bringing in a gourmet chef."

"A burger and some fries from the Cottage will do."

"Anything else? A massage and a movie?"

"I know you're just trying to do your job, Pat, and so am I."

Whalen gestured to say he wasn't all that moved by the détente.

Back out onto the street, Jim and I were swarmed by reporters. We pushed through their barrage of questions and ducked into Jim's car. He made a U-turn on Third Street and drove up until we were safely out of the hubbub before parking.

"Sorry about Steve losing it back there," I said.

"It's all right. If he's being falsely accused, he'd better be pissed. I'd be more concerned if he wasn't."

"Yeah, I suppose you're right."

"What about Vanderhof? What do you make of his name coming up?"

"You mean aside from the fact that Vanderhof's wife is divorcing him and I happen to be the guy who's been following him around for his wife's attorney the past few months?"

"Yeah, aside from that."

"I don't know. Coincidence? Connie and this friend's wife happened to have noticed his name in the news recently? He's had his fair share of publicity. I saw him at the police station just before you showed up, dropping off a $100,000 check to the Policemen's Association. Citizen of the year, they're calling him."

"What's your point?" Jim said.

I looked over at him.

"I don't know. I hate the son of a bitch for having so much money?"

Jim smiled, just the corners of his mouth turned up slightly, the eyes looking ironic.

"But as to Connie and Vanderhof, I never saw them together. For what that's worth."

"All right," Jim said. "You want me to send somebody else to chase after him?"

"No. I'm already all dressed for the occasion and they'd only be getting in my way."

Jim patted me on the shoulder.

"Go home and get some sleep. You look like hell. Anyway, there's nothing more either one of us can do for tonight."

"Yeah, as soon as I deal with Butch the miniature poodle."

"What's that all about?"

I explained.

"Well, there's a sign of true devotion," Jim said.

"Or the sign of a fool."

"You're getting to be cynical in your old age."

"Yeah, maybe. Well, keep me posted. I'll be in my office tomorrow morning. Hopefully somebody will darken my door dangling trinkets. Depending on how that goes, and the weather, I'll either be there, out on the road with the air-conditioning blasting or hiding out at the Surf & Sand. I'll have my cell phone on either way."

I got out of Jim's car and waded back down towards my office. The minute I crossed Beach, the sidewalk was packed again like a small-town carnival. I passed a couple speaking Farsi over ice cream cones in front of the art gallery next to my office door. That was Laurel Lagoon on a summer night. They should have put up a sign out on Coast Highway.

Little Tehran.

Back at my desk, I looked up Steve's parents and called them. His old man answered. He took the news pretty well, all things considered. I didn't expect it to go so well with Steve's mother. I mentioned the matter of bail, then Butch. The old man was ready to put up the house as collateral, if need be, but he didn't know what to say about the dog. Steve's folks lived down in North County San Diego. They were old and didn't drive much at night these days. I told the old man I'd take care of Butch for the time being and got off.

Jesus. What was I going to do with a poodle? I might as well walk around Laurel Lagoon with a purse.

I turned off the lamp and kicked my feet back up on my desk. A car went by, sending another kaleidoscope of geometric patterns across my ceiling and walls. I got lost in the ancient, unspoken feelings they seemed to evoke.

Giving in to a misguided notion, I flipped on a Coleman Hawkins CD. *It Never Entered My Mind* started to play. I hung my head. The old memories cut hard and deep. That first kiss, our first night out on the town, the pain of that still sweeter than anything else I had ever known.

So why had it come to this? Better yet, why couldn't I let it go? The woman was gone.

I had no answers but Solomon would have been proud of me. The heart of a wise man was in mourning, not mirth. So he had said. But all I had of wisdom was to regret the happiness I once held in my hands.

Unable to take another bar of the song, I reached to turn it off. Best to go up and take care of old Butch. I locked the door on my way out, went down to my car and pulled onto Coast Highway, headed south. Steve lived up in the hills on the far end of town.

I heard Butch barking away as I fished the key out of the fake rock. He went ballistic when I opened the door, like one of those miniature dogs you see locked up in a car at the supermarket. To Steve's credit, he had skipped the Westminster Kennel Club hairdo. Butch looked more like an overgrown piece of Berber carpet, apricot colored.

"It's okay, Butch," I said and squatted down to his level.

He sat down, still wary, but no longer barking.

"It's okay, Butch," I said again. "Come here. Come here."

He eventually slunk over, tail down like he anticipated a beating. Within moments, he was on his back, paws up in the air, in a state of ecstasy as I scratched his belly. He was awfully cute.

I looked around for Butch's leash, food and feeding bowls. Butch kept a watchful eye on the entire enterprise.

Back out at my Impala, I opened the passenger door and he jumped right up onto the front seat. A forlorn look followed.

A thought occurred to me so I went back inside the house, Butch still shadowing my every move. Out in the garage, I found a tall doggie seat in Steve's car and unbuckled it.

Back out at my car, and with the doggie seat installed, Butch jumped back in. We went down the road, Butch eagerly watching the world go by and Steve seemingly forgotten.

Back at the house, I fed Butch, let him outside to go potty, put some water out and made him a makeshift bed on the floor with some old towels. Then I took a long overdue shower. Butch parked himself in the doorway, Sphinx like while keeping an eye on me.

Before crawling into bed, I poured myself a stiff one from a bottle of bourbon—straight, no chaser. Butch stared on curiously as I had that one, and another.

When I finally crawled into the bed, Butch jumped right up there with me.

"No, no, Butch," I said and set him back on the towels.

"You've got the floor tonight, buddy."

I crawled back into bed with Butch staring at me from ground level, like some Sesame Street character, the mouth a straight line, inconsolable.

The little bugger was gunning for an Academy award. He certainly had my vote. After thirty seconds of that, I gave in.

"All right, goddamn it. Come on."

Butch jumped right up and lay down at my feet. This was not the way I had pictured my life turning out.

I lay there thinking about Connie's murder and trying to put two and two together but it was too damned late. My brain was mush. I promised to give them all hell in the morning and turned off the lamp.

3

I stepped back into my office the next morning at a little past nine with Butch on my heels. The temperature was already pushing ninety, with the humidity in the same general vicinity. That kind of sultry weather would drift up over the Mexican border from time to time; what the weathermen now referred to as monsoonal conditions. Since when, I wasn't sure, but mix in a bit of high pressure out over the desert and you had some kind of hell on your hands.

Feeling better than the previous morning, but not by much, another tactical retreat to the Surf & Sand Hotel was under consideration. I pulled the sweaty dress shirt loose from my back and glanced at the liquor cabinet behind me. A bit of the hair of the dog seemed to be in order.

I noticed Butch over there staring at me. Fine. I'll give it until noon.

In lieu of a drink, I grabbed the USB cable for my camera. Jake owed me money for that mission up to gangbanger land the previous day and I needed money. While the photos were uploading onto my computer, I reached for the phone and gave him a call.

"It's Devlin," I said when he answered.

"Did you get the photos of her?"

"Yeah, staggering out the front door with some biker trash."

"Fucking bitch."

I let him stew. If you hated the old flame, that probably meant you still loved her, so of course the idea of his wife doing another man had to be killing Jake. I assumed that would be true in spades if it involved some badass biker with chains and tattoos.

"But nothing of her inside," Jake said.

"You've got to be kidding me. I'm lucky I wasn't on the wrong end of a drive-by shooting."

"Shit," he said.

"Look, I IDed this biker character and he's got a rap sheet a mile long, including a meth lab bust, so these photos of them together is enough to prove intent. She didn't drive up there to get her nails done. With his history, let her explain this away to a judge."

"All right. What do I owe you?"

"Twelve hundred, minus the retainer."

"Shit."

"Look, I followed her around for two days and you already knew my rates."

"All right. Send me the photos and I'll send you a check."

"No, Jake. You come down here with a check and I'll hand you the photos."

"Come on, man. You've already got my retainer. I'm good for the rest. Just attach them to an e-mail and I'll put a check in the mail today."

I smelled a rat but did as asked.

"All right. They're on their way. Please don't screw me around."

"Don't worry about a thing, brother. I'll take care of you."

I got off the phone, plenty worried. Screwing other people around had become a career goal for a lot of folks in this world and I had no proof that Jake saw life differently. I added his invoice to a growing stack of unpaid bills and leaned back in my chair. There was a glance at the pink-brown smog gathering out near Catalina Island, then over at Butch. He was lying on the floor, panting away. I tried to unglue the cotton shirt from my back one more time and that got Butch's attention, but just the eyes.

27

What the hell was I going to do with the little bugger? I figured our relationship had a shelf life of about two or three days.

With a look back out at the coast, I had a sudden urge to head down south to my trailer in Baja. Once you got past all the garbage blown up against the border, and the clutter of Ensenada seventy miles farther south, the road jackknifed up into the coastal mountains and the journey took you back a hundred years in time. Vineyards carpeted the high valleys. Ramshackle farms dotted the hillsides here and there, slapped together with corrugated sheet metal, cardboard and old camper shells. After fifty miles or so of loping through oak and sycamore shrouded mountain passes, the road headed back down towards the coast along a rolling salt plain. The Sea of Cortez was to your back, just to the other side of a mountain range running north and south down the spine of the peninsula, and every afternoon, without fail, the high winds blew down from that direction like a venturi, turning the Pacific into a regatta; white caps and gulls and breaking surf as far as the eye could see.

My heart had grown lost in the imagery when the phone rang. I saw Jim's name on my caller ID and reached for the phone.

"Yeah, Jim."

"Giovanni just charged Steve with murder one."

"That prick. What for?"

"A couple of Connie's friends testified that Steve had been stalking her."

"Oh, goddamn it."

"You know about this?"

"Yeah. I guess he had been following her around when she first filed for divorce. The usual broken heart nonsense. Had to know if she was seeing another man. I told him to knock it off and leave that business to me and that was that."

"I don't like the smell of it."

"I'm telling you, Jim. I've known the man since we were kids. All through school, I never so much as saw him get into a fight. You never thought of Steve and violence in the same sentence."

"I'm trusting your instincts here, my friend, and stalking your wife alone isn't much to go on. It may just be a play of hand so Whalen and the DA can keep Steve behind bars for another seventy-two hours but he's headed to OCJ and there's nothing I can do about it now. Not until they arraign him. I'll press to get that done today but it'll probably take until Monday."

"All right. Did you have a chance to talk with this Tim Durant yet?"

"Spoke with him an hour ago. As best he could tell, Connie was chirping away about Vanderhof's wealth and good looks on the phone that day. Was she seeing him? Tim couldn't say, one way or the other."

"And his wife Lisa?"

"She's at work so I haven't had a chance to question her yet."

"All right. Thanks, Jim. Is Steve still up there at the police station?"

"Yeah, Whalen said it would be another hour or so before they could run him up north."

"Thanks. I'll give Whalen a call."

I had Whalen on the phone a minute later.

"Don't even try," he said upon hearing my voice.

"Come on, Pat. You got a murder weapon? A witness? Some DNA?"

"I've got probable cause and that's good enough for me right now."

"Shit, once you and the DA get a hard on like this, the good lord himself could come back to testify and it wouldn't change your minds."

"You done?"

29

"Yeah. I just wish you'd be reasonable for once. The man's not going anywhere. Why do you have to make his life miserable until you're sure?"

"It's done, Devlin, so why don't you get back to your husbands and wives stabbing each other in the back business."

I was about to give Whalen a piece of my mind but the phone went dead.

The bastard.

While I was still giving him a mental thrashing, the phone rang again. The caller ID read Cliff Black, a client who had called me from Seattle three days earlier. Purportedly, his wife was in some sort of trouble and the job description was to follow her around until he got back from his business trip. Only don't let her know I was doing so. A big red flag went up right there. It had been my thought to pass on the job. I needed another marriage going south like I needed another hole in the head but it was a job, and once again I needed the money.

I answered the phone and exchanged hellos with Cliff.

"What's the word?" I said.

"I arrived back to town late last night but my wife wasn't home when I got here. I've called her phone repeatedly but she's not answering. Do you happen to know where she is?"

'No, I..."

"When was the last time you saw her?"

"Two days ago. Look, she was at work and everything appeared to be fine so I left it there. I didn't want to waste your money. Did she leave a note or anything?"

"No."

"And you have no idea where she might be."

"None...Look, Mr. Devlin. I need to talk to you about what I had mentioned in our last conversation, but it needs to be in person."

"Okay. When were you thinking to stop by?"

"Right now, if that's possible."

"Right now, as in?"

"I can be there in fifteen minutes."

"All right. I'll be here at my office."

"I'll head out the door as soon as we're off."

I spun around in my chair and looked out the windows. Whalen was probably right. I was just a nickel and dime operator, with a specialty in husbands and wives stabbing each other in the back. Going by what Cliff had described to me on the phone from Seattle, it certainly sounded as if Mrs. Black was having an affair. Probably Cliff thought so, too. If she was in so much trouble, why were we being coy about me following her around?

According to Cliff, he had first grown suspicious when his wife took a sudden and unscheduled business trip to Phoenix the previous week. She had come home late that same night in a lousy mood, explained it away by saying a client was running her around and went off to bed without another word.

Over the next several days, Cliff became aware of Mrs. Black making hushed phone calls from their home office, the door conveniently closed each time. Sensing that something was up, Cliff decided to call me while on his business trip in Seattle. One of my former clients had referred him along.

Having related the aforementioned scenario, Cliff wanted to know what I thought. I told him it wasn't much to go on. It wasn't, but I had declined to reveal my suspicion that Mrs. Black was having an affair. Ditto my growing aversion to cheating wives and cheating husbands. I had had enough of infidelity and jilted lovers to last me a lifetime. I had seen one too many visions of marital bliss blown all to hell, and to me, Cliff sure sounded like one more jilted lover.

Unaware of my unstated reluctance on the phone that day, Cliff had pressed on. Before leaving on his business trip, he had stumbled across some information, something his wife appeared to have scribbled absentmindedly on her desk calendar while talking on the phone. It involved a very powerful individual and suggested to Cliff that his wife was in real danger. I had asked Cliff to go into more detail. He had declined to do so over the phone. As soon as he returned from

Seattle in a few days, he would stop by my office and explain everything in person. All he asked was that I keep an eye on his wife until he returned.

"I really, really love her," Cliff had assured me before we hung up. "Perhaps you can understand why I'm so concerned."

"Sure, sure," I had told him.

When someone hit you with the "I really, really love her" card, what were you supposed to say? Chances were, the woman's heart had moved on, but accept the fact? Like every other fool in this world, this one included, it appeared that Cliff was not ready to let go, at least not without a struggle. Faced with the obvious, few men ever were. Better to do a Kabuki dance in your head late at night. If only I did this. If only I did that. Surely I can make autumn leaves return to their trees.

Given my various aversions and reservations, I had gotten off the call with Cliff that day thinking, well, let's just leave things where they stand until he returns from Seattle. But then his deposit check had arrived the next morning, FedEx, first delivery, so I blew twenty-five bucks on a background check, learning, among other things, that Audrey had graduated from UCLA, class of '05, had acquired an MBA from Pepperdine, had done a ten year stint with a Fortune 500 company and now ran a private consulting firm with a go getter named Rick Duncan. They had a cozy little office up the coast. I smelled afternoon sex all over his back office.

My suspicions aside, I had called up to their consulting firm that morning and Audrey answered. I immediately liked the voice, with reservations. It was sweet and melodic, but way too corporate for my tastes.

I gave her a line about being a potential client and we talked. While doing so, someone shouted out in the background. I assumed it to be her partner, Rick Duncan. There was the sound of the phone being cupped in Audrey's delicate little hand and her muffled voice.

"Sorry," she said in coming back. "That was my business associate. He wasn't aware of me being on the phone."

I let her off the hook for their sloppy professionalism. Who was I to judge?

As to telling Cliff that I had seen his wife two days earlier, I was going by the phone call, but that was as good as a visual sighting in my book. My primary question had been answered. Secret affair or not, everything seemed to be peachy in Audrey's world. I had made a discreet exit from the phone call and was now waiting for Cliff to arrive at my office.

The fifteen minutes went by, then another fifteen, and still no sign of him. I did not mind people being late, but call me. My time was as valuable as yours. Apparently some folks disagreed.

While seated there, I heard the sound of children's laughter echoing up from the shore. It was summertime down at the beach — umbrellas and ice chests, beach towels and sun tan lotion — a crowd of carefree souls down there frolicking around in the surf. If not for Steve's problems, and this unwelcome appointment with Cliff, I would have headed down to the shore myself. Pulled off my loafers and stuck my toes in the surf for a spell.

I was lost in daydreams when a silhouette appeared outside my frosted glass door. I sat up, preparing to look professional, but it was only my neighbor Betty from down the hall. She cracked the door open and poked her head in.

I waved for her to make the complete entrance and she did.

"I heard you talking earlier and thought maybe you were still on the phone."

"Just talking to myself."

Betty laughed. Both her voice and laughter were gravelly from all the cigarettes. Her aura was tinged with gray from all the smoke.

"Oh my god!" she said, noticing Butch. "He's adorable!"

Butch went right over and let out with a coyote howl, a couple of them in a row, the mouth in a big "O", the front paws bouncing up off the floor with each one.

Betty and I laughed.

33

"What brought this on?" she asked.

"The poodle or the howl?"

"Both."

"The howl, I don't know. It's the first time I've heard it. The poodle? You know, when in Laurel Lagoon…"

She laughed again.

"What's her name?"

"His. Butch."

I explained the situation.

"Aw, I'll take care of him for you."

"You will?"

"Sure. You need a nice little home, don't you, Butchie?"

He was on his back now, paws up, all love and kisses.

Betty's husband Leonard went by out in the hallway.

"Look," Betty said. "One of Michael's friends got arrested so Michael's watching his dog. I'm taking him home."

Leonard nodded without a smile and continued down the hall. He and Betty had come out from Jersey the previous year, Italians, the last name right out of the mob. Together they ran an online cosmetic supply business. Betty handled the phones. Leonard handled collections. She was the dame. He was the goodfella with the oversized reading glasses hanging from a gold chain around his neck. Their specialties were hair products and a line of ponytails. Betty was sixty something trying to look forty with her stretch slacks, Barbie Doll shoes and empire-waist blouse. She had a figure. I'd give her that much. I was still trying to decide if the smoky blonde hair piled up on her head was real or not. The 'do was somewhere between Phyllis Diller and Farrah Fawcett. Probably a bit more to the Diller side of things.

"What's on your mind?" I asked her.

"Oh, this heat's driving me crazy. What do you say we hit up Lars for some air-conditioning?"

"We'd have better luck trying to find a couple of natives to fan us."

She looked askance, like I might try to bill her for the joke.

"You're a real character. Why don't you give him a call?"

"Why don't you?" I said.

"You're no fun."

"It's no fun asking Lars to make improvements. Look at the place. Besides, he'll just raise the rents. Is that what you want?"

There was another tap on the door and the mailman came in. He was mulatto looking with a blue bandana tied around his head.

"Here's your native with the palm fronds," I said to Betty.

That got another chuckle out of Betty. The mailman smiled warily, sensing he had been made the butt of a joke.

"Hot one," he said and reached out with my mail.

"Hot one," I said. "Betty here needs someone to fan her. Ten to four, if you're looking for extra work."

With another wary smile, the mailman did a double take on Butch and went out the door. I turned back to Betty.

"You were saying?"

"Okay, I'll just have Leonard call the landlord."

"Now you're talking. Sic the Italians after him."

"Thanks for nothing," she said. "Come on, Butchie."

"Here, you may as well take his bowls."

Butch did his howl and trotted after Betty as if I had never existed. I watched them disappear, feeling as if my life had veered way too close to a bad sitcom. Betty and the old man lived next door. I was the neighbor who stopped by for a glass of cheap cabernet and an episode of CSI now and then. Betty had Butch in her lap on a Bellagio sofa. Her ashtray was always filled with cigarette butts. I had other places to go but could never seem to get back out the front door. We were a movie within a movie, life imitating art.

I slumped down in my chair and turned the small fan on my desk more directly at my face.

Tough break for those two. They had sold their home in Hackensack, expecting to find orange trees and a Mediterranean climate. Instead, they had been greeted with monsoons. At least in Jersey they had four seasons.

35

The phone rang. Seeing it was my mortgage broker, I reached for the phone, my heart filled with hope. My finances were in shambles, most of my equity having evaporated with the recession and clients not paying their bills. A few years back I had been sitting on top of the world. Now the ship was going down. This had to be the Coast Guard pulling up...or...

"Sorry," the broker said. "But they turned you down."

"But I'm only asking to take out twenty grand," I reminded him.

"Yeah, but you missed a payment on that second mortgage."

"I took it out to take care of my dying parents."

"They don't care about your noble intentions. They only care about the bottom line."

"Goddamn it," I said and got up to pace, ready to kick something. "Those self-righteous, bloodsucking bastards. Screw us all and wave as we're going down."

"That's about it, but at least you're not alone. They're being pricks to most everyone.

"Oh, well, that makes me feel enormously better."

"Yeah, well, that's the way it is. You want me to keep trying?"

"No, screw it. I'm done. Send me a bill if you have to."

He declined. I got off, staring at skid row.

4

Seated back at my desk, I started thumbing through the stack of invoices again. Half a dozen clients and not one of them paying their bills, save for Mrs. Vanderhof. Then, with all of her money, she could have purchased the Dakotas and had enough change left over to make a bid on the Marianas.

What a world. Her soon to be ex had set up an online gambling site a few years back, designed to service the Chinese mainland. A bit of proprietary software, a nod from the Communist Party, the flip of a switch and, bingo, he was a multi billionaire before you could say mahjong.

Meanwhile, I was going broke. Fifty years old and there were itinerant Irish minstrels with more savings. I owned a home but was about to lose that.

With my back to the wall, I made several calls but it was the same story everywhere I turned. Clients tapped out, and those were the nice ones. Most of them didn't bother to answer the phone.

My mind moved on to its standard prosecution. If only I had done this. If only I had done that. Every lousy decision I had made over the course of a lifetime now came under indictment. It was, I assumed, the same thing that every man did when he was down on his luck, but I hadn't lived anyone else's lousy life, so I was the last to know.

I glanced up at the clock. Cliff Black was now nearly an hour late. Already down, I found him to be a convenient punching bag. You can take your failing marriage and shove it, pal.

With perhaps twenty minutes at best before they hauled Steve up to county jail, I pushed back from my desk and was headed for the door when a woman's scream tore apart the sultry morning. I rushed back to my windows and poked my head out.

A man wearing all black was sprawled out on the sidewalk directly below me. A pool of blood had begun to gather next to his chest. In keeping with the nature of fluids, the blood was quickly searching for lower ground.

In that instant, I was out my door and racing down the hallway. I hustled down the old wooden stairs and went charging out of the front door. A crowd of people had already gathered around the body, but mostly at a safe distance. Only a Mexican busboy from Mark's across the street had dared to squat down near the man. He stood up when he saw me coming. I squatted down in his place.

Best to find a priest, I thought with a closer look at the man's chest. He appeared to have taken one close to the heart. Blood had turned the front of his shirt into a pool of red paint. On a hospital gurney, he might have lived. Lying on a public sidewalk, I gave him two, three minutes tops before he joined the dearly departed.

"Did someone call 911?!" I shouted out to those around me.

A young man nodded with his phone held out.

"I did."

I turned back to the stricken man, wondering who in his right mind would be sporting a black coat, a black shirt and black pants in the middle of a heat wave. Never mind the gray streak dyed into his once perfectly coifed black hair. The guy looked like he belonged at a celebrity impersonator's convention. He should have been schlepping photos of himself on the Vegas Strip for twenty bucks and a kiss, not gunned down on the sidewalks of Laurel Lagoon on a blisteringly hot summer day.

Then it hit me. This must be Cliff Black. If so, some luck. A potential payday and the guy gets plugged twenty feet from my office door. I leaned down closer and whispered to him.

"Cliff?"

His eyes came around and looked at me, leaden but trying to say something.

"I'm Michael Devlin. What happened?"

He spoke in a raspy and barely audible whisper. I put my ear up closer to his mouth.

"What?" I said.

"My wife…Audrey…she's knows the…"

His breath gave way to a rattle. I leaned in closer and whispered again.

"Your wife knows what, Cliff? Who shot you?"

I felt his body heave ever so slightly and pulled back to look at his face. The mouth was open, the eyes blank. I closed the eyelids. There was a gasp from the crowd. A man pushed through everyone else on the sidewalk. He was wearing the collar.

"I'm the pastor from the Presbyterian Church. Someone up the street said a man had been shot."

I stood up and turned the last rights over to him. He saw the blood.

"Oh dear God," he said and knelt in prayer.

Just then, two squad cars came barreling the wrong way down the one-way street, sirens blaring. A moment later, I had Detective Whalen in my face. He had a quick look at the last rights in progress and looked back at me.

"You know this guy?"

"No," I said.

"Did you see what happened?"

"No."

"Do you know anything?"

"I know whoever plugged him must have used a silencer."

"So, no shots rang out."

"Nope, just a woman's scream."

39

"Do you know which woman?"

"Nope," I said.

He came closer.

"You didn't plug him, did you?"

"No, but maybe Steve did."

"Don't get smart with me, Devlin."

"Me get smart. Open your eyes, Pat. Something bigger's going on here."

"You know what your problem is, Devlin? You think too much. Now get out of here before I cook up something to charge you with."

"What about Steve?"

"What about him?"

"Is he still up at the station?"

"Nope. He's on his way to the rough house. Not to worry, though. Nice white boy like that? Those Mexicans up there will take real good care of him."

"Jesus, Pat. No one will ever accuse you of wearing your heart on your sleeve."

He smiled sarcastically and moved on to the business of dead bodies. I had a look around at the crowd. All of the neighboring proprietors had come out to gawk. Leonard had come downstairs. I looked up and saw Betty poking her head out their office window. The cops were busy rolling out caution tape. As they pushed everyone back, I trudged back upstairs. Betty peeked out into the hallway before I had a chance to disappear into my office. She was holding Butch.

"Is he dead?"

I nodded.

"God, how awful."

I nodded again. I would have assumed, given the crime family name, that she and Leonard had seen their share of dead bodies, but maybe not.

Inside my office, I grabbed a moist towel, cleaned the blood from my hands and sat down at my desk. What a lousy way to start the morning. Watch a man lose his life. But who would

40

want Cliff dead? He had known something. The same with his wife. Cliff had said as much. "My wife Audrey...she knows the..."

But knows what? The person who'd want to shoot him? Or whatever it was that Cliff had been reluctant to discuss with me over the phone that day? Maybe they were the same thing.

Filled with reservations about this case from the start, I had never thought to dig into Cliff's identity but went online and did so now. His name promptly popped up with a Facebook link. That was him all right, the guy lying dead on the sidewalk. A picture of Audrey was on his wall. By the looks of Cliff, I had pictured Elvira. Something gothic. Dyed black hair, tattoos and body piercings everywhere. Instead, Audrey was a beautiful redhead. The image of her kicked me right in the gut. I had a thing for beautiful redheads. In fact, I had loved one deeply not all that long ago and found myself falling far, far down into a tangle of ancient emotions. I closed the Facebook page before I fell too far.

Minutes passed with the feelings continuing to work on me. Audrey, beautiful Audrey, with your piles of radiant red hair.

Then I remembered Cliff's uncashed check. No doubt Audrey would notice it in his ledger. It was enough of an excuse to call her, and pole vault me over my questionable motives.

I reached for the phone, picturing the conversation.

"My condolences for your loss, Mrs. Black. Perhaps you noticed that your husband had written me a check."

"Oh yes. I did wonder about that."

"Yes. I'd be happy to explain things but perhaps it would be best if I did so in person."

My movie quickly segued into the two of us having tea, she in black, me being careful not to stare too much at her red hair. Segue again and Audrey and I were frittering away the

41

afternoon behind her closed bedroom door, the window curtains dancing lazily in a gentle breeze.

God, you are sick, Devlin…Well, at least I had the check

A moment later, Rick Duncan was answering my call, but Audrey wasn't there. In fact, she had failed to come into the office that day. Without pressing too hard, I gleaned that Rick had been trying to reach her by phone all morning, to no avail.

I excused myself from that call and phoned my friend and business associate, Kenny. A moment later, he answered. Kenny had a second story office directly across the street from mine. I looked over and saw his dimpled face smiling back at me. We could have hit each other with well-aimed tortillas, had we been inclined to do so.

Kenny had come out of college with a fine arts degree, a career path that had failed to pay his bills, so he put his minor in software engineering to work and had somehow drifted into the people search business. I liked using him over the big names online. It was more personal. Plus, he was good.

"I take it you can see the dead man lying down there on the sidewalk."

"Bummer," Kenny said.

"Yeah, well remember Audrey?"

"Yeah, from last week."

"Well that's her husband and I'm on a mission now to find her before the cops do."

"You think she did it?" Kenny said.

"I don't know, but something doesn't smell right."

I explained about Audrey not showing up for work that day.

"See if you can dig up her mobile number. Home number, whatever you can find."

"Okay…Hey, I just pulled up Cliff's Facebook page. Wow, same get up he's wearing now. What's with the gray streak dyed into his hair?"

"It was big in Hollywood some years back. Probably a bit before your time."

"I guess so."

"Yeah. I suspect it was part of his professional persona. It says here he was an industrial photographer, but his real passion was portraiture."

"The frustrated artist," Kenny said.

"Aren't we all…"

"Hey, this Audrey looks a lot like your old flame."

"Shut up."

Kenny laughed, which could have been mistaken for a man clearing his throat, or an act of self-deprecation, or both.

"Sorry. I'll call as soon as I have some info."

While waiting, I couldn't suppress the urge to open up Cliff's Facebook page again and thumb through the photos. There were several of his marriage to Audrey. She was wearing white, he a black tux. It looked like a big crowd. The ceremony had taken place about three years back.

Why Audrey had fallen for a guy channeling '50s matinee idols was beyond me. As romances went, it did appear to have its flaws, but who was I to say? I had spent half a lifetime looking for the right gal, only to see my best shot drop kicked off a cliff. What did I know about handicapping romances?

I jotted down the names of various friends and family members listed on the Facebook page and got back to staring at Audrey. God, the red hair and pug nose. I knew it was best for me to steer a million miles clear of this whole thing but my heart had other ideas. And there was my hunch. Something in my gut that told me that Connie's and Cliff's murders were connected.

Kenny finally called back.

"I found her social security number and hacked into her credit cards. She checked out of a hotel in downtown San Diego about two hours ago."

"Just enough time to drive up here and shoot her husband."

"Could have, huh?"

"Seems like a bit of a stretch, but she had just enough time to do it and I'm not very fond of coincidences."

"Yeah. So what now?"

"Kemosabe."

Kenny laughed.

"Just keep tracking her. Let's see where she lands next. And send me a bill, even though I can't pay it right now."

Kenny did his laugh again and hung up.

Aware of a renewed buzz down on the sidewalk, I looked out my window. The forensics folks had finished poking around with Cliff and were spreading a sheet over him. The cops had wasted a few rolls of caution tape trying to keep the crowd at bay.

I sat back, thinking again about the check. Audrey was bound to find the entry in Cliff's checkbook and I certainly owed her an explanation.

Lost in visions of her red-haired beauty, the phone rang again. With a glance, I saw it was Dirk Vanderhof.

Mr. Billion Dollars, I liked to call him. I grabbed the phone.

"Fancy that, Vanderhof. I was just thinking of you."

"Yeah?"

"Yeah, but I'll get over it. What's on your mind?"

"I've got a job for you to do."

"And that would be?"

"Meet me at the English Cottage in half an hour and I'll tell you."

"I can't."

"Why not?"

"Ethics. You may be a bit unfamiliar with the term but it goes like this. You settle with your wife. Then we can talk. Until then I don't meet you anywhere outside of a courtroom."

"Don't tell me you lack the balls to meet me in a quiet bar somewhere."

"I lack a penchant for folly. That's what I lack. Besides, I have a couple of murders to solve. You know anything about murder?"

There was silence.

"No. Why would you ask?"

"Just fishing."

44

"Sorry," he said after a moment of silence. "But that's one subject I know nothing about."

"Okay then. End of conversation. Give me a call as soon as Mrs. Vanderhof owns half your fortune."

Vanderhof had started to say something else as I dropped the receiver in its cradle. I spun around in my chair. There was one more attempt to unglue the blue, cotton shirt from my back.

Vanderhof playing dumb, when Steve had known him back in the day. Something definitely didn't smell right.

In the course of investigating Vanderhof for his wife's divorce attorney, I had unearthed everything from a statutory rape charge to backdated stock options. The statutory rape business had involved a sixteen-year-old girl. A few drinks late one night, a joint, a bit of extracurricular activity in his bedroom Jacuzzi and, boom, he was in big trouble.

"That was nothing but a bit of fun," he had told the district attorney when I brought his dalliance to light. Called me a slimy, groveling piece of shit for exposing him. That was no way to start a friendship. A grand jury was still trying to sort things out.

Then there was Mrs. Vanderhof, the silky blonde from Scandinavia. She was enough to make me forget about all the beautiful redheads in this world, but with her convertible Bentley and the teacup Yorkie in her purse, there were times when I didn't know whom to side with.

Then, it was hard to feel sorry for either one of them. All that money, a mansion the size of a concert hall and all they could wring from it was a penchant for stabbing each other in the back.

About the only thing that engendered sympathy for the Vanderhof's was their missing daughter. Someone had abducted her as a toddler about ten years back. Several ransom notes had followed, a botched attempt to pay the ransom, and then nothing, not another word. That was a hard one to take, and for all I knew, the ongoing grief of it was what had driven the couple apart.

I had a look back down at the sidewalk. Cliff was gone, and most of the cops along with him. A swarm of reporters had taken their place. I said a word of sympathy for the dead and got back to Cliff's final utterance.

Audrey…she knows the…

Audrey knows the…what?

I had my hunch, but it involved nothing more than circumstantial evidence. All I had in the way of facts was a man's purported devotion.

"I really, really love my wife," Cliff had said. "Perhaps you can understand why I'd be so concerned."

Yeah. I understood all right. Every time a lady tossed your heart away, there was an impulse to grab her by the shoulders and plead before she wandered on down the road, hoping to make the joy you once knew come back to life. It just rarely did.

The way I saw it, Cliff was the lucky one. One shot in the heart and he was on a fast track to oblivion, his troubles over.

I decided to grab a sandwich down the block and left the door open, hoping to catch a breeze through the windows.

Using the back door of the building, I expected to avoid the swarm of reporters, but no such luck. The alley in both directions was lined with news trucks. The vultures would pick the bones off this carcass and run off the minute someone else was killed.

A cop had positioned his squad car in the library parking lot directly across from my back door. I received a nod from him going by. My focus was on making the next block before Bernie or any of his pals noticed my escape.

5

I slipped back into my office fifteen minutes later. That hoped for breeze was nowhere in sight. The oppressive heat had the feel of wool about it; thick, heavy, the air dead, not a single breath of wind blowing in through the windows.

Across the street, the Mexican busboy who had knelt beside Cliff's body was now setting up tables over at Mark's. He had hosed off the sidewalk earlier in the morning and it still looked damp. Yellow caution tape circled the crime scene, keeping the gawkers up and down the street at bay.

The cops had blocked off access from Coast Highway and someone was out there honking, wanting to pull in and pissed off over the inconvenience. A uniformed cop walked out and read him the riot act. One of Whalen's underlings was still down there taking testimony from anybody who thought they might have something to add. Reporters were busy getting their own take from members of the crowd.

I glanced up at the dry hills behind town. They were wavering in the heat. A sense of disbelief permeated the summer morning.

I leaned back in my chair, doing what I could to make sense of two murders and not getting very far with it. About the time I was back to puzzling over Cliff Black's last words, I heard someone barge in the front door and footsteps hustling up the stairs. They marched down the hallway with the same urgency and my door flew open. It was Whalen. His deputy Fowler had tagged along for the ride. Fowler was the new kid on the block;

baby-faced, his whole persona pregnant with arrogance and hair oil. You might have guessed from Fowler's grin and the way he was chewing gum that the two of them had stopped by for a college prank, but Pat's look told me otherwise.

"I heard you and Mr. Black were sharing secrets before he kicked the bucket."

"Yeah?"

"Yeah. So let's hear what he had to say."

"He said 'my wife, she knows the...' We never got any further than that. I presume he was going to say 'she knows the way I loved her'."

"Don't get cute with me."

"I'm not. You want me to make up something, I will, but that's what the man said."

Pat shook his head.

"What?" I said.

"You're always holding back on me, Devlin, and I don't like it."

"Come on, Pat. I had just witnessed a man lose his life. You can forgive me for being a bit distracted."

He started for the door.

"Hey," I said. "Have you been able to locate Cliff's wife yet?"

Pat paused.

"What do you care?"

"Just thinking of Cliff. She was the last thing on his mind."

"No, I haven't. Apparently no one else has for the past three days. And don't go sticking your nose where it doesn't belong," Pat added before heading out the door.

Fowler tried the same tough guy look before disappearing but he was about twenty years and some acting lessons shy of pulling it off. I offered him an Italian salute and got back to Cliff. He had suspected Audrey of being in trouble. She goes missing for three days, then checks out of a hotel down in San Diego two hours before her husband is plugged. The woman had all the earmarks of trouble in high heels.

The phone rang again, breaking me from my thoughts. It was Jim Harrison.

"What do you know, Jim?"

"I couldn't get the arraignment scheduled until Monday. And the judge won't talk bail with me until then."

"All right. I'll drive up to visit Steve over the weekend. What about Lisa Durant? Did she know anything more about the Vanderhof connection?"

"Not much. Nothing useful. Basically, what Steve had told us. That the McPherson's and Vanderhof's were acquainted back in the day. Lisa denied any knowledge of Connie and Vanderhof screwing around together, then or now. As far as I can tell, Connie was just chirping away about Vanderhof being in the news and the fact that she had known him coming out of college. By the way, you know anything about that shooting downtown?"

"Surely you jest. The man was sprawled out here right below my office windows. A prospective client, no less. I was ready to place his check in the bank."

I shared what Cliff had told me and everything I had seen.

"Any hunches," Jim asked me.

"Haven't a clue at this point. Probably my best bet is to break into Audrey's place and see what she had scribbled on her desk calendar. That seems to be what really got Cliff suspicious."

"Breaking and entering can land you in jail."

"Yeah yeah. That's why I have an attorney."

"One of these days, I'm going to let you rot."

"So you've told me."

"All right. Keep me posted, and let's go grab a steak one of these nights."

"Sounds good," I said.

"You always say that. Then I never hear from you until the next time you're in trouble."

"Okay, I'll give you a call soon...Hey," I said before hanging up.

"Yeah," Jim said.

"Please get a message through to Steve. My neighbor Betty's looking after his dog Butch. I didn't want Steve worrying."

Jim promised he would and we got off. I sat there in the listless heat, faced with the contradiction of my life. I figured our only hope as a species was to return to our tribal roots, but I was about as tribal as a grizzly bear. I rarely called my friends anymore. My every other thought was about disappearing down to my place in Baja.

I really did want to get away, and heading south of the border sounded lovely, but I turned my attention instead to the list of names I had culled from Cliff's Facebook page. Audrey was first on the list so I called her business again. No answer. That seemed strange in the middle of a business day but I set that to the side and dug around online for some phone numbers to Audrey's family. Her mother promptly answered when I called and said she had just heard the news about Cliff. I explained that Cliff was an old friend of mine and there was something personal I needed to share with Audrey.

"Of course, there's no rush, under the circumstances. Just ask Audrey to give me a call whenever she feels up to it."

"I will," Mom said, sniffling away. "My God, this is all so terrible. And now I can't seem find my own daughter. I haven't heard from her in almost three days. You don't think she's in trouble too, do you?"

"No, no. I have no reason to think that."

I offered a few more reassurances, left my phone number and hung up.

I had the numbers for Audrey's three sisters and started down the list. With the first two, I got no answer. It being the middle of a summer afternoon, I fancied they were out having fun in the sun. That or on their way over to join the grieving party at Mom's place.

Audrey's youngest sister Diane was the last one in line and with her, I finally caught someone at home.

"Who are you?" she said when I told her I was looking for Audrey. The sound of her kids could be heard yelling in the background.

"My name's Michael."

I gave her the same line I had given Mom.

The yelling and screaming reached a new crescendo in the background. I became aware of the phone being cupped and heard the muffled sound of Diane scolding her kids. Then she was back.

"Sorry about that," she said. "Well, if you're looking for Audrey, I'm afraid I can't help. Everybody in our family's been looking for her. By the way, how did you get my number?"

"It's in the white pages online."

"Oh. Well I'll have to do something about that."

"Well, sorry for the intrusion and what I have to tell Audrey isn't all that urgent, in and of itself. It's just something in Cliff's personal affairs that she's bound to stumble over, so it would be best if I explained the particulars to her personally. Do you think she'll give you a call?"

"I doubt it. We're not that close. She hasn't stopped by my place for years, other than for the holidays."

"Well, again, I'm terribly sorry about Cliff and this can certainly wait until things settle down a bit."

"I'll definitely pass along the message, once we hear from her."

"Thanks."

"Sorry I can't be of more help but I really have to go. I was about to call my niece Sylvia when you phoned. She has a fortune telling business down in Doheny Beach and I've been waiting all morning for her to open up shop."

Diane had mentioned her niece's fortune teller shop like she was referring to a strip joint. I offered my condolences one more time, left my number, rang off and immediately went in search of Sylvia's phone number on the Internet. I knew her place. I had been passing by the neon sign out on Coast Highway for years. When the number came up, I called. When no one answered, I left a message. Nothing about Audrey this time. I was just a man looking to have his fortune read. It was a line, but fitting enough.

With a glance at my watch, I saw it was a little past noon. The phone rang a moment later. It was Kenny again.

"Have you read the news today?"

"Oh boy," I said.

Kenny did his laugh.

"I'm sending you a link. This story just broke."

A moment later, his e-mail arrived. I clicked on the link and quickly scrolled through the article. Magellan Ltd., Audrey's consulting firm, was mentioned as having brokered a shipment of small arms, destined for Liberia. According to anonymous sources, the Feds believed that some sort of top-secret technology had been hidden inside the shipping container and that the shipping container's ultimate destination was an unspecified Middle East country. There was no word on the exact nature of said technology, or if the shipping container had been intercepted at this point.

Meanwhile, a Saudi arms merchant involved in the deal had escaped to the wild backstreets of Abu Dhabi and an FBI agent gone bad was sitting in jail right then, getting used to steel bars and florescent lights. The Feds were still ransacking LA harbor for the shipping container. Towards the end of the article, there was mention of Vanderhof being one of Magellan Ltd.'s former clients.

"Did I ever tell you my dream about being from Orion?" I said.

Kenny laughed.

"Uh, no. I don't think so."

I explained. In the recurring dream, I had come here from a distant star but missed the spaceship ride back, haunted every day at dusk by this image of my wife cooking dinner over the stove, waiting for my return home. But of course, I never arrived.

"What brought this up?" Kenny said.

"Oh, escape, I guess. See, every time I have the dream and picture myself walking in that door to greet my wife, I have the most wonderful feeling of bliss. You know, like things were perfect back on Orion."

"You'd probably be on Orion, dreaming that things were perfect somewhere else."

"You have a way of ruining everything." Kenny laughed. "Well, anyway, listen. About this article. I want you to look into something for me."

I explained what was on my mind.

"See what you can find out. And let me know the minute Audrey starts banging her credit cards again."

"Will do."

I got off and leaned back in my chair, armed with just enough facts to drive a man crazy. Cliff's wife gets herself into a legal mess and goes on the run. Okay, but how did that have anything to do with Cliff being plugged? And how did Cliff getting plugged have anything to do with Connie being strangled out by Irvine Lake the other day? The latter conjecture represented a significant leap on my part, but that feeling in my gut just wouldn't quit.

As to the idea of dirty business going down in Orange County, I had always been a bit naïve on that score. 'What? There's nothing more sinister going on behind all those shopping malls and manicured lawns than a few extra-marital affairs, is there?'

But of course there was. A high tech corridor shot right down the backbone of our county, commencing amidst the crisscross of power lines and barrios to the north and terminating into the brick driveway of Mr. Billion Dollars' tony, gate-guarded estate, a corridor of wealth that divided the mountains from the sea and in some places had a view of both. Taking into consideration all the money at stake, the inherent greed of mankind and the shady deals for which our local government officials had been famous over the years, why would I assume there to be anything but a lot of foul play involved?

That's what happened when you lived a sheltered life in the once sleepy little beach town of Laurel Lagoon, a slave to your long-lost liberal arts education and misplaced beliefs. I went to bed each night thinking this world of ours was a fundamentally decent place, and that most everyone in it was worthy of being trusted. I had no idea how to square those assumptions with five thousand years of human history. People kept stabbing each other in the back. That seemed to be the enduring legacy of our species.

I spun around in my chair with a sigh. Of all the countless galaxies and worlds, I had to get stuck in this one.

I was back to daydreaming about Audrey and her piles of long red hair when I heard a man's footsteps cautiously coming up the wooden stairs. I listened to them approach slowly down the hallway. A silhouette went past my office. A moment later, whoever it was returned and stopped outside my door. Very quietly, I opened the top drawer to my desk and placed my hand on the Smith & Wesson I kept in there. Whoever it was on the other side of the glass, he remained stationary and staring my way. He was dark haired, sporting a mustache and had a bit of pot gut. I could tell that much through the glass.

Finally, whoever it was turned back down the hallway towards the stairs. His footsteps went down to the ground level and the back door opened and closed. I dashed out into the hallway and peeked from the fire escape but the man had already disappeared.

I was sitting back down at my desk when the phone rang again. It was Kenny.

"She just banged a card at the Doheny Beach Resort."

"Just enough time to drive from here to there."

"She's very coincidental."

"Yeah she is, but this one doesn't make any sense."

"How's that?"

"If you knew your husband was dead, why check into a hotel barely five miles away? Why not drive home? Or head for the border?"

54

"That's why you're the detective."

"Any idiot could have figured that out."

"Thanks."

"You're welcome. Do you happen to know what she's driving?"

"A white Mercedes SUV. Want the license plate number?"

"Yeah."

I jotted it down, thanked him, grabbed my laptop and headed out the door.

The northbound lanes heading into town on Coast Highway were bumper to bumper with morning commuters. A thousand souls, medicated on talk radio, Kenny G and rap, and none of them looking too happy about it.

Every time I saw this lemming march, I found myself wondering. Why not take a few days off? A few months. Think things over. Try to figure out how we had gotten ourselves into such a rush. But no. Someone somewhere had decided we needed to go about life with our hair on fire.

I turned left when the light changed, headed south, hit the air-conditioner and flipped on some Latin jazz. The traffic was fairly light in that direction. My trailer down in Baja was calling to me again. I owned a five-acre parcel of hillside property. The coastline curved out forty miles to a point looking south. There had always been a thought to build a proper hacienda down there. A five-hour drive and it was the end of the world.

Then the last time I had driven down to Todos Santos popped into my thoughts. Headed from there down towards Cabo, it was a dreamy stretch of coastline for fifty miles, the road wandering up and down alongside the bristling white surf, the pace as lazy as a Mexican siesta, not a care in the world.

With my mind looking for an escape, I was reminded of Jack Oliver. Jack was the grizzled old veteran who had taught me the craft of spying as a young man fresh out of college. Stay out of your head, he used to say. Keep your eye on the little things. Watch cars. Count telephone poles. Note every tree and shrub. Over and over, the same mantra, which had basically gone in one ear and right out the other. The truth was, I had practiced such discipline little back then and not all that much from then going forward. Like today. Rather than keeping my eyes on the road, I was daydreaming about redheads and the Mexican Riviera.

Arriving at the parking lot of the Doheny Beach Resort, I tucked away my errant dreams and went in search of Audrey's white Mercedes. I spotted it on the first lap but also spotted two men parked several rows back in a white van, their rig pointed straight at Audrey's. A magnetic sign said they were contractors for a local cable company. Both of them eyed me as I drove by.

I had my money on them being Dick and Tom, a couple of Feds. Dick was sitting behind the wheel, an older, military type, square-jawed, with his graying hair in a crew cut. Tom had a long face, with bulbous eyes and thinning hair, done in a comb over. You pictured him being the comedian of the two.

I shook my head at their preposterous appearance. A pair of overalls. They couldn't even get the blue-collar thing right. The wrong gear and not a smudge of dirt on them anywhere. It looked like their Linen Finders outfits had just been unwrapped.

I noticed a partition with a door closing off the back of the van as I went by. Whatever they were sporting back there, it was not for public view.

To make sure I wasn't playing a bit part in their movie, I picked a slot at the back end of the parking lot, marched off into the hotel grounds and snuck back to my car in a way that Dick and Tom could not have witnessed.

They sat there keeping an eye out for Audrey. I sat there keeping an eye on her and them. I had already looked over my shoulder to make sure no one was keeping an eye on me.

Half an hour later, Audrey hurried out in a clip clop of high heels, her piles of red hair swaying this way and that. If she had just learned of her husband's death, it had not filled her with any great grief. She had a latte in one hand and appeared to be late for a business meeting.

I heard the beep of her entry lock and watched as Audrey climbed in, backed out and quickly headed for the streets. The boys in the van pulled in behind her. I waited for the two vehicles to exit the parking lot before joining the pursuit.

By the time I had pulled onto Coast Highway, Audrey and the van were a quarter mile ahead and headed north. I lapped a couple of drivers and blew a red light trying to catch up. Audrey kept breaking various traffic laws on her way up the coast. The two Feds did the same. I blew several more red lights and pissed off a number of drivers while doing my part.

In this manner, the four of us meandered up and down that stretch of open coastline north of Laurel Lagoon, left it behind for the bumper-to-bumper traffic of Corona del Mar and were soon flying past the Balboa Bay Club. When Audrey took Newport Boulevard onto the peninsula, everyone followed. When she pulled down the long access lane to a rough and tumble shipyard, I pulled into an office parking lot across the street, perplexed. This was the gritty, backside of the harbor, where you'd expect to find the captain of a shrimp trawler, not a doll in high heels.

Dick and Tom had stopped at the top of the shipyard entrance to watch, then backed up and parked at the curb when Audrey disappeared into the shipyard proper. I jockeyed my car behind an SUV, where I could stay out of sight and still keep an eye on things.

Tom remained sitting in the shotgun seat, his eyes on the shipyard entrance through an open window. Dick had disappeared in back. I fancied they had a fortress of electronic gear back there. If correct on that score, those boys could listen in on any conversation within a few hundred feet of the van.

I sat there watching and searching for answers. Audrey's husband was dead, so why this? Maybe she didn't know yet. When your husband was shot dead, you went home to grieve with the family and Audrey did not appear to be grieving in the least. As to why these two clowns were tailing her around, I hadn't a clue. There was the logical explanation, based on the newspaper article. Audrey and dirty business were mixed up together and the Feds were holding back on arresting her, hoping she would lead them to bigger fish. Beyond that, and lacking more information, all I had were a handful of wild notions.

I knew one thing for certain. The three of them had my full attention.

6

With the adjacent SUV blocking the back of my car from view, I went around to the trunk and rifled through my surplus of stage props and disguises. I wasn't the least bit worried about Audrey picking me out of a line up but those two Feds had seen my face up close.

Having grabbed what I needed to change appearances, I closed the trunk and climbed into the backseat. While pulling off my clothes and getting into the new ones, I kept glancing in the direction of the street, just in case anyone had thoughts of running off without me.

With the change of clothing complete, I climbed back in front and donned a mustache and floppy hat with some dark glasses. It was Tom Selleck does Serpico — or maybe the other way around. Either way, I was fairly certain those two Feds would never recognize me.

With all that done and the car locked up, I crossed the street and started down towards the shipyard entrance like I hadn't a care in the world. Tom immediately pinned me in the passenger side mirror and watched my approach. If he had any discernible reaction, it was annoyance. I was just one more prick in an Armani jacket with too much time and money on his hands.

I turned from the sidewalk down towards the shipyard without the slightest look in Tom's direction. Even as I slipped past the sliding wrought iron gate and entered the haphazard world of the shipyard, I kept my focus straight ahead.

Inside the shipyard, I headed for the clapboard office. The business of grinding, welding and getting things done went on all around me. The scent of burnt carborundum blades filled the air. Several workers glanced over as I navigated the puddles of oily water. Their reception was what you would expect for a guy wearing Bruno Magli loafers.

The inside of the office looked to have been painted a light gray color at some point in the past, but soot and years of neglect had brought it closer to a charcoal shade. A seriously overweight and balding man got up from his desk with a grunt and walked over to the counter. This was a man who had ceased to care about his appearance long ago. His gut was spilling over his belt buckle. The buttons of his plaid shirt were about to pop. His face had not seen a razor blade in a couple of days. What remained of the hair on his head was in disarray.

With a dexterous move of his lips and tongue, he repositioned a spent cigar to one side of his mouth and nodded the chin of his oversized face in my direction.

"What can I do for you?"

"Phil," I told him and held out my hand.

"Jack," he said and offered me his calloused paw, but not before he had wiped at his pant leg with it.

"What can I do for you?"

"Oh, I was wondering if you fix motors."

"You mean, do we repair ship engines?"

"Yeah, that."

"What kind you got?"

"Perkins, 135 horse."

"An old one, eh?"

I nodded.

"What's it running?"

"A Gulfstar 44."

"Yeah? Helluva boat."

I nodded again.

"Well, it's not that we don't have room," he said with a nod of his chin out towards the yard. "Or that we couldn't do it, but you'd be lost like a show dog in a back alley full of mongrels around here. I'd be worried to death about getting a smudge on her."

Jack gave my attire the once over while he grabbed a pen. I watched him scribble something down onto a pad of paper.

"Here's the names and numbers of two shipyards in town. They specialize in that sort of thing. They may even be able to fix it in the boat."

I took the piece of paper from Jack, feeling a bit jilted.

"If one of these operations can't help you, they'll know who can."

This whole time, my eyes had been peeled for any sign of Audrey but she was nowhere to be found. I was about to leave when a man came down a hallway behind the counter and slipped into an office through a partially opened door.

"Hey," he said to someone unseen. "Sorry but I was in a meeting."

"Sorry, nothing," a woman's voice said. "Do you realize the mess I'm in? Someone just shot Cliff and they're probably going to shoot me next."

"Now, calm down, doll," the man said. "I'm not going to let anyone hurt you."

"Yeah, right. You're the one who got me into this mess!"

With that, an unseen hand closed the door.

"I told you not to worry, doll," I heard the man's now muffled voice say from behind the door. "Nobody's going to hurt you. I've got this under control."

"Yeah, right," she said. "And stop calling me doll. It sounds like we're boyfriend and girlfriend."

Jack and I stood there staring at each other.

"Well, best get back to work," he said as if we had just heard two people discussing the weather.

"Yeah, guess I'd better try these other outfits."

Jack lumbered back over towards his desk. I started towards the door but stopped.

"Say, you wouldn't happen to have a john around here I could use?"

Jack looked up from his desk.

"Sorry. It's out of order."

The two of us were left staring at each other again, with Jack having lied and me knowing it wouldn't do any good to remind him that he had.

I went out the door and started across the yard, looking for any way that I might slip around to the backside of the office but it was hard up against a chain link fence. Besides, half the shipyard was watching. My best shot was to retrace my steps up the sidewalk and see what I could see from next door. Tom watched me intently as I passed the van and headed in that direction.

The next business front was a marine supply outfit but it had no access to a parking area in back of it. That meant the parking area belonged to a restaurant next door. It wasn't open for business yet but I knew from experience that the big wooden doors would be unlocked for deliveries. Going in, I found a hostess and a handful of waitresses busily preparing for the lunch crowd. The hostess allowed me to use the bathroom on the basis of a kind word and my charming smile.

When she went upstairs to the office, I slipped out a side door and found my way around to the backside of the shipyard office. I hadn't been there two minutes, straining to hear more of Audrey's conversation, when I suddenly had my right cheek and ear crushed up against the chain link fence. Blood trickled into the corner of my mouth, the sweet taste of it incongruous with the feeling of nausea in my gut. Some goon had my left arm pinned up behind my back, high enough to scratch the back of my head, had I wanted to do so.

It was Tom, and when he peeled me back from the fence, I was staring at Dick.

"Look at this," Dick said to Tom. "He thinks he's Serpico."

Dick knocked the pork pie hat from my head.

"And now he's Tom Selleck."

Tom chuckled as Dick tore the mustache from above my lip. "And now he's not."

"What the hell do you think you're doing?" I said.

In response, Tom cinched my arm up a bit tighter.

"What the hell do I think I'm doing?" Dick said. "Well, first thing I'm doing is to make sure I know more than you do."

"Then you're in good shape, because I don't know a damned thing."

"He doesn't know a damned thing," Dick said to Tom. Dick nodded and Tom cinched me up again for good measure.

"You know," Dick said. "You had me fooled pretty good back there. And I don't like being fooled. If it wasn't for you getting nosy, I might not have made you at all. Which brings me back to where we started. Who are you and why are you poking around here?"

"No one and nothing that concerns you." Dick flinched as if I had insulted him and quickly had my wallet in his hand.

"A private dick," he said to Tom, then to me. "So what? You got a tail on the doll?"

"I don't know anything about any dolls."

"Yeah, sure you don't. But let me give you a fair warning. Get off the case. You don't know what you're dealing with here."

Dick nodded at Tom, who let me go. I licked at the blood in the corner of my mouth.

"You understand?" Dick asked me.

"I understand it's a free country."

"Yeah? Well it's not as free as you think."

He handed me my wallet and the two of them started towards the back door of the restaurant. I looked up and saw the hostess staring down from a second story window. Dick turned back once before going inside.

"Get off the case, gumshoe. Before you find yourself in a whole lot of trouble."

"Gumshoe," Tom said with a smile. "Gumshoe," he repeated as if he liked the sound of it and followed Dick through the door.

I gave Dick and Tom a good head start before following them back into the restaurant. All the waitresses were staring my way as I walked in. One of them was kind enough to hand me some napkins.

Back out at my car, I kicked a tire and cursed. It was one thing to be made by a cop. It was another thing to be made the butt of their jokes.

"Hey, it's Serpico...And now he's Tom Selleck...And now he's not. Ha ha ha."

Like they had been reading my mind.

I climbed in behind the wheel and checked my face in the rearview mirror. They had left me with a deep gash on my right cheek, and blood all over my $500 Armani jacket. I sat there with a napkin to my wound, fuming.

Having chewed on my anger for a few minutes, I went back around to the trunk. I wasn't done with those two bastards yet and they weren't done with me.

Having donned a new disguise, this time a baseball cap wearing redneck, I headed across town to a rental car agency. Outfitted with their latest SUV, I headed up the coast to Audrey's place of business. Expecting it to be a long day, I stopped to grab a turkey sandwich along the way.

As anticipated, those two Feds were parked outside Audrey's office building when I arrived. The building was five stories, black glass and surrounded by rolling lawns and eucalyptus trees. A set of broad, concrete steps led from the parking lot up to a central courtyard. With Dick and Tom commandeering that spot, I positioned myself in a parking lot across the busy boulevard and kept an eye on things through passing traffic.

The day wore on like eight hours waiting to be seen by a dentist. I had my windows down to the listless heat. I squirmed. I ate half of the sandwich. Several times, I almost gave in to my impulse and phoned Audrey's office but I may as well have placed a big neon sign over my head. With all the gadgetry those two Feds were packing, they could have triangulated me in Times Square on New Year's Eve, and had a number to go with the dumb look on my face.

Ultimately, as afternoon was fading to dusk, the two Feds gave up and pulled out of the parking lot. I gave them a few hundred yards and pulled into traffic behind them. Obviously, in their zeal to figure out who I was, and cuff me around a bit, those two pros had made a fatal assumption. That Audrey would be a good girl and show up to work that day, and she had not.

The ensuing chase led down to San Juan Capistrano. Pulling off the freeway, Dick and Tom turned right and then right again along the backside of the old mission. We passed a schoolyard playground. A series of short cul-de-sacs branched off to our right, all of the homes sporting a Spanish theme — heavy stucco texture, a few arches here and there, very non-descript — the sort of community that came with zero lot lines.

From there, the road narrowed and jogged up over a knoll into a much older neighborhood. It was as if we had entered a time machine. There were some real gems from the 1800s, back when the Spanish had owned the place.

Dick and Tom parked at the curb and I parked a hundred yards behind them. Figuring they had just led me to Audrey's house, I dug Cliff's check out of my briefcase and sure enough, this was the place. I Googled his address and zoomed in on the house. It was the one with a jacaranda tree overhanging the red tile roof. The jacaranda was in bloom and had littered the front yard with purple blossoms. Oleander bushes lined an old plaster wall on the opposite side of the road.

I was back to thinking about that note Audrey had scribbled on her desk calendar. If not for those two Feds, and the fact that there was still a bit of daylight, I would have broken in to find out.

After another hour or so of waiting and squirming behind the wheel, it seemed clear to me that Audrey wasn't at home so I drove back to the resort in Doheny and tried waiting for her there. When she failed to materialize at the resort, I drove back up to Newport and dropped off the rental car.

Back at my office, I spent the next half hour combing my office for bugs and peering out through the closed window blinds. At one point, I saw Kenny looking back from his office across the street. He smiled. I had already received an update from him by that point. Nothing new on Audrey. Wherever she was and whatever she was doing, she had stopped using her credit cards.

Satisfied that those two Feds had not bugged my office, I headed up to the police station on foot. It was another hot and muggy summer night, packed with restless souls.

The gay kid at the front desk was filing his nails when I walked in.

"Is Whalen in?" I asked him.

"Who should I say is calling?"

"Don't get cute. Just ring his office."

He buzzed Whalen and announced my arrival.

"Send him in," Whalen called out.

The kid released the door and went back to filing his nails.

"Try red," I told the petulant little prick. "It's always worked for me."

Pat glanced up from the file in his hands as I walked into his office. His eyes took note of the gash on my cheek and returned to his file.

"I thought you were mad at me," he said.

"I am. That doesn't mean you can't be useful."

"Funny. Who gave you the beauty treatment?"

"I was working a divorce case earlier today. Up in Newport and a couple of boys roughed me up."

"Must have been some pretty rough boys."

"Rough enough."

"Where in particular, if you don't mind me asking?"

"Behind the Sea Shanty."

"And what did you want from me?"

"Whatever you can tell me about Cliff's murder?"

Pat placed the file down on his desk and stared.

"Even if I did know something, why would I tell you?"

"Because I'm an honest, hardworking man with everyone's best interest at heart."

Pat scoffed.

"I'll give you hardworking…maybe."

We stared at each other. When it didn't appear that Pat would wax loquacious any time soon, I offered up a chip.

"The guy who was shot this morning?"

Pat nodded.

"He was a prospective client. He must have been on his way to my office."

"And you didn't tell me this…because?"

"I didn't know him from Adam. If you had seen the former client who referred Cliff along? You never would have made the connection. I've got a sunny, golf loving client over here and Cliff, the Roy Orbison impersonator over there."

While still staring at each other, a call came in and Pat took it. His conversation went on and on. I sat there watching what passed for fun at a police station on a summer night. Not much. A guy in shorts and a Hawaiian shirt came in, complaining that his wallet had been lifted at a sidewalk café. The rookie took a report with his usual petulance. In fairness to the rookie, it probably was a fruitless exercise. The man would never see his wallet again. Someone called in about a party making too much noise. There was an accident on the north end of town. A patrolman appeared in back and went about completing a drunken driver report. There was a disheveled young man caged in the tank behind him. He would not be having any more fun that night.

Setting aside the plaques on the walls, and the photos of baseball teams sponsored by the Policeman's Association, there never seemed to be any good news at a police station. To become anything but cynical under the circumstances would be a miracle.

About the time that my spirits were in a full tailspin, Pat got off his call and leaned back in that chair.

"So, tell me again. Why are you so interested in Cliff Black's murder?"

"I think it's connected to Connie's death."

Whalen scoffed.

"Go ahead, Pat, laugh, but I have this client coming by to see me, who claims to have some damning information. Only he won't discuss it with me over the phone. Insists that we meet in person. Then next thing I know, he's plugged down below my office windows."

"So?"

"So he thought his wife was in trouble. I figured she was having an affair. Now I'm thinking maybe he was right."

"Wait a minute. You're telling me that Cliff suspected Audrey of being in trouble?"

"Come on, Pat. You read the news. You know about Magellan."

"Yeah, but I still don't get where you're going with this."

"Look, Cliff told me that Audrey had gone off on an unexpected business trip last week and upon her return, she doesn't look so happy. Claims that a client had been running her around and sulks off to their bedroom. Only now Cliff notices her making a number of hushed phone calls from the back room over the next few days and figures she's in some kind of trouble."

Pat shook his head at me.

"What?" I said.

"You're always holding back on me, Devlin, and I don't like it."

"I'm not holding back. I'm here telling you."

"About twelve hours too late."

"What do you want from me, Pat? A man called, concerned about his wife and suddenly he gets plugged. Then a few hours ago, I learn his wife is involved in some kind of black-market deal, in which Vanderhof's name comes up, by the way, and my nose is telling me that something's going on here."

"You and Vanderhof."

"Yeah, me and Vanderhof."

"Yeah, well, this McPherson case is cut and dry as far as I'm concerned."

"Bullshit."

"He was stalking his wife."

"He wasn't stalking her."

"Yeah? And what do you call it?"

"I call it a guy with a broken heart, still in love with a woman who probably no longer loved him in return. It was stupid, but Steve doesn't have a mean bone in his body."

Whalen stared.

"He doesn't. It wasn't in him to strangle his wife. Or anyone."

"Yeah? Well then who did?"

"I don't have the foggiest idea at this point, but like I said, I'm betting it has something to do with Cliff."

"You're reaching, Devlin."

"Yeah. You were always a little slow in the uptake, Pat."

He gestured to let me know what he thought.

"The feeling's mutual."

We stared, stuck a game of chicken, in which Pat held all the cards.

"What else do you know?" I said, giving in first.

Pat came back forward in his chair.

"You want the inside scoop?"

"Yeah."

"Strictly off the record?"

I nodded.

"Nothing."

Pat leaned back.

"Funny," I said.

"Yeah, well, that's the way it is. The FBI's being pretty tight lipped and I'm sure they're expecting the same of me. Being that one of their own is involved. But as far as Audrey is concerned? And what I know? She's up to her ass in alligators. I have her checking out of a hotel down in San Diego two hours before Cliff gets shot. Just enough time to drive up the interstate and do it herself. Then a short time after he's shot, she checks into the resort down in Doheny."

"You found her."

"Not there but she finally showed up at her mother's place."

"And?"

"We questioned her for about an hour and found out she had a legitimate alibi for being at the hotel in San Diego."

"Business."

"Yeah, but not such a great alibi for checking into the Doheny Beach Resort."

"Marital problems."

"You know something you're not telling me, Devlin."

"I'm just reading between the lines, Pat. In one breath, Cliff's telling me how much he loves his wife. In the next, he's telling me to lay low while I keep an eye on her. It's not much of a stretch to think that Audrey wasn't fond of being smothered and that Cliff was the smothering type."

I stood up.

"Anyway, as usual, thanks for nothing."

"Yeah, same to you. I never get anything in return."

"I told you about Cliff and Audrey. Maybe it's not such a great love story, but it's all I have for now."

Pat nodded as if I had taken advantage of him.

"Try to stay out of trouble," he said as I started out the door.

I nodded and left with my guilty conscience. I had held back on Pat, he was likely to find out and I hated to think what would happen when he did. It wouldn't be fun.

From the police station, I waded back down to my office. It was still a hot and restless summer night.

Back at my desk, I kicked my feet up and took a few cheap shots at the world. There weren't many jobs for which I was so well suited. I had brains and had acquired a patina of cynicism

70

over the years. And I was still bristling from that cuffing around I had absorbed twelve hours earlier.

When a woman laughed down below, my thoughts returned to Audrey. Her words from that morning did another lap in my head. 'Sorry, nothing. Do you realize the mess I'm in? Someone just shot Cliff and they're probably going to shoot me next.' Such strange and dangerous words from a lovely redhead.

Just what did Audrey know? And who was the man talking to her? I had assumed him to be the owner of the shipyard, but whoever it was, Audrey didn't trust him as far as she could throw him. And where did Jack fit into all of this? With two people speaking of murder in the next room, Jack had barely flinched. Then, when a man looked like Jack, there wasn't much left to life besides booze, cigars, food and corruption, and not necessarily in that order. What was one more murder?

Then Dick came back to mind and his little warning shot across my bow.

'You don't know what you're dealing with here.'

I was guessing he did and in order to get to the bottom of what that was, apparently I'd have to mix it up with those two boys.

Get off the case, gumshoe, Dick had told me.

Well, sorry pal, but you're giving orders to the wrong soldier.

7

I had been sitting there in the dark for a good spell longer, still puzzling over two deaths and thinking to do a people search on the guy who owned the shipyard when my phone rang. It was Whalen. I watched it ring. Chances were, he had just figured out I was lying and I was in no mood to have him bust my chops.

When Whalen hung up and called back again, I finally answered.

"Yeah, Pat."

"Like to take a ride?"

"Why? So you can lock me up in the back of your squad car and beat me up?"

"Aw, poor Devlin. Got his feelings hurt."

"Yeah, yeah. So what have you got?"

"Well, didn't you say you were up at the Sea Shanty in Newport today when those two goons roughed you up?"

"Yeah. I've been trying to forget about it. So what?"

"So, the cops from the local beat just fished a dead body out of the harbor. They have him lying in a shipyard just to the other side of your restaurant. The driver's license says this boy makes his home up on Allview Terrace, and being that he lives in my beat, they wanted me to come down and have a look. Just wondering if you'd like to tag along."

"Yeah, sure. Anything to get out of this heat."

I hung up the phone and headed out the door. Tough break for that guy. If it was the same man I had heard talking with

Audrey that morning, someone had saved me the cost of a people search.

Ten minutes later, Whalen and I were skirting the coast north of Scotchman's Cove. I was staring out at some ship lights on the black sea. Whalen kept stealing glances at me as we drove along.

"What do you see out there, Devlin? Something you lost?"

"Maybe."

He looked forward again. I continued staring out at the ship lights. There was a strange longing to be out there with them, a longing that seemed to involve a doll, a bottle of booze and swells slapping lazily away at the boat hull.

I was working on that thought when Whalen got back to harassing me.

"You still think Connie and Cliff's murders are related?"

"We have three murders now," I reminded him.

"So we have. You think all three of them are related."

I shrugged, still staring out to sea.

"You're not being very talkative tonight. Those two girls really break your heart today, did they? Never kiss again?"

"Probably not."

Whalen finally gave up and went back to his driving.

A few minutes later, he was taking the loop onto Newport Boulevard. Across the bridge, he turned left and worked his way down to a dead-end street along the back side of the harbor. The shipyard and the lies I had told were straight ahead. If those two Feds were hanging around, Pat would soon start learning things I did not want him to know.

These various concerns came to a crescendo as Pat neared the entrance to the shipyard. Squad cars were parked every which way out in front, putting on a light show. A phalanx of news trucks and reporters was there too. The vultures had simply moved up the coast seven miles since the last time I saw them.

Whalen got out of his side of the car. Bernie was calling to me as I climbed out on mine.

"What do you know, Devlin?!"

I pointed at Whalen and followed him under the yellow caution tape, my ears pinned back for any sign of Dick and Tom. They didn't appear to be hanging around the shipyard but you never knew with boys like that. There were several restaurant balconies looking back our way from Lido peninsula and a handful of boats bobbing out there on the harbor.

Pat had waved to his counterpart from the harbor beat as we walked in. His counterpart waved back, wrapped up his conversation with a uniformed cop and started our way across the shipyard. Sgt. Hernandez was the name on the badge. His bearing was that of a bull looking for something to gore. Everything about him was way too serious for my tastes.

Otherwise, Hernandez looked a lot like Pat's Latino twin; the same butch haircut, the same workout build. He could have passed for a lifeguard, too, if you could picture a Mexican lifeguard.

He shook Pat's hand. Pat introduced me as a private dick and I received a nod instead of a handshake.

The three of us stood there taking in the crime scene. It was still as hot as hell. There were klieg lights everywhere and forensics folks at work, all of it made surreal by that armada of squad cars putting on a colored light show. Most of the cops were standing around the perimeter, shooting the breeze with each other. All the scene lacked was a box of doughnuts.

"Hot one," Hernandez said to Pat.

"Yeah, a hot one," Pat said to Hernandez.

Hearing that, my mind flashed back to a July evening long ago, when I had stopped to spend the night in Loreto, on my way down to Cabo San Lucas. It was nine o'clock when I stepped out of my air-conditioned car and the heat had slapped me in the face like a hot barber's towel. That sort of weather never relented. Midnight and the porches along the streets were still packed with restless souls. You couldn't sleep. There wasn't a breeze. Maybe standing right down next to the gulf, you'd feel one lapping up from the waves. Maybe, and it was just that sort of night in Newport. The heat made you want to dive into the harbor, as foul as it was with diesel fuel and boaters dumping their toilets on the way in from a day of fishing.

"What's the story?" Pat said.

"Like I said, a man dead and a ransacked office. Whatever else they were looking for, they took all the computers."

"Meaning, someone didn't want someone knowing something."

"Something like that. Better have a look at the corpse," Sergeant Hernandez added. "Before they toss him into the back of the wagon."

We circumvented the crime scene markers and walked down towards the water. The corpse was on the concrete ramp adjacent to the dock, covered with a plastic tarp. The harbor water was lapping not fifteen feet from the shoes.

Hernandez pulled back the tarp to reveal the man I had seen with Audrey earlier in the day. He was trim, a few inches under six feet and appeared to have put on some weight from his tour around the harbor. A few strands of sea grass were tangled in his coarse hair. The hair looked rust colored in the artificial light. I had an eerie sense of him smiling at me. For all his talk of dirty deeds with Audrey, he did have that look of a happy-go-lucky guy, everyone glad to see him when he walked into the party. He would have been in his early sixties, had he still been alive.

I had never grown accustomed to seeing a corpse, and this was especially true after one had been floating around in the brackish brine of the back harbor for a few hours. There was already a sad, surreal quality about the dead, as if someone had made up a copy of your Uncle Bob, only with the spirit noticeably absent. Add a bit of brine and they became especially grotesque. You could not help but think of how fragile your own hold on life was from minute to minute.

"Name's Dan Colby," Hernandez was saying. "And other than for bedding down in your town and owning this shipyard, we don't know much about him...You happen to know him?"

Pat shook his head.

"Where did you find him?"

"A couple in a power boat spotted him on their way in from Catalina. Called the Harbor Patrol. By the time the patrol arrived, he was bobbing around under the dock here. One slug in the chest. Looks like he took a brief tour of the harbor and washed right back up where he had started."

"Doesn't make any sense," Pat said.

"Nope," Hernandez acknowledged. "He didn't drown. And no one tied him to the bottom with rocks, so unless a swim at the end suddenly struck him like a great idea, you're right, it doesn't make much sense. There's blood up in the office, and a trail of it leading all the way down to the shore. There's also a big gorilla up there named Jack, who happens to be the shipyard foreman."

"Any motive there?" Pat asked.

"Who knows? The Harbor Patrol noticed him slipping out of the office as they pulled up to the dock. His story was, he had forgotten to write a check to one of their subcontractors. Saw all the blood and that the office had been ransacked and was heading off to call the cops. We asked him the usual. Why didn't you use the phone right in front of you? He told us the usual. He had panicked."

Pat had been listening to Hernandez without emotion.

"But motive?" Hernandez said. "Other than his mere presence in the office tonight? Not that I can see. Maybe you'd like to go up to the office and have a chat with him."

"Does he bite?" Pat said.

"Ask him. When we told him about Colby, his eyes got the size of saucers."

"You think he knows something."

"He knows how to get real scared. Or how to fake it real well."

I had been staring at the corpse throughout this entire conversation.

"You done looking at him?" Hernandez asked me.

I nodded and Hernandez dropped the tarp. He and Pat started up towards the office.

"Guess I'll take in the harbor," I told them.

"What's the matter?" Pat said. "Afraid you're going to see someone you know?"

Hernandez looked from Pat to me and back at Pat.

"Seems like a couple of goons roughed him up this morning. Over behind the Sea Shanty. Divorce case. That's how he got the gash"

Pat winked at me and looked back at Hernandez.

"That's his story anyway."

Hernandez eyed me with renewed interest. At the very least, he appeared to have some sort of tutorial about messing with crime scenes on his mind, but in the end, he let it ride and headed up towards the office with Pat.

As their voices trailed off into the distance, I walked out to the end of the dock. A trawler was tied to one side of me. Swells lapped lazily at the pilings beneath my shoes. A slight breeze had kicked up from the ocean side of the peninsula. The scent of the sea was trying to poke through the heavier scent of brine and diesel.

I heard a woman's playful scream and laughter from the direction of the fun zone and looked that way. The distant lights of the Ferris wheel were peeking over the rooftops. A bit of a ruckus broke out on the outdoor balcony of the Sea Shanty. Otherwise, the harbor seemed as peaceful as could be.

My mind returned to the jigsaw puzzle in front of me. I had hundreds of pieces scattered all over the board and at best a handful of them clipped together. One was knowing that Audrey had been involved in an arm's shipment deal gone south. Two, Dan Colby had been involved in some kind of dirty business with Audrey. Whether or not it was the same bad deal, I had no idea. Three, Dan Colby, Cliff Black and Connie

McPherson were all dead. Four, Vanderhof's name had come up in all three of the stories. Why? I had no idea but it appeared that knowing him was not particularly good for your health.

What else did I know? Audrey had a lousy alibi for checking into a hotel half an hour after her husband's death and she continued to act in mysterious ways. Jack had been caught sneaking around a crime scene and someone had found it necessary to make all of Dan Colby's computers disappear. Oh, and a silhouette had paused outside my office door earlier in the day. That definitely had my curiosity up, but add things all together and none of it made much sense to my tired brain.

Taking a wild swing at Jack's motives, it was possible he had come by to dispose of evidence; an e-mail sent by Audrey, a file saved on Dan Colby's hard drive, something that would have proven intent in a deal gone wrong, only to discover that someone had been there before him. And all that amounted to little more than a wild swing.

Looking back at Dan Colby's corpse, I wondered again why anyone would want to put a slug in him. On the face of it, it would seem that whatever secrets Colby had possessed, they had failed to extract them before ending his life. Or maybe they had and that's why they ran off with his computers.

My mind came back to Cliff and Connie. It was hard to see how Colby's death was related to their deaths, but something told me it was.

Well, my wild speculations aside, I imagined we were all as dumb as night crawlers about the mess we were in, the cops included, because once the feds got involved, a shroud of secrecy descended over everything. Not every citizen was created equal in their eyes. They were just equally dispensable. Of the people, by the people and for the people was just a convenient slogan you trotted out to cover your ass.

In the stillness of a hot summer night, I glanced up in the direction of the shipyard office. Pat and Hernandez were still in there grilling Jack. The forensics crew was preoccupied at the other end of the yard. In varying sized groups, the uniformed cops were hanging around in the darkness beyond the klieg lights, telling tall tales and no longer much interested in Colby's corpse, as far as I could see.

I was and walked back down to where his body lay by the base of the dock. With the tarp pulled back, I stared again at this trim man with the sea grass in his hair. It was a lovely look, if you happened to be frolicking in the breakers on a summer day. On a muggy summer night, lying on a concrete ramp, and with the chill of death overtaking your flesh, it left something to be desired.

Figuring Hernandez had already rifled through Colby's pockets, I didn't bother with repeating that exercise. Something else was on my mind, something that had caught my eye the minute Hernandez first pulled the tarp aside; the fact that Colby's left shoelace was partially untied. Possibly the tide had done that, but probably not.

With another quick look around to make sure no one was watching, I undid the lace the rest of the way and removed Colby's shoe. Something fell with a clatter into the base of it. When I turned the shoe over, a flash drive fell into the palm of my hand. The letters PNY and 32GB were printed on the case. I slipped the plastic case into my coat pocket. Mr. Colby's shoe went back on his foot. There was little point in bothering with the shoelace. No one seemed to have noticed it before.

With the plastic tarp back in place, I headed up towards the office. My heart raced a bit, passing various cops along the way. I had just committed a crime and had to worry that someone might have noticed.

There was also my impending encounter with Jack. Would he recall me from that morning? Would he see past the mustache, shades and pork pie hat? Probably not, but you never knew. There being no discreet way to disguise my voice under the circumstances, I made a point to keep my mouth shut.

Everyone turned as I walked into the office. I found Jack seated in the middle of the room. He looked like he had been tied to his chair, though he wasn't. Pat and Hernandez were batting him around like a shuttlecock in a game of badminton.

"We're still wondering why you showed up?" Hernandez said to him.

"Yeah, people don't just happen upon a crime scene in the middle of the night, Jack."

"And then leave."

"Not without a good reason, right?"

"That's right," Hernandez said.

"Say, why don't you just tell us the truth, pal?"

"Yeah, save yourself and everybody here a whole lot of trouble."

Sitting there and being grilled in his figurative stocks, Jack no longer looked so tough. In fact, he looked rather frightened. *Of Mice and Men* came to mind, only in this version of the tale, Lennie Small had shot George instead.

Pat smiled at me.

"You want to take a crack at him?"

"Who's he?" Jack asked, looking from me to Hernandez and back at Pat.

"I thought you knew him," Pat said.

"I don't know him from Adam."

"You want to take a crack at him?" Pat offered me again.

I shook my head.

"All right," Hernandez said with a nod towards one of the uniformed cops standing against the wall. "Take him downtown."

The cop assisted Jack's great girth out of the chair.

"What are you booking me for?" Jack wanted to know.

The question had come out somewhere between a grunt and a wheeze. Hernandez looked back over at him, annoyed.

"I'm not booking you for anything. I'm holding you for twenty-four hours. Or until I find out you've been lying to me. If you have, then I'll book you. If not, I'll let you go."

"I'm not lying," Jack complained in his now wheezy, piggly voice.

Hernandez didn't bother answering him. He just nodded and the uniformed cop led Jack out the door in handcuffs.

From the sound of Jack's complaint alone, I did not think he was lying, at least not about the murder. Maybe he was telling half-truths, but Jack did not sound like a man who had just plugged his boss. People who were lying could be indignant, or they could be whiny, but not both at the same time. It was in conflict with some unwritten law in our DNA. Probably Hernandez knew that too and was just shooting arrows around in the dark. Like me, there was a lot of darkness around Hernandez's fire, but probably a few less wolves.

Pat started to leave and nodded for me to join him.

"Give me a call," Hernandez told him. "I'd like to know if you find any computers up at Colby's place."

"Will do," Pat said.

The two of us went out the door.

"Find anything in his pockets?" he asked me.

My ears pinned back, the way any wild creature's ears will do when cornered. Pat stared at me until I looked back.

"Just some more sea grass," I said.

He grunted with a smile.

"That's all right, because Hernandez had already checked him out. Which is why he had the wallet. And why he called me."

Pat acted all full of himself, and I allowed him his moment. I had the flash drive. I probably should have turned it over to him, but I knew if Pat found anything on there with the potential to clear Steve's name, that information was not likely to see the light of day.

South on Pacific Coast Highway

8

All the way back down the coast, between blabbing away about his kids winning a soccer tournament and his perky blonde wife and their pink, Mediterranean style stucco house and their St. Augustine grass and how the city council was giving the police force a bum shake these days, Whalen still found time to take a few jabs at me.

"What's the matter, Devlin," he said after failing at every other form of harassment. "You still mad at me about McPherson?"

"It's not your fault that you're too dumb to see the truth right in front of your own eyes."

"I'll take that as a yes."

I gestured to let him know he was warm.

"Sorry, but the man's guilty. I'd bet my life on it."

"Then I don't give you long to live."

"Hey, he's your friend so I understand the sentiment, but you're wrong."

I nodded, tired of arguing with him. Whalen eyed me for a moment longer and got back to his driving.

As we approached Laurel Lagoon, I sensed him eyeing me again.

"You mind stopping by Colby's place with me before I drop you back at the office?"

"Not at all."

"Thanks. It'll save me making an extra trip."

"Anything to help."

"You're a real sport."

"So I've been told."

Whalen stared at me for a long moment, like he had something else on his mind but looked forward again without saying another word.

At the north end of town, the highway swung away from the coast and up past the knoll at El Morro Cove. Block walls draped with bougainvillea bordered both sides of the highway. Pines towered over the bougainvillea here and there. A gated community rose up into the hills on the inland side of the highway and down to the sea on the other.

A few hundred yards past the last guard gate, Pat turned left across a now empty highway and worked his way up a maze of darkened residential streets. Colby's house was up near the top of the hill, just south of the gated community. The minute Pat pulled onto Colby's dead-end street, it became clear that we weren't the first ones to arrive. The usual carnival of cop cars, klieg lights, news reporters and curious neighbors were out in front to greet us.

Colby's house was the very last one on the block. Pat braked to a stop and climbed out to face a crush of reporters. I ducked under the caution tape and went on alone.

Colby's place was a massive, three-story A-frame precipitously attached to a steep hillside. An undeveloped slope rose up behind the house and rambled off into a nature preserve. Below Colby's house, a mishmash of homes cascaded down towards Coast Highway. The sea broke against the cliffs some three hundred yards to the other side of the highway.

According to Pat, Colby's house had once belonged to a reclusive Hollywood starlet. It was easy to imagine her living up there all alone. The place had a view of the coast, from San Onofre all the way up to San Pedro, where a necklace of lights died into the black hump of Palos Verdes.

Pat joined me at the front door a moment later and we went up to the second story.

"Anything?" Pat asked Sergeant Burrell as we entered the living room. Burrell was the head of forensics and a matter of fact guy.

"Not much to go on," Burrell said. "He was divorced and didn't have a girlfriend. At least there's no sign of a woman having been around."

Burrell nodded towards a corner of the room.

"There's a cat."

The cat had responded to all the commotion by retreating to the top of a tall curio cabinet. It viewed Pat and me with part fear, part menace.

"I want his desk top," Pat said. "And every disk you can lay your hands on."

"Sure," Burrell said.

"Did you find a laptop too?"

"Nope," Burrell said.

"Well, keep an eye out."

"You got it."

"Anything else unusual?"

"Not unless you think expensive French wine with TV dinners is out of the ordinary."

Pat nodded.

"What happened to you?" Burrell said to me.

"He lost a fight with a couple of girls," Whalen said, speaking in my place.

"I'm having signs made up tomorrow. Just to save everyone the trouble of asking."

"Tough break," Burrell said. "Everyone giving you a hard time, eh?"

"Just Pat here," I said. "I'm guessing he's not getting any at home and taking it out on me."

"All right," Pat said. "Let's everyone get back to work."

"It works one way with him," I said to Burrell.

84

Burrell nodded knowingly and went back to dusting for prints. I followed Pat into Colby's bedroom. Pat was snapping on a pair of surgical gloves.

"Don't touch anything," he told me when I moved towards a photo on Colby's dresser.

"Not even you?" I said.

"Funny," he said and picked up the photo. It was of Colby and a woman. The woman was wearing Capri pants and high heels. She was a good-looking blonde and had a figure to match.

"His ex-wife?" Pat said with a glance in my direction.

"They look happier than most couples I know."

"Yeah, wonder what happened to her?"

"She got too tall for him."

"Funny," Pat said again. He took the photo out front and handed it to Burrell.

"See what you can find out about the doll, here. If you get her prints, check them against anything in the house."

Burrell took the photo, placed it into a plastic bag and set it down by his forensics case. Pat and I went up to check the third floor. Of necessity in an A-frame, each floor became smaller than the one below it, and in this case, the top floor was a spacious loft with a wet bar and half bath that had served as Colby's office. While Pat poked around in Colby's desk and file cabinet, I stood there looking out to sea. The precipitous view down the hillside left you feeling queasy. My gut kept telling me to back up a few paces but I didn't.

On our way out, Pat poked around the first floor but there wasn't much to see. It was the story of a man who had lived his life alone. What the world would probably learn about me when I bought the farm; few friends, little family and a handful of fleeting memories. At least Colby had owned a cat.

Back in town, Pat pulled into another left-hand turn lane and entered the tree-shrouded downtown street that ran past my office. He stopped in front.

The street had miraculously emptied out in our absence. Most everyone had gone home, or had ambled over to one of the late-night bars on the next block. I saw the same Mexican busboy mopping up tables over at Mark's. Every other establishment had closed their doors. The streets looked like the morning after Fourth of July; debris littered amongst the hangovers and broken hearts.

"Thanks for the fun," I said.

"Hey Devlin," Pat said as I was closing the door.

He hit the power window button and I leaned down onto the open window frame.

"I still think you're holding out on me."

I shook my head.

"Why don't I believe you?"

"Because it's your job not to believe me," I said.

"Prick. I know you've got something up your sleeve."

"I told you. I think Steve's innocent and I think all three of these murders are somehow connected. But it's just a wild guess at this point."

"You've got something you're not telling me."

"I've got a wild guess."

"Son of a bitch. See if I ever help you again."

Pat gave me an ominous look, hit the power window button and drove off. I watched him for a moment and considered how well I had parsed my words. Well enough, I thought. A lawyer would have been proud of me, a priest not so much.

I pushed open the door to my office building and dashed upstairs. It was an old habit from my youth, and one I was not yet prepared to abandon. I figured as long as I was able to dash somewhere, I was that much further from the grave.

Back in my office and famished, I took a bite out of the leftover turkey sandwich on my desk. The bread was leaning towards cardboard at that point. I reached behind me and pulled a bottle of Perrier out of the bar fridge.

While I got that mouthful of dry sandwich dislodged from my throat, I checked for phone messages. There was one from

86

Audrey. That meant she had heard I was looking for her. I returned the call but no one answered.

Hanging up, I tried retrieving the information on the flash drive but it came up gibberish. I called Kenny. He looked over at me from his windows.

"Why do you have all your lights off?" he wanted to know.

"I'm doing my part for global warming."

"Wow, what happened to your face?"

"Some people aren't very fond of my work on global warming."

Kenny laughed.

"Nothing yet on the redhead," he said. "She must be paying cash, or staying with someone she knows."

"Yeah, she went home. Whalen told me. She called here a short while ago but failed to leave a message."

"So what now?"

"Kemosabe."

Kenny laughed.

"Sorry," I said. "I just enjoy the hell out of saying that word."

"So what's going on?"

"Oh, I've got a bit of a tech problem. Mind if I stop over?"

"I'm here."

"I'm on my way out the door."

I headed downstairs and across the empty street. The entire front of Kenny's building was plate glass, including the door. Inside the foyer, a wrought iron stairway spiraled up to the second story. I hurried up the stairs and into Kenny's office. There was a rustling sound from behind a five-foot high bank of computers and Kenny's head poked out over the top. He smiled wryly before his head of wavy hair disappeared again. When he finally reappeared from between the wall and his computers, he had a piece of hardware in one hand.

"Upgrading one of my external hard drives." He laughed his dry laugh. "What's going on."

I held out the flash drive and sea brine spilled from one end. I imitated Kenny's dry laugh.

"This was on a dead man and they were both floating around in Newport Harbor for a spell."

"Not the worst idea in this heat."

Kenny looked pleased with his own joke.

"Yeah…So anyway, I tried to access the information but it seems to be encoded.

"Let's have a look."

Kenny sat down at one of his computers and went to work. I watched him try to retrieve the information in Word first, then as a PDF file, but everything remained digital gibberish on the screen. He tried a few more tricks but nothing worked.

"I'll bet it was encrypted with an RSA code," he said while still working.

"What does that mean?"

"It means you can probably forget about it."

Kenny spun around in his chair.

"RSA is basically unbreakable."

"We're talking absolutely no for an answer?"

"Look, here's what you're up against. One holiday a few years back, this computer geek, inspired by a bit too much Manischewitz, goes home and cooks up an encryption method. Called it RSA, after his initials and those of his two best buddies. In fairness, it probably should have been called ARS, but that's another story. The point is, the code is based on multiplying one prime number by another. If these two prime numbers are sufficiently large, it could take all the computers in the world the lifetime of the universe to break the code. Or one hundred million times the life of the universe, if we're just using my gear. Even a modestly large number would require many years of factoring."

"Give me a solution," I said.

Kenny laughed.

"Find the person who has the prime numbers. It only takes one of them to break the code."

"And that person was last seen floating around dead in Newport Harbor."

"He might have left a clue lying around somewhere."

"Like a vin number?"

Kenny offered up another variation of his laugh.

"Maybe if you were trying to protect your files from a casual hacker, you'd use a small number like that. But for important stuff, we're talking about something with three hundred digits."

"Shit."

"Yeah."

Kenny handed me the flash drive.

"You still want me to keep an eye on Audrey?"

"Yes, please. Call me if anything comes up. I don't care the hour."

"Will do," he said.

A minute later, I was back in my office with feet up on my desk and my mind back to puzzling over things. Why would Vanderhof's name keep popping up? Past business dealings with Magellan Ltd. and Audrey, okay. A murky past with Dan Colby, somewhat understandable. But knowing Steve and Connie back in the day? It was all too convenient, though for the life of me I couldn't see how any of it was connected.

And why start killing people now? Why not last month? Or last year? It hurt my head just thinking about it.

I got to my feet, ready to drive out to Mr. Billion Dollars' place. My only hope appeared to be putting a tail on him again.

I was halfway out the door when the phone rang. I went back and answered it.

"Yeah, Devlin here."

There was silence. Then whoever it was hung up.

I shoved my .38 into the shoulder holster, flipped on my desk lamp, wanting the caller to think I was still there, and hurried out the door.

Down on the first floor, I unlocked the back door and stepped into a closet at the underside of the stairs. A few moments later, the door to the street opened and what sounded like two men started slowly up the wooden stairs. From what I could tell, they were wearing boots and trying to be quiet. I waited until they were well down the hallway towards my office before I slipped out of the closet and opened the back door, my attempt at stealth foiled by a creaky hinge. As I dashed out the door, I heard footsteps racing back down the hallway.

Seconds later, I was fishtailing onto Laurel Avenue in my Impala. In my rearview mirror, I saw two men stumble out the back door of the office building. Culiacan boys, from the looks of them. Cowboy boots and belt buckles the size of your wallet.

A dark gray Suburban whipped out of the library parking lot and slowed long enough for the men to jump in. I blew the stop sign at Park and Laurel and heard a shot clink off the rear of my car. Two more bullets hit, all without a report. It wasn't much in the way of evidence, but they were using a silencer and someone had used one to kill Cliff Black.

With another glance in my rearview mirror, I saw I was losing ground. My only hope was to ditch these boys in that tangle of winding lanes leading up past the high school. I blew another stop sign, turned left on the next street and zigzagged my way up towards the hills behind town.

After careening onto Wendt Terrace, I quickly turned right onto a dead-end street called Griffith Way. Headlights were just turning onto Wendt Terrace behind me. At the first driveway, I turned in and followed it around to the back of a Tudor style house. A moment later, the Suburban went barreling down the street. Lights were flicking on in the house. I waited until my friends were well down the block before I backed out of the driveway at top speed. A man in a bathrobe was coming out the front door as I did.

I turned south onto Wendt Terrace and raced down the winding street going airborne with every speed bump. Before long, headlights were spraying the darkness behind me. I came to the stop sign at Thalia with the lights closing fast. Without stopping, I barreled across the street, made a few more wild

90

turns and was soon heading south along the dark, dead-end streets below Summit Drive.

With the headlights nowhere in sight now, I cut the motor at Carmelita and glided to a halt with my own lights turned off. My heart was pounding. My eyes were fixed on the rearview mirror. I felt like a submarine captain, waiting for the next depth charge to go off.

Fifteen minutes went by with me waiting and wondering how we had gone from Cliff and Dan Colby being shot to me being on the wrong end of a gun. Without answers, but convinced that I had lost those boys for the moment, I started my car, drove up to Pearl Street and turned left. Pearl was a narrow dead-end road at that point, with a deep canyon to my left and steep, tree shrouded driveways on my right. When two cars met, there was barely enough room for them to pass.

Motoring on into the darkness, I came to the very last driveway, turned up the steep ribbon of asphalt and parked under a deck. A set of 4X12 wooden stair treads led from the underside of the deck up to the house. Teresa, my part time bookkeeper lived there and you could not have found a more secluded place in Laurel Lagoon, not even my house.

It being late on a Thursday night, decency suggested that I call ahead, but not trusting anyone's phone to be secure at this point, I banked my fortunes on an unwelcome intrusion. Teresa forced a sleepy smile upon seeing my face at her door. It wasn't a happy smile and suggested a lot of things about her own life; that she was alone and hadn't enjoyed the comforts of a boyfriend for as long as I hadn't enjoyed the comforts of a girlfriend, that she was tired of that state of affairs, and though fond of me, not at all happy to find me at her front door at that hour.

"I have a phone," she said.

"Yeah. I'm sorry to be bothering you, but..."

"I knew that was coming."

"It's all right. I can leave."

"For god's sake, Michael. Quit being so melodramatic."

"Yeah, well, I don't respond well to people calling me melodramatic, either."

"Oh my god, Michael," she said, seeing my wounds. "What happened to you?"

"It comes with being melodramatic."

"Stop. Let me have a look at you…Oh my god."

Teresa waved me in through the door, her mothering instincts having kicked in.

"Go. Have a seat in the kitchen."

I slipped past her petite brunette form and did as instructed. Teresa closed the door and disappeared into the back of the house. When she reappeared, she was carrying hydrogen peroxide, Neosporin and gauze in her hands.

While she worked on me, Teresa's golden retriever Rusty sidled over and shoved his big snout into my crotch, the tail wagging. He was a sweetheart of a dog but smelled of bad feet — really bad feet. Teresa said it was some sort of skin disease. Give Rusty a bath and he would make your eyes water two hours later. The scent permeated Teresa's entire place. I didn't know how she endured it.

"Ow," I said.

"Hold still."

A minute later, she placed her medical supplies aside.

"So, to what do I owe the pleasure of your company at five past midnight on a Thursday night?"

I pulled the flash drive out of my pocket.

"I need that no one finds this thing."

"I don't know if I like the sound of that."

"I just spent fifteen minutes over on Carmelita making sure whoever had been following me wasn't still on my tail."

"I don't know if I like the sound of that any better. What might happen to the person who possesses this thing?"

"The guy who had it before me now sleeps with the fishes."

Teresa shook her head while staring. It was a look that I had seen once too many times in my life, a look that said I was not to be trusted, a look that had always left me feeling deeply wounded inside.

"You're right, Teresa. I shouldn't have come over here with my problems. I just didn't know what else to do with this thing right now."

"Do you mind explaining how you got into this mess?"

I did.

"The truth is, I don't know what's going on. I don't know what I've gotten myself into."

She stared.

"That guy who was killed down on Forest was your client?"

"Yeah. Well...he was going to be, before he got shot."

After a long moment, Teresa held out her hand. I gave her the flash drive.

"Thanks."

"You're welcome. And stop with the eyes already. You look like somebody just stole your bicycle."

"I'm all right."

She shook her head and herded me towards the door.

"Go home and get some sleep. You look like hell."

"Perhaps you'd better come down and get things organized one day soon."

"I will. But not until this business calms down a bit."

"Okay. And thanks again."

I gave her a hug before starting down the steps to my car.

It had been my thought to return to the office, but Teresa was probably right. I needed sleep, and going back there would only lead to more trouble. Besides, I wanted to give Dick and Tom a chance to rifle through the place. The sooner they knew I had nothing to hide, the sooner we could resume our chummy relationship. I assumed we were on the same side; a lot more than I ever would be with those three boys in the Suburban. And seeing the Feds come and go might just put a little fear of the Lord in the cartel.

Back at the house, I loaded my Remington pump-action shotgun and set it next to the nightstand, just for good measure.

After collapsing in bed, and tossing and turning in the dark for half an hour, I gave up, flicked on a light and reached for my hundred year old edition of Rudyard Kipling. Bound in blue leather, dog-eared around the edges and with pages as fine as a King James Bible, I grew lost in a story about a White Hussars regiment in India. Just before I drifted off into slumber, their presumed to be dead Regimental Horse had come galloping down a dusty road with a skeleton on its back.

South on Pacific Coast Highway

9

The following morning, I awakened to a warm, dry wind stirring in the eucalyptus leaves outside my windows. You would have thought there were rattlesnakes out there. Angry rattlesnakes. The wind had turned and was blowing down from the desert now, leaving behind a dry and empty world.

As I lay there, a gang of crows settled high up in one of the trees and started cawing. It was as if they had flown out of last night's dreams.

Actually, the dreams had been about the old flame, Caitlin. As usual, it had involved a wild chase of some sort, but chase as I might, I could never quite catch up. I had been chasing her from galaxy to galaxy for a billion lifetimes now, without any success. She was that wife on Orion, my portal to bliss, but the spaceship had left for home without me.

I rolled over in bed to escape the feelings, only to find them waiting for me on the other side. Caitlin's absence came with the sadness of a thousand lifetimes attached to it. God, just to see her once again.

When a dove cooed, my mind was carried back to the days of my youth, to the insects buzzing in the dry brush on late spring mornings, to the pepper trees drooping like willows in the heat, to the static electricity snapping in the plastic seats of our classrooms, to the restless boredom of waiting for school to let out for summer.

Then Caitlin was back. Jesus how I missed that woman.

Tired of my own thoughts, I crawled out of bed and wandered out to the living room. The sun was rising. The day was as dry as flour. A line of blue sea was visible beyond the shifting trees. My thoughts wandered down to my little trailer south of the border. I could see the waves breaking off for forty miles, certain that being there would make me happy. Why I thought I'd suddenly arrive at some Zen-like state of contentment by driving across the border, I had no idea. I had never been all that satisfied anywhere in this world. And still my heart was riding down the coast.

Due to testify in court at ten o'clock on Mrs. Vanderhof's behalf, I went in to shave. While staring into the mirror, Steve McPherson returned to my thoughts. Steve had been our star high school quarterback, a state champion in the hundred-yard dash, the owner of a million-dollar smile. Every girl at school had gone to bed with dreams of wearing his letterman's jacket and ring. Both of our lives had been sprinkled with fairy dust back then. Time had no end. What had happened to us? Steve was facing twenty-five years to life. I was on a downer I couldn't seem to kick.

In the background, I heard the fax machine kick in and start to print. I went to have a look. It was Jim sending me the police report on Connie McPherson's death. I dragged it back into the bathroom and scanned through the facts between swipes with my razor. A hiker had found her body up in an arroyo near Irvine Park, still wearing the short, red dress she had worn while out on the town the night before. Brush was tangled in her long, dark hair. One high heel was missing and the time of death had been confirmed to be sometime late afternoon to early evening, the day before.

Setting aside Steve and his lack of an alibi, why Connie? Who would want her dead and why? The police report had nothing to say on that score, only that they believed Connie had been killed in one place and then dumped there in the brush. There was no sign of her having been molested but forensics did find some dishwater blonde hairs on the dress. They weren't Steve's but what did Whalen care? With Connie having been out on the town the night before, the hairs could have come from anywhere. Besides, stalking your wife will turn you into a suspect every time.

During a long shower, my mind got back to beating up on me. What had I ever accomplished? Who had I helped? That sort of crap. The sum total of my legacy seemed to be romantic detours that turned out to be dead ends. As an antidote, I tried fixing the world. The prison system went first, then the national debt. By the time I was out of the shower, I had straightened out the entire planet, and still I felt lousy.

I dialed in Gromer Khan on my I-pad, put Samarkand Run on loop and went out to make breakfast. Dappled sunlight played on the floor while I cooked. I ate my bacon and eggs at the breakfast nook with the morning paper in front of me. The rattlesnakes were threatening but Gromer Khan had me on the midnight ship back to Orion.

A thought occurred to me. If gravity is mass, perhaps Zen is simply converting mass back into energy. With my life being a black hole these days, I had a lot of mass to work with. I set the dishes in the kitchen sink and went to dress, doing my best to convert a trillion tons of grief into weightlessness.

A few minutes later, I was looking snazzy in a beige suit, dark blue shirt and gold tie. I reluctantly turned off the music and headed out the door. There was a final longing glance back at my cottage, not really wanting to face the day and remembering Caitlin yet again, exactly the way she had looked the last time I saw her, remembering the peace I once felt with her in my life.

How nice it would be to have you call someday, doll. Let me know that you care. You are in everything I do, everything I think, everything I see. I still love you, more than I can say.

And there I was, trying to make autumn leaves return to their trees.

A small wooden bridge led from my front yard over a creek. My garage was twenty feet to the other side of the creek. I went in through the side door and hit the button. The wooden door rolled up, letting in the light of day.

Halfway into my Impala, I heard the neighbor's old gray-whiskered Lab growling in the narrow lane and went out to investigate. A black stretch limo had just pulled to a stop down from my driveway.

Seeing me, the old Lab came over, still growling low but wagging his tail. I petted him and stared at the limo. One of the darkly tinted windows lowered. It was Vanderhof. What in hell was he doing here?

"Come on inside," he said.

Against my better judgment, I did. The interior was decked out like a plush office with a master suite in back. We were a Jacuzzi and a couple of dolls short of a wild morning.

Vanderhof sat across from me grinning, but just with the mouth, not the eyes.

In all the time I had been investigating him, and even with crossing paths with him at the police station the other night, I had never seen him up this close. He was my height, a few inches over six feet, but also a few pounds heavier than I was. Bushy eyebrows, dark brooding eyes and a goatee accented his Slavic features. An oversized mouth dominated everything else. When he grinned, the mouth seemed to take up half his face. In keeping with the hot weather, he was impeccably dressed in his own cream-colored suit. His light brown hair was oiled and down to his collar and had a radiance to it, as if he had been out there frolicking in the summer sun.

"Coffee?" he asked.

I shook my head.

"Drink?"

I shook my head again.

"Whatever you want."

I shook my head yet again, but with a smile now.

"What?" he said.

"Oh, just having a Zen moment here."

"Devlin. You'd space out in front of a firing squad. Now I'm here to make you an offer, so let's get serious okay?"

"Okay. Let's get real serious, Mr. Vanderhof. I'm scheduled to testify against you in a civil suit in about an hour. And you see nothing unethical about the two of us hanging out together in your rolling disco?"

"Look around you, Devlin. Who's ever going to know we're having a chat?"

"Me."

He leaned forward, ignoring the comment.

"Like I told you on the phone yesterday morning. I have a job for you to do. So what do you have to lose by hearing me out?"

"My license."

He leaned back in the seat with a flick of his hand.

"If that's all you're worried about, I'll buy you another one."

"Look, Vanderhof. You want all your problems to go away, just settle with your wife. Then you won't have to come around here trying to bid on my loyalty. Or whatever it is you're trying to do here."

He stared, his head slowly nodding.

"Do you know how I made my fortune?"

"I'm going to guess by screwing a lot of other people."

I had half expected a grin. Instead, a dark shadow fell over his face.

"Getting warm, am I?"

"It's dog eat dog out there, Devlin. You don't think the Carnegies and Vanderbilt's had to step on a few toes in their day?"

"You may as well make Attila the Hun your role model."

"Look, you play rough in this world or you end up eating somebody else's shit. That's the way it is."

"Okay, so let's see if I've got this straight. You want me to come to work for you, so I can eat some of your shit."

He shook a finger at me.

"Goddamn it, Devlin. You really can be a pain in the ass."

99

"I know, but I figured as old chums and all, I was free to speak my mind."

"All right," he said with a check of his watch. "I'll give you one day to think it over."

"There's nothing to think over. Just settle with your wife and then we can talk all you want. Otherwise, there's the highway."

"You know, you're being a petty little prick."

"I know. I work hard at it. But it has left me with the freedom to tell most anyone in this world, go screw yourself. Including you. Now I suggest you try to stay out of trouble. At least until the ink dries on your divorce papers."

I opened the door and started to get out.

"Look, Devlin. I know you've got problems."

I stopped. Vanderhof's eyebrows went up.

"That's right. The minute my wife's attorney hired you to investigate me, I hired someone to investigate you. You're broke. You're behind on your mortgage. You're one medical calamity short of being out on the street."

"That's what happens when you tell enough people to go screw themselves."

"So, I'm offering you a bundle of money, and all you have to do is one little job for me."

"Which would be?"

"I need you to get rid of this Rick Duncan character." It was time for my eyebrows to go up. "You know him, huh?"

"Not really, but what do you mean, 'get rid of him'?"

"Get him off my back."

"Well, that could mean a lot of things. Some I'm willing to do, some I'm not. Why don't you tell me why you think he's on your back?"

"He claims to have some dirt on me."

"Which would be?"

"I don't know. That's what I want you to find out."

"Sorry, Mr. Vanderhof, but we're back to me jeopardizing my career. Not to mention my ethics. Which, as I said, I'm not willing to do. I don't care how much money you've got."

"You're getting on the wrong side of me, Devlin, and that's a place you don't want to be."

"What is it with people like you, Vanderhof? A few lucky breaks and you're king of the world. A finger in everybody's chest. All right, so you're worth a few billion. You can live in style for a few thousand years. Why don't you give something back to humanity now? Is there nothing else in this world that motivates you besides making a few more bucks?"

"What kind of statement is that? You think I do it for the money? You don't get anywhere in this world chasing after money, Devlin. I do what I do because I love it. I love the excitement of kicking ass and taking home the prize. What else would you do with your time on this earth?"

"That's a question that apparently has no answer when it comes to you."

"Son of a bitch."

"Yeah, I don't bowl over so easy. Now I've got some testifying to do, and after that I have a full day of investigating to do, so I'll be on my way."

"It better not be investigating my life any further," Vanderhof said.

"Why not?" I said. "You got something to hide?"

"Look, I'm giving you one more chance. Come work for me and you'll be on easy street. Or..."

Vanderhof held up his hands.

"Sorry, the answer's still no, but I'll make you a counteroffer. I own a little trailer down south of the border. There's a beachy little bar just up that abandoned stretch of coastline. All you need is a few bucks and some fishing gear. Settle up with your wife and we can meet down there someday for a drink and a long chat."

"Michael, I'm playing for billions here. I don't have time for being trailer trash down south of the border. Now are you going to work with me here or what?"

"You're asking me to sell my soul, Mr. Vanderhof, and I can't. I won't. At least not right this minute. Check in with me tomorrow. Maybe I'll be an easier mark by then."

He stared at me, playing with his goatee and as serious as venom.

"All right," he said. "I'll give you until tomorrow to think it over."

"I'll see you in court in about an hour."

I climbed out and started to close the door.

"By the way," he said.

I leaned back in.

"A word to the wise. Stop chasing that Audrey Black around. She's nothing but trouble."

Vanderhof grinned his deadly grin.

"Let's get onboard, Michael. You don't need me as one of your enemies."

I started to close the door but Vanderhof called me back again.

"Hey, are you coming to the Policemen's Ball next Saturday night. You know they're honoring me as Citizen of the Year."

"Yeah, so I heard."

"Don't be so sore. Come and I'll buy you a drink."

"I'll have to check my itinerary."

"You do that. I'll call you tomorrow."

The limo came to life. I closed the door and watched it start up the lane, shaking my head. What would Rick Duncan have on Vanderhof? And why ask me to shake him down? Vanderhof had plenty of his own monkeys to do his dirty work.

I walked back over to my garage, considering just when and how to put a tail back on Vanderhof. The man was trouble and I needed to know why.

Halfway into my Impala, I remembered it was low on gas and checked my watch. Half an hour before I was due in court. Damn you, Vanderhof. I jumped into my BMW 3.0, only to have the starter crank to a stop when I turned the key. I got out kicking tires again. If I worked for Vanderhof, he'd get me to court in a helicopter.

With the specter of barging late into a packed courtroom hanging over me, I jumped into my Impala, backed out into the gravel driveway and raced down the narrow lane in a cloud of dust. A cascade of red tile roofs and palms trees came into view. The ocean was off in the distance.

Down at the bottom of the hill, I turned right into heavy traffic, fought my way over to a gas station on Legion and was soon heading out the canyon with a full tank of gas and a total disregard for the rules of the highway.

A few miles east of town, I jumped on the toll road, headed south until I came to a major parkway and turned right back towards the sea. Three miles from the coast, I pulled into an overflowing courthouse parking lot. Vanderhof's limo was already parked off in the back of the lot, taking up four spaces. I parked over with the cops and judges and stuck a pass on my dashboard.

Being late, heads turned as I entered the courtroom. Mrs. Vanderhof noticed me and started to smile. Then she was doing a double take on my battle scars. Everyone in the courtroom was doing a double take on me and my wounds.

Mrs. Vanderhof's attorney pointed at a seat behind him. I waved him off and grabbed a seat against the back wall. Vanderhof was staring at me when I looked his way. He nodded. I looked forward again without responding. You got into a lot of trouble swearing on a stack of Bibles to tell the truth, the whole truth and nothing but the truth, and then doing otherwise.

The judge entered the courtroom and everyone rose. The bailiff called out.

"Please rise for The Honorable Abraham G. Hoffman."

The Honorable Abraham G. Hoffman sat down and struck his gavel twice.

"Please be seated."

The bailiff handed Hoffman the first case. He flipped through it quickly.

"Vanderhof vs. Vanderhof. Plaintiff's counsel, have we been able to arrive at a settlement yet."

Mrs. Vanderhof's attorney rose, an incorruptible, Ivy League looking type, with dark, wavy locks and soap opera good looks.

"No, your honor," he said.

"Defendant's counsel?"

Mr. Vanderhof's attorney rose, a tall, lanky fellow with a Patrician head and Huckleberry Finn face that had begun to age a bit. His florid, cocktail hour skin made him look every bit as corruptible as the other attorney did not. I pictured him as a USC grad, not a top-flight constitutional attorney, but not a flake, either. Knowing he worked for Vanderhof, I figured his ethics were sloshing around somewhere between his last highball and whatever he could get away with without being disbarred.

"Given the plaintiff's final offer, your honor," he said. "We're prepared to go to trial."

A dark cloud descended over Hoffman's pink face. His gray hair looked a little grayer all of a sudden. His frail body seemed to sigh.

"All right, plaintiff, call your first witness."

That was me. The bailiff stepped forward and let everyone know that it was. I went up and swore on a stack of Bibles. The truth, the whole truth and nothing but the truth. So help me God.

Vanderhof's attorney started to grill me with all those questions that are designed to drive an otherwise sane person out of their minds. Your name. Your address. Your occupation. Where you went to school. Have you ever owned a dog? A cat? I told the truth, except about Butch.

That done, the attorney went about trying to undermine my credibility. Wasn't it true that I had broken a few laws along the way? That my ethics were sloshing around somewhere between my last highball and whatever I could get away with without losing my license.

Mrs. Vanderhof's attorney rose up to object.

"Your honor, Mr. Devlin's prior record is immaterial to his testimony about the girl."

Judge Hoffman looked at Mr. Vanderhof's attorney.

"Your honor, we feel establishing Mr. Devlin's past behavior goes to his lack of credibility in this case."

"I'm well aware of Mr. Devlin's reputation, but he's under oath. I assume he'll tell the truth under the circumstances. Overruled. Let's refrain ourselves from anything but his specific testimony for today, please."

I had been sitting there with my good name being batted around the courtroom. Mr. Vanderhof's attorney did not seem to be at all concerned about my feelings and resumed doing what all good attorneys will do, which is to parse a simple matter into something far more complicated. I had testified to seeing the girl go into Vanderhof's mansion. I had testified to seeing her leave in Vanderhof's limousine a few hours later, looking quite a bit more disheveled than when she had gone in. I had used a laser microphone to pry on what could only be described as two people having sex.

"But you never saw them having sex."

"No."

"So, it could have been anyone up in that room with Mr. Vanderhof."

"I heard her voice, and I have heard it elsewhere, so I'm quite sure it was her."

"Having sex or simply in the same room."

"Well, she didn't sound like a spectator, if that's what you're asking."

That got a few laughs from the crowd, plus a couple of raps from Judge Hoffman's gavel.

"You will refrain yourself from that sort of stunt, Mr. Devlin, or you'll find yourself in contempt with a few nights in jail to think it over."

I took the additional beating without looking his way. Vanderhof's attorney lit back into me as soon as Hoffman was done.

"The fact is, you had met with her before she went over to Mr. Vanderhof's residence that evening, isn't that right?"

"No."

Vanderhof's attorney approached the bailiff with several pieces of paper stapled together.

"I'd like for the court to admit this as exhibit A. It's the testimony of Jane Doe from her deposition, where she admits to having spoken with Mr. Devlin. A photograph of the two of them meeting is attached."

The attorney turned back to me.

"In fact, didn't you coax her into going to Mr. Vanderhof's residence that night and coach her about what to say and what to do?"

"No," I said again.

Judge Hoffman flipped through the evidence and looked at me.

"Explain this."

"The counsel is implying that I met with her the night she went up to Mr. Vanderhof's residence, and I didn't."

Hoffman waved the evidence.

"But obviously you did meet with her."

"That was almost two weeks earlier."

"Mr. Devlin. Let's not parse the truth here. You met with her."

"Your honor, I swore on a stack of Bibles to tell the truth, the whole truth and nothing but the truth, so help me God and counsel is implying that I met with her the night she visited Mr. Vanderhof and that simply isn't true."

"Mr. Devlin, I appreciate your attention to detail, but if you feel there is some need to clarify your testimony, let the plaintiff's counsel know and he can bring it up in his cross-examination. In the meantime, just answer the questions. Counsel, you may proceed."

"Yes or no, Mr. Devlin. Did you meet with Jane Doe before she visited Mr. Vanderhof's residence?"

"No, not that night?"

Judge Hoffman looked to the heavens. I shrugged. The attorney and I went on locking horns for most of an hour.

Finally freed to go, I went outside into the hot summer sun, feeling dirty inside. A court was where you found justice administered, but not necessarily where the truth was to be found.

10

Out in the parking lot, I sat for a spell with my car running and the air-conditioner on full blast, stewing.

'I'm well aware of Mr. Devlin's reputation, but I assume he'll tell the truth under the circumstances.'

Who in hell did Hoffman think he was, calling my good name into question? Various forms of torture came to mind. At the very least, I'd stand that old bastard up against a brick wall; blindfolded, no last cigarette.

Lost in my thoughts of revenge, I was startled by a rap of knuckles against the driver's side window. Paul Bunyan was standing out there in a dark suit and sunglasses, staring down at me. He opened the door before I had a chance to roll down the window. A short, stocky man with a shaved head appeared next to him. He too was wearing a dark suit.

"Mr. Devlin," he said with a Russian accent. "I'll cut to the chase, as they say in your country. It appears you have something I want."

"Yeah? And who would you be?"

"I'm me."

"Real cute, Boris, but I don't have anything anyone wants and I'm already late for an appointment, so if you don't mind, I'll be on my way."

I started to close the door but his big goon blocked it for me.

"Mr. Devlin. We're not messy like those Mexican boys chasing you around last night. No bang, bang fireworks in the middle of the night, shooting up the town. You live as long as you play ball with me. If not?"

Boris gestured.

"Just like that. Very, very quiet. You're never knowing what hit you."

"I know. Like they say in my country." Boris smiled. "Well, as they also say in my country, you can't get blood from a turnip, so if you'll excuse me."

I again tried to close my door and again the big goon blocked it.

"Then tell me," Boris said. "Why are these Mexicans chasing you around last night? With guns going off?"

"I don't know. You'd have to ask them."

With that, Boris nodded and his goon yanked me out of the car like a rag doll. Boris was staring up at me now. The goon patted me down.

"Nothing, boss."

"Check the car."

The goon set me to the side and searched the interior. Boris stared at me as he did.

"Nothing, boss."

"Check the trunk."

The goon hit the trunk release button and went about making a mess of my props and disguises.

"Nothing," the goon said again.

Boris looked wounded by the news.

"Mr. Devlin. I'm a businessman and don't believe in wasting valuable resources. I also believe in rewarding performance. As long as our relationship serves some useful purpose, you live. The minute I find out you're fucking with me?"

He made his gesture again.

"Why don't you tell me what it is that you're looking for."

Boris stared.

"This thing you removed from Dan Colby's body the other night."

"Who said I removed anything from Colby's body the other night."

"Mr. Devlin. The hills have eyes. Hmm?"

"Oh they do, do they? Well, somebody's seeing things, because I didn't remove a damned thing."

Boris worked at an itch alongside his nose.

"All right. This is not the place to be making dead bodies. We see you tomorrow. I suggest you remember what it is that I'm wanting by then."

Boris started to walk away.

"Like I said, the hills have eyes…"

He looked over his shoulder.

"Yeah, yeah," I said. "Like they say in my country."

"Funny thing," Boris said. "They say that in my country too."

He nodded and continued over to a black BMW X-7. I dropped the Impala into drive and pulled out of the parking lot, adding Boris Badenov and his goon to my firing squad line up while wondering who they were. The news had mentioned an arms shipment being cover for the transfer of some top-secret technology, and it wasn't hard to picture some Russian thugs being behind that kind of mischief, or to imagine them lurking around the outskirts of that boatyard the other night and having witnessed what went down. But then why hadn't Boris searched Colby and found the flash drive? According to Hernandez, roughly an hour had passed between the time a passing boat had noticed Colby floating out in the harbor and when the cops found him bobbing around underneath that dock.

With all murders, there were these seemingly inexplicable loose ends, but I'd put my money on one thing for certain. Add together Boris, the Mexicans and an arms shipment gone south and somebody was trying to stab somebody in the back.

Having nothing better to do that morning, I decided to take a drive up and see Steve at the county jail. He was sitting in a cell right then, trying not to think about twenty-five to life for something he didn't do, and probably doing a lousy job of not thinking about it.

At twelve noon, on a hot and smoggy summer day, I found myself surrounded on all sides by an industrial wasteland and inching forward in bumper-to-bumper freeway traffic. In years past it would have been a breeze heading up to Central County at that hour but they had been widening Interstate 5 for most of a decade and it was always a virtual parking lot these days, no matter what time of day you passed through.

I hated traffic jams. I hated industrial wastelands. I hated hot smoggy summer days and was ready for more vengeance by the time I reached downtown Santa Ana. I had spent the whole trip steaming over Hoffman and Boris Badenov and trying to solve things I couldn't seem to solve.

I parked on a side street to avoid another traffic jam and headed on foot through what was the original part of town. Old Craftsman homes and sycamore trees lined the sidewalks with the nearby jail and black glass towers peeking through the rustling leaves here and there.

At the jail entrance, I was informed that the morning visiting hours had ended at eleven. If I wanted in, I'd have to come back at three. I flashed my license and informed them that I worked for Jim Harrison. That got me inside, but not without some hostile looks. Jim had done a lot of pro bono work for shafted inmates and the guards did not take kindly to you screwing with their meal ticket. Inmates meant one thing to them: job security.

As every metal gate slammed shut behind me, my spirits sank further. It was easy to champion law and order when you had never been on the wrong side of the law. All hope was abandoned in places like this. There was no describing the despair you felt, realizing you couldn't leave.

At the end of a long corridor, I was escorted into a small room. There was a glass partition and one phone on the opposite wall. The feeling of it all was grim, but nothing like Terminal Island or Folsom. If they convicted Steve, he would be sent to one of those places and men did not come out of them the way they went in.

I saw a metal door in the other room open and a guard escort Steve inside. Steve sat down and picked up his phone. I picked up mine. The guard stood with his back against the opposite wall.

"What happened to you?" he said.

I shook my head.

"I've been answering the same question for the past two days now. A couple of guys roughed me up. There seems to be trouble every which way I turn right now…So how are they treating you?"

"The guards are all right."

He leaned forward and whispered.

"A white guy? Without tattoos? I'm like one of their own."

"How about the rest of it?"

"I haven't been poked in the ass yet, if that's what you're asking, but I've had plenty of offers."

I smiled grimly. Steve didn't smile at all.

"Go ahead and spill it," he said.

I shrugged.

"I don't have any news yet, Steve. We won't know much until the arraignment on Monday. I've been working on Whalen but I wouldn't get your hopes up on that front. You may as well face it that this thing is going to trial."

"Yeah. They'll shaft me, sure as shit."

"Come on, Steve. Stay positive. You're innocent and we're going to prove it."

Steve glanced over his shoulder at the guard and back at me.

"Have you looked into Vanderhof?"

"Actually, I had a talk with him earlier this morning."

"You did? So? What did he say?"

"Well, the man isn't going to come right out and confess to murder, but I think you're on to something. His name comes up everywhere I look."

"What do you mean?"

112

I explained about the other two murders.

"I knew it. Connie was looking for trouble hanging around with that dude."

"This is a very wealthy and powerful individual, Steve. Not easy to get to, and frankly, I don't have anything on him yet, but I will be all over his ass. You can count on that. I just can't change the nature of time. I know you want out of here yesterday but we're stuck until Monday now. Let's just hope this judge grants you bail."

"Did you come by to cheer me up?"

"I stopped by, Steve. I could have gone home and screwed around for the rest of the day."

"I know. Fuck, I'm sorry."

"It's all right. I don't blame you for being pissed, but just hang in there. We'll get you out of here as soon as we can."

"Yeah, I know but try being falsely accused and knowing the person who killed your wife is out there running around with a grin."

I stared, not having any more answers for him. In the background, I heard an iron gate open and close and footsteps passing down the hallway. Steve and I sat there staring.

"My parents came by earlier," he said a moment later. "They said that there had originally been plans to bury Connie on Monday but I guess now there's a big fight in her family because Connie wanted to be cremated and some of the members don't want to honor her wishes."

"That's too bad."

"Yeah. I wish I could be there."

"Yeah."

"You know, I've been thinking a lot about those days when Connie and I first got married. Fresh out of high school. All the world in front of us, everyone so full of hope. Remember?"

"Oh sure," I said. "It was great being dumb."

He smiled a bit.

"Anything seemed possible back then. If somebody had told me it would end up like this, I would have shot myself."

We talked about the old days for another half an hour. I looked at my watch.

"Go ahead," Steve said. "I know you have other things to do."

"Yeah, as always. I'm running late. A few bad breaks and I'll be out on the street."

Steve stood up. I stood up with him.

"I'm doing everything I can."

"I know, Michael. I really appreciate it. And for getting Jim to help me."

I nodded, my mind on home and a steak for dinner that night and feeling like hell that Steve could not walk out with me.

"Hey, how's Butch?" he said.

"Fine. He's in good hands with Betty." I described her and the Barbie Doll shoes. "She's all dressed up for the part, I can tell you that much."

He smiled sadly again.

"Thanks again for taking care of him."

"Sure, I'll be by to see you again soon, all right?"

He nodded.

"And chin up. Jim and I are busting our asses every minute to get you out of here."

Steve nodded and hung up the phone. I hung up mine and started for the door, feeling his eyes on me and wishing they weren't.

Before going out, I looked back but Steve was already gone.

On my way through the old neighborhood, the sycamore trees were whispering to me again. High up there, trying to say something, like the spirits of my ancestors sending a message that I couldn't hear.

Back on the freeway, I decided to stop by Vanderhof's place before going home. I had overheard him telling a client once. "That's where I do a lot of my business." It was fair to assume that it wasn't always the kind of business you'd want to share with the Wall Street Journal.

Two exits shy of the highway leading down to Laurel Lagoon, I pulled off the freeway and worked my way back into the dry chaparral country. A few miles west of the freeway, I came over a knoll and down into a hidden valley. Every home there sported mission architecture and smelled of serious money. If you guessed two, three million apiece, you were kidding yourself. An empty lot would cost you that much.

Vanderhof's place stood well off by itself against the adjacent hills and was enough to make Frank Lloyd Wright hang his head. Amidst the desert mesquite and sagebrush, he had built himself a little Versailles. Some men had more money than sense. Vanderhof definitely had more money than taste.

I drove past the long driveway and around to a cut in the adjacent hills. Parking out of sight, I opened my trunk, changed into something more fitting for the occasion, took my binoculars, a hat and a laser mike and scrambled up to a nearby knoll. Vanderhof's estate spread out below me, his maze of Versailles style gardens and fountains dissipating into the surrounding desert chaparral. Closer to the back door, Vanderhof had built an equally ostentatious swimming pool.

Seeing Vanderhof's yellow Ferrari 458 Spider in the driveway, I assumed he was home. I took my binoculars and scanned the building, and did the same with the laser mike but there was no sign of him anywhere in the rooms facing my way.

While I waited for Louis 14th to make an appearance, my eyes drifted off towards the freeway. Traffic was inching along like columns of ants. The flat terrain rose up beyond the freeway in a tilted plateau towards Saddleback Mountain. In the days of my youth, that plateau had been carpeted with orange groves. You could ride your bicycle for miles and miles and never find an end to them. Now the same area was carpeted with tract homes, and what remained of those groves was managed like a museum. Even the rows of towering eucalyptus trees, planted by the old ranchers as windbreaks, were mostly gone.

I had grown lost in dreams of days gone by when I heard the scratchy sounds of a voice through the mike. I focused the binoculars at the mansion again and saw that Vanderhof had taken a seat in his office. I turned the mike in that direction and heard him talking.

"Listen," he said. "I don't want any loose ends. You know what I mean?"

There was silence.

"Okay, just so we're on the same page. If we can find a way to use them here stateside, fine. If not, we give them a post overseas. Just so they're out of my hair. You got it?"

Again, there was silence.

"All right, I know you two boys are professionals but let's get this done."

I waited for more but Vanderhof hung up the phone and leaned back in his chair. I felt the hot summer sun beating down on my head. There was a sick feeling in my gut. You had to assume these overseas assignments were dead-end jobs; very dead end, no future, no pension, no more sunlight or trees. But who had Vanderhof been talking to? He had said 'you two boys'. Beyond that, I hadn't a clue.

Fifteen minutes later, I was about to give up when Vanderhof's phone rang again. He answered it.

"Yeah," he said, and "yeah" again.

"Son of a bitch," he said a moment later. "All right. I'm heading down there right now."

I saw him hang up and spring out of his chair. He passed by several windows along what appeared to be a long hallway and then disappeared from view. Seeing he was on a mission, I scrambled back down to my car.

A minute later, Vanderhof tore out of the long driveway in his Ferrari. I allowed him a good head start and got on his tail. A wild ride through the dry, back country followed. The winding two-lane road eventually came to a T intersection at Bonita Canyon. Vanderhof turned left, cut over to Ford Road and turned down towards the coast at Jamboree. I had to blow several red lights trying to keep up with him.

At Coast Highway, I held back, waiting to see which way he planned to go and found myself blocked by both a yuppie mom in a giant SUV and an old geezer in his Jaguar, both of them gunning for brownie points at the academy of good driving. The light had turned green and Vanderhof headed straight down the hill towards Balboa Island. By the time I got around our two model citizens, the light had turned red again. There was no blowing this light so I had to sit there for five minutes, fuming. By the time I drove onto the island, Vanderhof was nowhere in sight. I crisscrossed the streets for half an hour before giving up and turning towards home. I had a head full of questions, the main one being, who did Vanderhof know on Balboa Island and why had he been in such a furious rush to go see that person? Whoever it was, their actions had been enough to make him swear out loud.

Back at my office, I found the mail waiting for me inside the door. Mostly it was bills, and no check from Jake. Harried by poverty, I tried calling him but got no answer. I tried reaching the various other clients who owed me money but no one answered. When someone finally did, I got another song and dance. Sorry, I'm broke. I can't even pay my rent. As soon as I have some money, you'll be the first to know.

What was I going to do? Sue someone for hard luck? A lot of people I knew had gotten rich over the past thirty years. Fools like me? Well, I had no one to blame but myself.

I heard the door open downstairs and the sound of high heels coming up the wooden stairs. My fantasies were brief. Betty popped her head in the door a minute later.

Butch quickly slipped in through the cracked door and proceeded to sniff around the premises. I laughed out loud. Betty had given him a trim. It wasn't exactly the Westminster Kennel Club look but Butch had definitely taken a hard right turn in that direction.

"You like it?" Betty said.

"He's definitely butch now."

Butch was on a serious hunt around my office and oblivious to my ongoing laughter. He seemed to have shrunk three sizes.

"Jesus, what happened to you?" Betty said, coming into my office all the way.

"She didn't like my line."

Betty examined my cheek.

"You should go see a doctor."

"Please. I don't need a doctor."

Betty patted me on the other cheek gently and smiled.

"The weather's a lot better."

"Yeah. Welcome back to your Mediterranean climate."

"You sure you don't want me to treat that? It looks like it could get infected?"

"No, I'm fine. I just want to be left alone to pout."

Betty laughed and started out. Butch hesitated. I pretended to go after him and he bent down on his front paws, in full play mode.

"I'll get you!" I said with another jab at him and the game was on.

Butch spun out on my hardwood floors like it was linoleum, went skidding out of the door and tearing off down the hallway towards Betty's office. There was a brief moment of silence, from which I assumed Butch was doing a donut down in her place, and back he came in a great tear. He dashed in the door doing sixty miles an hour, made a wild lap around me and my desk, went skidding wildly on his way back out and tearing off down the hallway again. After another moment of silence, I heard him hauling ass back my way.

In he came, and off he went again, ears flying.

Finally, after three complete laps, he stopped at my door, panting. I heard Betty call his name.

"Fun's over, buddy," I said with a salute.

Butch ran off, all full of joy. To be that simple. You had to wonder who was the real beast of burden in this movie.

I tried working for an hour or so and gave up. Who was I kidding? I had no clients. At least no one who was paying me.

I killed the rest of the day at home, growing lost in passages from Ovid and Homer and staring out to sea through the rustling trees, lost in my thoughts and dreams. Mostly my trailer down south of the border kept calling to me. I missed that desolate stretch of coastline. It was a place where the madness of modern times did not yet exist. I had dragged an old Burroughs typewriter down there a few years back, big and black and out of step with the times. My thought had been to sit at the kitchen table telling tall tales while the sea broke down the coast. It sounded lovely in theory but I had yet to do a damned thing about it.

As Friday afternoon faded to dusk, I considered giving in to the idea, but to head south on a weekend was to head into a hundred-mile traffic jam of Winnebagos and weekend fools, from here to Ensenada. And there was Steve to consider. Remembering him, anger burned in my heart. I hated injustice. How many times had the innocent been wrongly accused? And simply because there was someone in a position of power to do so.

But who would want Connie dead, and why? I went to bed early, plagued by that question. As a substitute for heading south, I thumbed through a tale about some wild young men, drinking wine and smoking opium in Tangiers long ago and telling tall tales of their own.

11

On Saturday morning, I awakened with my spirit still in turmoil. That barren stretch of coastline looking south from my trailer was calling to me. The whisper of the sea, the prospect of escaping this world and all its troubles, the allure of it was haunting. A part of me was already exchanging pesos at the border.

Then there was Steve, stewing away in a jail cell.

I crawled out of bed with the words of the good book doing laps in my head.

For now we set aside childish things…

I sighed on my way out to make some coffee. Okay. One more day. It was back to the business of finding Audrey. I could not think of anything else to do.

But where? And how?

While savoring the first cup of coffee, I realized that she had to be burying Cliff soon, probably on Monday, and nothing would stop me from making an appearance at the funeral. That said, the thought of waiting all weekend was too much for a man like me. I grabbed one of my burner phones and called Audrey's office. It was a long shot, that anyone would be around on a Saturday morning, so I was a bit startled to hear her partner Rick answer my call. I assumed it to be Rick. It was the same grating voice I had heard, the last time I had called looking for her.

"Okay, is this Nacho again," he wanted to know before I had spoken a word. His mistaking me for Nacho was understandable. My phone would say "private caller." It could have been anyone.

By the paranoid sound of Rick's voice, I pictured him with a desk wedged up against his office door.

"No," I assured him. "It's not Nacho."

"Okay. So who are you?"

Thinking on my feet, and mindful that Rick could probably authenticate my story, I told it straight, more or less. I was a private investigator and prospective client, with an interest in taking my business global.

"Okay. Are you the kind of detective who carries guns around and that sort of thing?"

"I've been known to carry a gun from time to time, sure."

"Okay. So look, I've got a situation here and maybe I'd like to hire you. Okay? So how long before you could be up here to my office?"

I glanced at the clock.

"It's a bit past eleven right now. I still have to shave and shower. Say, twelve-thirty at the latest?"

"Okay, the sooner the better," Rick said. "You know the address?"

"I do."

"Okay. So I'll be waiting here for you. And make it as fast as you can, okay?"

"I'll see you in about an hour."

"Okay. I'll be here waiting."

"Oh, hey," I said, having another thought.

"Okay, what?" Rick said.

"Jot down this number." I read off the number from a burner phone. "Be sure to call me if something comes up."

"Okay, just hurry up."

I hung up the phone, ready to beat my head against the wall. How many times could a man repeat the word "okay" without realizing it had become obnoxious? I pictured a movie scene, Rick dropped out of a Cessna from 15,000 feet, a wave goodbye as he went tumbling down and down into the abyss.

Everything "ookkaaaay" with you now there, big guy?

My mind returned to reality and Nacho. Could he be one of the narco thugs chasing me around the other night? The name certainly fit. How he and Connie and Cliff Black fit into one jigsaw puzzle, I couldn't see, but it sure smelled like I was getting close to something rotten.

On my way up the coast, suspecting that I might be about to cross some legal lines, I grabbed another burner phone and called Jim Harrison. He answered.

After the usual hellos, I asked if there was any news on Steve's case.

"Nothing, except for the judge we were assigned."

"Bad?"

"He's a world class pain in the ass but if I petition for a new one and we're denied, we're really screwed. Better to play nice and hope for the best."

"You're the one to know."

"Yeah. And what's on your mind?"

I explained about going to see Rick.

"What if he wanted to hire me and I didn't tell him about my involvement with Cliff and Audrey? Would I be on safe legal ground?"

Like any good attorney, Jim asked me several discerning questions and threw the matter back in my lap

"It's fairly simple, Michael. Could you confess to what you're doing with everyone in the same room?"

"Probably not."

"And there you have it. Are you crossing a legal line in the scenario you've described? Not yet, but I suppose you could very quickly. If he hires you to scare off Nacho and nothing else, that should keep you out of trouble."

"Thanks, Jim. Have your secretary send me a bill."

"Don't worry about it. Let's go grab that steak, or just drop by some night with a bottle of bourbon and we'll have a nice long talk."

"Well, maybe a steak but we'll skip the bourbon."

"Oh? Are we on the wagon?"

"Something like that."

"I see. And when did this come about?"

"You mean, why?"

"Well, I suppose I already know the answer to that one."

"Yeah. Anyway, one too many hard mornings."

"Hey, I'm glad to hear it. Just bring along some Perrier then, but stop by."

I told him I would and rang off.

Perrier. It just didn't have the same ring to it.

With another thought, I called Kenny.

"Any sign of Audrey?"

"She bought a casket and some flowers, and some other stuff that goes with people getting buried."

"Do me a favor, will you? Check for the funeral."

"I already did. The service is at St. Mark Presbyterian Church. Monday at noon. They're burying him at Pacific View Park and Mortuary."

I thanked Kenny and hung up. There was a thought to call Whalen and see if he had anything new on Audrey but I decided not to press my luck. She wasn't behind bars yet. That was news enough

Five minutes later, I was approaching Rick and Audrey's office building and pulled over to scan things from a distance. The parking lot was mostly empty and Dick and Tom were nowhere in sight. It being Saturday, maybe they had taken the day off, or had moved on to bigger things. Whatever the case, seeing no sign of them, I parked at the far end of the lot, marched across the sea of hot asphalt, dashed up the concrete steps to the central courtyard and went in through the black glass entry door on my right. The elevator was straight ahead. I pushed a button for the third floor.

Down at the end of a long, drab corridor, I found suite 323. A sign on the door said Magellan Ltd. The name did have a quaint ring to it. Not quite Dutch East Indies Company, but I got the picture. If you found yourself adrift at the end of the world, they would be there to rescue you.

The door was locked when I tried it. I knocked and waited. No one answered so I knocked again. Still no answer. Pissed, I headed back towards the elevator. The phone in my pocket rang as I did. It was Rick. I answered.

"I'm here at your office. Where the hell are you?"

"Okay. This Nacho guy called again and it kind of freaked me out."

"Then what am I doing here?"

"I don't know, but I think you'd better get out of there, okay?"

"Where do I find you?"

He gave me directions to a Tiki Tiki joint down by the pier. He'd be waiting for me in a booth in back.

"I'm on my way. Don't move."

I hung up, ready to wring his neck.

I had made it halfway down the long hallway when I heard footsteps rushing up the stairs. I ran to the elevator but the car was already on its way up from the ground floor. I ran back down the hallway trying doors until I found one unlocked and barged in. A trim businesswoman was staring up at me from behind a desk. I closed the door, placed a finger to my lips, pointed out at the hallway and made a gesture at my neck. Startled as she was, she seemed to accept my message. There were bad guys around and I wasn't one of them.

I locked the door, gestured again for her to keep quiet and went to check the parking lot from her windows. The dark gray Suburban was parked out there by the courtyard steps with its doors flung open.

I went back to listen at the door and heard footsteps charging out of the stairwell. Then the elevator door opened and more men went hustling down towards the far end of the hallway. When I heard a door being kicked in, I waited a moment before cautiously peeking out into the hallway. It was empty.

I gestured again for the woman to be quiet, slipped out the door and ran down towards the stairwell access. That door was closing behind me when I heard shots clip off the walls. I had made it from the lobby out to my car in the parking lot when footsteps spilled out into the courtyard behind me. There were men shouting in Spanish and more automatic gunfire going off.

Not liking the odds of circling back to the street entrance, I dropped the Impala into drive, jumped a curb and did a four-wheel number over a grassy knoll. Bullets were pinging off the trunk as I made the summit. I hit the street with the rear of the car beginning to look like one of those road signs on a dead-end country road.

From living in that town long ago, I knew my way around and quickly disappeared into a maze of back streets, tossing the two burner phones I had used that morning for good measure.

The adrenalin had mostly dissipated by the time I reached the restaurant, but not my temper. I barged past the hostess and into the darkened interior of the restaurant, searching for Rick. The décor was palm fronds, thatched bamboo panels and tropical plants. Martin Denny was playing in the background.

As promised, I found Rick seated in a booth in back, and as usual, I had done a lousy job picturing a man from his voice. In my mind, Rick was tall with dark locks. In reality, he was short with sandy colored hair, not unattractive, but half blind from the looks of his glasses. If you judged by the knots in his jaw muscles, I had gotten one thing right. He was wound tighter than a piano wire and one Lithium prescription this side of legal sanity. I literally felt the energy field warping around him.

Rick had a leather notebook on the table in front of him, with a smaller one next to it. They had been neatly arranged with great care, the margins between them perfectly square and equal. A pen lay next to the notebooks, also nice and square to the world. A cocktail napkin was part of the mosaic, also carefully arranged.

"What happened to your face?" Rick said as I sat down.

"Never mind my face. What do you think you're doing, setting me up like that?"

"Okay, what do you mean, 'setting you up'?"

"I mean, a gang of what I presume to be some Mexican cartel boys just kicked in your office door. And were taking shots at me as I four-wheeled out of your parking. That's what I mean. I get paid good money for putting up with that kind of shit and you haven't paid me a damned cent yet, so I'm asking you again. What is going on?"

"Okay, I don't know either."

"Well, you'd better know something. And if I hear you say "okay" one more time, I'm going to throw you in that waterfall over there."

"Okay, I..."

I went for his throat but he lurched back.

"Okay, okay. I mean, all right. Shit...just calm down, will you?"

"I'll calm down as soon as I know what almost got me killed."

The busboy appeared with another menu and my obligatory glass of water. I smiled for him through the tension. He sensed things weren't right in the universe and got out of Dodge. I leaned towards Rick again. He was back to fiddling with his notebooks.

"So? Spill it."

When he failed to answer me, I swiped both of them onto the seat of the booth.

"I said spill it."

Over the next several minutes, Rick did so, offering up mostly what I already knew from reading the papers; a business deal gone south, a Saudi arms dealer skipping town, the Feds all over Rick's back, etc., etc.

One thing was new. Rick blamed Audrey for getting him into this mess. He figured she was up to no good. I sat there wondering if Rick was just a lousy friend or more generally a lousy human being. I was leaning towards both.

The waitress came to take our orders. Famished, I ordered the teriyaki chicken. Rick ordered barbecued ribs. He also ordered another drink.

With the waitress gone, I leaned back over the table. Rick stared back, looking a bit like a man in a fishbowl behind the thick glasses.

"There's something you're not telling me. What about Vanderhof? I read in the paper that you've done business with him in the past. Did he have anything to do with your arms deal?"

Rick hesitated.

"What?" I said. "Does he have something on you? Do you have something on him?"

Rick leaned over the table in my direction.

"Look, I'm not supposed to be discussing my client's deals with other people, okay?"

I reached to grab him by the neck again.

"All right, all right. Look. I don't know what Vanderhof's up to half the time. He mostly deals with Audrey and it's all hush, hush, but he's definitely playing on a global scale and obviously for some big-time money. We're talking sheiks and princes and leaders of the world."

"And maybe some Russians?"

"Look..."

"Look, nothing. I want some answers."

Rick leaned a little closer.

"Okay," he said and winced. "Look, there was a guy named Colby involved, but somebody shot him the other night and..."

"Whoa. Back up. What do you mean, a guy named Colby was involved?"

"Colby had a small network of shipping containers and Audrey liked to use him from time to time. He was nimbler than the big guys. I'll give him that, but to me he was just a two-bit player."

"Who shot him?"

"I don't know. All I know is, the Feds have been all over our case. They've been by the office four times already this week, asking us all kinds of questions."

"What kind of questions?"

"Basically the same ones, but from a thousand different directions. How and where did we meet this black-market dealer? What did we know about him? Who else knew about the deal? On and on. Then two of them came back yesterday morning and seemed pretty pissed off to find out that Audrey wasn't around."

"How many of them were there originally?"

"Four. I think one day there were actually five."

"And the two guys you saw yesterday. Were they part of the original team?"

"No. They didn't even dress like the other guys."

"Describe them."

"The two guys?"

"Yeah."

He did so, in enough detail to convince me it had been Dick and Tom.

"And what did they want?"

"Mostly they wanted to know where Audrey was."

"And the other guys. What did they want to know from you?

"Like I told you before. All about the deal."

"And not about Audrey."

"Why would they ask about Audrey? She was sitting right there."

"But she wasn't there on Thursday."

"No. She called me to say she was on her way that morning but never showed up. And I haven't heard from her since."

The waitress arrived with our food and Rick's gin and tonic. I let her know with a wave of my hand that my club soda was fine.

Rick worked on his plate of ribs with wary glances at me. I dug into my teriyaki chicken with equally wary glances at him, doubting I trusted the man as far as Audrey had trusted Colby.

"Tell again me what you told the Feds."

"That the government agent had identified himself as a licensed exporter, this Saudi guy had all the right papers and the shipment was supposed to be small arms and some sort of standard issue military replacement parts. I had no reason to believe it was anything but legitimate. Obviously the Feds have other ideas."

"And the two guys you saw yesterday. What? They finally just gave up and left?"

"Yeah."

"And they never asked you about anything other than Audrey?"

No. They grilled me about her for a couple of minutes. Told me not to leave town. Nodded like a couple of tough guys and left. Once they got into the elevator, I hurried down to that window at the end of the hallway and watched them climb into a white van. And as far as I know they sat out there watching and waiting the entire day."

"What?" Rick said as he was polishing off his second cocktail.

"What? I'm trying to make sense of this mess, that's what. Why would these Mexican heavies be chasing you around? And taking pot shots at me? And who are these Russians."

"I don't know about either of them."

I scoffed.

"I don't."

"And you had no reason to think this arms deal was rotten before you got into it."

"I've never known one that didn't smell a bit rotten up front, but I had no specific knowledge of this one being on the wrong side of the law."

I stared at him.

"Okay…I mean, all right, so you don't believe me."

"I don't know if I do, but nothing you've told me explains the mess you're in. The mess I'm in."

"Look, the shipping container was bound for Liberia. That's what Al-Hamad had filed on the manifest for customs and that's all I know."

I finished the bite I was chewing and wiped at my mouth.

"All right. Al-Hamad. Who is he and what do you know about him?"

"Nothing really except that he's a Saudi arms dealer and what you can read in the papers."

"All right. Back to these men who were questioning you for a minute. Did any of them ever identify themselves?"

"The original guys, yeah. They said they were with the FBI."

"And you saw badges?"

"Yeah, but shit, anyone could have one made up."

"And the two guys yesterday?"

"Nothing. They just acted like tough guys."

I nodded.

"So, what? You think I was stupid to play along?"

"I don't know. Consider yourself lucky it wasn't those narco boys or you wouldn't be sitting here eating ribs."

I pushed away from my own meal and considered what I had learned. Maybe there were two separate government agencies at work here, maybe not. Maybe there were two separate crimes, maybe not. Something was rotten in Denmark and Vanderhof had his hands in most or all of it somehow. That was all I really knew, which was just enough to give me a headache and not much more.

"What about a phone number for these Mexican boys?" I asked Rick.

"If there is one, it would be on my caller ID at the office."

"Are you able to retrieve your calls from here?"

"Yeah, sure."

"Then please do it."

I watched as Rick called into his voice mail. When he got to the right message, he jotted down the number on his notepad. I took the piece of paper from him as he hung up. Rick seemed to be looking for a third Tanqueray. A burner phone started ringing in my pocket. The call was from Sylvia. I answered.

"You left a message about a reading yesterday morning."

"Yes. I was wondering if I could possibly stop by today."

"I can tell you're in a lot of pain," she said.

"I'm an easy mark that way."

"But today more than most. I feel some great shift about to take place in your life. I think we know each other."

"Sure. Another galaxy, another lifetime."

"Another lifetime."

"Yeah. So what about seeing you today?"

"What time were you thinking?"

"I could be there in an hour."

"I won't be able to see you until seven."

"Okay, seven it is."

"I will be here. When you get to the front of my shop, call me. My residence is in back."

"I'll call you as soon as I'm there."

My regular phone started to ring in my other pocket. Rick was watching as I hung up the one phone and answered the other. Now it was Teresa.

"Where are you?" she asked.

"I probably shouldn't say."

"Well, you'd best stop by here. The sooner the better."

"Okay. Got it. I can be there in half an hour."

I hung up. Rick was shaking the ice in the bottom of his drink.

"I take it you have to leave," he said.

"Yeah, where are you going to hide out?"

"Over at my girlfriend's place, I guess. Hey, what's up? I thought you were going to get these fuckers off my back."

I grabbed Rick's pen, pulled apart two cocktail napkins and drew up two brief but identical contracts.

"Sign these. Give me five hundred bucks and I'll go looking for Nacho."

"You're sure you can get rid of him?"

"I said I'll go looking for him. If you've got a better deal, take it."

Sullenly, Rick signed the contracts. While I signed them, he wrote me a check. I shoved that and a copy of our newly minted contract into my coat pocket. For all his fussiness, Rick had failed to notice that I had backdated both copies three days.

I wrote down the number for another burner phone and gave it to Rick.

"Call me the minute anything else comes up."

I started to throw some money on the table but Rick pulled out a wad of cash and insisted on paying. He had to act like a big shot at some point and I let him. I headed off through the Tiki Tiki décor on my own, relieved that I now had some sort of alibi, if and when Whalen came to shake me down.

12

Motoring along that open stretch of coastline south of Corona del Mar, blocks of blue sea and russet-colored hills came to surround me. The sun was high in the summer sky. Beach crowds peppered the shore. A postcard memory of childhood popped into my head. I was a boy again, dashing down to the sea in my trunks. It was a place where mistrust and heartache did not yet exist, where loved ones had yet to die and leave this earth, where you could depend on something other than disappointment. Then the shoreline along Scotchman's Cove disappeared in my rearview mirror and those reveries of distant days fled into the whispers of a summer afternoon.

As the highway wound left and up into Lagoon Laurel, my brain moved on to blocking movie scenes with Sylvia the fortune teller. I sat waiting in a darkened room, a crystal ball before me. Time passed. Then Sylvia appeared from behind a beaded curtain, this gypsy beauty with long dark hair. She lit candles, read my fortune and we fell in love.

Devlin, you really did make a wrong turn back down the road somewhere.

I grieved again briefly over my misplaced romantic illusions and got back to the business at hand. What was going on with Teresa? Clearly something was amiss or she wouldn't have called me.

With the gated community in my rearview mirror, I took a left, skirted the hills over to Broadway, and from there worked my way south along the backside of the high school. There had been a thought to stop by and check on things at my office but I dispensed with that notion as fatally flawed. Nacho and Boris and all my new pals might be hanging around waiting to see me and dragging them over to Teresa's place was the last thing I wanted to do, and that assumed they had not already found her.

Driving along, I kicked myself for having involved her in the first place. Out to slay dragons, I had dragged an innocent person into my suspect affairs.

Those were my thoughts as I wound out Pearl Street and pulled to a stop in Teresa's driveway. She was watering her garden out in front. I climbed the stairs and took the end slot on her lover's bench, ready for a flogging. Teresa offered me a token smile, which from her was pretty damned close to a flogging. She had a truly glorious smile, so when you got the token one, you felt like nobody loved you.

Teresa continued watering as if I wasn't there. I stared out at the rooftops sloping down towards the sea. A cat jumped into my lap. Rusty moseyed over and shoved his snout into my crotch. I petted him gingerly. Such a sweet guy, but god, the scent. It was enough to make your eyes water.

I moved on to considering my symbiotic relationship with Teresa. Maybe we were too much like brothers and sisters, some sort of friction always simmering below the surface, though for the life of me I could not explain what that was. The astrological, probably. The only thing I had going for me when it came to Teresa was her propensity for being an earth mother. Nothing else could explain why she stayed on keeping my books. As long as Teresa saw me as a wounded animal, oh god, the compassion. Teresa glanced at me once and I did my best to look wounded.

After several minutes, she finally turned the water off and sat down on the bench beside me, brushing at some loose strands of hair in her face. I was offered a better, if reticent smile. I started to speak but she gestured and shook her head.

"I found a hummingbird's nest up among the trees yesterday. Would you like to see it?"

"Sure," I said and followed her out into a grove of eucalyptus behind the house. The weather was still dry, but not nearly as hot as it had been.

Off to our left there were mulberry trees going down a slope. A couple of big pines had grown up among the eucalyptus. Rusty went off ahead of us silently. Our footsteps snapped in the brush. The eucalyptus and pines whispered their differing songs above our heads.

A few hundred feet into the grove, Teresa stopped and pointed up into an adjacent cypress tree. A hummingbird bolted out, did its version of a fan dance, offered its alien-like staccato whistle and retreated back among the limbs. Teresa talked to the bird in a singsong voice, transformed suddenly into her rapturous earth mother persona. She looked at me with a wistful smile. Then she was back from wherever she had been and sighed. She looked from me to the ground and whispered very quietly.

"I went out this morning. When I returned, I knew someone had been in the house. I'm very conscious about keeping the doors to my armoire closed. Moths, you know. One of the doors was slightly ajar. There were other signs."

"And..."

Her eyes snapped at me. She paused to consider her words and whispered again.

"You're worried about your precious little flash drive."

"I'm sorry, Teresa. I do little more than bring trouble into other people's lives."

Teresa offered me a cautious hug with one arm.

"You can't save the whole world, Michael."

"Yeah, but I keep trying. It's some comfort when my seemingly pointless existence rises up to face me."

Teresa studied my face, looking sad now.

"And never a word from Caitlin?"

"Please, let's not start with that again."

I looked away into the trees. They whispered around us.

"It's a woman's intuition, Michael. I sense she regrets her decision and still loves you but is afraid to call."

"And if you're wrong?"

She threw up her hands.

"No, Teresa. I'm better off not knowing."

"So, what? You sit here with a dream that she secretly longs for you? What good does that do anyone?"

"It's a nice dream," I said.

Teresa sighed, let go of her determination and reached out to wipe at my cheek.

"Maybe I'll call her for you," she said.

"Maybe we'd better stick to business."

"Okay. What do you propose we do?"

"Leave things as they are? If that's okay with you."

"I suppose it's just as well. They've had their chance to look around. I doubt they'll come looking again."

"I truly appreciate your ingenuity and stealth, Teresa. As long as this thing is hidden somewhere, a bullet in my head would be rather imprudent."

"I hope that can be said for both of us."

"You're killing me, Teresa."

"I think it's the other way around."

"Yes," I said. "Yes, you're right."

A faint smile crossed her serious gaze.

"I'd better get back. The animals need to be fed."

"Yeah, where did the day go...?"

Teresa started out. I followed at her side. The leaves rustled overhead. The sky was quickly darkening with the late afternoon.

"You're sure you don't want me to reach out to Caitlin," Teresa asked with a hand on her back door. I stood there staring. Every bit of me wanted to say yes. There was no way to express how much I loved that woman, how dearly I wanted her back in my life, but I wasn't about to undo what destiny had ordained. I reached out to touch Teresa's shoulder and started down to my car.

Stopping by to check on things at my office turned out to be one more ill-fated decision. The roads were jammed with cars, no matter which way I turned. Even the secret back ways locals used were bumper to bumper. A Saturday afternoon in the summer was just a lousy time to be heading into the guts of that town.

Already in a foul mood over my traffic debacle, I had not been back at my desk two minutes and waiting for the computer to boot up when Pat and his sidekick Fowler barged in through the door.

"You putting a tail on me these days, Pat?" I asked him.

"You'll be lucky if I don't put a pair of cuffs on you."

He came around and hovered over me, one palm on my desk, one on the back of my chair. Fowler came around and hovered over me from the other side, working away at his chewing gum. I didn't like any of it, but especially not Fowler and the smirk on his face. A rookie cop, and all of a sudden, he was judge, jury and executioner.

"What's eating you?" I asked, leaning back to look at Pat.

"Stop playing dumb with me, Devlin. I know enough about your activities to throw you behind bars, and that's leaving aside all the shit I haven't heard yet."

"Like what, Pat?"

"Like my town getting shot up last night and witnesses testifying that the car trying to get away looked a lot like yours."

I stared back at him in silence.

"Yeah, don't give me that look. I already saw the back of your Impala. It looks like somebody shot up a road sign."

"Since when is getting shot at a crime?"

"Maybe it's not, but add to that, the fact that you just happened to be getting cuffed around at a restaurant yesterday, and that restaurant just happened to be next door to my crime scene and I'm getting real suspicious here. As in handcuffs kind of suspicious."

"We've already been through the particulars, Pat."

"Yeah?" he said.

"Yeah. A man was shot underneath my office windows yesterday morning. I took a ride with you last night and saw another dead body. The guy who used to own that dead body had a pretty nice house, odd as it was. And he had a not too bad looking ex-wife. Did I miss something?"

"Yeah, the part about telling me the truth."

I glanced up at Fowler and back at Pat again.

"Yeah," Pat said. "That look said everything I need to know."

"Look, Pat. Why don't you quit screwing around here and tell me what you know?"

"That's the problem with you, Devlin. You're always getting me to spill my beans and I get nothing from you."

"That's because you always know more than I do."

We stared at each other.

"All right, shit, I'll tell you what I've got. I've got a hostess who remembers a guy with a pork pie hat and mustache getting cuffed around by two gentlemen behind the restaurant yesterday, and funny thing, this guy just happens to look a lot like you when the hat and mustache come off. Meanwhile, back at the shipyard, I've got Jack the three hundred pound ripper, who confesses to a strange convergence of people in his office yesterday morning, a redhead who just happens to be Audrey, and a guy who just happens to look a lot like the guy getting cuffed around behind the restaurant next door, before he loses the hat and mustache."

"Sounds like you've been reading one too many of those dime-store novels, Pat."

I tried a smile on him, but it didn't come off very well, from either end.

"Careful, Devlin, or I'll knock more than a hat off your head."

Fowler chuckled.

"Do you think I shot Dan Colby?" I asked Pat while staring at Fowler.

"No," Pat said.

"Or Cliff Black?"

"No," Pat said again.

I stood up.

"Well then, you had better charge me with something. And get junior here off my back while you're at it."

"Big tough guy," Fowler said with a smile.

"One more word and you'll find out just how tough."

"All right, all right," Pat said and shoved Fowler towards the opposite chair. "Go on, sit down. And you, too," he said to me.

I did, steaming. Whalen leaned over me again.

"That's your problem, Devlin. You get your teeth into something and you don't know when to let go."

"Yeah, well, you can bet your ass I'm not going to let go now."

"All right, all right. Let's get back to business. You lied to a police officer while in the pursuit of a criminal investigation, and unless you can come up with a real good reason why you did, I can't see any reason why I shouldn't take you in on perjury charges."

"I didn't lie to you. I've got a client and told it to you as straight as I could."

"Client, my ass. The only client you had that was remotely related to Audrey and Colby was Audrey's husband and he's dead. So you'd better come up with a better excuse than that or you're coming down to the station with me."

Both men flinched as I reached into my coat pocket. When I pulled out the cocktail napkin with Rick's contract on it, Fowler chuckled. Whalen had a look and scoffed.

"Bullshit," he said.

"Call him if you want."

"On a cocktail napkin. I've seen everything now...All right. Go on. Give me your cock and bull story."

139

"It's no cock and bull story. Cliff hired me to look after Audrey so I called up to Magellan, looking for her. Audrey was nowhere to be found but Rick was there and asked me to meet him for lunch down by the Huntington Pier. That led to a story about someone shaking him down. When he found out I was a gumshoe, he hired me on the spot. Next thing you know, I've got Pancho Villa and his sidekicks chasing me around."

"You signed him up on a cocktail napkin."

"I told you. He wanted to hire me on the spot. What was I supposed to do? Drive back to Laurel Lagoon for a proper contract while he waited?"

"You knew all this the other night and didn't tell me?"

"Look, Pat. How many times do I have to say this? I have a fiduciary responsibility to protect my clients and their interests."

"Don't give me that legal crap."

"It's the truth, Pat."

"You wouldn't know the truth if it hit you over the head."

"All right," I said, feeling raw. "Rub it in."

"All right, Devlin. Tell me something I don't already know."

I glanced at Fowler with his smirky ass grin and back at Pat.

"Before I tell you my story, tell me one more thing."

"Here we go."

"I just want to be clear on this point."

"Go on."

"The ballistics. Did they match on Cliff and Colby?"

"Nope."

Pat smiled at the look on my face.

"There goes your pat little theory, huh?"

"I suppose."

"Yeah, talk about having a hard on for something. Now spill it. What do you know?"

"This is what I know. With Cliff shot and Audrey's partner having hired me to find out who was shaking him down, I got curious and went looking for Audrey. Her partner seemed to think she was the bad seed in this arms shipment deal so it was only natural for me to put a tail on her. Next thing I know she's driving up to Newport and…"

"Wait a minute, wait a minute. How did you happen to find this Audrey?"

I stared.

"Oh, right. You moonlight as a private detective."

Fowler had a laugh. I stared. Whalen waved a hand.

"All right. Maybe that was a cheap shot…Go on."

I stared another long moment before continuing.

"So Audrey drives up to Newport and turns into the shipyard. I went down there to look around and see what she was up to. I never actually saw her go into the shipyard office. I never saw her there. I never saw her leave, and I haven't seen her since. I can also tell you that her partner hasn't heard a word from her either, if that eases your mind any."

"But you talked with Jack," Pat said. "Why didn't you level with me about that?"

"I went in to see if Audrey was there. To me, Jack had nothing to do with it."

"Okay, Devlin. We'll leave that to the side for the moment, and the matter of your disguise, but all of a sudden, you're at the backside of the restaurant next door, getting cuffed around by a couple of boys."

"I thought maybe I could see something from the backside of the office that I couldn't see from the front."

"And you say those boys were from the big leagues."

"That's the way they played it."

"Did they show you a badge?"

"No."

Pat stared at me.

"You knew all this yesterday and you didn't say a word."

I stared at him.

"To hell with you, Devlin."

Pat started to leave but stopped at the door. Fowler piled up behind him.

"Don't come around the station looking for any more favors from me."

"What's eating you?" I asked him.

"I'll tell you what's eating me. Someone showed up last night. Maybe your boys from the big leagues. Maybe someone even higher up. I don't know but whoever it was had an order from a federal judge. Said it was a matter of homeland security. Ran off with the desktop and files we had collected at Colby's place. That's what's eating me, Devlin."

"I take it you and Hernandez never found his lap top."

"What do you know about a lap top?"

"You mentioned it to Burrell the night we were over at Colby's place."

"So I did. So I did. Well, just for the record. Hernandez is on my case about you too. In fact, we're both wondering what you were doing out there with Colby's body while no one was watching."

"Minding my own business, Pat."

"Yeah? Well, just remember. Disturbing a crime scene can land a person in jail."

Pat let that soak in for a moment before starting down the hall. Fowler offered me a wink on his way out. He left the door open. I got up to close it and sat back in my chair to sulk.

Not that I had intended to play Pat for a sucker, but maybe he was right. I wouldn't know the truth if it hit me over the head. Thinking I knew best how to clear Steve's name and save the world, I had perpetrated a number of deceptions and probably committed a crime.

Speaking of deceptions, this whole disguise business was beginning to have a rather perverse symbolism to it. Who was the real Michael Devlin? I was losing sight of the truth myself.

Just call me trouble. On that much everyone could agree.

There was a thought to go home and have a glass of milk. Crawl into bed. Take a nap. Maybe things would look better to me when I reawakened.

Before I got too far with that idea, the phone rang. It was Kenny.

"She just banged a card in Doheny Beach. Looks like a take-out place. Japanese or something like that. Do they have Japanese take-out on Orion?"

"Oh yeah. Orion rolls. They're big."

Kenny laughed.

"Okay. Just wanted to let you know she was down in Doheny again."

"Thanks. It just so happens I was heading that way to have my fortune read."

"Hey, I want to have my fortune read."

"I'll get her card. In the meantime, please keep an eye on Audrey. And call me on my cell if anything comes up."

"Will do."

I hung up, went out into the hallway, locked the door and headed downstairs. Out in the back alley, I found Dabney, the town meter maid in the process of ticketing my Impala. As bleached blondes went, she wasn't a sore sight but could not seem to lay off the potato chips and candy bars. At five foot two, she was a load packed into a set of tight shorts. Just the kind of gal who'd make herself at home in a small-town police station. An endless stream of men to flirt with and always dreaming one of them was about to lead her down the aisle. Never knowing, or at least never admitting to her innermost self, that in the backroom world where those cops played out their lives, Dabney and her fullback frame were good for little more than a parade of nasty jokes and sick laughs.

Poor Dabney, only I didn't pity her one bit. She had the same smirk on her face that Fowler had. Probably Pat had sent her over to ticket me. The whole lot of them had been talking behind my back.

"Try to stay out of trouble," Dabney said before driving off in her three-wheeled cart. I nearly tore up the ticket in her face.

Heading south on Laurel Avenue a few moments later, I grabbed one of my burner phones and dialed Nacho's number.

"Jess," a gravelly voice said with the obligatory accent.

"This is the gringo with the Impala. What do you want from me?"

There was a pause. I pictured Nacho pulling the phone away from his ear to check the name and number on his caller ID. I heard rustling and Nacho was back.

"I tell ju what I want from ju, ju motherfucking gringo. I want my fucking shit?"

"How can I help you get your shit when I don't even know what I'm looking for?"

The phone was cupped and I heard muffled voices. Nacho was back again, only playing nice now.

"Okay, we meet for a drink somewhere and I explain everything ju need to be hearing."

"What I need to be hearing is the truth. What are you missing?"

"Okay, I tell you, gringo. That fucking Colby, he's supposed to be delivering me a chipping container, only he's dead now, so I figure out real fast, because I'm one smart motherfucker, maybe he told the bitch, and maybe even that pinche cabrón she works with, only I can't find those fucking pieces of shit anywhere!"

Having gotten himself all worked up, Nacho took a moment to calm down again.

"Okay, listen, gringo. All ju need to do is have them tell ju where to find the chipping container, then ju can be telling me and we all go our separate ways, like amigos. Or people are going to start dying. ¿Sabe?"

"Yeah, I sabe. I'll call you back as soon as I have some answers."

"Hey hey hey!" Nacho said before I could hang up.

"Yeah, what?"

"Ju have my word, gringo. We meet for a cerveza, nice and friendly. Ju tell me what I'm needing to hear and it's adios. No questions asked, just like old compadres."

"Yeah. It'll be adios, all right, with me six feet under."

"No, no, my friend. Ju tell us where my shit is and we call it good."

"All right. I'll call you as soon as I know something."

"Hey, don't fuck with me, gringo!"

That was the last thing I heard as I hung up the phone.

My mind immediately went to work, stitching together a story from what Nacho had just told me, and from what I had read in the papers. The Feds were purportedly looking for a shipping container up in San Pedro, said to be filled with small arms, but also likely to contain some sort of illicit, top-secret technology. One could go with type and assume that Boris was hunting for the top-secret technology while Nacho was looking for the small arms. Assuming that much, you could picture Al-Hamad having snuck his stolen technology into that shipment of small arms, only Colby comes along with plans to divert the container down to Nacho and his pals in Mexico and now everyone's plans have been turned upside down and everyone's at each other's throats.

One thing jumped out at me above all else in what Nacho had just said. 'Only he's dead now', referring to Colby's death as something out of his control. I had never really bought into this theory of Nacho and his boys going by Colby's shipyard to shake him down and all of a sudden Colby's floating face down in the harbor with a slug in his chest. You didn't shoot someone before you got answers, and now even Nacho's own words seemed to discount the idea.

Nacho had also said, "...and people are going to start dying." A manner of speaking, perhaps, the meaning lost in translation, but that was worlds apart from saying "people are going to keep dying."

Well, with one more piece of the puzzle in hand, I now had short odds on someone other than Nacho having shot Dan Colby, none of which explained who had shot Cliff or strangled Connie. Meaning, I was no closer to getting my friend Steve out of jail.

Sometimes you just felt like a lousy detective.

13

Heading down the coast, I saw the last glint of sun, disappearing below the rooftops in my rearview mirror. The trees along the road quickly filled with the ink of dusk. I saw three seagulls, winging down the shore in the fading light, off to wherever they go as evening fell. My date with destiny and Sylvia the fortune teller was straight ahead.

A thought popped into my head. What if she could read minds? That could make things awkward. I made a mental note to control what I was thinking, then laughed at myself.

Having come to the sprawling point at the north end of Doheny, I followed the highway up and over a rise and down into town. The highway split around an arrow shaped property and the ensuing commercial strip steadily widened until it was an entire block separating the north and southbound lanes.

I turned left a few stoplights farther on, crossed the northbound lanes and turned south again into an alleyway behind the storefronts, boxed in now by apartment buildings on my left and the back of commercial buildings on my right. It was everything that had become seedy about Doheny Beach over the years, commercial right alongside residential, single-family homes in the shadow of towering triplexes, dumpsters across the alley from someone's front lawn. If you discounted the sweeping coastline looking south towards the Mexican border, and the clapboard architecture, the clutter of cheap storefronts and power lines along Coast Highway almost gave South Central LA a run for its money. It was as if someone had sold out a quaint New England seashore village for a quick buck. The place could have been a bungalow dream from the '40s. Instead, it begged for a bit of dynamite.

I crossed one street going down the alley and turned right on the next. When I pulled to a stop at the curb, I was fifty feet back from the highway. A two-story, World War II era stucco duplex was on my left, the duplex joined to the commercial building on Coast Highway by a fence and courtyard. The commercial building had been constructed of block and was painted ship gray. It had all the charm of a Navy tanker.

The storefront to Sylvia's shop was in that block building. The entrance was around the corner on the highway side.

Over the years, on countless late-night odysseys, I had passed by Sylvia's shop, wondering what mysteries lay hidden behind the neon hand in the window. It had always been my intention to go in one day and find out, and now that hour had finally arrived. Audrey was the ostensible reason for my visit, but that did not seem to be the point of it anymore. She was simply a trick the gods had used to get me through Sylvia's front door. The real issue was the ball and chain around my life.

Deciding it was best not to leave my car where it could be spotted, I made a U-turn and parked farther up the block. There was a thought to wear my .38. It was always possible for trouble to follow me, but it was also possible to bring it along in the form of a gun. In the end, I shoved the holster and gun under the front seat, called Sylvia to let her know I was there and headed back down the block towards Coast Highway on foot. Sylvia had told me to wait out by the front door. She would be right there.

The storefront could have been a Laundromat; plate glass with a nondescript glass door and a set of cheap blinds over the whole lot. There was a small barbershop on the left, a two-seat hair salon to the right, both of them already closed. The sidewalk out front looked as if it had not been washed down for a couple of years.

Late at night, with the highway empty and the stars twinkling high up in the black sky, the setup had a far more romantic air to it. Even in the fading light of a dying day, gypsies and romance and mystery were hard to imagine.

I heard the sound of the lock being turned and Sylvia opened the door from the inside. The heat of a stuffy room wafted out and promptly doused my romantic visions. There was a certain baby-faced beauty to Sylvia, but she was built along the lines of a sumo wrestler. Not at all the petite little gypsy gal I had envisioned.

I smiled and tried my best to hide my thoughts. That my search for love had come to one more dead end.

I placed Sylvia in her thirties and guessed that her mother had hailed from some dark, Eastern European country. Sylvia had black hair, black, fathomless eyes and a birthmark on the right side of her nose.

The room behind Sylvia was decorated with French provincial furniture, highlighted by a sofa against each long wall. Two matching high-backed chairs were positioned around a small table at the back of the room, the pale-green velvet fabric on each piece variously worn, faded or stained. Along with the matching coffee table and buffet in back, it was as if a middle-class dream from the Bronx had gone south.

Besides the furniture and two mass production paintings on opposite walls, there were candles, crystals and figurines scattered all around the room. The figurines were predominantly gnomes and wizards. An altar dedicated to Jesus, the Virgin Mary and various Christian saints had been arranged on the buffet.

Sylvia looked at me and my wound without any sign of emotion. I was invited to take a seat at the small, round table near the back of the room. Sylvia cracked the door open with a floor stop and came to join me. The pace of her movements was elephantine, her line of sight on things up near the ceiling.

She settled her significant girth into the opposite chair. Her posture was upright and calm, her gaze intense. I stared back into her black eyes.

A wave of highway traffic rushed by outside the front door. I was back to wondering how well Sylvia could read other people's minds. Thoughts of Caitlin danced in my head.

"I can tell right now," she said. "A palm or psychic reading won't be enough for you. You're after something more. I think it would be best if we did the tarot cards."

"Okay," I said, already aware of her pricing from a small sign by the front door. Palm readings thirty dollars, psychic readings fifty. The tarot cards were seventy-five.

Sylvia lit a candle and some incense. She placed four crystal pyramids together around the candle, then moved a set of worn tarot cards from her side of the table over to mine.

"Shuffle them," she said. "Then cut them into three piles."

I tried to do as instructed but the thickness of the cards made that nearly impossible. They did not respond at all like player cards. The deck became skewed in every direction. I laughed like Kenny at my seeming ineptitude.

"How much?" I asked Sylvia.

"It doesn't matter. Whenever you're satisfied. They just need to have your energy in them."

It took another minute for me to get all the cards realigned. That done, I made three separate piles. Sylvia made those back into a single deck and began to place the cards on the table face up, first one, then two split off the bottom of the first card, then three split off the bottom of those two, and then a row of four. At this, she stopped, studied the pile and began to speak.

"You are what we call an old soul," Sylvia said without looking up at me. "Your karma is very ancient. I see pharaohs and some curse from those ancient times. Not something you did, but something done in your name and you have been trying to clear your name of this curse for many, many lifetimes now."

Sylvia spoke English awkwardly and with an accent, as someone who used it as a second language. She studied the cards. I studied her.

"You will never be happy until you let go of this ancient wound," she went on finally, "and though romance is how you've tried to resolve it, it has never worked."

She stared at my face now, though it seemed as if she was looking through me.

"I see that you want to get up on your steed and be a gallant knight for a particular woman."

She waited for an acknowledgement. I shook my head, then nodded.

"But you feel she has never truly appreciated this part of you."

I performed more or less the same gesture.

"You fail because your aura is broken. It is powerful but broken in places. When this woman lets you down, the dark places in your heart take over. You need to heal your aura and only then will you be able to fulfill this destiny you seek."

Sylvia went on to recount the high points of my life, which included a brief but disastrous marriage and as a whole represented an uncanny appraisal. But she had yet to lock onto Caitlin, and I was wondering how on earth she could miss the most obvious thing.

Then it came, and with sudden accuracy.

"I am seeing a woman. Catheri…Cat…"

"Caitlin," I said.

"Red hair, yes?"

I nodded.

"She is why you are here."

I frowned.

"No, I mean she sent you here. I have heard her screaming since the first moment we spoke on the phone."

The traffic rushed by. The light of day continued to fade around us. I was running fast from my ancient wounds.

"This woman is a very sweet soul," Sylvia went on. "But she is in an enormous amount of pain. And she is not dealing very well with that pain on this earth."

"Michael," Sylvia said. "This is a soul mate, but the two of you have very different karmas and it will be hard for the two of you to reconcile them in this lifetime. You have an ancient karmic destiny to fulfill. This woman is only concerned with happiness right here and now. She loves that gallant knight in you, but she doesn't understand what drives it. She only wants you to make a little cottage for her in the woods, right?"

"I suppose that was true once."

"It is still true now and you should do it."

"This woman's gone from my life," I said.

"No," Sylvia said. "She is not. I feel her here with you right now."

I clamped down firmly on my emotions and stared at Sylvia. She stared back.

"It's all right," she said. "You can let it out."

I shook my head and looked away.

The room had grown nearly dark by this point, lit mostly by flickering candlelight. I was in something of a trance, waiting for Sylvia to continue when the back door opened abruptly. I looked up to see a red-haired woman approaching the table. As her face appeared in the candlelight, I saw it was Caitlin and rose up out of my chair. All the love I had kept buried in my heart over the past five years propelled me forward, my intent being to take Caitlin into my arms, but she rushed right past me and over to Sylvia.

"I think those same men are here."

At hearing those words in the darkened room, the spell was broken and I realized this woman was Audrey, not Caitlin. And still I was drawn to pull her into my embrace, the match between them was so heartbreakingly uncanny.

"What men?" I asked Audrey.

"Who is he?" she said to Sylvia as if I were an intruder.

"What men?!" I asked more demonstrably when Audrey had failed to answer me.

Just then, the shadows of two men moved across the drawn shades at the front of the shop. Immediately, I knew one of them to be Nacho and herded the two women towards the back door.

"Go on," I whispered. "Get out of here."

I handed Sylvia one of my cards.

"Text message that mobile number as soon as you're someplace safe. But only text messages. No calls."

"Who are you?" Audrey asked me. "What's going on?" she asked Sylvia.

"It's all right," Sylvia said. "He came here to help you."

Audrey looked at me as if she had no interest in being helped; by me, or anyone.

"Go on, get her out of here," I whispered to Sylvia again. "And remember to let me know where you are."

I quietly pushed the back door open and Sylvia went forward into the enclosed walkway. Audrey followed her with another look back my way.

Once both women had disappeared into the back door of Sylvia's apartment, I locked the door and turned back to face Nacho and his pal.

A man was trying to peek in through the cracked front door. Then a hand reached down to lift the doorstop. That man slipped in, followed by Nacho. They waited as the door closed behind them.

Unsure of themselves in the darkness, they moved cautiously in my direction—Nacho straight towards me, the other man over to retrieve a candle from the table. He used it to illuminate my face.

"What the hell, Nacho? I thought you were going to give me some time to figure things out."

Nacho pulled a Five-seveN pistol from his pant waist and shoved it under my chin. With the silencer, the barrel looked nearly as long as a rifle.

152

"Check for the mujeres?" Nacho said to his sidekick.

Nacho's pal placed the candle down and went out the back door.

"Okay, gringo. What do ju know?"

"Nothing yet."

Nacho nearly broke my front teeth shoving the gun against my mouth.

"We're not fucking around, gringo. Now somebody is going to be telling me where my shit is or we take ju someplace nice and quiet and start cutting off pieces one by one."

The other man rushed back in.

"Those two gringos just parked down the street and are coming this way."

"What are they packing?"

"Some serious fucking cannons. I told ju we should have brought the pinche machine guns."

Nacho let loose with a string of expletives in Spanish.

He looked back at me.

"Ju want to live, gringo, ju come up with my shit within twenty-four hours, or that's it."

He made a gesture at his throat.

"Jou're fucking dead."

Just then, the silhouettes of two men passed by the curtains out front. Someone tried the door.

"¡Vaminos!" Nacho whispered angrily to his partner.

I was about to rejoice over the cavalry riding in when something flashed in the darkness and pain exploded in my brain. Nausea followed and the curse was cast. I went tumbling down through three thousand years of bad luck. A pharaoh's tomb with torches was straight ahead.

14

I came to in the darkened room with a solitary candle flickering above me. The gnome and wizard figurines stood sentry on the nearby hutch. Crucified on the carpet, more or less, I watched their shadows dance on the ceiling and walls. The back of my head throbbed with a stabbing pain.

I tried to sit up but quickly lay back down from a wave of nausea. While I worked on keeping the contents of my stomach in place, Audrey came to mind. Feelings of abandonment followed. That seemed to sum up my place in this world. All the dearest people in my life had gone away. My cherished lover had dismissed me with little more than a shrug. Nothing was turning out the way I had planned.

I closed my eyes to the nausea and watched a parade of faces pass through my head; Nacho with his deadly smirk, the elephantine Sylvia, Audrey, Whalen, Fowler, Dick and Tom. I remembered that flash of something in the darkness and felt nauseous again. I tried to think of something pleasant but nothing came.

A moment later, I heard voices and became aware of several shadows passing by the closed blinds. Laughter carried off into the night, along with the bustle of footsteps down the sidewalk. Then all was quiet in the flickering candlelight again.

For unknown reasons, my mind went to work on the puzzle of who these people were and arrived at an almost instantaneous conclusion. By the pitch of their voices, by the boisterous, bustling, happy-go-lucky nature of their gait, and by the freedom it would take to be out at this relatively late hour, and yet still unable to drive a car, I concluded it was a group of young teenagers and was so confident in my assumptions, gauged in the blink of an eye, that further analysis seemed entirely unnecessary.

What a marvelous bit of instrumentation the brain was, able to distill trillions of bits of disparate data into a coherent snapshot of the world in an instant. So why did mine keep getting me into trouble?

At least Nacho had failed to put a bullet in my head. I wondered where Audrey had gone.

With my nausea beginning to subside, I sat up and leaned back on my hands. My head fell back in that direction. The associated rush of blood sent another jolt of pain through my head. I touched the wound and groaned, feeling all the more nauseous for having done so.

I was about to get up on my feet when the outline of two human forms flashed into my peripheral vision and my heart nearly jumped out of my chest.

It was Dick and Tom, sitting on one of Sylvia's threadbare French provincial sofas.

"Jesus Christ," I said. "You scared the hell out of me."

"Good morning, sleeping beauty," Tom said. "We were wondering when you'd wake up."

"I had odds that you wouldn't," Dick said.

"Yeah, you might just owe us your life," Tom said, "Can't be sure but someone was rushing out the back door as we slipped in. You've seen the movie. A screech of tires and gunshots. Only we held off shooting our cannons this time."

He patted an M-37 Falcon lying on the sofa next to him.

"What were you planning to do with that thing? Bring down a passenger jet?"

Tom smiled.

"You should have seen those two beaners flying out the back door."

I felt the blood at the back of my head again.

155

"And you didn't bother shooting them because?"

"You want the whole sheriff's department down here poking around?"

"No, I suppose not."

"Well, neither do we. Besides, I never had a good shot. No sense in taking out one of those apartment buildings across the street while we're at it."

"Did you get a name?" Dick said.

"In all the fun, we forgot to exchange cards."

"You're a barrel of laughs," Tom said. "Considering that we may have saved you from a cold night at the morgue, you're not showing much appreciation."

"Okay, I'm eternally grateful. Now what?"

"I'm not sure, but I think we'll keep an eye on you for a little while longer. Trouble seems to follow you around like a lost puppy."

"That's why I came to see a fortune teller. What brought you here?"

"I've always fancied having my fortune read."

Tired of the bullshit, I used Sylvia's round table as a crutch and got to my feet. Dick and Tom stood up with me, Dick on my right, Tom to my left. Dick was the linebacker with a butch. Tom was his paunchy, somewhat disheveled looking coach in a nylon parka.

Tom cocked his head and had a closer look at the Tarot cards. They were still spread out precisely the way Sylvia had left them.

"Hmm...the hanged man. Maybe you'd better go home and get into bed."

"Funny. I was just thinking the same thing."

Dick had a closer look at my skull.

"Somebody gave you one hell of a pill. Maybe you'd better stop by the emergency room and have your head examined first."

Tom chuckled at the double entendre. I gave him a look, still pissed about being roughed up by them the previous morning and not at all amused.

"Thanks," I told Dick, "but I think I'll take Mr. Comedy's advice here and go home where it's safe."

I blew out the candle.

"Yeah, well maybe we've got a few questions for you before you go," Dick said.

The three of us stood there staring at each other. Traffic rushed by. Light and shadows played on our faces. The figurines stared on like silent sentinels.

"It's a free world," I reminded Dick.

"Yeah, but not as free as you think," he reminded me.

"Yeah? And what do you want to know?" I was foolish enough to ask.

"Like why you went on that little love cruise late last night?"

"And left fifteen minutes later," Tom added.

"Hot flashes," I told them.

"Yours or hers?" Tom asked me.

"What do you care?"

Tom stood there smiling in his jocular manner. Dick looked to be chewing on some bile.

"Look," I went on. "Go back and search the place again. Help yourself but I've got nothing to hide. And neither does she."

"We just might," Dick said.

"Fine, but it's plain and simple. I'm just a private dick working a private case, so if it's excitement you're looking for, you'd better aim that bazooka of yours at bigger game."

"Yeah? Well yesterday you didn't even know about a doll. And as far as I can tell, you've been chasing one around. So who knows when you're telling the truth?"

"And when you're lying," Tom added

"Why does talking with you two always end up sounding like a cheap B movie?"

Dick got into my face and pretended to dust off my collar.

"I told you to get lost, didn't I?"

"I don't remember any law against having my fortune read."

He studied my eyes.

"Let me tell you how this works, Devlin. One day you're getting into your car. Then all of a sudden there's a bag over your head. A wild race across town follows. Then you sit shivering in the gutted belly of a C-17 for about twelve hours at thirty-five thousand feet. Next thing you know, you're in a cold cell somewhere, counting seconds and minutes. And nobody cares. Nobody ever hears from you again."

"I had the same vacation offer from some Russians the other day. You know anything about some Russians?"

Dick shook his head and dusted off my collar again.

"Just be a good boy and get back to your divorce business."

"You done with the lecture?" I asked him.

He nodded with a gentle slap of my face. I nearly decked him. Instead, I went around to the front door and turned the deadbolt. Dick and Tom were waiting for me in back. They went out with a final review of the room. I turned the knob on the entry lock, closed the door and followed them through the side gate at the back of Sylvia's apartment.

"You always get into this much trouble?" Tom wanted to know once we were out on the sidewalk.

"Every few weeks or so. I get bored without it."

"I guess you're just not very good at what you do, huh?"

"I was thinking the same thing about you two. In fact, I'm beginning to think you're just a couple of civilian hacks."

"Don't you kid yourself," Dick said. "We're the big boys working for the company."

"Yeah. And I'm here selling encyclopedias."

"I can see why people keep hitting you over the head," Tom said with another smile.

I stared back.

"Look," Dick said. "The doll's in deep and we were told to bring her in. So, like I told you, be a smart boy and get out of the way, before you find yourself in even more trouble."

We were back to staring at each other.

158

"Well, like the guy with the punch lines here suggested. Guess I'll go home and crawl into bed."

I wanted those two clowns to think that was exactly where I was headed, when I had no intention of going home. Even if I did, it would not be for very long. I would only toss and turn all night, wondering where everyone had gone without me.

When Dick turned towards the highway, Tom followed, but not before he waved goodbye, just the tips of his four fingers moving in unison. I turned the other way up the sidewalk. The narrow, darkened street wound up a hill to my left. The three-story triplexes loomed over me from both sides. The street was empty save for a crush of parked cars.

When I looked back, Dick and Tom were nowhere in sight. Betting my two pals weren't done with me yet, I went up past my Impala and slipped behind the side gate of a duplex. Sure enough, they cruised by a minute later, turned onto the next side street and crisscrossed back and forth several times before they finally headed back down to the highway. I gave Dick and Tom a few more minutes before heading back down to my Impala.

Once inside, I sat there considering the latest pieces to the puzzle. Given the lag time between my arrival and Nacho's, it wasn't likely he and his friend had followed me. The same could be said of Dick and Tom. That meant, in their separate ways, both of them had made the connection between Audrey and Sylvia and had then stumbled in on me as a matter of blind luck. Certainly, if Dick and Tom had been tailing Nacho, things would have played out differently, not with my Mexican pals slipping out the back door of Sylvia's shop as Dick and Tom slipped in the front.

Several minutes went by without me arriving at any further insight on the matter, except to say that I doubted Dick and Tom were working for the firm. Maybe as contract players, but other than Dick's bile towards me, there wasn't the gravity you expected of someone who felt the fate of the world was in their hands. In fact, take away all their gadgetry and those two clowns came off as second-rate detectives.

To their credit, if they hadn't stumbled in when they had, who knew what would have happened, so I guessed I owed them a big thanks.

With the facts sorted out into my best theory of the day, I still knew next to nothing. My hunch was, Audrey knew something. What, I had no idea, but somewhere in her secrets, I had my money on there being a missing link.

I started the Impala and headed down the street, faced with a choice — head home for the night or stay on the chase. My impulse was to sleep for a thousand years, but with Steve looking at life behind bars, I opted to follow the hounds.

At the bottom of the block, I parked across from Sylvia's apartment and crossed the street to her front door. The door was protected by a prison grade wrought iron screen. I tried to open it but it was locked. I knocked quietly and a minute later, the front door itself cracked opened. The room was dark behind the screen. The outline of a form was visible in the darkness. I could not make out the features but it was another hefty soul. Then I heard a high, boyish voice.

"My Mom's not here."

"Do you know where she is?"

Another form materialized behind the first form, a bit taller than the boy, but of equal girth. I saw both their eyes flashing in the darkness. They seemed to be taking in the Band-Aid on my face.

"She went to the Indian reservation," the other voice said. It was a deeper voice, but belonging to a girl.

"What Indian reservation?"

The boy and the girl looked at each other. I heard them whispering.

"It's all right," the girl said to her brother, then to me. "It's the Cahuilla tribe. They're out by the Salton Sea. At the north end. The people on the reservation can help you find my Mom."

"Thank you," I said. The two of them stared for a moment before the girl closed the door.

I walked back to my car, both in awe and repulsed by Sylvia and her brood. The bloodline probably went back five hundred years, the whole lot of them as gifted as Rasputin but with the societal manners of inbred Appalachian hillbillies. Sylvia must have weighed three hundred pounds and both her children were already giving her a run for her money on that score; telling fortunes while beefing themselves up on Cheetos and Oreo cookies.

Back in my car, I sat there weighing whether to head straight out to the Salton Sea or to drive home for a shower and a change of clothes first. I decided on the shower and change of clothes and turned back towards Laurel Lagoon. I wasn't losing much in the way of time. The new toll road started a few miles beyond the outskirts of town and loped out to the 91 freeway in one straight shot. Unlike the old days when you had to drive up and around the old packinghouses in Pueblo Hills, I could leave my place, have the road and some hauntingly unspoiled country all to myself and hit Corona in less than twenty minutes.

Driving back up the coast, the pieces of the puzzle continued to work in my brain, sometimes fitting together rather neatly, sometimes not making one damned bit of sense. From all those years of listening to Jack Oliver, I had learned to follow the money. Money did indeed make the world go round, but where did it lead you in this sorry affair? To the wild back streets of Abu Dhabi? To a drug cartel south of the border? No matter how I parsed things, nothing came close to explaining the deaths of Cliff and Connie.

Back in Laurel Lagoon, I took the precaution of parking on the street up behind my house and scampered down a wooded slope to the rear entrance. Going in through the laundry room, I left the lights off and deposited my dirty clothes in a pile on top of the washer.

In the shower, there was a repressed yelp as the first torrent of hot water hit the back of my head. A stream of reddish water swirled down around my toes. I shampooed gingerly around the wound and felt nauseous every time my fingers came anywhere near it.

Once I had dried off and had gotten into my robe, I used two mirrors and various contortions to see what those boys had done to me. I quickly looked away with renewed nausea. This was going to require stitches.

I had a favor to call and was dialing Dr. Gunderson's phone number a moment later. He answered groggily.

"Doc, it's Michael Devlin."

"What on earth time is it?"

"Going on midnight."

I heard him groan.

"What can I do for you, Michael?"

"Sew up my head."

I heard him sigh.

"All right. Meet me down at the clinic in half an hour."

"Better make it ten. I have a long night ahead of me."

"All right. I'll head down right away."

I went to the fridge and poked around for something to eat. Nothing looked appetizing. I settled on a piece of leftover chicken breast, added some salted nuts and chased everything down with a big gulp of milk.

I dressed and headed out the door. The chicken and nuts were trying to come back up. I should have been in bed. The concussion had left me feeling as hollow as a box.

My regular phone beeped as I was climbing into the Impala. It was a text message from Vanderhof. Call him. Not yet, buddy. Go ahead and stew. The only person I wanted to hear from right then was Audrey and she couldn't be bothered.

Heading through town was a breeze at that hour. There were folks spilling out from the late-night bars and the standard hubbub of a hot summer night in Laurel Lagoon but few actual cars wandering around on the streets. I quickly found a parking

162

space near the clinic and parked. Dr. Gunderson pulled up a minute later. I got out to greet him. His ruddy, bearded face usually had a cheerful look, but not tonight. He nodded and went straight to unlock the door. Fluorescent lights flickered on in the reception area ahead of me.

"Come on in back and let's have a look," he said.

Seated in an examination room, I waited while he washed his hands and then winced as he probed around the wound. Satisfied, he went to retrieve some supplies from an upper cabinet. He returned with a pile of stuff, including a razor blade.

"I'll give you a local but this still may hurt a bit," he said.

"Yeah. I needn't tell you it already does."

"Dare I ask how?"

"Ouch," I said as he started poking around with the Novocain.

"Sorry."

"Some Mexican boys."

"Hmm. Doesn't sound good."

"No, they're not very polite, when you get right down to it."

While we waited for the Novocain to take effect, I told the Doc about a story I had read in the Rolling Stone many years earlier. This was when the Mexican cartels were first starting to flex their muscles across the border. A few happy-go-lucky hippie kids got involved with them, having no idea they were messing with such deadly killers. When a few of these hippies got greedy and decided not to pay up their tabs, the cartel sent up a couple of hit men to leave a message. The cops found this one college kid dead on his bathroom floor. The narcos had cut his dick off in roughly one-inch pieces. The cause of death was shock.

"Lovely story," Dr. Gunderson said.

"I read it in Rolling Stone."

He nodded and went to work with his razor. With a spot on my skull shaved bald, he started to stitch me up. A few minutes

163

later, he was throwing the last of his sutures into the stainless-steel tray. A bandage followed.

"All done," he said.

I looked in the mirror. I now had a yarmulke to go with the scab on my cheek.

Before he washed his hands, he examined the scab.

"You might want to take it easy for a few days."

"Yeah. I tell myself that same thing every morning."

He washed his hands and turned to face me.

"Even?"

"Sure, even," I said. "And thanks."

I started for the door.

"Must be on my way. I've got miles and miles to go before I sleep."

Dr. Gunderson smiled.

"Lovely words, but I suspect there's nothing lovely about what you're up to."

"There's no sneaking anything by you, Doc."

He smiled again.

"The next favor's on me," I said before letting the door close behind me.

Winding out through the canyon, I had nothing but the dark hills and the stars twinkling high above me for company. There was even less of civilization as the new toll road climbed up through the oak and sycamore dotted open country, and fewer cars with every passing mile, just the occasional set of headlights stabbing out of the darkness and into the heart of a man all alone.

Weariness started to settle over me and the questions came. Where are you going, Devlin? Why can't you live a normal existence like everyone else? Settle down, get a wife and have some kids? Why did your life always have a cheap, desperate feeling about it? Like John Garfield on the road to no good. In place of answers, I had more weariness settling over me and the long dark road up ahead.

164

About the time I hit the interstate, the oppressive desert heat started to bleed through the leather interior and my air-conditioner went on. So did a Lester Young CD. *Guess I'll Have to Change My Plan.* Yeah I will. I listened to the song until I had tired of beating myself up.

For thirty miles, a string of heartless cities passed by, the newest developments trailing off into the darkened hills like a necklace of lights. Half an hour later, the towering mass of Mt. San Gorgonio appeared off to my right, its remaining splash of snow illuminated by a waning moon. The surrounding hills and vast desert terrain seemed utterly small and insignificant in comparison.

Then I was passing by the fields of white windmills turning slowly in the night wind. The lights of Palm Springs and Palm Desert spread across the distant valley floor, restless, throbbing and chewing up all that free energy as fast as the windmills could make it.

Half an hour later, I was passing through the date orchards of Indio. At the far end of town, I took a turn onto Highway 86 and bore right again when the highway split at the top of Salton Sea. Halfway down the sea, I noticed a sign announcing Ray & Carol's Motel and turned left onto North Marina Drive. The ensuing streets brought to mind ancient mariners. Sea King, Sea Port, Sea Kist and Sea Nymph. The scenery was gutted buildings and trash filled lots.

I did come across one, well kept, single family home, done up in a pseudo Mediterranean style, but all alone on an empty street, as if someone was desperately hanging onto their own forsaken dreams, hoping to ignore the fact that the Salton Sea's vision of paradise had gone south a long time ago, to paper over the yearly fish die offs and busted out windows and the trailers with their plywood veneers peeling off beneath a relentless desert sun, to ignore that the Salton Sea had been a cosmic accident and was now more symbolic of a cancer eating away at the American soul than anything else, a reminder of how close we were to our own little third world bummer, that the

American dream could easily rot back into the earth with what was, geologically speaking, the blink of an eye, that some future civilization might one day pick over the bones of this dying town, like the carcasses of so many beached whales on the shores of a forgotten sea, reading the portents of an ancient empire's curious demise.

Half-delusional from my weary journey and desperately needing to lay my head down to sleep at two in the morning, I found myself rooting on the side of whimsical hopes and dreams.

After several turns, I stumbled upon Ray & Carol's place on Ontario Avenue, which, from Sea Kist and Sea Nymph was a big letdown but more in keeping with the looks of the overall town. So was the chain link fence around the motel. At least the roof was still on and the windows had yet to be busted in.

15

A bell jingled above the door as I walked into the office. An old calendar hung on the wall behind the desk — The Fabulous Salton Sea — one of those art deco numbers from the '60s, with a couple of dolls water skiing behind a motorboat.

Moments later, Ray appeared from in back. He looked to be in his eighties, wiry, with bad teeth, rummy eyes and a hunchback. His thinning hair was plastered over with Pomade. He bled cheap bourbon and cigarette smoke.

"Welcome to the Salton Sea," he said with a gravelly voice.

Ray was a long, long way from channeling anything fabulous.

"I'm looking for a room," I said.

"Got some ID?"

I dug out my detective license. Ray had a good look at my war wounds while I did.

"I prefer to keep things quiet, if you get my drift. I'll pay with cash."

"Make it a two hundred dollar deposit."

I handed him the money. He handed me a key.

"Don't want no trouble," he said.

"No trouble."

"Just follow the building around the corner to your right."

"Thanks," I said and went out the door.

The room did nothing to change my perceptions of the Salton Sea, from the fraying beige curtains to the obligatory cigarette burn marks on the faux marble bathroom countertop.

The geometric patterned bedspread was enough to short circuit a man's brain, especially one as tired as mine.

I threw my overnight bag on the bed and stood there for a moment, lost between the smell of rotting fish and my reasons for being there. With the temperature hovering in the nineties, I faced a long restless night. It was that or bake the planet a bit more. For me to remain cool, I would need to burn some more fossil fuel, which would lead to more global warming, which would require more air-conditioning and the burning of more fossil fuel. It was a vicious circle.

After tormenting myself for a moment, I said a word of penance to the planet this once and hit the air-conditioner. I had never slept all that well in a steam bath.

Crawling into bed, I flicked on the late-night news. It was the same old mind-numbing crap. Another man had blown himself to hell in a far-off country. A sizable gathering of people had been blown to hell along with him. There was a film clip of people wandering around lost amidst the debris and rubble. Dead pigs and chickens littered the ground. It was a reminder of how hard peace was to come by in this world, and why I loved my hideaway down in Baja so much. A man could never entirely escape the modern world, or do entirely without it, but how lovely to forget the whole thing for a week or two.

The drone of the air-conditioner finally lulled me off to sleep. Visions of a beautiful red head and a sea filled with dead fish haunted my dreams. They were the dreams of a man moving blindly by impulse, a man who had no idea what had brought him out there to the Salton Sea or what he had hoped to find. The true reasons for my quest were a mystery. I was trying to make the world turn out the way I wanted it to turn out. How foolish of me. It was all a distraction. You spent a lifetime fighting the indomitable tide, and left this world exactly the way you had found it. The only peace was to accept things as they were.

But of course, I couldn't.

The next morning, I was startled awake by a pack of Harley-Davidsons roaring by the motel. The unsettling sound shook the walls and only slowly echoed off into the distance. It took a minute before there was complete silence again.

Concerned, I crawled out of bed and peeked through the curtains. No sign of them. Screw bikers, anyway. They evoked the apocalypse, a version of history that had gone down the road to perdition. Maybe the world was already heading in that direction but I didn't need anyone nudging things along.

I crawled back into bed, still draped in dreams. The darkness of the room was cut in half by a sliver of brilliant light left by a gap in the heavy curtains. A hot day was already in full swing outside.

With a glance at the clock, I saw that I had slept past ten. I checked my phone. Nothing. Damn it, Audrey. They're burying your husband in less than twenty-four hours. Where are you?

With the air-conditioner still humming away, I attempted to hide in the safety of my cocoon for a little while longer, wondering again why I had driven out to the Salton Sea. I could have been hanging around my own pad feeling lost, and a lot more comfortably.

Needing coffee, I went in to shave and found a dead fly lying legs up on the bathroom counter. It looked as if someone had posed it there. Headed off to the great hereafter, hey, buddy.

I looked in the mirror, aware of my own mortality. Blessed Sunday. What was I going to do? I was a man without salvation.

Fresh from a shower, I left the fly in its sacred posture and went to see about breakfast. I had noticed several signs for cafés while motoring into town the previous night but the fate of the associated eateries was along the lines of most every other establishment I had stumbled upon in Salton City so far — closed for business long ago, the roof gone, the windows blown out — just one more abandoned carcass rotting down to its bones beneath the relentless sun.

I had not seen a café still open for business, in any case, and was hoping the old man could point me in the right direction.

I left the coolness of my room, hurried over to my car in the glaring desert heat, tossed my luggage into the trunk, started the engine, turned the air-conditioner on full blast and hurried over to the office. Ray was standing behind the front counter when I went in, going over the books. A cigarette burned in the ashtray. I caught the scent of bourbon in Ray's coffee. I saw Carol through a doorway to the other room, half Ray's age and twice his weight, no makeup, the roots of her dark hair showing through the bleached blonde dye job, the hair itself pulled back as if it had been done so with considerable torque. The extra pounds were peeking through a space between her spandex pants and a sleeveless stretch blouse. A man could wish she had been a bit more modest under the circumstances.

"What can I do ya fer?" Ray asked as the automatic door closed behind me.

"Point me in the direction of a café. And hopefully one where those bikers didn't go."

"There's only one. Down at the boat marina. Cody's Café and the bikers are mostly harmless."

My mind stalled on "marina" and "mostly harmless." I had never known bikers to be harmless, and there was something more than the scent of a marina in the air.

"Where is the marina?" I asked.

Ray was taking a puff from his cigarette and pointed with that hand.

"Head down to the end and turn left. The state and federal folks are about to do a big restoration down there. Guess they finally realized, you let the sea turn to dust and you'll have one hell of a disaster on yer hands. They're gonna try and duplicate what they done with that wetlands up there on the north end."

A big fan when it came to deterring disasters, and headed up towards the north end myself, I thought to pick Ray's brain on the subject but decided I had already left enough of a trail.

"Know where I can find a market instead?"

"There's one down at the other corner."

I pushed away from the counter.

"You checking out?" Ray asked me.

"Yes and no. I've already tossed my things into the car but I'm waiting for a call. If a convention comes through before I return, feel free to rent the room."

Ray eyed me and counted out my change.

"We'll be here."

"There's a chance I'll be back."

"Ray!" Carol shouted out from the other room. "Where's my goddamned pink pants!?"

That was my cue to slip out the front door. The very hot day beat down on my head as I did.

My car air-conditioner had cooled the leather seats down to a bearable temperature. I sat there in the front seat, wondering what to do next. The thought of a cup of yogurt and one of those packaged muffins sounded grim. Anyway, I had my heart set on bacon and eggs and started down towards the marina. It was easy to find. Just follow the scent of rotting fish.

Parking to the side of Cody's, I negotiated around the pack of Harleys out front and pulled open the front door. The place went silent as I did. Every biker looked up. The same with the cook working at the grill in back.

"Morning," he said through the opening.

I greeted him back and nodded ever so slightly towards the bikers. They resumed their conversation. I took a seat as far from them as possible without appearing to be unsociable.

The cook appeared.

"Coffee," I said and entertained myself with the menu until he returned.

"Need some more time?" he asked while pouring my cup full.

"No," I said, snapping the menu shut. "Bacon and eggs. Orange juice. Rye toast if you have it."

"It's on the way," he told me and left.

When the food arrived, I quietly asked the cook about the restored wetlands.

"Yeah, everybody's coming out here to see them these days."

The bikers all looked up at the sound of his voice. I pretended not to notice them and spoke quietly again.

"How do you find the place?"

"Go north on the highway," the cook said in a hushed voice now. "You'll see a sign for the Torres-Martinez Reservation. The entrance is up before the highway splits. If you head down towards the sea from there, you'll find it. If you have any trouble, just ask the first person you come across. There's quite a few of the tribe down there along the water."

"Thanks."

He went back to his grill. I dug into my breakfast. A handful of boats were bobbing around in the marina across the road. The Fabulous Salton Sea. With the sunlight refracted just right, the brackish waters almost looked like Ray's poster.

An old couple stepped in through the door before I was done with my meal; weather-beaten, hats and shorts, and doing their best to make things seem fabulous. They had been drinking the previous evening. They had probably been drinking that morning and were soon chirping away with the cook. When they tried to drag me into their conversation, I offered a wink and refocused on my breakfast.

The bikers finally got up and left, but not without a final look in my direction. It came with the air of hyenas marking territory.

Fine, I thought. This is your personal fiefdom? Knock yourselves out.

I watched them climb onto their bikes and ride away.

Once the bikers were well out of sight, I threw some money on the table and headed out the door. Still no news from Audrey or Sylvia. That was the story of my life. Chasing after women with no time for me in return.

I climbed into the Impala, started the engine, turned on the air-conditioning and sat there thinking. My trailer in Baja was back in my thoughts. Escape. That's all I really wanted.

Maybe Vanderhof was right about me. I was trailer trash. At least my trailer had an ocean view.

Once the inside of my car had been restored to something resembling an arctic winter, I started slowly back up towards the highway. Salton City hadn't been much to look at on a star filled night. It fared even worse in the glaring light of day. Seeing all the abandoned buildings, it was hard not to think of the abandoned dreams that had gone with them.

The carcasses of rotting trailers dotted the shore on my drive north, more beached whales festering out there in the sun, as if civilization had wandered down to the sea and taken its last gasp before expiring. The turn off to oblivion was straight ahead.

About twenty miles farther up the highway, I saw a sign for the reservation. Well shy of where the main road split, I turned down a dirt road and followed my nose back among a scattering of weary looking stucco homes. Half a mile or so farther on, I caught a glimpse of the blue sea. Egrets and great blue herons dotted the shoreline. Islands of reeds and cattails surrounded their stilt-like presence. The sense of something cool came on the listless breeze.

I parked adjacent to a gate at the end of the dirt road. The edge of the wetlands was several hundred yards beyond the gate. I slipped through the fence and walked as close to the water's edge as possible without disturbing the birds. There, in the shade of a mesquite tree, I sat down and took in the sight. Water rippled around the egrets and herons. Two of them took flight and settled in again. A barge of gulls floated a few hundred feet offshore.

Off to the east, the Chocolate Mountains were bright and pink in the hot sun. I glanced over my shoulder. An arc of high cirrus clouds was bending in from the west. The sky over San Jacinto had turned ominously dark.

Odd, I thought. This was the sort of front you expected to see swooping down from the Gulf of Alaska in winter, not during the summer months.

I turned my attention back to the rippling blue water. A few minutes later, my phone vibrated. It was a message from Sylvia. She and Audrey were at the Salton Sea. Could I come to meet them.

So much for clairvoyance. I wrote back to tell Sylvia I was already here.

Where? The message came back a few moments later.

At the wetlands, I wrote back and added directions. Look for Lincoln Avenue. My car is parked where it ends. Go through the gate. I'm not far from there.

Okay, came back. I placed the phone in my pocket and stood up to wait. The arc of the cold front had now clipped the sky in half directly above my head. Off to the east, the hills and mountains still wavered in the blazing sun but the sky to the west was brooding with great darkness and the approaching storm had turned the blue water of the wetlands a choppy gray.

A few minutes later, the two women appeared in the distance. The wind stirred wildly in the brush as they approached. Sylvia was wearing a purple muumuu and scarf over her head. Audrey wore a sky-blue sundress, matching blue tennis shoes and a straw hat. She had a straw bag over her shoulder.

They joined me in the shade of the mesquite. I searched both their eyes.

"Why did you come out here to the Salton Sea?"

"Why don't you tell us…" Audrey started to say but Sylvia cut her off.

"When the energy's not right, I come out here to commune with the tribal people. It helps to guide the spirit back onto the right path."

"Would said communing lead to telling me the truth?"

I looked at Audrey. She looked at Sylvia and back at me.

"Sylvia said you were trying to help me but I don't see why."

"At this point, I'm not entirely sure, either."

Without prompting, Sylvia started down the path towards the wetlands alone. I watched her move away at her elephantine pace then looked back at Audrey. With her red hair and pale skin and pug nose, it was everything I could do to keep from pulling hard at the back of her waist.

"What is it with you two?" I said.

"What do you mean?"

"I don't get the connection. You're a bit of an odd couple."

"Sylvia is very wise and has always given me good advice."

"I'm guessing you haven't always taken it."

Audrey winced a bit but continued staring.

"What happened to your face?" she asked without emotion.

"I got into a heated discussion with a fence...The fence won," I added.

Audrey glanced from that wound to the one on my head.

"And that little boo boo I took for you last night."

I watched her eyes, a bit wounded to see my words had failed to humor her, or my gallantry make her swoon. Audrey came off like the opposing counsel in a lawsuit; as cold as a conference table, no emotional sparks whatsoever.

"I still don't understand why you're following me," she said.

"Your husband hired me to look after you. He thought you were in trouble. Then he was killed on Thursday morning. Right below my office windows. My original purpose was simply to return his deposit check. But then..."

I gestured.

"But then what?"

"But then another man you knew was killed and a friend of mine has been falsely accused of murdering his wife and I've come to believe that all three of these deaths are somehow connected. My guess is, both Cliff and my friend's wife learned something they shouldn't have known, which is why they were killed. I'm guessing you know what that is too. Why it hasn't

175

gotten you killed yet, I have no idea, but I think we both know it's only a matter of time. You've got a mark on your head."

"I didn't kill anyone," she said as if we were speaking of embezzlement.

"I never suggested you did, and you're avoiding my point."

A clap of thunder shook the sky and Audrey nearly jumped into my arms. Both of us looked up at the clouds closing in. I was facing west and could see a curtain of rain starting to fall over the distant hills. Audrey was facing east where the sun was still brilliant out over the Chocolate Mountains. We had half an hour, maybe, before it was time to run for cover but Audrey appeared to be ignorant of that fact.

Her eyes turned back to meet mine. I grew lost again in her red-haired beauty, wishing for some of that old magic, but I may as well have tried to pry passion from a rock. Audrey displayed no apparent interest in men. If anything, she exuded disdain.

The wind tossed some loose hair ends into her face and she brushed at them.

"Look," I said. "I'll make this easy for you. If you're guilty of a crime, you're guilty. If you're not, you're not. I have no stake in that game, one way or the other. I'm only out to learn what got my friend Steve falsely accused and to clear his name. So we can play nice, or we can do this the hard way."

"Why do you think I was involved in any of those murders?"

"Partly intuition, partly circumstantial evidence."

"Is that all it takes to be accused?"

"Sometimes."

She stared, still impassive, still unwilling to speak.

"All right. I can understand your reluctance so let me break the ice. The morning your husband was shot, I ran down to see what I could do to help and his last words were, 'my wife, Audrey...she knows the...' Then he was gone. Any idea what he could have meant by that?"

She continued staring, the shake of her head almost imperceptible.

176

"No?" I said.

She shook her head a bit more demonstratively.

"He also mentioned seeing something you had jotted down on your desk calendar. Something that had alarmed him enough to want to hire me. Any idea what that might have been?"

She gazed off, looking puzzled.

"No? No idea at all?"

"I jot down a lot of things on my calendar," she said, looking back.

We stared.

"So?" she said. "Is that it?"

"No, not even close, Audrey. In response to your husband's death and a business partner being murdered, you go on the run? It's hard for me to paint a picture where you aren't involved in some way. Or at least have knowledge. And that's leaving Connie McPherson to the side for the moment."

"Look, Michael, I didn't kill anyone. If that's what you want to hear, there. I've said it, but that's all I'm going to say to you. About any of this."

"All right, let's go," I said and grabbed her by the arm.

"Stop it!" she said. "What do think you're doing!?"

"Taking you back to Laurel Lagoon. If you don't want to level with me, we can sort this out with the police."

"Let go of me!" she said and yanked her arm free.

Seemingly overcome with emotion, Audrey reached into her straw purse. I assumed for a hankie. Instead, she pulled out a Pink Lady .38 Special and pointed it at my guts.

"What the hell?"

"If you touch me again, I'll shoot you. You know I can say it was in self-defense."

"Fine. Let me make it easy for you."

I bellied up to the barrel.

"I'm a man with nothing to lose, Audrey."

Seeing her hand tremble, I brushed the gun away and wrenched it from her grasp.

"What the hell's wrong with you? You think these things are a goddamned fashion accessory?"

I checked the chamber, found it loaded and emptied the bullets into the brush.

"Here," I said, handing the gun back to Audrey.

She dropped it into her purse as if I had handed her a dirty sock. Her eyes were locked onto mine now, and no longer with the cold, impersonal look of a corporate lawyer. It was as if by playing rough with her, I had flipped her biological switch.

"You liked that, huh?" I said.

She took a step closer.

"Oh come on, Audrey. This isn't the least bit credible."

She kept searching my eyes, seemingly spellbound.

"Oh for the love of god...Okay, let's start with who killed Colby and your husband. Do you have any idea?"

She shook her head.

"Then why did you run off? You keep acting like you couldn't care less about either one of those murders."

She looked away in thought.

"Maybe you found their deaths convenient?" I said.

Her eyes snapped back.

"I'm a human being, Michael."

"So was Atilla the Hun."

Audrey winced again.

"Look, you want to know how I felt when I learned that Dan Colby had been killed? Mostly indifferent. He was nothing more than an occasional business partner to me, and not always an entirely scrupulous one, as I came to find out. If anything, I had grown concerned for my own safety by that point."

"And your husband?"

Audrey took another moment to reflect.

"It wasn't the happiest of marriages, but you seem to know that already."

"That fifties matinee idol look just wasn't doing it for you?"

She sighed.

"That was part of it, yes. He started dressing that way after we got married. Said it was his new professional persona. The first time I saw it…I didn't know what to say."

"Do you think he knew how you felt?"

"Probably. I never said anything but I suppose he must have sensed over time that the passion had gone away."

I stared at Audrey, liking her less by the minute. She made a face.

"Come on, Michael. You've never felt that way about a woman?"

"Yeah, sure. I've had my share of reconstruction projects over the years. But I've never thought of marrying one. Or shooting her."

"I can't believe you really think I'd shoot my husband. Or anyone else."

I darted a look at her straw bag.

"It's for protection."

"You were pretty quick to put your finger on the trigger."

"I wouldn't have done it."

"Fine, we'll leave that to the side for the moment but we still have a dead husband on our hands, and a dead business associate. In response to which you ran off, for reasons you can't seem to explain. There are also a couple of hit men from a Mexican drug cartel on your tail. And a Russian character, who seems to be looking for the same thing that the Mexicans are looking for. But you wouldn't know anything about that either."

Audrey grabbed my arm.

"What do you mean, Russian character?"

"As in the Russian mob, I'm assuming."

"You're really freaking me out, Michael. I don't know anything about any Russians."

I glanced down at her grip on my arm and she slowly let go.

"Sorry, but please tell me you're kidding."

I shook my head.

"When did you see these men?"

179

"Yesterday."

"And what did they say?"

"Not much. Like the Mexicans, they seem to think I have something they want. And were ready to rough me up if they didn't get it."

"Michael. I honestly don't know who these people are or what they could be after."

"Okay, fair enough. You're innocent. Let's go tell the cops what you know."

She reached for my arm again, but tenderly this time.

"Michael, please. You have to trust me. I'll explain things when the time is right, but I can't right now."

"Sorry, Audrey, but I'm not buying your lost little girl routine. Anyway, I've run out of gallant knight chips for the week. You can check in with me on Monday."

16

Audrey remained staring at my forearm, seemingly spellbound as her fingernails slowly brushed through the dark hairs. If she had heard my snarky comment, it failed to elicit a response. When her eyes came up to meet mine, it was with a dreamy look. I shook my head in response.

"Let's try to stay on track here, okay? According to your husband, you made a business trip to Phoenix last Monday and were in quite a state upon your return. Why did you go and what happened while you were there?"

"I went to meet Al-Hamad."

"The arms dealer who fled to Abu Dhabi."

She nodded.

"And what happened?"

"He wasn't there"

"What do you mean, he wasn't there?"

"He wasn't there. I should probably go back. I had started to receive these mysterious phone calls and…"

"What mysterious phone calls?"

"Just like in the movies. I'd pick up the phone and hear only silence. Then whoever it was would hang up."

"Did the name on your caller ID suggest this person hailed from Culiacan or Vladivostok or somewhere along those lines?"

"It read private caller."

"Okay. Go on. You went to meet Al-Hamad."

"Yes. He called and asked me to meet him at the airport but sounded so totally stressed out, I almost didn't go. The whole thing just didn't feel right."

"But you went anyway."

"Yes. In the end I figured it was business."

"And…"

"He never showed. Then, when I got back to the airport later that night, I found two men waiting for me in the parking lot. I got away but…."

"Wait. Tell me about the two men. Were they the same ones you saw at Sylvia's place last night?"

"I never actually saw a face last night. Someone tried Sylvia's front door. Then I saw shadows moving across the windows outside and sensed something was wrong."

"When you came into Sylvia's studio, you said, 'I think those same men are here.' What did you mean by that?"

"Two men came to Sylvia's door one night when I was there but she quickly told everyone to be quiet and we never answered the door. We heard them poking around outside for a bit, trying to see in through the windows. When it sounded as if they had left, I peeked out and saw them getting into a gray Suburban."

"And they were the same men you saw in the airport parking lot."

She nodded.

"Describe."

"They were Mexican. I'm guessing from their looks and accents. The one with the potbelly and mustache seemed to be the boss. Does that sound like who you saw last night?"

I nodded.

"Then what happened? What did they want from you?"

"They asked me, 'where is it' and I said 'Where's what?' and they said, 'The shipping container' and I told them, 'I don't know. I guess still somewhere up in LA Harbor.'

"Then what did they say?"

"They started getting rough with me, but just then, this couple came along two cars over and the husband turned out to be an off-duty policeman. He identified himself and asked if I needed help. The one Mexican was suddenly all diplomatic and saying it was just a minor disagreement over a car they had sold me. The police officer came around to confront them and I used the opportunity to drive off. I guess from what happened at Sylvia's last night, they're still after me."

"And the Russians? You have no idea why they would be chasing you around?"

She shook her head.

"Hmm."

"What does that mean?"

"It means that either you're lying or none of my theories make sense."

She stared.

"Probably both," I said.

"Thanks, Michael."

There was another clap of lightning and thunder and Audrey looked over her shoulder this time.

"It's going to rain, isn't it?"

I nodded.

"Finish your story," I said.

"That's all there is."

"Nonsense."

"I'm being honest with you. That's all I know."

"You know something you're not telling me."

She gazed out over the white-capped water.

"I suppose no one really appreciates simplicity until they've had this kind of trouble. I've wanted so much to change everything over the past few days. To fly away somewhere and leave this crazy world completely behind me."

Audrey turned back to meet my stare. A wild gust of wind blew up just then and we both reached for her hat before it flew away. With our eyes locked, I slowly let go of Audrey's hand. A flash of lightning lit up the gray sky and thunder rumbled across the land. The birds rose up in a great white brushstroke before settling back onto the restless waters.

"So beautiful," she said.

I nodded, studying her, the unanswered questions lingering between us. What was Audrey hiding? And how was it related to Connie McPherson's death?

Without thinking, I put a hand to Audrey's back and we started down towards the shore.

"Tell me more about Al-Hamad," I said as we walked.

"You know, I always thought our relationship was a bit odd."

"Why's that?"

"The first time we met, it was in a bar…At his suggestion."

"Is that so odd in your business?"

"It's odd in any business, isn't it?

"I suppose not if you're in the mob."

She smiled bleakly.

"And you went?"

"I went."

I studied her profile, waiting, but nothing else came.

"Were you aware that he was wanted for a shady bank deal in Jordan?"

"No, not then. And how did you find out?"

I stared.

"Oh, yes. I keep forgetting. You're a private detective."

"Yeah, a private dick, but in this case, I simply read the papers."

"Well, I guess I didn't read the papers and really didn't know a thing about the man."

"Wouldn't that be standard practice? I mean, making sure everything was kosher before you got into a business deal with someone like that?"

"Of course, but that arms dealer? The one who turned out to be a government agent?"

I nodded.

"He had all the necessary papers to export from here. Al-Hamad had the necessary licensing papers to export from the emirates to anywhere in the world. Magellan was simply acting as a stateside broker and, oh Michael, do we really have to keep going over all of this?"

"We do, unless you'd prefer talking to the police."

"I just don't see how any of this helps to explain my husband's death."

"And Dan Colby's," I reminded her.

We had come to the water's edge and stopped. The sky and water were a collage of blues and grays and whites in the blustery wind.

"Back to your business deal. I'm guessing there must have been a lot of money involved."

"Yes, that's the truth of it, Michael. A lot of money was involved."

"Enough to make you step all over your customary business practices."

She rubbed her forehead.

"Some of them, but Al-Hamad kept insisting that there was nothing shady about it."

"Your clandestine meeting in a darkened bar aside."

"I know. I've asked myself a thousand times over the past few days. What was I thinking? I graduated from college with a goal of making a lot of money and retiring at a young age. I had no intention of going to jail in the process."

"Is what I've read in the papers true? That some sort of top-secret technology was in that shipment?"

"According to, Al-Hamad, no. Just small arms, ammunition for the small arms and some spare helicopter parts for a repair facility."

"How about where it was headed?"

"Again, according to Al-Hamad, Liberia. I subsequently learned that Liberia doesn't even have a helicopter repair facility."

She opened her eyes wide for effect and looked back out over the water. The wind was moving in great gusts and the rain was closing fast. I found myself staring at Audrey's delicate little hand, wanting to hold it. The scent of perfume came on the wind, evoking everything feminine about her.

I looked back up and found her staring.

"So? What are you thinking?" she said.

I cleared my throat.

"Oh…back to this helicopter facility. Did you ever confront Al-Hamad about the discrepancy?"

"Yes, but by then the government was breathing down our necks and Al-Hamad had stopped talking. And you know the rest."

"Not really. How did Colby get involved?"

"That's simple. He owned a modest network of global shipping containers and told Al-Hamad about our company. And that led to our deal with Al-Hamad. Then those government agents came around asking questions and I went to see Colby. I had no proof that he had done anything illegal, but like I said, he wasn't the most scrupulous person in the world and I wouldn't have put it past him."

"And what did Colby have to say when you confronted him?"

"He gave me a bunch of sweet talk and swore he'd never do anything to hurt me."

I nodded. That much at least jived with what I had overheard at the shipyard.

"Is that it?" she said.

"No. We're not anywhere close to the truth yet."

"Please, Michael. I'm tired. What else can I possibly tell you?"

"Whether or not Dirk Vanderhof is involved in this mess."

And with that, Audrey's Blanche DuBois routine vanished into thin air.

"Push a button, did I?"

"Look, Michael, I like you. A lot. I don't think I've ever felt this way about a man, but I'm not saying another word. This is way too much like talking to the police."

"Audrey, Audrey, Audrey."

"What?"

"What? The cops think you killed Dan Colby, and maybe even your husband. And now those Mexican boys are putting the squeeze on your partner. Add in the Russians and I don't know where you think you're going to hide."

Audrey rubbed her forehead.

"I don't understand. What do you know about my business partner?"

"I'm working for him."

She gestured dramatically now, as if she might go mad.

"Michael. Go ahead and haul me in to the police. I don't care, but we are so done talking here."

She looked away and back.

"Please stop staring at me."

"Sorry but Vanderhof's name keeps coming up everywhere I turn, so either you tell me what you know about him, or..."

She looked away, brushing at sudden tears.

"Hey," I said, pulling her chin around. "I'm only trying to help you. I just won't do it at the cost of my friend going down for murder one."

Seeing she was sincerely overwhelmed, I put my arm around her waist.

"It's really best if we go talk to the police."

"Please, Michael. You've got to believe I'm innocent."

She cocked her head fetchingly while wiping at tears.

"Audrey, it's not that I don't. There's just got to be some way to exonerate you and my friend in the same story. If not, then..."

Audrey bit her lip while slowly shaking her head, then leaned into my chest. I wrapped my arms around her tiny waist.

After a moment, she looked back up at me.

"Please, Michael. Help me. Isn't that what you came out here to do?"

I looked down at my little red-haired Mata Hari, at once falling madly in love and deathly afraid of her.

"Please," she said again. "I have nowhere else to turn."

"You've got to tell me about Vanderhof."

"I can't," she said.

"Why not?"

"I just can't."

She stared up at me. After a moment, her hand reached up to touch the wound on my cheek tenderly.

"Please," she said again.

"No. Not with my friend still in jail. Until I hear the truth, I'm not sticking my neck out for anyone, I don't care how much I fall for you. If you tell me the truth and help me to free my friend, I'll do everything I can to protect you."

Audrey put her head against my chest and looked back over her shoulder at the wetlands. My eyes followed hers, my heart drawn to protect this woman, even if it meant the two of us going up in flames. As long as I got Steve out of jail, I didn't care what happened next.

I kept staring until Audrey looked up into my eyes.

"Okay. Take me somewhere safe and I'll tell you everything I know."

With the wind again gusting wildly around us, I was about to kiss her lips when something like a clap of thunder rang out and Audrey jumped in my arms. I looked over my shoulder, knowing that something other than thunder had torn the fabric of space and time.

Off in the distance, Sylvia appeared from the wetlands, hurrying back as fast as her elephantine girth would allow it. A moment later, three men appeared on her tail, but not in any particular hurry. I recognized them from the café that morning. One of them had a sawed-off shotgun over his shoulder.

Sylvia joined us with a look back at the men. I passed Audrey to Sylvia.

"You'd better use all your clairvoyant powers and get to someplace safe. Go on. I'll stall these dudes for as long as I can."

"No," Audrey said as Sylvia started to pull her away.

I reached out and touched Audrey's hand.

"It's all right. I'll see you at the funeral tomorrow. And Sylvia, call the tribal folks. Let them know I'm here."

Audrey still hesitated.

"Go on," I said. "I'll be all right. Just let me know where you are as soon as you can, okay?"

She nodded with Sylvia dragging her off through the brush.

"And remember, only by text message," I called after them.

Audrey looked over her shoulder one last time before disappearing into the mesquite. I turned back in the direction of the three bikers. They were now about a hundred yards off. Thinking it would give the women a bit more time to escape, I walked in their direction. We met halfway.

"Hey, this is the dude we saw having breakfast in the café earlier this morning," one of them said.

"There's no law against having breakfast, is there?"

"The fucker thinks he's funny."

I nodded. They didn't.

"What's going on?" the one with the shotgun said.

"Oh, just enjoying the wetlands. Beautiful, isn't it?"

"We're going to be riding home in the fucking rain," the one who had spoken first said to me. "I guess you think that's fucking beautiful."

"I'll tell you what I think's beautiful," the third man said. "That big hoocha momma who came walking up here a moment ago."

He made a lewd gesture to suggest how he'd like to have her.

"Leonard's partial to big women," the one with the shotgun said. "I kind of fancied that little redheaded pastry you had over here. Where'd they go?"

"I have no idea."

The shotgun came up in the general direction of my chest.

"I'm thinking you do."

"Then we appear to be having a fundamental disagreement."

The barrel of the shotgun was suddenly at my neck.

"And maybe your head is going to be having a fundamental disagreement with your body if you don't wise up."

He nodded at Leonard.

"Go on. See if you can find your big momma. And don't forget to bring that other little bitch back here with you."

I started to move but the barrel was shoved a bit more firmly into my throat.

"Careful, partner."

He nodded at the other man.

"See who he is?"

A moment later, the other man had my wallet flipped open.

"A fucking private dick."

The one with the shotgun took the wallet with his free hand.

"Yeah. Here, take his money," he said and looked back at me.

"I hate cops, but I enjoy the shit out of watching bodies flop around after they don't have their heads attached anymore and if Leonard doesn't come back with those two bitches, I don't know what else I'm going to do to keep myself entertained for the rest of the day."

I was considering what to do for my last rights when a shot rang out. The guy with the shotgun wheeled around to find the source and another shot quickly followed. He dropped to the ground with a yelp. Part of his left knee had been blown off. When the other man went to pick up the shotgun, another shot rang out and clipped him in the hand. Both of these tough guys were now lying there on the ground, one of them cursing, the other one whimpering like a dog.

Five members of the tribe appeared out of the brush a moment later. The leader had a short, black ponytail and was graying around his temples. There was another man beside him, more or less the same age, and three younger men. All of them were carrying rifles. It had the air of the cavalry riding in.

"What are you doing here?" the leader asked as if he didn't think me all that worthy of being rescued.

"I drove out here to enjoy the wetlands. Then these two came along making trouble. There's another one out in the brush somewhere. He may be armed."

The man in charge nodded and the three younger men lit out into the brush.

"And bring back the truck," he called out softly after them, then to the lead biker. "Doesn't look like you'll be going anywhere on your own any time soon."

"Fuck you, Injun," the biker cursed back, his eyes red with rage. The wind was blowing his hair all around. The comment earned him a rifle barrel up against his chest.

"Yeah?" the tribal leader said. "Well it just so happens that we're the cowboys in this movie. And it's your turn to be the Injun."

Another bolt of lightning lit up the sky off to the west. I looked in that direction. Thunder followed and rumbled across the land. The rain was now barely five miles away and coming fast. Two of the younger tribal members reappeared out of the brush with a rifle at Leonard's back.

"Fuck," he said when he saw his two partners. "Are you all right, Axle?"

"Fuck no, you dumb motherfucker. And where the fuck is the rest of our gang?"

"Shut up," the tribal leader said with another shove of his rifle at Axle's chest.

Axle went on fuming at Leonard and the tribal leader.

One of the young tribal men set Leonard down by his two partners. The other one came up and whispered in the tribal leader's ear. He nodded and looked at me.

"Why didn't you tell us you were with Sylvia?"

"I didn't think it was any of my business to say so."

He nodded and searched my eyes.

191

"Sylvia's blood with us, so you're blood. Anything else you want to do here?"

He nodded at the three bikers.

"That one has my wallet and cash."

One of the younger tribal members quickly rifled through Axle's pockets and found both. Axle spat at my feet. I counted the money.

"Here," I said to the tribal leader. "This belongs to him."

Axle spat again.

"We'll use the rest for his funeral if he keeps that up," the leader said. "Best if you move on now. And next time, come see us before you visit the wetlands. We like to know who's down here."

I nodded and started up the road towards my car. The other young tribal member soon raced by me in an old truck, kicking up dust. I looked back once as I slipped through the fence. You had to smile, the Injuns being the cavalry.

South on Pacific Coast Highway

17

I climbed back into my Impala with the day growing dark around me. A raindrop slapped at my windshield, then another one. I spotted two crows high up in the sky, being tossed about in the wind like pieces of paper.

I started the engine, cranked up the heater against the sudden cold and dashed off a message to Sylvia. Where are you? A minute went by without a response. I dropped the Impala into drive and headed down the desert road, beginning to feel like a fool. In my effort to clear Steve's name, I had fallen for a dead man's wife, and one who appeared to be all dressed up for murder. I could assume Audrey to be at Cliff's funeral in the morning but had no idea what more I could hope to extract from her, at least willingly, and even fewer ideas about what to do with myself in the meantime.

Back out on the highway, I found myself driving into the teeth of a squall. More madness, I thought. Summer rain was rare enough in Southern California, but a cold front like this? Blowing down from the north? With gale force winds? You never saw something like that in August, or even June or July. The latest I could recall a cold front barreling down from the north was on a Memorial Day weekend, decades earlier. And setting aside that anomaly, April was usually the latest you saw this kind of mischief. Maybe in early May, but certainly not in August. It was as if the world had been turned on its head.

It did make for a lovely drive back to Laurel Lagoon. The rain had turned the desert floor dark. The shrubs and mesquite were glistening bright green. The unbearable heat of recent days had been completely washed away.

Lost in thought, I was nearly to Interstate 5 road when an idea struck me and I made a quick exit at the next offramp. It took me most of fifteen minutes, working my way through a labyrinth of city streets, but I eventually came to an old country road, heading northeast. Rolling hills now surrounded me, oaks and sycamores and ranch signs. The rain had let up but the sky was still mottled with dark storm clouds.

For the better part of ten miles, there was hardly a sign of civilization. Then I came over the crest of a hill and was confronted by a shopping center and car dealership. Long ago, there had been nothing at this crossroads but an old general store. Now I waited for the light to change with SUV's barreling through the intersection. This was the place of my youth and, as always, it saddened me to see what they had done to it. In less than three decades, a once bucolic world had been bulldozed into a clutter of asphalt streets and strip malls. As kids, we had grown up in a Tom Sawyer world but only a few signs of that once pastoral past now remained. Everywhere you looked was conformity, and either you grew dulled by it, or moved away, or went mad, and I had done a little of each.

A few miles farther up the road, I came over the crest of another hill and started down a long, steep grade into the densely populated flatlands. With the remnants of the storm off on the horizon now, I pulled into an old plaza at the bottom of the hill. This one plaza had withstood the onslaught of years, anchored by the same old market, hardware store and ice cream parlor I had known as a kid. A chicken joint that specialized in broasted chicken still straddled the corner in front. An aging neon sign displayed a proud rooster.

I parked in front of the hardware store and dashed up the wooden stairs to a second story veranda. A diamond dealer maintained a business in one corner. A tax accountant occupied the middle. Jack Oliver had an office down at the far right end. In fact, Jack owned the entire plaza and commandeered that wing of the second story as his homestead. The sign on his door read Private Investigator but that only served to scare off the riff raff these days. Jack had stopped doing business long ago.

While waiting for Jack to answer the doorbell, his oft repeated mantra played in my head. Don't daydream. Watch, look and listen and keep your eyes on the little things. I had bristled at having Jack beat those words into my head as a young man and had failed at them more than I cared to say. I wasn't a very good student. Hell, I probably wasn't a very good detective.

My mind had wandered far down the lane of forgotten memories by the time Jack finally opened the door.

"What are you doing here, Devlin? And who knocked you around this time?"

He walked away from the door in his terry cloth bath slippers. I went in after him.

"Close the damned thing," he said over his shoulder. I did and passed through Jack's ersatz office. It had been a proper affair in years past, but not long after retiring, Jack had hired a contractor to cut a large opening through to his living room and the two rooms were now more or less of a piece, and both of them darkened to the point of feeling like someone's siege bunker.

Jack had the news blaring in the living room end of things. He returned to his recliner and grudgingly muted the television.

"You don't look happy to see me," I said sitting across from him.

"Why would I be? I know it's no damned social call."

"Yeah, well I'm in a bit of a mess and wanted to get your opinion."

"Look at you. When aren't you in a bit of a mess?"

"All right, all right. Everybody keeps giving me the same line of bullshit."

"Well, that ought to tell you something right there."

"Yeah, well screw you and the horse you rode in on."

He half smiled.

"Anyway, I'm feeling like hell right now."

I explained to him about Steve McPherson.

"That's a raw deal. Any leads?"

"I've had a few wild ideas. How about something to eat and I'll tell you everything I know?"

"Aw damn it. I knew you were going to try and drag me out of my cocoon."

"I'm famished. I just drove in from the Salton Sea."

That got Jack's attention.

"What were you doing out there? You in love with rotting fish or something?"

"Well, at least you'd never starve."

There was another half-smile.

"You know, Jack. I got to thinking there was something terribly prophetic about that place. It's hard to come up with a better metaphor for what's happening to this country these days. For the whole damned world, for that matter."

Jack got up out of his chair with a grunt.

"We'd better get you something to eat. Your brain's running on fumes."

He shuffled off in his slippers and returned wearing white tennis shoes.

What was it with old men and tennis shoes? You could write it off as a need for comfort, but it made them look so odd, Jack growing smaller and ever more feeble with age and the tennis shoes looking ever more massive in comparison, like a puppy with its paws out of proportion.

"I hope we're talking chicken," he said as I followed him to the door.

"I wouldn't think of anything else."

I waited on the veranda while Jack turned all three locks.

"Okay, Devlin," he said once we had reached the bottom of the stairs and were walking along beneath the second story veranda. "Tell me what you got?"

I suppressed a smile. I knew it wouldn't take him long to be grilling me over every last detail. The man couldn't help himself. His brain had been hardwired to pick things apart in the womb.

Between there, ordering two half chickens at the front counter and taking a window booth, I explained the events of the past few days as best I understood them, and in fact felt relieved to get the whole thing off of my chest. I had not felt free to do so since the day of Cliff Black's death. Jack listened, but with his eyes focused out the window. Jack hated crowds as much as I did and seemed to be enjoying the empty restaurant as much as I was. Late summer, three in the afternoon and the place was deserted.

When our meals arrived, I shut up and we dug in. The chicken came with homemade slaw and broasted potatoes, the broasted potatoes amounting to a big russet cut in four slices and deep fat fried until golden brown. A bit of salt and you couldn't find a better homespun meal in the world.

Halfway through the chicken, a Mexican family came through the door and stood at the counter, ordering their meal. Jack glared at them between bites of his food. One of the little girls had turned to stare at us with her back to her mother's dress. When I winked, she quickly hid her face in the dress.

"Goddamn Mexicans," Jack muttered to himself. "It's bad enough they come here illegally. Then they have to breed like rabbits."

I continued with my meal in silence. What were you going to say to him? We had taken the land from the Mexicans and they were on their way to taking it back from us. If anyone had gotten screwed in the deal, it was the native people. They had been here long before anyone else, but the gringos and Mexicans went on with their little pissing contest as if the tribes had no place in the discussion.

"What?" Jack said when I had failed to respond. "You're probably thinking some of that bleeding-heart liberal crap of yours."

197

Ignoring Jack, I looked out the window, somewhat grateful for the Mexicans being here. Without the primitive qualities of their culture, our world would be essentially sterile. Walk into one of their markets and you saw raw meat and flies. There were smells. It wasn't all florescent lights, Muzak and packaged crap.

"What?" Jack said to me again.

"Oh, just thinking. For them, this is probably like those glorious years right after World War II. The world so full of hope and possibilities. They have no idea it's all going to turn to shit."

"Sometimes I wonder if you ever learned a damned thing from me."

"I sometimes wonder too."

I was thinking it was just as well that I hadn't.

We went back to eating. Then, somewhere amidst the chewing and finger licking, Jack looked back up and studied my face.

"Getting smoochy with a dead man's wife."

I set down my piece of chicken and wiped my hands.

"I've admitted to my feelings, but I didn't throw myself at the woman. She threw herself at me, and one embrace doesn't amount to having an affair. Besides, for all I know, she's the next incarnation of Mata Hari. She could be planning to put a slug in me next."

"Maybe," Jack said. "But I doubt it. If she needed a fall guy, she wouldn't have to look any further than that dumb partner of hers."

"Yeah, well, I'm not entirely convinced of Audrey's innocence, but my mind keeps coming back to Dan Colby. Who was that man trying to protect? And why?"

"Maybe her."

"I've considered that, Jack, but I just can't see it."

"See? You never learned a damned thing from me."

"What?" I asked.

"You're so caught up in your head, you've forgotten the most obvious things. Love and money. One or the other of them, Devlin. That's what makes the world go round."

I had a sudden thought and threw my napkin on the table.

"Did I see a light go on in there?"

"Yeah, maybe. I'd better get back to Laurel Lagoon."

We were soon on our way out the door.

"Thanks," I told Jack at the bottom of his stairs.

"For what?"

"A second opinion. A short talk with you always seems to get my mind back on track. Your cantankerous right-wing bullshit aside."

I offered Jack a wink. He almost smiled back.

"Figure out who the Feds aren't already following around and tail that poor bastard for a while. Somebody somewhere knows something, and if you can figure out who and what that is, all the other answers will fall into place."

"I know. More or less the same thing occurred to me back there while I was listening to your bullshit."

We stared at each other.

"Good chicken," I said.

"Good chicken," Jack said. "And keep your hands off that woman," he added for good measure. "How would you feel if you were three days in your grave and someone was screwing your wife?"

"I wouldn't be feeling a damned thing, Jack."

He groused on his way up the stairs. I was about to expound on my feelings but turned away without another word. It wasn't any use. The man had spent his entire life married to the same woman, with whom there had never been a whole lot of passion or bliss, as far as I could tell. Yet Jack took to fidelity like a good Marine took to marching. You did your duty and didn't screw around, a lack of true devotion aside.

Somewhere deep inside my brain, the bells of admiration rang out for his constancy. But when I recalled how neither he nor his wife had been particularly happy, I died inside to imagine myself living out a similar destiny.

Half an hour of road time flew by with my head going around and around about love and heartache. Fools rush in, as the old song went, and in this story, there appeared to have been an even bigger fool than me, someone who had been ready to sell his soul for a bit of kindness. Then why had Dan and his fetching wife gone their separate ways? I couldn't explain the feeling in my gut but was certain the answer to that question would bring me one step closer to solving this case. I didn't expect it to provide me with all of the answers, but I'd be a lot closer to the truth than I was now.

By the time I came out of my thoughts, I was backed up in bumper-to-bumper traffic at the outskirts of Laurel Lagoon. It took me another fifteen minutes to negotiate all the hubbub around the three art festivals, only to discover that someone had taken my parking spot behind the office.

Inclined to call a tow truck, but having neither the time nor the stomach to ruin somebody else's day at the beach, I drove over to the adjacent library parking lot and flipped the old Filipino guard a twenty to look the other way.

Up in my office, I promptly ran a people search on Dan Colby and learned, among the other tidbits about his personal life, the name of his ex-wife. I then put out a search for Doris Colby and found she was comfortably ensconced in a place up on Balboa Island.

Well I'll be damned, Vanderhof. So that's where you were going in such a rush that day.

Back in my Impala, and like the king's charge now, galloping off to save the kingdom, I encountered another traffic snarl heading north out of town and was back to cursing every soul who got in my way. While doing so, my phone rang. It was Rick. I answered the call.

"What's new?"

"What's new? Okay, I'll tell you what's new. I drove by my place after we had lunch that day and found it had been ransacked. I've been bouncing around between hotels and my girlfriend's place ever since. Not that you give a shit."

"Who's your girlfriend?"

"This older gal I met in a bar a few months back, and what does that have to do with anything? I thought you were going to get these bastards off my back."

"I'm working on it."

"Well, apparently you're not working very hard."

"Hire somebody else then. Or better yet, go to the cops."

That shut him up.

"I still say you're hiding something, Rick, and I'm betting hard money it has to do with Vanderhof."

I waited in silence.

"What's the matter? Getting warm, am I?"

"I don't know what you're talking about. I already told you. Vanderhof's Audrey's client. He has a lot of money and thinks he's a big shot. That's all I know about him. If you want some answers, talk to Audrey."

"I already did and she wouldn't tell me."

"You talked to her?"

"Yeah. For about fifteen minutes and now she's disappeared again."

"Well, I'm done doing business with that bitch. I've been calling her for three days and not a peep in return."

"Yeah, well, not that it's bothering either one of you very much but her husband's dead, so I suppose we have to cut her some slack. In the meantime, I know you're both hiding something. What that is, I have no idea but I'm done sticking my neck out until somebody starts talking."

I heard Rick going off as I hung up on him. He tried calling back a second later but I let it ring. I was thinking of Vanderhof and wondering what had happened to him. His absence was rather eerie. Not a word in almost two days. Maybe he was hiding out at Doris' place. Maybe he had bolted to the high plains of Bolivia.

While I puzzled over his role in this mystery, the open stretch of coastline at Scotchman's Cove appeared off to my left again. Waves broke lazily along the shore. Kids down there playing with their sand pails. Then the highway dovetailed into Corona del Mar and ten minutes later, I was parking in a narrow alley behind Doris' house. A two-car garage commandeered the backside. Decades earlier, the neighborhood had been made up almost entirely of quaint little cottages. Now nearly every one of them had been turned into a mini mansion.

18

The storm was swiftly blowing off to the east, with the blustery afternoon now slowly fading to dusk. All that remained were some clouds barging along the horizon and a strange autumn-like feeling to a midsummer day.

I killed the next two hours, waiting and trying to piece together a set of circumstances that seemed to make no sense. Even when you factored in love and money, they didn't add up. Then, maybe I did not understand love and money all that well.

At a little before eight, the door to Doris' garage opened like the maw of a Toltec god, preparing to devour its sacrificial victim. A Jaguar backed out with Doris behind the wheel. Mystery and mischief were on her heels. I was a hundred yards behind them.

Keeping an eye on Doris did not turn out to be much of a chore. She circled around to Marine Avenue, drove up to Coast Highway, turned south and three miles later pulled into the valet parking at the backside of Five Crowns. I made myself comfortable on the adjacent side street and got back to counting minutes.

Just as I was feeling restless enough to go in and check on things, what had been beyond my wildest imaginings a few hours earlier materialized in front of me. A silver Range Rover careened into the Five Crowns' parking lot. A valet snapped to attention and Rick popped out of the driver's side door. The pieces of the puzzle were starting to fit. I had no idea what they might mean at this point but fell prey to the most obvious conclusion. Brash young man meets svelte, older woman. Money and passion start sloshing around in a couple of highball glasses and suddenly some very questionable decisions are being made, one of them involving murder.

That represented a whole new set of assumptions, and I had been proven wrong enough times to feel comfortable about going down that road without more evidence, but as I sat there considering what I knew, I was unable to come up with a more plausible theory to the case.

Like Jack had said, love and money make the world go round, and where those two souls had chosen to meet, and that they had chosen to meet at all suggested that both passion and money were involved. Where Vanderhof might fit into this scheme, I had no idea but would have given a lot to be seated in the booth next to Rick and Doris. The only problem being, my cover had already been blown with Rick, leaving me to don another disguise in order to fool him and I had had it up to here with donning disguises.

I was also constrained from placing a bug on either of their cars by the presence of three valets. That left me sauntering in and pretending it was kismet, a plan that would gain me nothing, even if Rick happened to buy into that bit of theater.

So I waited with the pieces of the puzzle still going around and around in my head. And one piece went around more than any other, the one that had been dogging me since the very first moment I laid my hands on that flash drive. What sort of information did it contain and why had Colby been willing to give up his life over its secrets?

Of course, it was possible he had not. Maybe the flash drive was purely incidental and had nothing directly to do with his death, but that still left the question of who had shot him, and why they had done it. It was easy enough to cook up a story tying Colby's death to Rick and Doris playing lovebirds in a high-class restaurant, but not one that involved them personally pulling the trigger, a fact that may or may not have helped to explain Nacho's role in this escapade.

Finally, I had to wonder why I even cared, beyond saving Steve, and that brought me back the feelings that had welled up inside of me the night I was standing inside of Colby's pad; a bottle of Bordeaux, a cat and some TV dinners; the images of a life that were way too much like my own. All I had to do was substitute grilled chicken and ditch the cat. And though it wasn't my job to stop every jilted lover in this world from feeling lonely, they didn't have to shoot Cliff or leave Colby floating around the brackish waters of the back harbor for a last hurrah.

I tried to imagine my own last moment, my anguished final thoughts about Caitlin, and a grief-stricken realization that my hopes towards her would never be realized. I would never again have a chance to make things right in this world. Perhaps both Cliff and Colby had felt something similar in their final moments. Never mind that neither Audrey nor Doris had shown any sign of giving a damn in return. I doubted the torment would be any different. If you loved someone that dearly, with all your heart, and felt the shot dig into your flesh, you would still be left there thinking, oh god, not yet. There's something I still need to do.

Not feeling overly sympathetic towards Doris, and already suspecting the worst about Rick, I came back to my growing frustration with Audrey. I had trusted that she wasn't involved in this mess. If nothing else, I had believed in her sincerity. Hell, I was ready to throw my life down on her behalf and she couldn't be bothered to return my calls.

It was too damned much like Caitlin. At the first sign of friction, she would disappear, not a word of kindness to be found for days and weeks on end. But that's what you got for falling in love with a woman who had clinical depression. If only someone had warned me in advance, but no. Caitlin dropped the word on me one day, two years into our romance, this "ah ha" moment, where her penchant for isolation suddenly had context. Not that it had changed anything. I was now warned, but no rescue was forthcoming. I had already been lured into the event horizon, falling far, far down into a black hole as Caitlin escaped in her spaceship. The last thing I saw was her waving goodbye, my every second of time now stretching out for all eternity, my every midnight slumber haunted by dreams of what might have been.

Tired of listening to the crap in my head, I made a tactical decision, hit the ignition, turned on the lights and made a U-turn. Rick and Doris would no doubt be distracted over dinner and drinks for a good long spell. Best to use this opportunity to plant a bug at Doris' house. If Rick and Doris threw another body into Newport Harbor while I was gone, so be it.

While I waited at Coast Highway for the light to change, my regular phone rang. It was Vanderhof.

"Hey, pal," I said. "Long time no see."

"They're trying to keep me down, buddy, but I'm not going to let them."

Vanderhof was juiced and sounding as if his combative streak had taken a hard right turn into maudlinville. I was shocked to see him show the least bit of vulnerability.

"Who's trying to keep you down?" I asked.

"The whole world…Hey, listen. Why don't you come down and have a drink with me?"

"Sure, where are you?"

"At the Quiet Woman."

"Okay, hang tight. I'll be there in half an hour."

The light changed and I pulled onto Coast Highway, headed north.

Being that I only intended to plant a wireless mic under Doris' bed, along with a paging signal to let me know when she had arrived home, and having no plans to poke around among her personal effects, I did not bother with bypassing the entire security system. Instead, I picked the side door lock to her garage, hit the main breaker outside, dashed inside to do my job, locked everything up behind myself and turned the main breaker back on before slipping silently down the block. I had never stuck around to verify my suspicions in a situation like this but was willing to bet that long before any cops arrived, the dispatcher from the security company would call to say everything was back in order. Must have been some sort of power outage. If the cops did bother to show up at that point, and they usually did not, they would check the doors, peek in through a window with their flashlight, see the stove light blinking and call it a night.

Whatever else had transpired as the result of me breaking into Doris' Balboa Island cottage that summer night, I was in and out of there without being noticed. I was also in there long enough to be reminded of how completely a woman can make herself comfortable in the absence of a man. The photo gallery of Doris' family on the antique credenza in her living room spoke volumes. She had a family. She had lots of friends. Who needed Dan?

A picture of Dan and Doris together back in the day had been among the many photos, in fact more or less the same one Dan had placed on his dresser, with Doris in her Capri pants and high heels, but the photo was well off in the back row at Doris' place, suggesting the memories attached to it were no longer of any great importance to her.

That's the way I figured it anyway. With her former husband having been shot dead two nights earlier and lying cold in a morgue, she was out on the town with another man. Not much to grieve over there, not that I could see. A man had made her comfortable but had somehow failed to keep her heart. Whatever the reasons for them splitting up, Dan Colby had ceased to serve any useful purpose in Doris' life. Maybe there would be one more life insurance policy to sweeten the deal.

I had a few wild ideas about how Doris became involved in this sordid affair, but they were of the wildest sort, so I was content to wait until I heard her side of the story. I wasn't too keen on hearing everything else that came with the process but assumed I would not learn much of anything until those two lovebirds had slipped into bed and extinguished their passions. Until then I was down to waiting for dinner and drinks to conclude at the Five Crowns. I wished them the best and headed back towards the Quiet Woman.

Vanderhof was sitting at the bar when I walked in, wearing a pair of pleated tan slacks and blue shirt. His hair was a bit disheveled but he looked debonair. He also looked half crocked. His fingers were etching Euclidean geometry on a glass of Scotch on the rocks.

I took the stool next to him and offered the obligatory handshake.

"Wow, Devlin. You look like you've been through a war."

He nodded at my assortment of wounds.

"Yeah, and there's nothing fair about it."

Vanderhof gave me his big, clownish grin, a grin that now had a decidedly downcast patina to it. Even his eyes looked leaden. The law was on his tail. His women were nothing but trouble.

I had a look around the bar. It was mostly empty. The usual din of voices and laughter and tinkling glasses filtered in from the dining area.

The bartender came and took my order for a club soda with a splash of cranberry and a twist of lemon. He went off to make my drink. Two junior executive go-getters did a double take on my right. So did Vanderhof.

"What, you don't drink?" he said.

"I'll skip the usual impertinence," I said. "About being 86% water."

"I get it," he said, tossed back his drink and called to the bartender.

"Hey, buddy. Back me up."

Vanderhof raised his eyebrows at me.

"I hope you don't mind."

"Not much."

Vanderhof went back to etching Euclidean geometry on his glass of Scotch. We were both studying the results.

"Like I said, Devlin. Some people are trying to bring me down right now but I'm not going to let them."

Vanderhof glanced over at me.

"Are you still up for citizen of the year?" I asked.

"Yeah, why wouldn't I be?"

"I don't know. You're the one who mentioned trouble."

"Don't you worry, pal. I'm still sitting on top of the world."

He smiled again, a smile that suggested anything but on the top of the world.

"That trailer on the beach down in Baja starting to sound attractive to you?"

"Maybe. How long does it take to get down there?"

"You know somebody who owns a Cessna?"

"Me."

"Then a little over two hours, as the crow flies."

"A nice little beachy bar, you say?"

"Beachy as they come."

"Hey, maybe we'll fly down there tomorrow. Just you and me."

"Just you and me and a beachy bar, old pal."

Our drinks arrived and we toasted. I took a sip. Vanderhof took a healthy slug of his Scotch. There was silence.

"You know, Devlin. I took your advice and settled with my wife."

"I know. I heard. That's why I'm here talking to you...It's probably for the best."

"Yeah. The truth is, I kind of miss her. You wipe away all that snooty, highbrow culture of hers and there's a good soul down in there somewhere."

"There usually is."

"Yeah," he said. "So anyway, now you can come work for me."

"Oh, I don't know. I'm pretty happy with the way things are."

"Bullshit."

"Yeah. I suppose happy isn't exactly the right adjective."

"You're broke and on the edge of disaster."

"It's all uphill from here."

"Goddamn it. You're coming to work for me, all right?"

"Yeah, yeah…How about you and the wife. Did you part as friends?"

"I've got all the money in the world and she won't talk to me."

I drank from my club soda and stared at myself in the bar mirror.

"Did you ever really love her?" I said.

"Of course I did."

Vanderhof looked in my direction. I kept staring into the mirror.

"What kind of question is that?"

I looked over.

"I don't know. I saw the two of you in court and thought, for the life of me, I can't see the connection."

"I guess you're pretty sure of yourself when it comes to handicapping romances."

"Vanderhof, when it comes to handicapping romances, I'm not sure of anything."

"Now you're being cynical."

"I'd like to think I'm being realistic. Then, being realistic, I suppose I would have given up on women a long, long time ago."

"Hang in there, buddy. There's all kinds of fish in the sea."

Vanderhof finished off his Scotch and waved to the bartender.

"Hit me again and get my pal here another one of these club sodas."

I waved the bartender off. Vanderhof studied me. I looked over at him. People were drifting into the bar around us. We were increasingly lost in the din of their voices.

"So you really think Elfie and I were doomed from the start."

"I don't know. I'm not much of a marriage counselor. I spent half a lifetime looking for the right gal, only to have it come to ruin. I don't know what to make of things anymore."

"Tell me about it, pal."

"Not much of a story, really. A few exquisite years. A senseless breakup and now I'm looking into some Tibetan monasteries."

I took a drink from my club soda. Vanderhof swished his Scotch around and did the same.

"I don't know, Devlin. I think you're making too much of it. I figure all a man needs are a nice set of legs, a tight ass, someone who likes to have a bit of fun in the sack and you're happy."

I looked over at him with a thought to explain how a certain kind of beauty will cause a man's heart to dream. And not necessarily great beauty. In fact, it was probably best if perfection wasn't involved, just something in a woman's face and spirit that leads the right man to feelings of eternity and devotion, but I saw there wasn't any point in it. I took another drink, suddenly wishing there was something more potent than club soda inside the glass.

"Come on," Vanderhof said. "Tell me your story."

"There's nothing to tell. I once loved with all my heart. I haven't been able to love since. End of story."

I finished my drink, my thoughts jerked back in Caitlin's direction. Despite her abundant flaws, she was such a sweet and charming woman. You really had to work hard to imagine her all alone in this world.

Jesus, Devlin. After all this time, the thing is still killing you.

The bartender tried to top off my glass again, and again I waved him off.

"I've got to drive," I said. He nodded and looked at Vanderhof.

"I don't," he said. "My limos out in the parking lot."

The bartender hit Vanderhof with another good shot, wiped at the bar around his drink, took my empty glass and left with all the loose napkins.

"Where are you headed?" Vanderhof said.

"I've got a case to solve."

Vanderhof reviewed me with suspicion.

"I hope it doesn't involve me, buddy."

I stared back, my suspicions about him renewed. You poked around too close to the man and there was a feeling of menace, a feeling that Vanderhof would kill before he'd let you discover his secrets.

"I'm off your case," I said. "If that's what's got you worried."

"All right," he said. "I hope so, for everyone concerned." He took a stiff drink. "So, are we headed down to that beachy bar tomorrow?"

"Not tomorrow. They're burying Cliff Black in the morning."

"Oh, yeah, yeah. I'd almost forgotten."

"Are you planning to go?"

"Yeah. I suppose I'd better go pay my respects."

"Then I'll see you there."

Vanderhof held up his drink to me. I left with him pouring down another good slug.

I was turning down towards Balboa Island when my pager started to beep. Good, I thought. The prey had entered the trap. I had prepared myself for a long night squirming in my car and not much liking the idea.

19

I parked several houses down the alley from Doris' place. Rick had parked his Range Rover lengthwise up against her garage door. I waited for several minutes, just to make sure my arrival had not alerted anyone in the neighborhood, then climbed out and placed a tracer on the underside of Rick's car. With that done, I returned to the Impala, pulled up a program on my laptop and locked onto the microphone in Doris' house. As expected, the two lovebirds were in her bed. The signal was faint and scratchy so I turned up the volume. The obligatory grunts and groans were in progress.

Doris, it turned out, wasn't much of a screamer. Rick, on the other hand, was everything I had imagined him to be. I heard "yes" repeated a lot and calls to god and all that interspersed with scatological references. At one point, Rick took to calling Doris a bitch. This was accompanied by the sound of flesh being slapped. I hung my head. What was it with men and this bucking bronco crap? Love was a tender art. You did not turn those loving affections into a rodeo.

At last, their passions reached a crescendo and came to an end, during which time I did not hear one word spoken from the heart. This was the raw thing, no illusions. You got what you needed and lay back on the pillow with a cigarette.

At least that appeared to be the case with Rick. Doris did say, "I love you" afterwards, but she was not offered any words of assurance in return. I pictured her lying on Rick's shoulder, waiting for a hug. As a man, you had to do that much. It was that or get dressed and hit the road.

Relieved to know their passions had been extinguished, I waited for one or the other of them to strike up a conversation. It did not take long. Doris expressed a few words of remorse about Dan being murdered and moved on to his funeral.

"I've arranged it for Wednesday," she said. "You'll come, won't you?"

There was silence.

"You don't have to, but I wish you would."

"I've got a lot on my plate right now, okay? Besides, I don't know if it's such a great idea, the two of us being seen in public together."

There was more silence.

"My agent said the life insurance policy will fund within a week. Wouldn't it be nice to take a nice long trip when all this is over?"

"Yeah, sure," Rick said.

Doris went on about world cruises and the two of them living abroad. Rick said not a word in response. Evidently, the idea that she might be the next one floating face down in the harbor had not entered Doris' mind.

Before Rick was obliged to say anything further, the phone rang. There was the sound of sheets rustling. Then Doris said "hello." That was followed by "yes" and a long silence.

"Well, I suppose I could do that. Yes…"

There was a long pause.

"Yes," she repeated. "I'll see you tomorrow morning at ten."

There was the sound of someone struggling to get the phone back into its cradle and then Doris saying "shit."

"What?" Rick wanted to know.

"It was that detective with the Newport Beach police. He says they've uncovered some new evidence about Dan's murder and wanted to go over things with me again."

"Okay," Rick said. "I don't know why you're getting all worked up about this shit. They don't have a thing on you. Or me."

Doris did not respond.

"Okay, so what? Is there something you're not telling me here?"

"I already told you everything but I'm sure they're going to check my phone records, so they're going to know I was talking to Jack."

"Okay, so you were talking to Jack. He worked in your ex-husband's business. Big deal."

Again, Doris failed to respond.

"Anyway, I never understood why you had to get that big goon involved in the first place."

"Jack has always been nice to me. Ever since I knew him in college. And he didn't always look like a big goon."

"Yeah? Well he's nothing but a big, disgusting goon now, okay? Besides, I'm sure he was just trying to get into your pants."

"I'm sure," Doris said sarcastically.

"Okay. Do you think men have anything else on their minds?"

"Do you?"

The question appeared to have knocked Rick off stride a bit, but he was quickly back at it.

"I've got plenty on my mind, okay? I'm going places and if you want to come along for the ride, fine. And if you don't, that's fine too. We'll just cut things loose right here."

"You don't have to get all worked up about it."

"Then don't yank my chain, okay?"

I almost felt sorry for Doris in the ensuing silence. The family photos suggested she was a decent human being and possessed a modicum of character. For all I knew she was a lost soul, looking for love in all the wrong places. Rick, on the other hand, was the human version of a hyena. He had gone straight from childhood to ambition, and from there to avarice, from being a little boy being bullied as the short kid in class to being a belligerent little prick. The tribal instincts had never developed in him. Doris afforded him comfort, but she had a very narrow window of value. One step out of line and he'd throw her to the sharks. Not that Doris was pure as driven snow, but compared to Rick, she was Mother Teresa.

I heard rustling, the sound of door hinges creaking, the sound of a man urinating, the toilet flush and the door hinges creaking again.

"Are you going?" Doris said.

"Yeah, okay. I've got to go track down this Michael Devlin."

"Who's that?"

"A private detective."

"You hired a private detective?"

"Yeah, because of this arms shipment deal, I've got some strange people breathing down my neck."

"Great. And now he'll probably end up stumbling onto this business with Jack."

"That's not why I hired him, okay? And as far as I can tell, Jack was just trying to sell Dan down the river. He's lucky he didn't get shot instead."

"Jack wasn't trying to sell Dan down the river."

There was a pause, I assumed in honor of the dead.

"How do you know that?"

"I just do…. Okay?"

"Hey, fuck you."

There were the sounds of someone getting dressed in a hurry.

"I've already had that dick Devlin teaching me the finer points of diction. Thinks he's some big shot arbiter of how people ought to talk, on top of being a big shot private detective."

"You're the only one who thinks he's a big shot."

There was the sound of someone being slapped, a tender little yelp, and then Doris quietly sobbing.

"You didn't have to do that," she said after a spell.

"Yeah, well, I'm trying to give an old maid a break and this is the thanks I get?"

"I didn't mean anything by it."

"Yeah? Well I can tell when someone is mocking me, okay?"

"Don't go," I heard Doris say, followed by the sound of a door being slammed.

I saw Rick pile into his car out back fifteen seconds later and off he went, racing down the alley. I got on his tail. My phone rang almost immediately. It was little Caesar. Two blocks down the road and he was all ready to give me orders.

"Hey, I've been trying to reach you," he said when I answered.

"I've been busy," I said.

"Yeah? Well I hope it's busy working for me, okay?"

"Actually, I have been, Rick, and there's something I need to ask you."

"Yeah, what?"

"Do you know a guy named Jack? I guess he ran the boatyard for Colby?"

There was silence.

"Hey, I hired you to get rid of Nacho for me. What does Jack have to do with it?"

"Sure, fine, Rick, but when I spoke with Nacho yesterday..."

"You spoke with Nacho yesterday?"

"Sure did. Gave him a call and next thing you know, Jack's name came up. Nacho seems to think you and Jack are mixed up in something together. Any idea how he got that notion?"

"I told you. I don't know anything about Jack."

"Nacho thinks otherwise and the cops are grilling Jack. Meaning, I'm not sticking my neck out any further. Not until you come clean and I get some answers."

There was more silence. Rick had pulled to a stop at the red light on Coast Highway. When it changed, he turned north. I gave him a few hundred yards and followed.

"We need to talk, okay?" he said. "Where are you?"

"We are talking."

"What I need to tell you I'm not saying over the phone, okay?"

He was back with his 'okays' and I was ready to slap him around again.

"Come down to my office tomorrow afternoon," I said.

"You said it can't wait. So, okay? Where are you right now?"

"Working on another case."

"Shit, you're about worthless. I don't even know why I hired you."

"I don't either but we'll have to continue this discussion at a later date."

I heard Rick being imperious as I hung up on him. He was still in my gun sights straight ahead. At Newport Blvd., he turned onto the peninsula and called me back. I saw Vanderhof calling at the same time and answered him instead. There were voices and laughter and the tinkling of glasses in the background.

"I take it you're still at the Quiet Woman."

"Yeah, where are you?"

Just then, Rick turned left down towards the waterfront.

"Hang on a minute," I told Vanderhof.

"Don't go putting me on hold, Devlin."

"Just hang on."

"What's going on?"

"I'm watching a bad movie."

Rick had come to the shipyard and turned down the long, dead end alley leading up to it. I parked across the street, hit my lights and watched his progress. He came to a stop alongside the closed gate. His lights went out but I could tell from his tailpipe that the motor was still running.

"What's going on?" Vanderhof said again

Just then, Rick saw something he didn't like and wrenched his Range Rover around hard. As he barreled back up the alley, a guard appeared at the gate with a Doberman Pinscher.

I gave Rick a lead and got back on his tail. By the time I caught up with him, he was making the loop from Newport

Boulevard onto Coast Highway, heading north, and pissing off a parade of motorists as he did. To hell with him, I decided, and headed south. I had the tracer on his rig. If he went back to Doris' place, I would know it. I wasn't sure anything else about the man held much interest for me, except to know why he had gone poking around at the shipyard.

"Damn it," Vanderhof said. "Tell me about the movie."

"Oh, just somebody fishing around at a shipyard."

"Yeah? Don't tell me you're over at Colby's old place."

My ears pricked up.

"What do you know about Colby?"

"I knew him. Everybody knew Colby, Devlin. Besides, like I told you. I've been keeping an eye on you buddy."

"Yeah? Like right now?"

"Maybe. I'd have to call the boys and see if they lost you."

I looked in the rearview mirror.

"See anybody?" Vanderhof wanted to know.

"No. What do your boys look like?"

Vanderhof was silent. I pictured him tossing down his Scotch, all full of himself.

"All right. Tell me more about Colby."

"Colby, yeah. Talk about silk. He could have sold sand to an Arab. And the women loved him. He was the life of the party."

"Really," I said.

"Yeah. His ex-wife was a real doll, too."

"Yeah? What did you know about his ex-wife?"

"What do you mean, 'did'? Did somebody shoot her too?"

"I don't know. I don't know anything about the woman."

"Don't lie to me, Devlin."

"I'm not," I told him and waited, assuming he would start up of his own volition again. He did.

"You know, when we were young, Colby and I played around a bit together in real estate. I hate to admit it but Doris and I played around together a bit too. Times what they were, you know. I don't think Dan ever knew about it."

"No one's perfect," I said.

219

"No, I'm sure not. She was one hell of a good lay, though," Vanderhof added. "And a damn good soul."

Setting aside the fact that 'one hell of a good lay' and 'a damned good soul' did not seem to fit very well in the same sentence, I understood. Once a lady had been kind to you in bed, your view of her would never be entirely objective again.

Another line started to ring in.

"Hey, I've got another call," I told Vanderhof.

"Don't go starting any more trouble, okay Devlin?"

"I'll try not to."

"Good…So, hey, how about Tuesday morning? We'll jump in my plane and take that ride down to your place in Baja."

"Maybe. Let's see if we can both stay out of trouble until then."

"You're all right, Devlin."

"You're all right, Vanderhof."

"Hey, who knows how many years we have to live. No sense in living your life like some clown just cut you off on the freeway."

"Sage advice," I told him. "But not so easy to follow."

"I'll see you in the morning."

I started to add something but Vanderhof had already hung up. I was left there staring at my lie. I didn't really think Vanderhof was all right but what did I know? Maybe he was headed in the right direction. I decided to cut him some slack and answered the other call. It was Jim Harrison.

"Got time for that steak?" he asked me.

"Oh shit, I don't know, Jim. I'm still working."

"Come on, Michael. Don't make it so painful to spend a moment with a friend."

"All right. Where are you thinking?"

"How about The English Cottage?"

"All right. I'll be back in town in about fifteen minutes."

"That's just about my timing. First one there grabs a table."

I rang off with the darkness of Scotchman's Cove alongside my car. The bristling white surf against the black water was all you could see.

Back in town, I found a parking spot a few slots up the block from The Cottage. The phone number I had given Rick had been ringing the whole way up the coast. I took a moment to delete all his messages before going in. With a quick check of the GPS signal on his Land Rover, I saw that he was up by the airport, probably in a hotel. Good, let him twist in the wind for a spell. Maybe Nacho would find him and put both of us out of our misery.

A prospective client had also called on my regular line. He had heard I was great on divorce cases. Please ring him back. Like hell I would.

I threw both phones on the seat and started for the restaurant. Not a damned word from Audrey, the civility of answering my calls seemingly of no importance to her at all.

I found a line of people queued up just to the other side of the hostess kiosk as I went in, waiting for their shot at the next open bar table. The bar itself started just beyond the kiosk. It was two rows deep with dolls on barstools and a pack of men milling around behind them.

I pushed my way through the crowd and found Jim seated at a window table, his tall physique framed by lace curtains. Every bar table around him was spilling over with patrons. I noticed a handful of resentful looks back at the hostess kiosk as I sat down.

"Who'd you bribe?" I asked Jim.

He nodded at the waitress working the bar tables.

"She just got her third DUI," he said with his whispering willows southern voice. "I'm keeping her out of the gray bar hotel."

He stared at me.

"Speaking of trouble, what happened to you? You look like you've been through a war."

"So I keep hearing."

Jim smiled, as much as he ever did.

"I'll tell you all about it after we order," I said.

The house musician was ten feet behind Jim, surrounded by electronic equipment and a grand piano. The guy was a magician, working the foot pedals with just his socks on, lost in his work. You hardly noticed he was there. He acknowledged me as an old hand around town and I tipped my hat in return. A bit of Hendrix was in the works right then, *Third Stone from the Sun*, just the guitar riff, soft, mellow and melodic. Then he segued into a Cole Porter number without missing a beat. I smiled as the knife jabbed into my heart. I've got you under my skin. Jesus. Any other song.

I turned my attention to a gaggle of firemen in the street behind Jim. They had just returned from a run and were backing their truck into the station. The station was kitty-corner across the road. Two of the firemen were out holding up traffic at the intersection. The rest of them were alongside the fire station in their battle gear. Fifty feet behind them, Whalen was probably warming up his seat at the police station.

"It's a bitch, isn't it?"

"What is?" Jim said.

"Those firemen. If we tried something like that, the cops would have us face down with a gun at the back of our heads."

Jim had a quick glance over his shoulder and looked back at me.

"Fighting the wrong battles, as usual."

"Yeah, but I can't seem to help myself. All these years and I'm still mad at the world."

"Give me the story behind the wounds."

"Oh, this I got when a couple of clowns cuffed me around up in Newport on Thursday morning. This boo boo I got when two completely different SOBs clocked me with a pistol last night down in Doheny Beach. The two in Doheny were from south of the border. By the way, women love it when you call them boo boos."

Jim smiled again. I forged ahead with my best explanation for what had been happening over the past few days, in twenty five words or less, but it was more like five hundred and nothing seemed a whole lot clearer to me when I was done.

"Russians, huh?" Jim said.

"Yeah. I had a pat little theory going until they came along. Then Whalen told me the ballistics from the Cliff and Colby murders didn't match and that let the rest of the air out of my balloon. Whalen refused to tell me what was what, but he got a big kick out of knowing I was on the wrong track."

The waitress appeared. Jim and I both ordered a New York steak from the bar menu. Jim ordered a glass of pinot noir. I ordered a stiff club soda.

"So?" Jim said once his client in distress had run off. "Where does that leave you?"

"Not much of anywhere. One thing I don't get is how everyone comes to know everyone else. It seems way too pat. Too much of a coincidence."

"There aren't all that many rotten people in the world," Jim told me. "At least that's my experience. Like rats on a sinking ship, they tend to swarm together."

"Yeah? Well I'm not buying your polling data on that score, but we'll set that aside for the moment. Who do you think killed Cliff and Dan Colby?"

"I don't have enough to go on," Jim said. "Nor am I convinced that it was the same person."

"Take a wild guess."

"I'll tell you who I don't think it was."

"Okay."

"Audrey. There's no motive for money there with the husband, and if she was planning to shoot Colby, I don't see why she stops by earlier in the day to chew him out."

"I'm with you so far."

"Jack. It sounds as if Colby was long dead before the cops caught up with him there."

"I don't know," I said.

"Well, accessory, maybe, but I don't think he pulled the trigger."

"I don't know," I said again.

"Okay, we'll come back to him, but as to the others, this Nacho seems to present a major mystery, agreed?"

"He definitely presents a nice whack on the head."

"Well, I think your instincts were right on the mark there. You don't kill someone first, then start asking questions."

"It does tend to complicate the interrogation...However, from my encounters with Nacho over the past few days, I wouldn't rule out his emotions getting away from him."

Jim and I were left staring at each other.

"That leaves us with Rick and Doris," I said.

"Don't forget about Dick and Tom," Jim said. "And Vanderhof."

"Dick and Tom. That's interesting."

"Until they have a note from the President, I'm not buying their story."

"Well, I'm more inclined to point a finger at Vanderhof, but one minute I think he's guilty, the next, I think he's the proverbial red herring."

"Playing devil's advocate here," Jim said. "He had a connection with Magellan Ltd. and he's everywhere in your story and sometimes the most obvious guy is the last person you'd expect. It's possible Colby had something on Vanderhof and Vanderhof wanted to keep him quiet."

"Yeah," I said. "But in that case, why not shoot his wife while he's at it?"

"The one is obvious, the other not so much."

"And none of that explains who shot Cliff and who strangled Connie."

"Like I said, I don't know if I buy that there's only one killer. Or one motive."

"Yeah."

I shook my head.

"And like I said, one minute I think I've got it all figured out. Then I find a million reasons to think I'm on the wrong track."

The waitress brought our steaks. They were served with a slab of horseradish butter on top, a salad and some onion rings on the side. We dug in. A few bites later, I wiped my mouth.

"Well, back to Rick and Doris, I'll tell you this much. They sounded as guilty as sin while talking in bed. I mean about killing Colby, but even at that, their involvement doesn't make any sense to me. Rick's got plenty of money. Doris is comfortably ensconced on Balboa Island. Why shoot someone over a few more bucks?"

"It happens all the time," Jim said between bites. "An aging woman is blinded by her love for a younger man. Sees them sharing a lifetime of happiness together. If only there was enough dough lying around. She might even have enticed Jack into pulling the trigger."

"You believe any of that?" I asked him.

"Not really," he said. "But I don't have enough to go on."

"Oh Christ, I give up," I said and grabbed an onion ring.

"Yeah, why don't you see what happens at the funeral tomorrow. Audrey will need a shoulder to cry on, sooner or later."

"Yeah. All I have is bad luck with women these days. A lot of fireworks and then they disappear on me."

"Maybe you make too much of the fireworks."

"Yeah, but I love the fireworks. I just hate it when they're over and it's time to sweep up. If it wasn't for Steve, I'd drop the whole thing and head south."

Jim and I finished our steaks in silence.

"Did you hear about this Connie funeral business?" I asked while wiping my hands and disposing of the napkin.

"Yeah. Steve mentioned it yesterday. Too bad. They would have granted him a temporary release under the circumstances. They usually do if you're burying an immediate family member."

Jim shook his head.

225

"Too bad."

"Yeah. Too bad."

I looked at the bill and slipped fifty dollars inside the plastic holder.

"You got a faraway look all of a sudden," he said.

"Oh, just thinking a nice long walk along the shore sounds in order. I need to clear my head."

20

I stood up. Jim stood up with me and started out past the hostess kiosk and all the resentful looks. The queue was ten deep. The wait was thirty minutes and Jim had cut in line.

I tossed a five-dollar bill in the musician's glass jar and received a nod of appreciation. The last strains of *Midnight Rider* followed me through the bar. That song transitioned into *Satin Doll* and that melody kicked me in the ass as I went out the door.

I had to stop frequenting this place. It was impossible to walk in the door without thinking of Caitlin. Our second dinner together had come back to me right then. "So, are you glad?" I had asked her as we settled in with our candlelight and drinks. "Yeeaaaahhh," she had said without hesitation. Both of us so happy to have found each other.

So why this pointless ending? I assumed I would never know.

Out on the street, the night was far more autumn like than summery after the storm. Jim had his hands in his coat pockets and his nose up in the breeze. The trees were stirring. The stars were sparkling up in the black night.

"Be nice to know what's on that flash drive," he said.

"Yeah. I've thought about breaking into Colby's old place and poking around for the code."

"Better be careful," he said. "Breaking the law in order to enforce it could land you in jail."

"And you? Don't you ever break the law?"

"Some lawyers cross that line. Not me. I see my profession more like walking through a succession of rooms. Sometimes the rooms are big. Sometimes they're small, but the walls are never that far away. Something's always telling me, no, not this way, no, not that way."

I touched my boo boo.

"Me too," I said.

Jim let out one of his rare laughs.

"Try to stay out of jail," he told me.

"The man's already dead. I presume his cat is gone."

"Try to stay out of jail," he said again. "I've got a court date tomorrow morning. I don't need any more trouble."

"Yeah, I'll do my best, and thanks for the sounding board."

"Learn anything?"

"Probably not. In fact, you're likely to get a call from the local gendarme in about an hour."

"Don't make it too late," he said and went over to unlock his car.

Mine was a few parking spots up. I grabbed my regular phone out of it and started down the sidewalk on foot. My office was a block and a half down towards the sea. For a Sunday evening, the streets were surprisingly empty. The cool weather had taken the itch out of everyone. I went along with a good steak in my gut and a head full of lousy thoughts.

Passing by the door to my office building, I glanced inside the salt water taffy shop next door. The taffy barrels were full. The place was mostly empty. Same with the art gallery and the ice cream parlor sitting kitty-corner on Coast Highway. Given the chill in the air, there wasn't much of a run on anything that evening, but definitely not on ice cream cones.

I hit the button, waited for the light to change and hustled across to the wooden boardwalk. From there I headed north. A couple passed me walking their two St. Bernard's. Two lovers sat on a bench to my right, snuggled up under a shawl. The surf was riding high from the storm. A fine breeze was blowing in towards shore.

At the far end of the boardwalk, I turned right up the concrete steps and past the adjacent public bathroom. The smell of urine mixed with the salty air.

The stairs led up to a winding trail along the bluff. A hotel with a Mediterranean motif cascaded down among the palm and cypress trees.

At the top of the bluff, the path led into a grassy park skirting the coast. Wind-battered cypress trees hugged the successive rocky coves on my left. I stopped at one of the coves to enjoy the breeze in my face. A lone cypress tree moaned quietly beside me.

Having followed the park to the north end of town, I retraced my steps back to the boardwalk. The lights of downtown were off to my left now, the surf churning against the black sea off to my right. A band was playing at a bar over on Ocean Avenue. People were still milling around outside the bar, looking for a final thrill to their weekend. It was the two halves of life, the guilelessness of nature over here, the world of mankind over there. The world of man seemed like gum on the sidewalk in comparison.

With regrets, I parted ways with the guilelessness of nature and crossed back over Coast Highway, and was doing all right until I arrived at the top of the old wooden stairs in my office building and saw my office door flung open and broken glass all over the carpet.

I paused outside to take in the mess. It must have been Nacho and his pals. They had punched a hole in the frosted glass to let themselves in and had really gone through the place.

My thought was to lock up and go crawl into bed. A bottle of whiskey sounded hopeful. My only consolation was to know that, having hit me, those Mexicans probably did not know about Teresa yet.

Just in case, I stepped over the debris, hit the bankers lamp on my desk and called her house. It was a little past eleven, not too terribly late for a Sunday evening.

"What's up?" Teresa said after saying hello.

"Nothing. Just checking in on you."

"Everything's fine," she assured me.

"Okay. I was wondering if you could stop by tomorrow and clean things up around here. It's gotten to be a bit of a mess."

"Sure," she said. "Any particular time?"

"Make it the afternoon if you can. I'll probably be here in the morning working."

We said goodnight. I hung up and stood there lost amidst the chaos for a moment before going to work. The top of my desk got straightened up first. The drawers went back into the oak filing cabinet next. I found a piece of cardboard, taped it over the broken glass and had just cleared a decent pathway back to the door when I heard the unmistakable sound of high heels coming in through the door downstairs. Castanets did a number in my heart. They always did at the sound of a woman in heels.

Being it was the fairer sex, I saw little point in brandishing my .38. Instead, I went to stand behind the desk. The scent of fine perfume hit me a split second before the lady who came with it. And not a cloud of perfume. Just enough to give a man that dumb look on his face. I presume that was how I looked when Mrs. Vanderhof stepped into the open doorway.

"Good evening, Mr. Devlin," she said.

There was a subtle accent to her words, as if she had said, "Darlingk."

"Oh my," she added. "Your office is even messier than I recall it."

"I had it done all for you."

She smiled. A knowing smile, a smile that said somebody in this universe might actually appreciate me.

"Here," I said, cleaning some papers off of the worn leather chair. Mrs. Vanderhof had a better look at my head and the other wound.

"Oh my," she said again. "You're a bit more of a mess than I remember."

"I try to get out of the way. It doesn't always work."

She smiled again, did a little extra housekeeping on top of the leather seat and settled in with her silk slacks. She was lean, enough so that the silk slopped around on her a bit, but she had lots of soft parts. Her skin was pale, her cheeks rosy. Her blonde hair was as silky as her blouse and spilled down over her shoulders. The teacup Yorkie had been left down in the Bentley, or so I assumed

"It's a bit chilly," she said with a nod at the open windows. "Do you mind terribly?"

"I'm Irish," I said by way of explanation but did as she had asked.

"Something to drink?"

"Oh. Scotch on the rocks sounds lovely. Do you have some?"

"The finest single malt."

Her smile said she was impressed. I arranged her drink, handed it across the desk and sat in my chair.

"You're not having one too?"

I considered my usual impertinence but demurred.

"Actually, I have to run out again this evening. Never drink and drive, as they say."

"Oh, well, if you have to go," she said and looked for someplace to set her drink down. I rushed to stop her.

"Mrs. Vanderhof, please. There aren't that many beautiful women in my life these days. At least none who come up to visit."

I waved as if to offer her the place.

"Please enjoy your drink. It's a pleasure having you here."

In honor of our détente, she sipped at the Scotch and watched me over the top of the glass. Anticipating the next move, I slid a coaster over to her side of the desk. She put the glass down and had another look around the office.

"Do you know why I like you, Mr. Devlin?"

"Michael, and I haven't the foggiest."

"You're unpretentious. You are what you are. Crude at times."

I frowned to let her know I had been wounded.

231

"Sophisticated at others," Mrs. Vanderhof added, as if to soothe the wounds she had left behind. "In fact, I find your frankness very attractive."

"Everybody's trying to get me into trouble."

She watched me over another sip of Scotch.

"Do you know why I divorced my husband?"

"I haven't the foggiest notion about that either. I can see why you might be inclined to do so, but what got you started? No idea. Had you hired me first, I would have asked. Once you hired an attorney, it ceased to be any of my business."

"Oh, I've had no illusions about his dalliances over the years, and might have looked the other way. Losing Zoe was hard on both of us. Hard on our marriage."

"I'm truly sorry about your daughter..."

"It's all right, Michael. You look around and see so much tragedy in the world these days. It seems entirely unfair to go on worrying about yourself at the expense of everyone else."

"Still," I said.

"Yes," she said. "I grieve over her a little every day. However, we were talking about my husband and in the end, I had simply tired of his pretenses. Unlike you, he has tried to be something he's not. Take away his online gambling fortune, which was little more than a stroke of good luck, and my husband is nothing but a two-bit street thug."

I did my best to hold back the smile.

"It's true," she said, recognizing my efforts.

"Forgive me, but it was your turn of phrase, not the intent behind it."

"You are an educated man, Michael. I like that."

I gestured as if to feign modesty.

She smiled and held her empty glass of Scotch my way. The eyebrows went up. I splashed a bit more Glendronach over her ice cubes.

"Thank you," she said and took a sip.

"And to what do I owe the pleasure of your company, Mrs. Vanderhof? And it is a distinct pleasure."

"Elfie."

"Elfie."

I was lonely. I had your final check here. And being in town already…"

"Everybody's trying to get me into trouble."

"Well," she said and produced an envelope from her purse. It was slid over my way. "I would enjoy just sitting here to chat for a spell. If you don't mind."

"Of course not. I have plenty of time. And a full bottle of Scotch."

"Were you aware that my husband finally settled with me?"

"The word's gotten around. I'm happy for you."

She smiled and got up to peruse the books on my bookshelves, her glass in hand.

"Lawrence of Arabia. Caesar. Alexander of Macedon."

Elfie looked back over her shoulder at me.

"Jack London? I take it you're fond of adventure stories, Michael."

"Just looking for any form of escape."

She eyed me.

"No, it hasn't worked, if you're wondering."

She smiled and went over to examine the world map on the opposite wall more closely.

"You know, Michael. I have this sense that you would have made a tremendously powerful figure on the world stage…"

"If I had wanted to be a tremendously powerful figure on the world stage."

"If you had wanted to be a tremendously powerful figure on the world stage," she repeated with a smile over her shoulder. A sadder smile now. Her delicate hand fingered a rubber dart stuck to a world map on the wall and it fell to the floor. She looked at me. I gestured to let her know it was all right. She left it and stepped back to my desk, but remained standing.

"Why not?"

"Become a tremendously powerful figure on the world stage?"

"Yes."

"Oh, I've had my share of daydreams. King of the world and all that."

"They still have sultans, you know."

"A sultan would do just fine too. His Grand Suzerain."

Elfie smiled.

"But not politics."

"Oh no. I'm far too blunt for that role. Politics is the art of compromise. First, you compromise your integrity to get into power, then you compromise whatever's left in order to stay there. That's not me."

"But don't you worry that you have failed to live out the fullness of your destiny?"

"Every day. In fact, I got up this morning grieving over it. And I'll probably do a little encore before tucking myself into bed tonight."

"And?" she said.

"And what?"

"Have you come to a conclusion?"

"No. I suppose I sought peace of mind over power, and have found little of either."

"But it's not too late to turn around, is it?"

"Is this Krishna grilling Arjuna above the field of battle?"

"Oh dear," she said. "I seem to remember something about that from my comparative religion class at Vassar. And what does happen to Arjuna again?"

"I believe he goes off and gets himself killed, like any good soldier."

"And you?"

"I'll probably get myself killed someday, but not because I'm a good soldier."

Elfie smiled again.

"What about you living out your destiny on the world stage?" I asked her.

"Oh, I'm sorry, but I enjoy talking about you so much more."

"We could just as easily talk about you."

"Perhaps you think I should give away everything I own and join a convent."

"How about donating a good portion of it to a worthy foundation?"

"How prescient of you to say so."

My eyebrows went up, both over her ten-dollar word and whatever was behind it.

"Yes, I've actually been thinking to start one in Zoe's honor. I suppose now that this divorce is over, I'll have the time to concentrate on such things."

Elfie smiled her sad smile again, put her glass down and came around to lean against my side of the desk. Her delicate feet and ankles were peeking out of the silk pants. Her red toe nail polish was peeking out of her high heeled sandals.

"You never answered my question," she said.

"You mean about living out the fullness of my destiny?"

"Yes."

"Oh, there was a time when I thought I was."

"How so?"

It was my turn to smile sadly.

"Oh, I see. We're speaking of love now, aren't we?"

"Romance, to be more specific, and I was deluded."

"But we've all been deluded once or twice in our lives."

"Terrible state of things, isn't it?"

"Yes, but…"

"Yes, but," I said, interrupting her. "I can assure you that I've been more deluded than most."

"Oh dear," she said. "This is beginning to have a tragic air about it."

I shrugged.

"So, you dispense with your illusions and live out the days as best you can."

"More than a bit tragic."

"Many a time the harmony of their tongues hath into bondage brought my too diligent ear."

"Oh, I believe I know that too," she said. "Shakespeare, isn't it?"

"Yes. And I'm quite sure he wrote that line for me."

"Tell me how it all ended, Michael?"

"Oh, I think this is probably a good time to close the book on our little bedtime stories."

"I'm sorry, Michael, but a woman can't help but be curious when it comes to men and their broken hearts."

"Ah, such a charming little double entendre you said there."

She stared, the sad smile having acquired something of a sly look about it.

"Oh, Elfie. I'm so tired of talking about it, and I'm quite certain the world has tired of hearing me. I loved a woman once. With all my heart. I was forty then. I'm fifty now and can't seem to get started again. I don't know what else to say."

"Oh, dear, dear Michael," she said with a hand to my face.

There was a most sincere look of sympathy in her eyes, a look that came with the scent of her very fine perfume.

"Joy?" I said.

"Yes," she said. "You know it."

"Yeah. When a man loves a woman with all his heart, he knows perfume."

Elfie's hand gently stroked my cheek.

"Oh, Michael. If I didn't tell anyone, and you didn't tell anyone? Would anyone ever know or care?"

"That's a lot of ifs," I said.

"Oh, now I've completely embarrassed myself. I saw you...I saw you being quite comfortable with danger in your professional life and assumed, well...you know, that the same daring applied to your personal life as well."

"Trying to put the bit in my mouth, are we?"

"No, no. I'm sorry. You're right. I shouldn't be saying these things."

I stood up, having decided long ago to accept the bit. Elfie's silk slacks came up softly against me and what was beneath them felt warm against the cool, summer night. I looked down

236

at Elfie's red toe nail polish. The toes wiggled to say hello. I looked back into her eyes. She stared for a long moment, then rubbed her nose against mine.

She was adorable, from her head down to her dainty little feet. So why not give in to romance? Forget Audrey and this 'all my heart for all eternity' business. I just wanted someone who sincerely cared and appreciated me in return.

After a moment of passion, I reached to close the blinds and returned to the sweet, waxy taste of Elfie's red lipstick.

21

The next morning, I awakened to a cool ocean breeze rustling in my window curtains. Thoughts of Elfie were rustling around with the breeze. The image of her naked torso leaning over my desk, wearing only high heels, felt corporeal in the morning air. I was suddenly aroused again, just recalling the act. A woman, no matter her station, was suddenly made vulnerable in that position. The higher her station, the more exhilarating it became. The more delicate the high heels, the more erotic the exhilaration. Come, do it hard, Elfie had said, and I had, and it had felt so damned good. I was ready to do it all over again.

I climbed out of bed and went off to shave, a tug of war over three women ongoing in my heart. The sane thing would be to give up on these temperamental redheads. Caitlin and Audrey were like a roller coaster ride compared to Elfie. And Elfie had been so completely adult. And still I was drawn down the rabbit hole of my romantic illusions.

After a shower, I picked out a black suit, a white shirt and a checked tie to wear. At a little before eight, I was headed down to my office, ready to pay my respects to the dead.

Walking upstairs and down the hallway, my spirits sagged again at seeing the broken glass door. The mess inside only added to the lousy feelings.

I opened my office windows to the ocean breeze, did what I could to straighten things up a bit more and sat down to call someone about repairing the glass. Then I had a look at my finances. The bank had told me my mortgage needed to be current within a week. I was behind three payments. Elfie's check took care of two of them. The day after tomorrow was D-Day. If I didn't come up with another three grand by then, the foreclosure would start.

Faced with disaster, my mind started scrambling for answers.

The mailman popped in a few minutes later.

"Wow, what happened here?"

"I was taking out my frustrations with the world."

He smiled while sorting through the mail.

"It does kind of look like you've been through a war," he said, handing it to me.

"That's what happens when you take out your frustrations with the world."

We stared at each other.

"I guess it would be a bummer, getting beat up and then having to explain it to everybody."

I nodded sarcastically to let him know he was getting warm.

"Hey, it looks like you're going to a funeral."

"I am."

"Oh, yeah, that guy."

"Yeah, that guy."

"Sorry."

"What are you sorry about? You didn't shoot him. Or did you?"

He smiled again and started to leave.

"Nice day," he said. "I guess you won't be needing those natives with the palm fronds for a spell."

I nodded. He stopped just outside the door.

"Smells like nice perfume in here."

Cornered, I nodded yet again. The mailman winked and left.

Smart ass. I got back to business. My first call was to Sylvia's number. It rang and rang. I was ready to hang up when she finally answered. I dispensed with the pleasantries.

"Look, Sylvia. I'm trying to help the woman and she can't even be bothered with answering my calls? You'd better believe I'm getting pissed here."

"I can't speak for Audrey. We returned here from the desert and she left in her own car."

"Do you have any idea what she's hiding?"

"I'm sorry. I really can't answer your question."

"Fair enough, but just so you know. I'm not sticking my neck out for her any further. Not until she tells me the truth."

"The mist will start to clear in about twenty-four hours."

"Shall I look for the heavens to part?"

"The key will come to you. I don't know about Audrey. I feel badly for her. If she doesn't change, I don't see a happy ending."

"That certainly sounds ominous." There was silence. "Are you going to the funeral?"

"Yes."

"All right. I guess I'll see everybody there. Can I count on you to keep our conversations confidential?"

"Yes."

"Thanks. I suppose it would be best for now."

We hung up. I turned on my computer and made another attempt at cleaning up around my office while it booted up. Then I called Rick.

"I guess I can forget about seeing any results for that five hundred dollars I spent," he said in answering the phone.

"I told you everything I know, Rick, so why don't you tell me something I don't."

"Like what, okay?"

"Like how you got involved with Colby's ex-wife? And why you went poking around down at the shipyard late last night?"

There was a moment of silence.

"Okay, that's it. You can keep the five hundred dollars. Just get off my case. I don't need your help. I don't want your help."

"Yeah? Well, sorry, Rick, but when you hired a private investigator, what did you expect? That I wouldn't find out you were lying to me?"

"I'm not lying, and we're done, okay? Just get lost."

"Okay, big shot, but I'm up to my neck in this mess and as long as I'm not working for you anymore, I may as well go to the cops. Spill my beans. Let them know everything I know, before they start thinking I'm the one who shot Dan Colby."

There was another long silence.

"Okay, so I've been playing around with Doris, but I had nothing to do with this Jack business. Okay? You want to go to the cops, she's the one who's up to her neck in this mess, not me."

Some pal, I thought. Throwing Doris to the sharks at the first sign of trouble. Never mind his reversion to that obnoxious "okay" syndrome.

"Explain what you mean by 'this Jack business?'" I told him.

"This is what I know, okay? She was having trouble with Colby and asked Jack to talk to him and next thing you know, Colby's dead."

"What do you mean, 'trouble with Colby'? About what?"

"Okay. I thought you knew."

I saw a shadow and heard a knock on the door.

"Just a second," I told Rick. "Come in," I said to whoever was outside.

It was the glassman.

"This it?"

"Yeah. Hey, I'm on the phone so do whatever you need to do."

He nodded and started taking measurements. I got back to Rick.

"Okay, I don't know anything. So spill it or I'm going straight to the cops."

"Okay. Doris had called Colby to discuss his will, and when they got into an argument about it, she started worrying that maybe he had changed it and went to Jack for help. And next thing you know, Colby's dead."

"You think Jack killed Colby?"

The glassman looked up from his bid. This was the most excitement he'd had all week. I winked and got back to Rick. He had asked me who else would have done it.

"Doris," I said.

"I've wondered the same thing, okay? And I wouldn't put it past her. But the way I read the situation? I don't think so."

"Look, Rick. I told you from the start. I'm not an attorney. I can't shield you from the law. If you know something, you'd better spill it right now."

"Okay, she had some dirt on Colby and asked me to play along."

"What kind of dirt?"

"I don't know."

"Bullshit."

"Look, whatever she had on him was her business. I had my own dirt and thought I might get a little better deal on some shipping with this other stuff hanging over his head. But I never expected it to come to this."

"To murder?"

That got the glassman's attention again.

"Okay," Rick said. "Doris called to tell me about Colby's death and next thing I know, she has us running off to the Caribbean somewhere. Hey, that's not what I bought into. I've got a business to run. She's an all right looking gal for her age, and a pretty good lay. I don't know anything else."

"I've got to run," I told Rick.

"Hey, what's this shit? I spill my beans and you're going to the cops anyway? That's not the deal we made."

"My gut tells me you're lying so I'm giving you twenty-four hours to spill the truth. I'll keep my mouth shut that long. Now I've got to go."

"Hey," I heard him saying as I started to put the phone down. I put it back up to my ear.

"What?"

"I want to know if you're still following me around."

"I don't know," I said. "You'd better act like I am."

I hung up. The glassman was waiting for me.

"I take it you want the same frosted glass."

"Yeah. Just like it was."

"Then it's $350 with installation."

"There goes my trip to the Bahamas."

"It's mostly labor. It's a lot of work getting the old glass out and installing the new piece.

"It's fine. How soon can you do it?"

"A couple of days. If I put the order in today, I'll have the glass day after tomorrow."

"All right."

"It's fifty percent down."

I wrote him a check. He gave me a receipt and left.

I leaned back in my chair with the various faces involved in this case doing a dance in my head. Rick, Audrey, Doris, Nacho, Vanderhof; sometimes the mist seemed about to lift, then I was filled with confusion again. Sometimes I thought I was starting to grasp the motivation driving these people. Then I was back to being surrounded by darkness.

Just as I was starting over, trying one more time to fit the pieces of the puzzle together, I heard footsteps hustle up the wooden stairs and down the hallway. I opened the top drawer of my desk and got my hand on the Smith & Wesson. Shadows appeared at the bottom of my door. Then it flew open and Whalen barged in, followed by his sidekick Fowler. I closed the drawer. Whalen was busy taking in the wreckage around my office.

"Who the hell hit you up?"

He came closer and nodded at my fresh wound.

"Whoever it was, I see you lost again."

"Leave it alone, Pat."

"Sure, because you've got enough troubles. I'm placing you under arrest."

"Arrest for what?"

"For harboring a fugitive. And maybe withholding evidence."

I looked around my cluttered office.

"What fugitive? What evidence?"

"Don't get cute with me, Devlin. You want to call your attorney now or wait until I book you down at the station?"

"What's eating you, Pat?"

"Don't think you're going to charm your way out of this one, Devlin. Now come on, let's go. We're pals enough to do this without the handcuffs."

Fowler came around to my side of the desk and motioned for me to stand up. I could smell his hair oil and chewing gum through the ocean breeze. I was ready to deck him again. I looked back at Pat.

"I'm asking you again. What fugitive and what evidence?"

"Audrey. She's disappeared again and I'm guessing you know where she is. I'm also guessing you're not prepared to tell me where, so I'm taking you in until you start talking."

I shook my head.

"Yeah, go ahead and cook up some more bullshit," Pat said. "But I'll know it's bullshit because your poker face isn't worth a damn."

"Pat. Are you charging Audrey with murder?"

"Yeah."

"Of her husband? Or Colby?"

"Maybe both."

"And you believe that?"

"I don't know, but I've got to start someplace, and she's all dressed up for the occasion. Motive in both cases. A failing marriage and fingerprints all over that shipyard office. And when I went to talk with her at her mother's place an hour ago, no one knew where she was."

"What's wrong with you, Pat? They're burying her husband in a couple of hours. You don't suspect she might be there?"

"Is that what you heard?"

"That's what she told me yesterday morning."

"You saw her yesterday morning?"

"Yeah, before I knew you were charging her with murder, mind you, so I'm not so sure your harboring a fugitive charge is going to stick."

"You knew where she was and didn't tell me?"

"Pat, look. I had a tip that she might be out at the Salton Sea and…"

"Just like that. A tip that she might be out at the Salton Sea."

"No, not just like that. I had gotten in touch with her niece Sylvia, the fortune teller, and that's what Sylvia told me."

"Oh boy. Sylvia the fortune teller."

Pat looked at Fowler with a smirk.

"Now I've heard everything."

"You done?" I said when he looked back.

"Yeah yeah. Go ahead."

"Like I said, I took a trip out there and was poking around, looking any kind of clue when Audrey called me."

"And just like that, she calls you."

"I had left my number with her mother."

"Okay. We'll just say she conveniently called you. Then what?"

"Then we met out there and she started telling me a story."

"A story about what?"

"About a business trip she took to Phoenix and how when she arrived back, some cartel boys confronted her in the parking lot. And from her description, I'm guessing the same ones who were chasing me around Laurel Lagoon the other night."

"And you got any wild guesses as to why they'd be there confronting her in the airport parking lot?"

"I haven't the foggiest, but the way I read her emotions, she's in the dark about the whole thing too."

"What else did you learn from Audrey?"

"Not much."

I explained briefly about the bikers, Audrey's disappearance and my own frustrations.

Pat shook his head.

"What?"

"What? Once again, you don't tell me shit until I've got your balls in a vice."

"Pat. You and I both know Magellan's involved in this mess up there in San Pedro. So she's up to her ass in something, but killing Colby? I admit to having my own suspicions but she flat out denied it when I cornered her on Sunday."

"And you don't know where she is right now?"

"I told you. She's left me high and dry, just like every other woman in this world, but go to the funeral. That's where I'm headed. If she doesn't show up there, maybe you've got a case on your hands. If she does, you'll be able to grill her with all the questions you like."

Whalen stared at me.

"Look, Pat, why don't you answer something for me."

"Yeah? What do you want to know?"

"Is Jack singing?"

"Squealing is more like it, but you know I can't translate that into words for you."

"All right. But he hasn't confessed to killing Colby, right? And he hasn't implicated Audrey."

There was a pause.

"He's confessing to a lot of things, but not to any of that."

"But you still think he had something to do with Dan Colby being killed."

"I don't know. Maybe. What do you think?"

"On the face of it, I think there are five or six people who might have had a motive for plugging Colby. The same could be said of Cliff, but as far as Jack and Doris and Audrey go, and even that little prick, Rick, Audrey's partner, I'm beginning to think it's all a red herring. The rest of what I've got? Nothing but a bunch of wild hunches."

"So go ahead and tell me one."

246

"I don't traffic in hunches. Anyway, they're the same ones you probably have."

"All right," Pat said. "Let's go."

"Look, Pat. I'm trying to help you here but I need forty-eight hours to work things out. If I'm right, I'll drop the whole thing in your lap and you can take a big victory lap, no thanks needed, no questions asked."

"Go to hell, Devlin."

"You have something better to go on?"

"It doesn't matter if I do or I don't. If you know who killed Colby, you'd better spill it right now."

"I already told you. I don't. I have my hunches, but upon further examination, none of them seem to hold water."

Pat kept staring

"Look at it this way," I said. "If I'm wrong, I save you a lot of egg on your face. If I'm right, you come out looking like a hero. That's the best deal I've got."

"You've got a lot of nerve, Devlin. That's what you've got."

I stared back until Pat pushed away from my desk.

"All right, damn it. I'll give you forty-eight hours, but if you run me around like you did on that last case, I'll let Fowler here cuff and perp walk you up Forest Avenue."

"You give me too much credit, Pat."

"I don't give you any credit," he said and waved at Fowler. Fowler gave me his punk smile as they went out the door.

I picked up the phone, dialed a number and sat there licking my wounds while it rang.

"Hello," a woman's voice said finally.

"I need to talk with you, Doris."

"Who's this?"

"Who I am is less important than what I know."

I waited while her gears spun around in the silence.

"I don't know who you are, but if you're thinking to blackmail me, you can forget it. I've already told the police everything I know and I don't have any money to give you, even if you did have something on me."

"I know Jack, and I know Rick, and I know one of them is trying to stab you in the back. I just don't know which one yet."

"Who are you?" she said again.

"The only way you're going to find out is to have lunch with me."

"I don't go out with strangers," she said.

"I don't bite, and if you want your troubles to go away, you'd better play along."

I waited.

"All right. Where?"

"Pick a place over on Marine Avenue. There are plenty of joints right around the corner from your house."

"Amelia's," she said after another pause. "Were you talking today?"

"Yeah, if you can make it," I said.

"All right," she said again.

I glanced at the clock.

"Let's say eleven-thirty. We'll beat the lunch crowd."

"What do you look like?" she asked.

"Tall, dark and handsome."

"Ha," she said.

"All right. Tall and dark. You can decide on the rest. Take a table if you arrive before me. I'll find you either way."

Both of us lingered in silence for a moment before hanging up. I dug out Nacho's number and dialed it from my office phone. It took several rings for him to answer.

"Jess," he said.

"This is your friend from the fortune teller."

"You got what I want, cabrón?"

"Look, I want you off my back. I want you off my client's back. That's all. I don't want any money. I don't want any blood. I don't want to know anything about you or your business. I just want you to go away. Fair enough?"

"If you got what I am wanting, my friend, chingon. You're the kind of business partner I'm always liking to have."

While Nacho was trying to romance me, I pulled up LA harbor on Google map and zeroed in on an out of the way spot.

"All right, here's the deal, Nacho. Call me superstitious but I'm not taking any chances. I want to see the smile on your face when we open the shipping container. Then I'll know we're good. Otherwise, I'm sitting around here waiting for the next shoe to drop. You got something to write with?"

I heard Nacho shouting for someone to bring him a pencil. When he returned to the line, I gave him directions, short the container number.

"There's a building with a white, metal roof where you turn in. Meet me behind it at two o'clock. No cops. No blood. No bullshit, okay?"

"We see ju at two, my friend."

The phone went dead. I hung up mine and leaned back in my chair, hoping that someone higher up the chain of command had been listening. I was going to look awfully stupid showing up in the ass end of LA harbor all by myself.

But who? Dick and Tom? Or the boys who had grilled Rick before Dick and Tom showed up? Maybe Dick and Tom were working for 'the company' after all. I was the last to know.

Either way, I needed to hear Doris's side of things. Then maybe the pieces would start to fall into place. Until then, I made an oath to stop speculating and headed out the door.

I ran into Betty downstairs. Sixty something and she was still all sex and high heels. She had Butch on a leash.

"Hey Butch," I said.

He was all ready for action.

"Well aren't we looking debonair," Betty said, giving me the once over. "Let me see that face of yours. Oh Jesus, what happened to your head?"

"People keep trying to knock some sense into me…And, no, it didn't work."

She shook her head with a smile.

"You should see a doctor before that wound gets infected."

"Who do you think stitched me up?"

249

She slapped me gently.

"Try to take care of yourself, handsome."

She started upstairs with Butch. I watched her backside for a moment. If that was all you ever saw of Betty, she'd give you a thrill. I shook my head and continued on my way, mildly concerned that the woman had just raised my pulse.

22

From my parking spot at the back of the building, I turned right onto Laurel, then took the first left and proceeded to where it intersected the bottom of the precipitous 3rd St. hill. When traffic allowed, I turned left, drove past city hall and the downtown district, turned left again onto Broadway and right up the bluff on Cliff Drive. That winding lane flung me out onto Coast Highway a few hundred yards north of Main Beach. The art museum was on my left, a long row of art galleries on my right, the galleries and raised sidewalk well above the highway. The supermarket at Boat Canyon came and went, a burger stand, the drive thru espresso shack, a handful of antique stores and a hodgepodge of commercial buildings. Four traffic signals later, I was motoring past all the pine trees and bougainvillea hemming in the gated communities. A minute after that, I was loping up and down the bluffs alongside Scotchman's Cove again.

The breezy early morning had already turned into another hot and listless day. The usual bank of pinkish-brown smog had gathered out near Catalina Island. I was bounded by undeveloped coastline on my left and multi-million dollar homes rising up a steep hillside to my right. San Pedro Harbor and the oil refineries around Signal Hill were in my sights, thirty miles up that long stretch of crescent coastline. That was Southern California, exquisite natural beauty backed up to an industrial wasteland. Nothing was sacred and you just shrugged.

At the north end of Corona del Mar, I turned right on MacArthur Blvd. and, a mile further on, left into the parking lot of St. Mark's Presbyterian Church. Limos lined the driveway from end to end. I circled around and found a spot at the back of the parking lot.

Bells were tolling as I headed for the church entrance. They stopped before I walked in. I found a spot in the back row. A pastor was up in front, offering an opening prayer. After the prayer, he did what men of the cloth do, give meaning to why people lived and died. A number of Cliff's family and friends then went up front and paid homage to his life. The pastor offered a final consecration and everyone joined in another prayer. Not in the mood for small talk, I departed for the cemetery before the other mourners rose to their feet.

Pacific View Park and Mortuary was roughly a mile south across the coastal bluffs from the church and straddled the top of a hill. I parked a safe distance from the grave and waited for everyone to disembark. The hearse carrying Cliff's casket pulled to a stop first. Audrey and her immediate family were right behind it, followed by that fleet of limos. Audrey had worn black and had her hair pinned up. The colors and long pale neck were all too familiar. I remembered Caitlin looking that exact same way at my father's funeral.

I waited in my car until everyone had gathered around the casket before joining the outskirts of the crowd. The mood was somber. The sea was off in the distance. Staring at the casket, I was reminded of that fly out at the Salton Sea. Be prepared, fair voyager. The end is never that far up ahead.

After the service, I held back as people filed by to offer Audrey their condolences. Whether real or conjured, Audrey's face was red with tears.

When it was Vanderhof's turn, he embraced Audrey tenderly then held both her hands. I stared as they spoke. Another tender embrace followed and Vanderhof whispered in Audrey's ear. I imagined him saying how they ought to get together. She seemed disconcerted by whatever he had said but the next person quickly came along, offering condolences, Vanderhof drifted off to chat with some other folks and the moment passed.

When the line was down to the last few stragglers, I went over and took my place at the end. Audrey gave me a warm hug.

"Thank you for coming."

"I'm sorry for your loss. Obviously I didn't know your husband very well but when he called, asking me to look after you, he expressed how much he really, really loved you, and…well…there aren't many people in this world who have been loved in that way."

Audrey fought back more tears. I touched her shoulder.

"Wherever you go and whatever you do, I hope you'll always remember his devotion."

"Please give me a call," she said. "There's so much I need to explain."

"I did call you."

"I know. I'm so sorry. It's just been too much for me, dealing with all of this."

"All right. We'll talk. I wish you peace. It's always right there, if only we can see it."

"Thank you. Those are actually very sweet words."

"We'll talk," I said again.

On the way back to my car, I saw Whalen jawing away at Audrey. He could have asked her to come down to his office tomorrow, but no.

I had a look around for Dick and Tom and Nacho and his gang but it looked as if they had skipped the event. With Audrey being there, I had to wonder why.

Vanderhof caught up with me as I was stepping into my car. From his maudlin state of mind the previous evening, he had made an amazing recovery. Then I remembered his money. That would tend to smooth over a lot of rough edges.

"Hey, buddy," he said. "You've got a way with the women, huh?"

Reflexively, my ears turned red. I assumed he was talking about Elfie and was in no mood to lie to him, not that early in the morning, and not at a funeral.

Vanderhof nodded in Audrey's direction. I followed his eyes and looked back at him.

"She's a beautiful woman," I said.

"Yeah she is. So listen. I had completely forgotten about this shoot we're doing up at Point Duma today. Why don't you join me? We can talk about setting up your new operation on our way up the coast."

"Shoot?" I said. "As in the movies?"

"Well, as in TV."

"Really?"

"Yeah, I'm diversifying. In a few years the online gambling business will be overrun with upstarts. It'll be like flipping burgers. Content. That's where it's at, partner."

"Really?" I said again.

"Yeah. Anyway, we're doing a pilot for our own reality TV show. It's sort of like all this vampire, hero shit the young people are all into, only it's set during medieval times in Europe. You get the picture."

"Yeah, vampires and young hero shit. But why Point Duma? Why not Italy?"

"The director. He's world renowned but a bit of a prima donna."

"I suppose they go together."

Vanderhof smiled.

"Yeah, we couldn't get him to go to Europe so we brought medieval Europe to him. Props and what not. It's amazing what they can do. Come with me and you'll see for yourself."

"I can't. I've got a case to solve."

"I already told you. You'd better not be looking into my life again."

"And I already told you. Your case is closed."

Vanderhof studied me, filled with suspicion. Then his sunshine returned.

"All right," he said. "But I'll be up there all day if you change your mind. It's at the state beach. Just drive up from Malibu. Look for all the cranes and equipment in a parking lot down by the sand. You can't miss it."

"I'd rather run away to Baja," I said.

"Hey, we can do that tomorrow. The world's at our fingertips, my friend."

"Yeah? Well, good luck with your shoot."

Watching Vanderhof walk back over to his limousine, I felt sick in the pit of my gut all of a sudden. How had the two of us gotten so chummy?

Down at the far end of the cemetery, I parked behind an out building and changed from my suit into a cotton shirt and khaki pants, then continued down the hill towards Coast Highway. I was listening to Cannonball Adderley's *Autumn Leave*. Audrey's long, pale neck and piles of radiant red hair were doing a waltz in my heart, trying to forget one redhead by falling for another.

My phone rang. It was Jim. I answered.

"Hey Jim. How did it go in court?"

"The judge denied bail."

"Shit. What for?"

"Apparently Steve has some kind of real estate investment down in Micronesia? Did you know about that?"

"Yeah, but what does that matter?"

"It matters because he's spent a lot of time down there in the past few years, he's got money in the bank and Micronesia just happens to have no extradition treaty with the US."

"Shit."

"Yeah. I did my best but the DA convinced the judge that Steve was a flight risk and that was that."

"Damn it."

"Yeah. I don't know what else to say. I got discovery set for two weeks. That's the best I can do at this point. Speed up the trial."

"Yeah, bummer. Well, thanks Jim. I'm sure you did the best you could."

"Yeah. You come up with any evidence that will help to exonerate Steve, let me know and I'll go back to the court. Otherwise, he's stuck in there through the trial."

"Man, what a bummer. But thanks again. I'll be in touch."

I got off the call, disgusted with this part of law and order. Steve had just enough money to make him look suspect, but not enough to have the courts look the other way.

Down at the highway, I turned north, then left at Jamboree and down onto Balboa Island. What money could do. All of a sudden, there wasn't a care in the world.

Thinking the place looked a bit barren, it struck me that all the old Ficus trees along Marine Avenue were gone. Then I recalled a story in the papers from a few years back. The city council had wanted the trees gone. Their roots were ruining the sidewalks. A great many pitchforks showed up at the next council meeting. Remove the trees and we'll have your heads. I hadn't followed the story but it certainly appeared that the pitchforks had lost.

I found a parking spot and started up the sidewalk towards Amelia's with the sun beating down on my head through the missing the Ficus trees.

The entrance to the restaurant was tucked away at the back of a tiled courtyard. The interior was pleasantly dark against the brilliantly sunlit world outside. I spotted Doris at a table in the back corner, pointed her out to the hostess and walked over alone to greet my date.

"Michael," I said and held out my hand.

"Hi," she said, looking guarded as she shook it. "I guess you are tall, dark and handsome."

I sat down.

"Foolish too. At least when it comes to women."

"Somebody got to you," she said.

"Are we talking about the boo boos or the jaded heart?"

"The boo boos," she said. "Both, I guess."

I nodded and stared back. Doris had aged from the photo on Colby's dresser but she was still something of a doll in her sixties. Nice figure, nice teeth, nice skin. As in the photo, her hair was short and I guessed she had always worn it that way. It went well with her face. It wasn't that old lady look, where a woman has simply tired of the upkeep. It was more like Janet Leigh, the features precisely cut, but with the eyes a bit more quixotic. Either way, she had come to be noticed, and I noticed.

From listening to Doris' conversation with Rick the other night, I knew she was searching for a guy on a white horse. How she had mistaken Rick for Prince Charming, I hadn't a clue, but my money was on Doris being a Taurus. Loyal and doting...to a fault. Maybe even stifling to a fault, if you happened to enjoy your solitude as much as I did.

Still, if it weren't for my fascination with redheads, Doris and a handful of dreams would have gone a long way down the road of life.

"Did you order already?" I asked her.

"No. I wasn't sure if we were eating or just tossing Scotch in each other's faces."

I smiled.

"I'm hungry. Why don't we start with that and if there's time left over, we'll move on to the Scotch tossing contest."

She smiled. A bit. I studied her as she attended to her hair.

When the waitress arrived, I ordered the capellini with fresh basil and tomato. Doris ordered the chicken marsala. When I ordered a large bottle of Pellegrino, she said she would just have a glass of mine.

"It's all right," I said to Doris, then to the waitress. "Bring the lady a glass of your finest Pinot Noir."

The waitress disappeared.

"Are you trying to get me drunk, or just impress me?"

"Loosen you up a bit, maybe. I wasn't sure if being a gentleman would impress you."

She smiled circumspectly. Her eyes drifted out from the darkened interior to the bright street outside. My eyes

257

followed. An open archway with an ornate wrought iron grill faced out onto Marine Avenue. Cars passed by, pedestrians too. I saw an older man go down the sidewalk wearing a captain's hat, blazer and cravat. The look went well with life on Balboa Island. It seemed to be all about shopping and eating and being lazily rich.

I looked back to find Doris staring at me again. The Pellegrino and Pinot Noir arrived. The waitress poured my goblet full of sparkling water. The waitress left and I offered a silent toast.

"I wish you'd just spill what's on your mind," she said after taking a drink.

"Well, first of all, I'm sorry about your husband."

"Is that why we're here?"

"I said I'm sorry about your husband, that's all. He seemed like a decent enough guy. He had your photo on his bed stand."

"Okay, you're just another cop."

"No. Just another private eye. But I happened to be there when the local cops were rifling through his place. I also happen to know that they're growing suspicious of your relationship with Rick."

Doris choked a bit on her Pinot Noir.

"It's all right. I have my own agenda here, so if we're keeping score, nothing you say to me will ever go beyond this table."

Doris stared, thinking.

"Dan had my photo next to his bed?"

I nodded.

"You were wearing high heels and Capri pants. The two of you looked pretty happy."

"My God, after all these years."

I nodded. I understood…after all these years.

"Well, I've made my share of mistakes," she went on. "And maybe divorcing Dan will go down as one of them, but I don't know what you're supposed to do when the passion has gone out of it."

"Go see a fortune teller."

"I did, or the equivalent. I hung around for seven more years, until what remained was like a glass of Scotch and soda leftover from last night's party. With a cigarette in it."

I gestured to let her know, I sympathized with that sentiment, too.

"But talk about feeling jilted," she said. "When I learned Dan had fallen head over heels for some schemer and changed his will…"

"What schemer?"

"I don't know. I only know he left me high and dry and gave everything to her. Even the life insurance policy."

"Is that why you got Jack to put the squeeze on him?"

Doris choked again on her Pinot Noir.

"So that's it," she said. "Who hired you? Dan's floozy?"

I shook my head.

"Well, I'm not saying another word until you tell me what's on your mind."

I nodded.

"What's that supposed to mean?"

"Just this," I said and nodded again.

She had a good sip of her wine and studied me. I waited, having learned long ago that most people abhor silence, in the same way that nature abhors a vacuum, and sure enough, Doris soon got going again.

"Jack was always an honest and hardworking employee, but he was my friend first. I knew him in college. At UCLA. Jack had lettered in football. From the news, I knew that he had bounced around a bit in the pros but never really made it big. When I ran into him at a bar down on the peninsula one Sunday afternoon, you could see he was growing lost in the world. This was a few years after he got out of the pros and he had already put on a lot of weight. Nothing like now, though."

Doris had another sip of wine and wiped daintily at her lipstick with the cloth napkin. The lunch crowd kept piling in around us, spoiling our quiet little corner of the world.

"So?" I said, hoping to encourage Doris along.

"So, I was already going with Dan at that point. Dan had already started the shipyard and I got Dan to hire Jack. Within a year, he was running the place, and has been ever since. "Well…" she added, remembering that Dan was dead and Jack was out of a job.

"You asked Jack to go down and reason with Dan, for old time's sake."

"Something like that."

Our food arrived. The waitress asked if we needed anything else. I asked for red pepper flakes and some extra parmesan. The waitress ran off to retrieve those things. Doris and I busied ourselves with napkins and buttering our bread. The waitress returned with my request and I dug in.

"Something like that," I repeated to Doris at the first wipe of my mouth. She looked up from her chicken marsala and wiped her mouth too.

"I called and asked Jack to talk with Dan, like you said. I didn't ask him to shoot anyone."

"Do you think he did?"

"I don't know. I think the police want me to believe that he did, figuring it would scare me into talking, but I have nothing else to tell them.

"Have you been able to speak with Jack since Dan was murdered?"

"No. Do you think Jack shot Dan?"

"I don't know either. When did you call Jack that day?"

"The police say it was around two in the afternoon but I honestly don't remember."

"And Jack never called you that night from the shipyard?"

"Nope. The police know that too. They were the ones who called me with the news."

I had a bite of my capellini, chased it with a belt of Pellegrino and wiped my mouth.

"What did you have on Dan?"

"That's none of your business."

"Fair enough. We'll leave that to the side for the moment. How did you come to know Rick and what did he have on Dan?"

Doris dabbed her mouth.

"Why don't you tell me all about your girlfriends?"

"For one thing, I don't have any. And two, none of the girls I know get involved with murder. At least as far as I know."

Doris leaned over the table and spoke so no one else could hear her.

"What do you want to know from me, Michael? If I asked Jack to kill my ex-husband over money? I didn't. If I know whether or not Jack decided to pull the trigger himself? I don't."

She leaned back into her chair.

"Shall we call it a day then or move on to the Scotch tossing contest?"

"We'll have to make it cheap Scotch. I'm a bit broke after that glass of Pinot Noir."

The look on Doris' face slowly softened.

"You are a charmer, Michael, but you haven't answered my question."

"No. You haven't answered mine. What did you have on Dan and how did you come to know Rick?"

She looked down as if penance was in order, then back out towards the street.

"I'll tell you about my relationship with Rick."

"That was my second choice."

"I know, but that's just the way it is."

I nodded and waved for her to go on.

"Okay, so all the girls I know play this game. If you want to meet someone who's a bit younger. And with a bit of money? You go to hang out in the bar at Five Crowns. You'll meet some frogs. But you'll meet some hunks too."

"And some jerks," I added.

Doris made a face, something between a grimace and a smile.

"Well, I was going to say, they all have money, Rick included."

"Does that really make it go down any easier?"

"A few days ago, I might have said yes. Today? Well, I think I've learned my lesson."

"Which is?"

"Stick to men my own age."

"How about just finding someone who'll be nice to you."

"They always are at the start."

"Rogues, aren't we?" I said.

Doris looked askance at me.

"So, are you satisfied now?" she asked me.

"No."

"I didn't think you would be."

I kept staring with my smile that wasn't really a smile.

"You want to know what I had on Dan and I can't tell you."

"It'll come out sooner or later, Doris. It always does."

She looked out towards the street.

"All right," I said. "I'm not going to grind on you but how about the object of Dan's affections. Can you tell me who that is?"

"No."

"You can't or you won't?"

"I don't know."

"Then how did you find out there was one?"

"Jack stumbled across some poetry on the company computer."

I raised my eyebrows.

"Yes, poetry. So, one day Jack asked Dan about it and Dan told Jack to keep his mouth shut. Guess he figured Jack's loyalty was greater to him than it was to me."

I waited but nothing more came.

"Is that it?" she asked.

"No."

"Okay, what else? I have to bury my ex-husband in two days and I'm really getting worn out by this."

"Did you kill him?"

"No," she said without hesitation.

"Do you think Rick had some reason to kill Dan?"

"I can't see why."

I pushed away from my meal and a Mexican busboy quickly ran off with the remains. Doris was still playing with the chicken part of her chicken marsala.

"What do you know about Dirk Vanderhof?"

Doris choked over her chicken.

"That's an old name," she said with a dab at her mouth.

"I understand he was friends with Dan at some point."

"A long, long time ago. About the time you saw me in those Capri pants and high heeled sandals."

"Nice look," I said.

"Thanks," she said.

"Were you friends with Vanderhof too?"

"We were all friends. Dirk was a number of years younger than we were, and something of a player. Always a different girl on his arm, but he and Dan did all right in real estate for a spell. That's how we ended up with the house in Laurel Lagoon."

"Do you think Vanderhof had some reason to kill Dan?"

"I don't know."

"You don't know."

She shook her head and looked away.

"Well, I have to tell you, Doris. I'm perplexed. Everybody loved Dan Colby."

"So?"

"So where's the motive for shooting him?"

"I don't know."

"I think you do."

"Look, if you're dying to know, I was saddened to hear of Dan's death. I've had pause to think of all the good times we once shared and they're not so easily replaced. That, if nothing else, has become clearer to me as the years go by."

263

I had been staring out through the ornate wrought iron grill while listening to Doris' soliloquy. A eucalyptus tree was rustling out there. The lunch crowd kept piling in and growing more animated around us.

"Who do you think killed Dan?" she asked me.

I looked back at her.

"I don't know. Maybe it has something to do with why Vanderhof came rushing down here to see you the other day?"

Doris' ears turned red. I shrugged.

"Sorry, but I just happened to be following him around."

"I don't even know why I'm talking to you," she said.

"Because you don't have much of a choice. See, I'm in this place where I know too much. In fact, just about enough to put me in a position of withholding evidence…The smart thing for me would be to go to the police and come clean. But guess who they're going to come looking for next if I do that?"

Doris absorbed what I had just said, took a sip of her wine and stared out at the street with a sigh.

"You know, I saw him about a month ago. Over on the peninsula."

"Saw who?" I said.

"Dirk Vanderhof. He was driving with the top open on his yellow Ferrari, and of all things, had Connie McPherson sitting next to him."

It was my turn to choke on my Pellegrino. I put my drink down and cleared my throat.

"What do you know about Connie McPherson?"

"Oh, she and her husband Steve came out of college about the same time as Dirk and quickly became a part of our crowd. That's all, really. They were the model couple, Connie a cheerleader, Steve the student body president. The all-American types. But getting married right out of high school the way they did? That's a lot to ask of two people."

"You mean sticking it out for sixty years?"

"People change," Doris said with a nod. "Anyway, this was long before Dirk became filthy rich. And before he and Elfie

264

had their little girl. When that happened, they quickly drifted off into their own little world and we rarely saw them."

"What do you know about the little girl?"

Doris looked away again, biting her lip, lost in thought.

"She was such an adorable little thing. Cried a lot but she was adorable."

Doris looked back.

"I mean a real screamer. It might have been colic. I don't know, but like I said, once Dirk and Elfie had her, we didn't see much of them anymore, so I don't know if she got any better. Of course, then..."

Doris drank from her wine and looked off in thought again.

"Anyway, back in the day, I always suspected Dirk had a thing for Connie, but my god, that was twenty years ago. I have no idea how they reconnected, but it sure looked like love that day."

I had been fiddling with my cloth napkin and threw it on the table. When I slipped a hundred dollar bill in the check holder, Doris looked disappointed.

"I guess we're skipping the Scotch."

"Sorry. I just realized I'm running late for an appointment."

"Oh," she said. "I hope it wasn't something I said."

"No, no. You've been very helpful."

I handed her my card.

"Oh, so you're that Michael Devlin."

"Yeah, that Michael Devlin, and before I go, I need to level with you, and to ask for your silence."

"Okay, I guess," she said.

"I had a connection with Audrey's husband. When he was killed, I had reason to go talk with Rick. When I did, he let on that these Mexican cartel boys were shaking him down and hired me to go look for them. The last I saw Rick, he left your house late and drove straight over to the shipyard. Then a guard appeared with a Doberman Pinscher and Rick raced off. But it was enough of a red flag for me."

"So you've been snooping around my house this whole time?" Doris said.

"I followed Rick over there. I followed him when he left. That's it."

Doris' ears were red again.

"Look. I understand how you feel but I think Rick is knee deep in trouble of some sort, and I think your life might be in danger because of it, so I'm advising you to stay away from him, if you can restrain yourself. And I'm asking you to keep your mouth shut about all of this. At least for a few days. All right?"

She stared, still looking violated.

"Please," I said.

"All right," she said finally. "I pretty much wrote Rick off the other night anyway."

"You're a smart girl to get away from him. With your looks, you ought to be able to find someone who truly appreciates you. Look for a kind heart first. It hasn't worked out all that well for me, but I like the way it sounds when I tell someone else."

"What about your heart?" she said.

"Oh, I'm damaged goods. And I definitely don't have any money."

I stood up. She stood up with me.

"Aren't you going to wait for the change?"

"It's close enough," I said. "She'll remember me as the last of the big spenders."

Doris offered a sardonic smile. We walked out to the sidewalk.

"I wish I had met you instead of Rick," she said.

"Those are the breaks," I said.

"So, am I going to hear from you again?"

"You've got my card. You call if something comes up. Either way, I'll touch base with you in the next few days. Just don't mention my name to Rick, whatever you do."

"I won't," she said. "You can count on me."

It was said by a woman who meant it, for better or worse, through thick and thin. Why she had decided to ditch Colby, or why Colby had failed to appreciate her was beyond me to understand.

Thinking it was appropriate, I offered Doris a cautious hug with one arm.

"Sorry about Dan."

"Those are the breaks," she said.

I watched her walk away. She looked back twice, once over her shoulder and once more as she turned onto the side street that led to her house.

I checked my watch. There was time to spare so I drove across the island and took the ferry over to the fun zone. As I turned right onto Balboa Blvd., the Ferris wheel was climbing high into the sky with the sound of screaming kids on a summer day.

At Coast Highway, I turned left and headed north. There was a nice stretch of coastline ahead and an hour or so for me to try and tie together all the loose ends.

South on Pacific Coast Highway

23

Barreling out over the river jetty, I left Newport Beach in my rearview mirror. Huntington Beach and a long stretch of crescent shoreline were straight ahead. Surf pawed all along it for miles. A jamboree of sunbathers littered the hot sand, like cookies on a flat sheet. There were beach umbrellas and suntan lotion and billows of smoke from all those hot dogs and hamburgers being grilled.

As a kid, I had been a denizen of these same beach towns and my mind flooded with images of those summer days long ago, the boys and me rushing home from the shore in the late afternoons and jumping into someone's backyard swimming pool with the sand still on our feet, this cheery vision of how middle-class life ought to be again in my heart, only that vision appeared to have careened out a highway to nowhere now, the arc of Southern California culture littered with more stragglers and loners than it was with the all-American dream. At least most of the people I knew had failed to follow the script. And even the ones who had tied the knot had failed to fill in the kids' part of the questionnaire and what remained in the wake of those decisions was often a lot of aimlessness, boredom and vice, and not necessarily in that order.

Where you might have bent a little here and there in the course of a marriage and found ways to compromise, you ended up in bed with another man's wife. Where you might have seen through to old age with a pile of grandkids and lasting memories at your feet, you were chasing around bars in your fifties and sixties, looking for a few more cheap thrills — hoping to fill in the emptiness and regrets left over from your questionable decisions.

Accepting my part in all of that, and tossing aside what remained into the scrapheap of heartaches and bad luck, my mind raced back to Steve McPherson's call a month earlier, telling me that Connie had filed for divorce. Saddened to see these childhood sweethearts calling it quits, I had reluctantly agreed to keep an eye on her, ready to strangle Connie myself after a few weeks of watching her clique of newly divorced, fifty-something girlfriends out playing the singles game; dancing until all hours, getting their panties wet at male stripper clubs and running personal ads on racy match sites. Grace alone said give it a year. Make sure the ink's dry on the divorce papers before you start calling the next clown in line a hero. You're breaking a man's heart, but suddenly Little Ms. Cheerleader could not have cared less.

And in all of that, I remembered a night when Connie and her friends had closed their favorite disco, only when their limo left at three in the morning, Connie was nowhere to be found. I had wondered that night where had Connie gone and with whom, and was back to wondering about it now.

I snapped out of my reveries to find myself passing through the shantytown looking commercial district of Sunset Beach. All these years later and its hippie era wooden facades were still intact. Some things died hard, for better or worse.

That brief stretch of highway quickly faded in my rearview mirror and I came alongside a shallow wetland. The rippled water was dotted with egrets, sand pipers and a colony of seagulls. Then the highway jogged away from the shore and up into a tangle of commercial development. I soon crossed a narrow saltwater inlet on a bridge, turned left onto 2nd Avenue, then left again onto Bay Shore Avenue, with Naples and yachts and million-dollar homes off to my left now, and everything smelling of money again.

At Ocean Boulevard, I turned right and started up a stretch of crescent coastline with a forest of high-rise condominium towers anchoring the sand. The jetty and harbor works jutted out into the bay just beyond the towers and the hump of Palos Verdes loomed as the last punctuation mark to this collage.

Ten minutes later, I was wandering back among the guts of the harbor. It did not take long to find the general area where I had instructed Nacho to meet me. I had played long odds, hoping the Feds were listening in on our conversation. If not, I was out on this island all by myself.

I passed the building with a white roof and continued on through that sea of cracked and aging asphalt. Mirages boiled up in the distance. I was definitely on a rendezvous with desolation, whatever else I had hoped to find.

Turning left past a truck crane, I parked in its shade and climbed out. It was hot. It was smoggy. It was hard to imagine anything good coming of a place like this.

I went along searching among the rows of containers. After a minute or so, I stopped in the shade. There was no sign of Nacho.

I noticed the door to the container in front of me was unlocked, so out of curiosity I pulled on the slide bolt and opened the door. I had my head half inside when I heard a voice barking out from behind me.

"Get down! Down on the ground! Right now!"

I looked back to find six men dressed in black, legs spread and guns drawn, taking aim at me with both hands. Having dared to look back, the one barking at me barked even louder.

"Get down!!! Right now!!!"

As soon as I was prone on the hot asphalt, they collectively ran up and someone cuffed me. I was lifted up like a sack of potatoes and shoved face first against the hot metal of a shipping container.

Having searched me, I was turned around. All six men surrounded me, none of them looking happy.

"Private dick," one of them said with my wallet open.

"Yeah, I'm a private dick. Where's Dick and Tom?"

"What are you talking about?" one of them said. The name tag on his shirt read Decker.

"I was roughed up a few days ago by a couple of boys, claiming to be from the big leagues. I figured you must be them, if you know what I mean."

"Somebody roughed you up, all right, but I don't know any Dick and Tom. There's just us, if you know what I mean."

He turned to the other men and nodded.

"Take him in out of the heat so we can have a chat. You, Daniels, search the car and bring it around."

Decker turned back to me.

"You'd better have a good reason for poking around up here or you won't be going home tonight."

They put a bag over my head and assisted me into the back of a car. From the direction, I assumed we were driving farther back into the harbor. When the car stopped, I was led out and into a building. From the echo and the heat, I suspected it was an empty metal warehouse.

We went up some stairs and into a smaller room. Once I had been seated, they took the bag off my head. There were no windows or décor, save for a couple of extra chairs. Decker sat across from me, chair turned around backwards, his arms across the back. One of his goons had leaned against the wall, keeping an eye on things.

"You mind about the handcuffs?"

Decker nodded and the other man came over to remove them. I rubbed my sore wrists and stared at Decker.

"What were you doing up here?" he asked me.

I had a couple of cute answers in mind but decided to try the truth and see how that went — at least part of the truth. I wasn't really sure what I could tell Decker, without getting myself into further trouble.

"It started with these Mexican and Russian boys shaking me down."

"Describe."

I did.

"So?" Decker said.

"For some reason both of them think I have something they want. The Mexicans, knowledge about a shipping container. The Russians, I don't know what they're after. Anyway, the Mexicans had been shaking down one of my clients and went through my office last night. Made a real mess of things. I'm guessing it was the Mexicans. I had a number for them and called to arrange a meeting up here. Gave them a story, figuring my phone was being tapped and that Dick and Tom would show up. Maybe the Russians too. It was all a tidy little plan, with a happy ending, until you showed up prematurely and scared everybody off."

"You have reason to think these boys are still up here in the harbor right now?"

"Who knows? They could be halfway to Cancun by now. Or Vladivostok."

Decker nodded at junior leaning against the wall. He poked his head out the door and whispered to somebody on the other side. Then he was back to leaning against the wall.

"This Dick and Tom," Decker said. "You have any idea who they are?"

"Like I said, I figured they were you. Now I don't know what to think."

"Who's the client they were shaking down?"

"I'd tell you about my fiduciary relationship, but I'm guessing you're not going to buy it."

"You're guessing right. Not if you do want to go home tonight."

Knowing I had to give up somebody, I chose Rick.

"Rick Duncan," I told Decker. "He owns Magellan Ltd."

Decker nodded as if he wasn't the least bit interested but he shared a look with junior and this time junior left the room. Decker looked back at me.

"What do you know about Rick Duncan?"

"Everything you can read in the papers."

"And why did he hire you?"

"To get rid of the Mexican boys, and maybe to find out if his partner was on the wrong side of the law."

"Who's his partner?"

"Why are you asking me questions you already know the answers to?"

He nodded.

"Did you find her?"

"Yeah."

"And?"

"She ran off again."

He waited until I told him a tale about the Salton Sea. He seemed to like the tale all right, but not the ending.

"And you haven't seen her since."

"Give me a break," I said. "Had I known about you beforehand, I would have waved at her husband's funeral a few hours ago."

Decker nodded.

"And you don't know anything more about these Mexican or Russian characters?"

"Don't know them from Adam."

"You got that number for the Mexicans with you?"

I read it off to him from memory.

"You got some other numbers up there in your head?"

"That's the only one that comes to mind right now."

Junior came back in and whispered into Decker's ears. He looked back at me.

"You've got a lot of phones that don't go anywhere. How come?"

"I like my privacy."

"Or you've got something to hide."

"They're the same thing, when you get right down to it."

"All right. You're free to go. Your stuff's in your car, but don't run off anywhere."

Junior waved at the door.

"Maybe I'm not done yet," I said to Decker. "Maybe I've got some questions for you."

"Like what?"

"Like who are you?"

"We don't discuss that."

"Then who are Dick and Tom?"

"Don't know them from Adam."

Decker offered a smile.

"I'll look into it, but maybe you've been running around with the wrong crowd."

"Maybe I have."

Junior waved again and I followed him out into the brilliant sunlight. The inside of my Impala was hot enough to bake cookies. I climbed in, hit the power window buttons and turned the air-conditioner on full blast.

Working my way back out of the harbor, I puzzled over why Decker hadn't known more about Nacho. That seemed to reinforce my present theory. That Colby had gone off the reservation in his deal with Nacho. It fit with what Audrey had told me about him too. It fit with everything I knew. The core issue here was some sort of espionage business involving the Russians. What that was, I had no idea.

As to Dick and Tom, either Decker was lying to me or those two clowns were pulling my leg. Sure, these intel folks had long been known for their aversion to working together, but I was inclined to believe the latter. Dick and Tom had been so eager to track down Audrey, and yet had failed to make Cliff's funeral. That made no sense, unless they were a couple of goons, working on something private. But private for whom? I had a theory on that too, but I wasn't sure it made any more sense than the other theories I had cooked up.

With nothing better to do while I mulled over this mystery, I decided to drive up and see Vanderhof and his big shot Hollywood production. I had visions of megaphones and scarves around the neck and lots of barking.

Before heading north, I located the nearest AT&T store and bought a new batch of burner phones. Back out in the parking lot, I threw all my old ones into the bed of a construction pickup and smiled at the vision of Decker and his pals screeching to a halt in front of a residential remodel.

Back in my car and with the air-conditioner blasting, I checked Google map, considering which route to take. Going over Palos Verdes and up the coast through Manhattan and Hermosa Beach was the straightest shot, but it was to confront a twenty-five mile tangle of boulevards and stop signals. I jumped onto the Harbor Freeway instead, took the 405 north and cut back down to the coast through Santa Monica. From there going north, it was a lovely drive. Save for a few more stoplights and a lot of rich folks building gaudy castles down on the shore, it could have still been the sixties.

When I reached Malibu proper, I took a loop de loop down towards the coast. A maze of back streets eventually dumped me out onto Westward Beach Road, which I followed down to an asphalt parking lot that bordered the shore. Vanderhof's circus was at the far end of the parking lot, out near a point. I parked a quarter mile away and followed a hiking trail along the bluff. A chain link fence separated me from the street. An embankment sloped steeply down from the path to the parking area. The slope was sparsely covered in shrubs and shaded with regularly spaced cypress trees.

When I came abreast of the action, I sat down in the shade of a tree to watch. There was enough motorized crap down there to give the Seabees a thrill; cranes, semi-trucks, booms, skip loaders and a boatload of box trailers. One of the trailers served as the wardrobe department. Six more had been placed end to end as dressing rooms. A twenty-foot long grill had been set up in front of a catering truck, serving everything from steak to salmon. There must have been fifty grips scurrying around at work, a good handful of them scurrying directly around Mr. Big Shot Hollywood Director. He had skipped the scarf and traded his beret in for a straw hat. I spotted Vanderhof off to

275

the side, talking to some doll. Good-looking dolls were loitering all over the set.

At Mr. Big Shot Director's instruction, a crane started to move a handful of enormous set pieces from a storage area to center stage. The pieces amounted to three hills and the parts of an ancient ruin. A long, narrow pool of water was made to look like a stream in the country. I guessed it was Tuscany, circa 1000 AD, made from steel frames and painted foam.

With everything in place, the actors took their places for an intended skirmish. Mr. Big Shot called "action" then "cut, cut" a moment later. The hills weren't right. The actors went back to their dressing rooms while the hills were repositioned.

My god, I thought. All this to keep us from boredom at night. They could have fed ten thousand poor souls for the rest of their lives at what it cost. Some values. If this wasn't madness, I did not know what was.

There was a thought to go down and let Vanderhof know I had made it but my heart wasn't into it. Instead, I called Nacho. He wasn't happy.

"Listen, cabrón. Why ju bring all your friends along?"

"I didn't invite them along. They must have traced your phone."

"Or jours, ju pinche gringo."

"Yeah and they're probably listening in on us right now. Would you like to say hello?"

"No, I just want my fucking shit, cabrón. Now where is it?"

"I already told you, Nacho. Your shits up in the harbor but this thing is way too hot to touch now. You'd better call me back in a day."

He went off in Spanish. Not having any better card to play, I tried beating the bushes a bit, just to see what it might flush out.

"Look, Nacho. Why don't you get in touch with Vanderhof and see what he can do?"

"What are ju talking, gringo? I don't know no one named Banderhof. Now get my shit or jou're dead. ¿Comprendez?"

"And I'm telling you. We need to let things cool off for a few days. Try me again on Wednesday. I'm not touching this thing again until I know the Feds are off my back."

I hung up on Nacho and stared down at Vanderhof. He had his arm around another Hollywood doll, all full of himself and rotten to the core, but maybe not quite as rotten as I had thought him to be. I ditched the phone under a bush and got up to leave. There was an empty feeling in my gut. All my theories were leading me nowhere.

Walking north, I passed by a handsome, middle-aged gentleman on the other side of the chain link fence, sitting atop his beach cruiser and taking in the action with a smile. The pair of washed cotton pants and flip-flops and polo shirt spoke of money. He smiled and nodded as I went by. I nodded back.

Wow, I thought with a quick look over my shoulder. It's the winner of the Pierce Brosnan look-a-like contest. Then it hit me. Hey, that is Pierce Brosnan. He didn't look quite the same without all the camera work. Then probably nobody did.

In need of a good, long drive and a chance to think things over, and wanting to avoid rush hour traffic on the 405, I reversed my route back to Long Beach and took Coast Highway heading south. Day was fading to dusk and dusk to shadows and shadows to thoughts of romance.

When I came to a traffic jam backed up at the north end of Newport Beach, romance went right out the window. The traffic going into Corona del Mar was even worse. A brief respite followed as I loped along the open country north of Laurel Lagoon. Then I was back in another traffic snarl.

Like every local with an affection for controlling his own destiny, I took a left up the first side street and worked my way south along High Drive. Passing by Dan Colby's old dead-end street, I considered going up there to poke around but felt a stronger urge to get back to my office. Sit down and draw a diagram with everybody on the same page, arrows and the likes.

Stepping into my office, I nearly gasped. It never failed. No matter how many times I had arranged for Teresa to stop by and clean things up, I always forgot she was coming until I walked in the door.

The wood desk glowed. The stack of mail was arranged neatly on top. The glass on all the pictures sparkled. The place smelled of furniture polish and Pine Sol. It looked as tidy as a British officer's headquarters.

I sat down at the desk and quickly sorted through the mail. No checks. Thanks, Jake. I'll get the check in the mail first thing tomorrow. Oh well. What was the worst thing that could happen? You died, and I feared death less than living these days.

I pulled a blank piece of paper out of the printer, made a big circle and wrote down everybody's name around the edges of it. Then I started drawing arrows here and there, until it looked like a kid's version of an astrology chart.

Aw hell, I thought and wadded up the piece of paper. Everybody knew everybody and Vanderhof was right in the thick of it. So what did that prove? Like a chess player, I kept thinking I had my opponent cornered, only to find myself checkmated instead. My tired brain wanted there to be one person, one gun, one victim, when it had probably taken two or three people and a boatload of bad motives to get Connie and Cliff and Dan Colby all killed in a couple of days.

There was a thought to have one of those dinner parties. Tuxedos and gowns at seven. Everyone darting looks around the table. We'd solve the whole mystery over snifters of sherry and beef medallions.

I flicked on Cannonball Adderley and settled into the growing darkness with *Dancing in the Dark* beginning to play, and with those age-old feelings doing battle in my heart. How did you start anew? I thought of Audrey's colors and red hair and my heart was swept away. Devotion, that's all I wanted. I missed that feeling of purity.

When *Dancing in the Dark* came to an end, I played it again, thinking of Elfie now. I saw her reaching up with a hand to my wounds. "There, there."

So sweet. So why did I not feel devotion towards her? I had no idea. The things that passed for sanity in a man's heart.

Somewhere around the tenth time the same song had repeated on my CD player, I heard the sound of high heels come in the front door and smiled to myself. At the first knock, I went to answer it. The hallway was filled with the umbrage of twilight and Elfie's eyes flickered in that darkness. She wore nearly the same thing she had worn the previous evening, only in a lime color now instead of cream. I liked that in a woman. She had a style. She stuck with it. If only she filled me with devotion instead of desire.

I invited her in and closed the door. She stood close, looking up at me.

"I'm in big trouble," I told her.

"Aw, there, there," she said and touched my face.

"I've dreamed of you saying those words all day."

"There, there," she said again. "It's very touching to see a man's emotions."

"May I get you a drink?" I said.

"Perhaps later. I was thinking of Sorrento's and a bite to eat first…What?" she said at seeing me hesitate.

"Sadly, it's probably best if I'm not seen with you in public at this point."

"Even with Dirk having settled?"

I remained staring at her.

"Well, all right," she said, looking a bit hurt but ready to be a trooper. "Let's call for take-out and I'll hide behind the door when they deliver."

I smiled at her joke through the burden of my own mixed up emotions.

"Forgive me?" I said.

"There, there," she said with a gentle touch of her hand to my face.

279

24

At a little past one in the morning, I turned up Dan Colby's dead-end street and pulled to the curb several houses down from his driveway. The neighborhood was completely dark and quiet but I sat there for a long spell, watching and waiting to make sure no lights flickered on in the adjacent homes before I climbed out and headed up towards the house. Yellow caution tape still circled Colby's front yard. I slipped under it and followed a path around to the back. The barren hillside rose up behind me.

When something snapped in a gathering of trees halfway up the hill, I froze. The sound continued until it became clear that it was a wild creature of some sort. Probably a possum, grubbing around for a meal, or a skunk. It was something slow moving.

Reassured that I was alone, I quietly ascended a short set of wooden steps to a back porch. The entry door on the landing was locked. Peering inside, I saw the door led into a laundry room and from there into the kitchen. I got out my lock kit and went to work. Several times, I stopped to look and listen. That creature was still grubbing away up above me but all else was quiet.

A few minutes later, I slipped inside and was greeted with the lingering scent of cat litter and TV dinners. The cat was gone but I could still picture it perched up there on the curio cabinet, fur raised, pricked with fear and menace.

Stalled there in the dark, the memory of Elfie returned to my thoughts. Her scent was all over me. I wanted her again, but that desire was haunted by my longings for devotion. There was no understanding it.

I got back to the purpose of my visit — to see if Colby had left the code for unlocking the flash drive lying around his house somewhere. My first impulse had been to go poke around the shipyard, but as Rick had learned, a reception party was waiting for you down there. Whether or not the house still held any secrets, at least I had it all to myself.

I went up to the third-floor loft first and grew lost in the view. There were lights from a pleasure craft a mile or so out on the black sea. Why that always seemed so tremendously romantic to me, I had no idea, but it did. Just you and a doll and a bottle and some fun.

I looked down at the hillside below the house. It sloped off precipitously, leaving one to feel as if you were leaning over the edge of a hundred-story building. With one last look out at boat lights, I turned to face Colby's office. There wasn't much to offer hope, aside from his desk and a filing cabinet. As already well noted by Whalen, his computer was long gone, though I did not see that as a major setback. A man of Colby's age was just as likely to scribble the code down on a piece of paper as he was to file it away on a hard drive.

I opened the top drawer of his oak filing cabinet and checked the labels of each folder with a pen flashlight in one hand, searching for any suggestion of a hidden code. Having checked all the labels, I started rifling through the contents of each folder. I did this with all three drawers and gave up. It would take a day to examine each piece of paper properly.

I was about to close the bottom drawer when the heading on one of the folders jumped out at me.

Yours, Always, it read.

I opened the folder and found a dedication page. It read like a testament of unrequited love. Everything Colby owned, he was giving to this woman. Who the object of his affections was, it did not say, but all that would become clear upon his death. I quickly thumbed through the accompanying collection of poems, hoping to discover a name.

As poets went, there were worse hacks than Colby. His words were in places humorous, self-deprecating and even touching at times, but I found nothing clearly identifying the woman. These were the words of a man who, at least according to Vanderhof, had been a swinger at one time, the life of the party, but had retreated into a monk like shell in his final years, writing poems to a woman who, from all appearances, had not loved him in return. Yet Colby persisted, hoping that one day she would come to reciprocate his devotion.

Then, with another last shuffling through the poems, a line caught my eye. The woman Colby loved "had too firm a grip on her own destiny," and the poems were his attempt to "crack open and reveal her more vulnerable core."

I put things away, closed the file cabinet and stared back out at the lights on the black sea. What fools we were. The more we invested our deepest and most ancient dreams in another human being, the more unattainable those dreams became. Hopefully you enjoyed the chase itself because the prize would always be one step out of reach.

Maybe the young starlet who had settled into this house all alone had it right; a couple of cats, a boy servant to fulfill your primal needs and none of the heartaches. Her fans could all take a hike if they didn't like it. She'd wave to them once a year from the Swallows' Day parade over at the mission and get back to her private world of debauchery.

It was me, without the cats, the beauty and the fortune. I wasn't even sure we shared the debauchery. All we had in common was our love for solitude and a sense that no one could hurt us. We'd do that all by ourselves.

With one last look around the room with my flashlight, I headed down to the second story. Jack Oliver had once told me that he kept his most vital papers hidden away in the freezer in case of a fire and that sounded like something Colby might do.

I found the refrigerator still purring away in the kitchen and opened the freezer. It was still packed with frozen TV dinners and Häagen-Dazs ice cream. Like the ice cream, the TV dinners were gourmet. I shoved things this way and that, looking for something hidden but came up empty. If I wanted Stouffer's lasagna tomorrow night, I was in luck.

I checked the refrigerator section too and was about to move on to the rest of the house when something struck me. One of the ice cream containers had felt empty. I reopened the freezer door and removed the lid from a quart of butter pecan. There was a plastic bag inside with a piece of paper inside the bag. I opened the zip lock, unfolded the paper and found a number with at least a hundred digits written on it.

Well I'll be damned.

I took the piece of paper, put everything else back the way I had found it and slipped out through the laundry room door. There was no sign of anyone watching as I walked down the street to my car.

Some animal instinct was urging me to return to my office but I headed home and tossed and turned for a few hours with my thoughts of three women. Boats out on a black sea were involved, faraway places, dreams of things that probably could never be obtained in this world.

Around midmorning, I went into the office and called Teresa.

"I need to talk with you."

"I'm here," she said.

"I'm on my way over."

She was out watering her garden when I arrived. Rusty walked over to greet me. I petted him with the usual sense of trepidation.

"It's okay. I gave him a bath this morning."

I nodded, no less reluctant. Three hours later and he already smelled of ripe old socks.

"I came to pick up the flash drive. Is it conveniently nearby?"

She turned off the hose and went to retrieve it in the back of the house. She was gone several minutes.

"Dare I ask where it was hidden?" I said when she had returned.

"Inside a door lock," she said quietly. "There's just enough room to slip it in next to the striker mechanism."

I smiled, amused by her precise use of mechanical terms. Most men would have referred to the striker as a "thingy"

"Did you find the code?"

"I think so."

"Off to save the world then?"

"I'd much rather pack up and head down to Baja for a few weeks."

"But," she said.

"But…Amazing how much that one conjunction can get you into trouble. Yes, but two men and a woman are dead and another man is looking at life in prison. That means somebody is getting away with murder. I don't know how you can throw up your hands under the circumstances. My mind certainly won't leave it alone."

"I know it's the noble part of you, Michael," she said.

"But," I said.

She smiled. I started to leave and turned back.

"Thanks for cleaning up the office. It's always a delight to open the door."

"You're welcome."

"I'll send you a check when I can."

She nodded and turned the water back on.

Back at the office, I immediately called Kenny.

"We need to talk."

"I'm here."

A minute later, I was bounding up his stairs.

"Here," I said, holding out the piece of paper. Kenny rolled his chair backward across the office and took it.

"Far out. Looks like a respectably long prime number."

"Maybe half the length of the universe to crack it?"

"Something like that."

I stood at Kenny's shoulder while he pulled up some software and methodically typed in the hundred digits. When he was done and hit enter, the gibberish on the computer screen magically became legible.

"Far out," Kenny said again and rolled out of the way. "The printer's on if you want to make copies."

He went to work at a bank of computer screens across from me. I sat down and scanned through the file, page by page. There were records of various transactions, for the most part. Al-Hamad's name came up, Magellan Ltd. Rick and Audrey, but not Nacho or Vanderhof.

A series of scanned documents followed, what appeared to represent some form of blackmail. One of the documents was heavily redacted. On the bottom of that page there were a series of numbers in feet and inches. It read like the coordinates on a set of blueprints.

Not knowing what to make of it, and having reached the end of the file, I leaned back with a sigh. Dirty deeds, maybe, but nothing specific about the shipping container or any kind of espionage.

I deleted the temporary file from the screen and slipped the flash drive into my pocket. What in god's name now? Nothing was any clearer to me than when I had started.

Kenny looked up from his work.

"You don't look very cheery."

"It's not exactly what I had expected."

"Not to be philosophical or anything, but when is life ever exactly what we had expected?"

"Not to be cute or anything, but some disappointments are more disappointing than others."

"So, end of story?" he said.

"No, just that much more I can't explain. By the way, anything more on Audrey?"

"She's banged her credit card a few times, but nothing out of the ordinary. She hasn't been any farther than San Clemente."

I stared out the windows, shaking my head.

"What?" Kenny said.

"Oh, I saw her yesterday at Cliff's funeral."

I looked back at him.

"The red hair and pale skin. They utterly disarm me. I can't seem to stop myself from falling in love with her."

"I could see that. The colors aren't very common. Think maybe you knew her back on Orion?"

"Pretty sure of it. I think she's supposed to be home making me dinner."

I stood up.

"Anyway, Whalen won't let go of the idea that she shot her husband and Dan Colby, so before too long she'll be wishing she was back on Orion, too. Probably already does."

I stopped at the door.

"Keep an eye on her."

"Will do. Oh, by the way. Where do I send my bill?"

"Send it to Whalen. That ought to perk him up."

Kenny laughed. I shrugged and left. He was always a good sport about the money, but I still felt lousy about not being able to pay him.

Back at my desk, I sat there for over an hour, drumming my fingers and considering what to make of the flash drive. Nacho and Vanderhof did a couple of laps in my head, Dick and Tom, too. In less than twenty-four hours, Whalen would be showing up with handcuffs. Something had to give. I had few options left. Maybe stir up a hornet's nest and see what happened. One more time, I had sensed the fog lifting only to have it close in on me again. I needed more to go on, one more piece to the puzzle.

Thinking of Rick and Doris, I pulled up my GPS program and found the little general had returned to her nest. That was curious. Doris had said she was done with him. Then why let the punk back in? Cutting her some slack, I pictured Rick barging in and Doris being too acquiescent to resist.

There was a thought to drive over and listen in on their conversation but what was the point? Whatever Doris and Rick knew, they were no longer sharing it with each other.

Nacho, Audrey, Vanderhof and the Russians, therein laid my best shot at solving this mystery, but two of them weren't talking, the Russians had mysteriously disappeared and Nacho was ready to pull my fingernails off one by one the first chance he had.

I glanced at the clock. It was a little before twelve. I decided to feed my empty stomach and started down towards the beach on foot. There had been a thought to hit the Surf & Sand but I was in no mood to fight the traffic. Besides, you could take in the blue sea from any beachfront eatery in Laurel Lagoon, be it five-star or a dive. I hoofed it across Coast Highway to this French restaurant owned by a Persian couple. Their rear veranda overlooked the rolling lawns and wooden boardwalk of Main Beach and was nicely hidden away by two Ficus trees. The food was lousy but I was mostly there for the view.

I tried their version of an ahi sandwich, thinking no one could screw that up, but they did. The sourdough bun was hard. Everything inside of it was dry and tasteless. I sat staring out at the sea, wondering why these folks didn't serve up something they knew, like couscous.

When a breeze stirred in the Ficus trees, the riddle of Zen returned to my thoughts. Zen did not require that you abandon this world and retreat to a cave in order to experience it. Zen was right here, right now, and yet nowhere. It was moving through space and time without duality.

With that thought, I had a sudden feeling of weightlessness, yet the minute I tried to hold the feeling fast, it disappeared. That was Zen. The act of wanting something was to become duality again.

I settled on this image of my spirit on the wind and left it at that.

When the waitress stopped by with the check, I told her she could take away my half-eaten sandwich. I lied about the thing being any good.

With a check of my watch, I decided to take a stroll down the boardwalk. The sun was high and hot on my head as I walked along. A fine dusting of sand covered the worn, wooden planks.

It took me all of two seconds to realize that I was out of my league. Kids splashing in the surf, dolls in bikinis playing beach volleyball, football jocks playing paddleboard down by the shore, this was for the half-naked and habitually young at heart, and, somehow, I had forgotten how to be either of those things.

What has happened to me? But a few years back, I was down here every afternoon frolicking in the surf like a dolphin. Now I could not remember the last time I had thrown on a pair of swim trunks. It was the black hole of love. I had fallen in and could not get back out. Once you had loved with all your heart and it went south, you had passed through the event horizon and were doomed forever to live in that singularity. Or so it seemed with my destiny.

At the end of the boardwalk, I started up the narrow, winding path along the bluff. A nice breeze stirred up from the ocean as I ascended. Near the top of the bluff, I found my favorite bench uninhabited and sat there beneath a whispering cypress tree. The coast unfolded in blues and whites to the south. My little Baja beach place was far, far off somewhere in that direction.

I glanced back at the shore directly below me. Wall-to-wall beach towels continued en masse all the way up to the old Laurel Lagoon Hotel. The hotel's foundation was anchored in the sand. The walls were brilliantly white in the sun. People packed its upper terrace, having lunch. Lounge chairs were lined up directly below the terrace, the hotel guests all oiled up and getting a tan. I watched a waiter come down the stairs to the sand with a tray of cocktails.

Beyond the hotel, the beach towels slowly dissipated along a sweeping crescent cove, that cove followed by a rocky point, then another sandy cove, then another rocky point, beyond which, the coast disappeared from view until the headlands at Doheny. Looking up at the hills behind town, million-dollar homes cascaded down the slopes, draped in bougainvillea and palm trees. The smell of money was everywhere you looked, and without it, you couldn't buy into this town anymore.

My thoughts turned back towards Steve. He was sitting there right now, looking at twenty-five to life for killing his wife. In one of my darker moments, lying alone late at night, I had found myself questioning his innocence. The idea of him strangling Connie was nearly impossible for me to conceive, or strangling anyone, for that matter. And still I wondered. What if he was playing me for a fool?

I tried to put the thought out of my mind and headed back towards Coast Highway. At the crosswalk, I heard some kids screaming down at the shore and looked back through the tinted windows of a fish joint, the days of my own youth calling to me again along that blue and white coastline.

The light changed and I turned back towards the world of men. Halfway across the highway, my phone rang. It was Audrey.

"Michael."

She sounded desperate.

"Yeah. What's going on?"

"Please. Can you come help me?"

I hesitated.

"Please," she said again. "I'll explain everything as soon as you get here."

"All right. Where are you?"

"Where I was right after Cliff got killed. Do you know what I mean?"

"Yes."

"Can you come right away?"

"Yes. I'm in Laurel Lagoon. I'll jump in my car right now."

25

I took the alley around to the backside of my office building and climbed into the Impala. The trunk was symbolic of my life, shot full of holes, but one call and I was off on my steed, ready to save a princess.

In that state, I broke various traffic laws, made Doheny Beach in under ten minutes and turned right just before the highway went over the knoll and down into town. The sprawling, undeveloped point at Smuggler's Cove was on my right. A spur on my left led me down a precipitous bluff to the harbor. That tree shrouded lane wound alongside the boat docks and waterfront restaurants. Directly adjacent to the yacht club, I took another spur back up towards Coast Highway and pulled into the wooded, resort entrance on my right.

I had been listening to a satellite radio station and a news bulletin came on as I was parking. A shootout had taken place somewhere in San Juan. Looking that way, I spotted two helicopters circling up in the general vicinity of Audrey's house. I hurried into the hotel.

"Audrey Black," I told the receptionist at the front desk.

"Your name?"

"Michael Devlin."

The receptionist checked my name off a list.

"Room 243."

I skipped the elevator and dashed up the stairs. When I knocked on the door, Audrey quickly opened it. Her hair was up and her ears blushing from the heat. Sweat had beaded up on the back of her neck. The French doors were open to the harbor and coastline looking south.

She waved me in, looked both ways down the hall, closed the door and threw herself against my chest.

"Thank you for coming."

My lips were at her neck and ears. I wanted to kiss them, and almost did.

After a moment, I pulled away and looked into Audrey's eyes.

"What's going on? I saw helicopters circling up by your house. Does that have something to do with you?"

She nodded.

"Some men showed up at my mother's place a couple of hours ago looking for me and were holding her hostage."

"Were?"

"Yes. It sounds like the Russians you had mentioned came first and then the Mexicans and there was a big shoot out and by the time the police arrived, everyone had disappeared."

"How do you know all of this?"

"My sister called."

"Just like that? 'Hi. I'm over here at Mom's place and just wanted to let you know we're in a big shootout?'"

"No. My Mom called my sister as soon as the men had disappeared and my sister hurried right over. And then she called me, asking where I was. She's such a bitch."

I smirked.

"She is."

"But they're all right."

"Yes, thank god."

"Okay. What else do you know?"

"I know someone went through my place last night while I was gone. Made a complete mess of it."

"But you don't know who."

Audrey shook her head.

"I assumed the Mexicans but I guess it could have been the Russians. Anyway, the police have turned the whole

293

neighborhood into a big circus so I don't think it would be such a great idea, me showing my face over there right now. I told my sister I was out of town on business and she gave me a bunch of crap."

Audrey hid her face in my chest again. I lifted her chin.

"I'm going to ask you again. Did you kill Cliff?"

She shook her head.

"Colby?"

She shook her head.

"Connie McPherson?"

She looked away. I pulled her chin back gently.

"What are you hiding from me?"

She stared.

"You know what I learned yesterday?"

She shook her head.

"That Connie McPherson and Vanderhof were having an affair."

I watched Audrey's eyes dart about to the rhythm of her thoughts.

"Still think Vanderhof had nothing to do with this mess?"

"I don't know." She sighed. "I'll tell you anything you want but there's one thing I just can't discuss."

"Audrey. How can I possibly help you if you won't level with me?"

"What I refuse to discuss has nothing to do with what's happening now."

"How do you know?"

"Because it's ancient history. I don't even know if what this person told me is true but I promised never to repeat it, to anyone, and that's the way it's going to stay."

"Christ, Audrey. You're leaving me with one hand tied behind my back."

"I'm sorry."

I stared at her.

"At least tell me one thing."

"What?"

"You said someone had told you. Who was that person?"

"Dan Colby."

"And to honor of the dead, you're going to keep his secrets."

She stared for a long moment before looking away. Again, I pulled her chin back.

"Do you have any idea what Dan was up to with this shipment?"

"No. He had said something about making a small fortune on the deal but that's all I know."

"And then the two of you would live happily ever after."

"That was his idea, not mine."

"And you never led him on."

"No. Never."

I kept staring.

"Okay, Michael. Dan and I had some fun after my marriage stopped working. Is that what you wanted to hear?"

"As your occasional business partner."

She sighed.

"Really? You've never gotten carried away like that? Someone makes you laugh and seems to understand all your problems and the next thing you know…"

"You're in the sack together."

"Please. You make it sound so cheap. I did enjoy Dan's company. It just wasn't love for me, so when he started talking about the two of us living happily ever after, I grew really uncomfortable and started pushing him away."

I kept staring.

"Please don't look at me like that."

"No, it's all right, Audrey. I understand. We've all been there. It just doesn't get us any closer to solving our problems."

"Actually, it might," she said. "At least part of them."

My eyebrows went up.

"Dan told me once that he had a secret safe in his house. The idea was that if something ever happened to him, he wanted to be sure I was taken care of. I suppose if he had anything those Mexicans wanted, that's probably where it would be hidden."

"And you know where this safe is?"

She nodded.

"And the combination?"

"I think I know how to figure it out."

"And you never thought to go look for yourself?"

"I thought about it."

I waited.

"I'm not nearly as corrupt as you think."

"No, I suppose not."

"Thanks."

I held her close for a moment as penance and pulled away.

"Sorry...Go on."

"Dan had said there was a folder of poems written for me in his file cabinet and the combination would be hidden inside it somewhere. I don't know exactly how you were supposed to figure that out. I guess a person would understand by looking."

"And you want me to go look?"

She nodded.

"All right."

While we stared at each other, Audrey fell into my arms again.

"Oh Michael. I've got to put an end to this but I don't know how."

She pulled back to look at me.

"Do you understand how mixed up I am? My husband's death? And this crazy mixed up arms deal?"

I nodded.

"So? Is this making any sense to you?"

"About Colby?"

She nodded.

"Yeah. I had already talked to this Nacho character and basically knew what was going on."

"You already knew? And have been playing me along this whole time?"

"I needed to know what you knew."

"Oh god. You don't even trust me."

"Trust you? Where have you trusted me in all of this? One minute you're here, the next minute you've disappeared again?!"

She looked down, rubbing her forehead.

"I'm sorry, Michael."

"Yeah, well, just to be clear, that kind of behavior's never going to cut it with me. There when you need me but nowhere to be found when I need you?"

"I said I'm sorry."

"Okay. But I've got to be perfectly clear about this. I've had enough of that kind of crap to last me a lifetime You want my help? That's got to stop."

She looked up and nodded. After a moment, I nodded back and continued.

"I talked with Nacho yesterday and it sounds like Colby was planning to divert that shipment down to Mexico somehow. A container full of small arms like that? Delivered to a cartel? It would be worth four or five times its value in Liberia. Maybe ten, twenty million. Enough to get you started on a little island somewhere. But as to the Russians and what they want? I have no idea."

"I guess Al-Hamad would know the answer to that one."

"I suppose. Not that it's going to do us any good. Because until these people get what they want, or they're dead, or in jail, this will keep happening. Are you ready to go to talk to the police now?"

"I already told you. I can't. That's why I called you."

She pressed herself up against me tenderly.

"Michael. I've never really trusted a man before in my life but I'm trusting you now. I'm in your hands. Tell me what you want me to do."

"I already told you."

"Michael, please. Anything but that."

"Yeah…Well, first of all, Nacho can forget about getting his hands on those guns. Not with the Feds buzzing around. Our only hope is to find a down payment in Colby's safe and make peace. He won't like it but if we can get rid of these cartel boys, we'll only have the Russians to deal with. That and three murders to solve."

I raised my eyebrows again.

"Of course, you still don't know anything about that, right?"

She shook her head.

"I honestly don't."

"Okay. Well, whether or not Nacho killed Colby, I'm guessing we can pin his death on him. That leaves Cliff and Connie. No ideas at all? Any reason to think Colby might have killed your husband?"

"I don't know. I don't think so."

"Okay. Well, remember what you just promised?"

She nodded.

"Okay, because I can only solve so much and things can only be so clean between us if you're being completely level with me."

"I told you everything I know."

"Almost."

"I don't know who killed Cliff or Connie. Or Dan."

I stared.

"I don't."

I stared.

"Can we just try to get rid of these Mexican guys for now and deal with the rest of it later?"

"You're not playing me for a sucker here, are you, Audrey?"

"I told you where I think the money's hidden."

I nodded.

"I could have taken it myself and disappeared."

I nodded.

She stood on her tippy toes and kissed me. It was a nice kiss, her lips as gentle as falling snow. I pulled her by the waist and kissed her hard in return. She caressed my head in a way that said she truly cared.

"Do you know how much I like it when you hold me in your arms?"

"I know it now."

"Do you think we can ever get to a place where you can hold me like this, without all the other stuff in the way?"

"I don't know. That depends on how we get from here to there. I can see a way where it's clean. I can see a way where we've dragged along all the other baggage."

"But we can try?"

"We can try if you want...Tell me about this safe."

Audrey kissed me one more time for good measure and explained where to find it.

"All right. I'll see if I can get these Mexican boys off our backs. You're sure your mother's safe for now?"

"She's staying with one of my sisters."

"All right. Well, I'm off to do what I can."

"Will you come back tonight?"

"I don't know if I can, Audrey. I have a lot of problems right now. People not paying their bills. The world's closing in on me fast."

I went for another kiss but Audrey went for a hug. I unlocked the door.

"You all right?" I said.

She nodded.

"You're sure?"

She nodded again.

"You know the police will be looking for you."

"I know."

"Okay. It would be better if you went to them but I'll leave that to you. Call me if they arrest you and we'll bail you out."

I started out the door.

"Oh," I said, turning back. "I won't be able to get into that safe until late tonight. I'll call Nacho in the meantime. If the money's there, maybe we'll have things settled by tomorrow morning."

"Thank you, Michael."

"You're sure you're all right?"

"Yeah."

Audrey came over and gave me a quick kiss.

"Call me," she said.

"I will, but it may not be tonight."

Audrey stared for a moment before closing the door and locking it behind me. I headed out to my car, kicking myself the whole way.

"I don't know, Audrey. I have a lot of problems right now. People not paying their bills. The world's closing in on me fast."

I should have kept my mouth shut. At the first hint of penury, Audrey had blanched. You want to play Prince Charming for that woman, you'd better be playing for big stakes.

I felt shame, but anger quickly followed. To hell with you and your love of money, Audrey. If you don't think I'm chivalrous enough for you, find some other fool to do your dirty work.

I had brooded for a mile or so down the road before remembering Nacho. Regardless of what Audrey did or didn't do, Nacho would never be off my back until he got what he wanted. I grabbed one of my new burner phones and called him.

"¿Bueno?" he said in answering.

"It's your favorite gringo."

"Fucking gringos, all right. What do I have to do? Put twenty fucking people in the fucking ground to get my shit?"

"How soon can you meet me where we first met?"

There was a pause.

"Ten minutes."

"All right. Out in back. I'll be waiting for you there. And ditch your phone."

I tossed the one I had used to call Nacho at the first opportunity and headed for the alley behind Sylvia's shop. When Nacho pulled to a stop behind me, I got out of my car.

300

Nacho and his two pals piled out of theirs. The four of us stood there staring at each other, like so much dried kindling. All the situation needed was a match.

I skipped being coy and laid my cards out on the table, starting with the part about Nacho never seeing his guns. He cursed in Spanish. I let him get it out of his system before I went on about our limited options.

"You want to go shoot it out with the United States government, Nacho, knock yourself out. I can't help you there, but I'll know later tonight whether or not Colby left your deposit lying around. If so, I'll make a straight up deal with you. You take the money and go back to Mexico, or wherever you want to go. Just leave the doll and me alone. She doesn't know anything and neither one of us can help you get those guns back."

"Let's see the money. If it's all there, we make the peace."

"Okay. How much am I looking for here?"

"Why am I going to be telling ju that, gringo?"

"Because if you don't tell me I'll take the doll and the money and disappear down into the Caribbean somewhere."

Nacho let off a bit more steam in Spanish.

"You done?" I said when he appeared to have calmed down.

"Fucking gringo."

"Come on, Nacho. What's the point of not telling me? Either the money's there or it's not. For all I know, you could be bullshitting me about how much."

"All right, pinche gringo. Ju win. Two million. And it all better fucking be there."

"If it is, it's all yours. Just don't make any more trouble until you hear from me again, okay? Neither one of us want the police involved."

"Yeah, gringo. We don't want no fucking cops involved."

"All right. It won't be until late tonight or early tomorrow morning when I know, but I'll call you as soon as I do."

We exchanged new phone numbers and got back into our cars. I made sure no one was following me before I headed back towards Laurel Lagoon. My thought had been to go home and take a nap. Maybe grab a rifle and a bit more ammunition while I was at it. That did not seem like the worst idea in the world, though a very fine line existed between too many guns and not enough of them. A man could get himself killed either way.

Instead, I went back to my office and tried to find one of my clients with money, but it was the same old story. People broke, people being pricks, people dodging me at every turn.

When it came to money, I wasn't much of a Prince Charming.

26

I had been there about an hour when I heard the front door open and footsteps dash up the stairs. The footsteps continued down the hallway at a more leisurely pace. I opened the drawer of my desk and positioned the Smith & Wesson to my liking, just in case.

Whoever it was stopped outside my door and knocked. I had started to say "come in" when the door flew open. It was Vanderhof. He did not appear to be packing so I closed the drawer.

Vanderhof had the Beachcomber Bill look going that day; sandals, washed cotton pants, a Hawaiian shirt and a couple of days growth on his face. With the oil missing from his sandy-colored hair, he was giving Pierce Brosnan a run for his money.

"So, this is it," he said and took in my office like he owned the place.

"This is it," I said and reached across my desk to shake his hand.

"You don't mind, do you?" he said and came around to have a look down at the beach.

"Nice view," he said. "Nice view."

He went over and had a closer look at the world map on the opposite wall. There was another smile back my way.

"You know, Devlin. You've got your own kind of style but I'll be damned if I get it. What's your brand?"

"My brand? A person has to have a brand?"

"Sure. Everyone has a brand these days."

"Really? Well how about Jesus in the temple? We can do a shot of me upending tables."

Vanderhof smiled.

"Knock yourself out, but you won't get far in this world being the angry prophet."

"It's fun trying."

He gestured at my office.

"And this is what trying got you."

I gave him a nod to say, fine. Have your joke on me.

Vanderhof sat down.

"Look," he said. "Why don't you come to work for me? I'll set you up in a big, splashy state of the art office. A handful of operatives working for you. A doll up front taking calls. Red carpet all the way. You won't have to worry for the rest of your life. How does that sound?"

"Splashy," I said.

Vanderhof studied me, nodding and thinking, that big, mirthless grin taking up half his face.

"I'm afraid to ask," I said.

"I just don't understand why you're trying so hard to be a bum in this world."

"I really don't know either. I like to blame it on my early days, vagabonding around the world. And then there were the psychedelics."

"Really? You did psychedelics?"

"Really? You didn't?"

"Hell no."

"Well, that would explain a lot. Visiting the fourth dimension does tend to put a damper on all this king of the world bullshit."

Vanderhof laughed.

"Devlin. You really would space out in front of a firing squad."

"I guess it wouldn't be the worst thing that could happen to you."

"No, I guess it wouldn't."

"Don't you ever wonder?" I said. "I mean, about why you're here? This universe might be just one of billions in the cosmic foam of existence. Where would that leave us?"

"It doesn't change a damned thing, Devlin. In this world, we're eating shit sandwiches, so the more bread you've got, the less shit you have to eat."

"Funny."

"But true."

"Yeah, but I still don't get it. You just settled with your wife. What do you want from me now?"

"You worry me and I've learned never to leave my flank open...Ever."

I shook my head in return.

"Hey, all your problems," he reminded me with a snap of his fingers.

"I know. You still want me to sell my soul, and as tempting as that might sound, I'm still pretty sure that's not what I want to do."

We stared at each other, our horns locked. The sleepy little town of Laurel Lagoon was murmuring away down below us.

"What's with the outfit?" I said, breaking the silence. "You heading down to Baja?"

"I thought that was the plan. Just you and me and a beachy little bar for a couple of days."

"I wish I could but something's come up."

He sat there, nodding, studying me.

"Something to drink?" I said.

He waved me off.

"Too bad you missed that shoot up in Malibu yesterday. It's amazing what those people can do."

He went on and on about how they had recreated a medieval setting, and I tried to look both ignorant and impressed. I was back to working on how the two of us had gotten so chummy all of a sudden. As I had already surmised, being chummy with Vanderhof did not appear to be good for your health. People died, or ended up in jail.

305

"Come on, let's head down south," he said with eyebrows raised.

"I already told you. I can't but why don't you fly down there yourself?"

"You ever go down there alone?"

"Every chance I get."

"What's it like? Can you slip in and out of there without being noticed?"

"Sometimes. Not so easily with a plane, though."

"Sounds awfully grim. I mean, just you and a trailer."

"For some it would be. Not many people view isolation with the fondness that I do. You can't get much farther away from everything after a three hundred mile trip. Not and still find yourself on the coast."

"And you really never go nuts down there all by yourself?"

"I already told you. I do. So I rush home and two days later I'm sick of this world and all ready to rush back down there again."

"Come on, Devlin. Give it a break. We'll chase some chicks and have a ball. Talk about how we're going to set you up for the rest of your life."

"The day after tomorrow, maybe. Let's see how much I can get done in the next two days."

"Hey, have you got an hour right now?"

"Not really. Why?"

"I'd like to show you my place."

"Come on, Vanderhof. I'm not like you. I have to work for a living."

"No, come on. We can dash up there in my Spider and be back before you know it."

"I'm telling you no."

"All right, all right. Have it your way. Hey, about my wife."

I held up a hand.

"We can say we're friends, but let's leave her out of it, okay?"

"Sure, buddy. I just wanted to say, no hard feelings."

"No hard feelings."

"I need to know something from you before I go."

"Go ahead and ask and I'll try not to lie."

"You have any reason left to cause me trouble?"

"I can't think of any."

"You're sure."

"Like I said, I can't think of any. If something comes up, I'll be sure to call you first."

"Don't, Michael. I like you and I'm giving you fair warning right now. Stay out of my business. I'm trying to make your life a walk in the park. I can just as easily make it a journey to hell."

"Well, on that note."

Vanderhof stood up.

"Hey, I'm still ready to go if you change your mind. I'll probably be in one of the local bars for a spell. Just give me a call."

There was a thumbs up before he headed back down to the street. I sat there weighing everything I knew and realized there was not one damned bit of evidence to prove Vanderhof was involved in any of these crimes. His path had left tire tracks in and around every murder scene in this story, but nothing directly. What I had on him was entirely circumstantial. It wouldn't make it as far as the newspapers, let alone a court of law.

Damn him and all his wealth. A private jet, a second home in Aspen, another one in the Bahamas. It did make you want to sell your soul. Virtue seemed awfully hollow in comparison.

I had been sitting there for about an hour alone when the phone rang. It was Doris and she sounded distressed.

"What's the matter?" I said.

"It's Rick."

"It's Rick, what?"

"They shot him."

"Who shot him?"

"I don't know. He's just dead."

This was where you were supposed to feel sorry for someone, and strangely enough, I did. The little Caesar deserved a lot of things. Being slapped around had frequently come to mind, but not murder.

"Explain to me exactly what happened."

"I don't know. I don't know anything anymore."

"Stop being emotional, Doris, and tell me what happened."

"Oh god. Okay. Well, Rick was here drinking and pacing around and getting himself all agitated. You know, in my face every other second."

There was a pause while she dealt with her sniffles.

"Then he went off about you. He seemed to know we had been communicating so I confessed to us having lunch. Then he was really in a state. I swore our conversation had nothing to do with him. That it was all about Audrey and Dan but nothing could calm him down at that point. I thought for sure he was going to strangle me."

She paused again for her sniffles.

"So then he went outside to make a call and came back in and drank for another half hour or so. Then his phone rang and he went outside to answer it. When I didn't hear his voice for a spell, I went outside to look around but he was gone. A short while later, I heard sirens from the direction of downtown and walked over to have a look. There was a crowd gathering where Park crosses Marine Avenue. The police had blocked off the bridge but someone told me a man had been killed. I pushed my way through far enough to see a body lying down by the canal and knew right away it was Rick."

"Did you go down there?"

"No. I hurried back here. I had no heart to get involved. I'm just sick to death of dead bodies right now."

"You haven't talked to the cops yet."

"No. I figure they'll be here soon enough."

"Look, first of all, I know a good attorney."

I gave her Jim's name and number.

"I'll call him as soon as we get off to let him know what's going on. In the meantime, you don't say a thing."

"Okay," she said less than convincingly.

"I mean it, Doris. I don't care if the cops come around beating your front door down, you say, 'I want to talk with my attorney' and that's it. Even if they drag you down to the station, you keep saying the same thing until they give you a call. You got it?"

"Yes, I've got it," she said.

"Now, do you have any idea who did this?"

"No."

"Don't lie to me, Doris. Everybody's been lying to me and I've had it up to here with the bullshit."

"Oh, for God's sake, Michael. Don't you know the state I'm in? Rick's been shot and I'm supposed to be burying my ex-husband tomorrow morning. I'd forget it was Sunday."

"All right. I know you're already carrying a heavy load but I need to hear it from you again. You had nothing to do with Dan's murder either, right?"

There was a moment's hesitation before she said, "Nothing."

"You're sure," I said.

"Nothing, Michael. I'm telling you the truth."

"Okay, because I'm about to go out on a limb for you here and I don't want to be caught with my pants down."

I grilled her for a few minutes about the period right before Rick's murder. When did he initially show up? When did he make the first call? How long was it until the second call came in?

"All right," I said when my curiosity had been satisfied. "If the cops take you in, I'll make sure Jim dashes over the minute they let you make a call."

I got off the phone with Doris, still certain she was covering for someone but having only the wildest of ideas about who it might be and why she might be doing it.

I called Jim while still pondering that question.

"I'm guessing you're not in the pokey yet," he said.

"No, not yet, but Whalen says he's going to let Fowler perp walk me down Forest Avenue tomorrow morning if I haven't brought him someone's head on a platter by then."

"Any particular head he wants?"

"He's still got his mind set on the redhead."

"You think she's guilty of anything?"

"I don't think so, but I've been wrong before."

"So what's going on now?

"Oh. You know Audrey's partner, Rick?"

"Yeah?"

"He's dead. Somebody shot him over on Balboa Island a short while ago."

I explained about Rick stopping by Doris' place for a few drinks and the phone call he had made and the phone call he had received.

"You still didn't say what you want from me."

"Go bail Doris out if she gives you a call. I gave her your number. Some of her friends may be rotten but I don't think she is. It'll be worth your time. Picture Janet Leigh back in the day. And Doris has the outfits to go with it."

"Is that it?" Jim said.

"Well, you may be springing me loose, too, if I don't come up with that head on a platter. I don't know. With the company I keep these days, you may be identifying me in the morgue, but either way, I'll probably need your help in the next twenty-four hours."

"I'll be around."

"Good. I'll keep you posted," I said and hung up.

I looked outside. The sun had gone down behind the two-story buildings across the street. The Ficus trees were filling with dusk. All the long-buried yearnings sprang to life in my heart.

Tired of dwelling on them, I headed for home. High up in the hills, the last glint of sunlight was flashing brilliantly in all the windows. Down on the highway, twilight was settling over the rush of traffic. Then Caitlin was back in my thoughts. So many times, I had driven over to her house at this very hour, her door left slightly ajar for me, a glorious smile as I came around the corner of her kitchen opening and found her chopping away at a cutting board.

It was a joke to think she would ever come back, but my life seemed to have no meaning without her. I once knew eternity. Now eternity was merely something to dread.

Already at war with my feelings, I walked up to my house and found a foreclosure notice tacked to the front door. I tore it off and stared at the words without seeing them. Goddamn it. I knew it was coming, and still it was a punch in the gut.

I went inside and wandered from room to room. I opened the refrigerator door and stared inside without appetite. I went out to the living room and sat on the sofa. There was a thought to take a nap but I couldn't sleep.

Sometime later, as darkness set in, I heard something crack in the brush out front and sprang to my feet. Expecting the worse, I slipped out the back door, moved up among the eucalyptus trees behind my house, followed them along the base of a slope until I came to the creek, leapt over it and worked my way back towards the far side of my garage behind a wall of oleander bushes.

Through the trees in my front yard, I saw three figures moving around inside the house. One of them was clearly Boris, another one the giant he kept around for muscle. Their empty X-7 was sitting out in front.

I released the garage door and opened it manually. As I backed out into the narrow lane, I saw the Russians piling out of my gate. I peeled out in a cloud of rubber, turned right onto Bluebird and then left at the park, blowing through that remote intersection with tires screeching. The X-7 had appeared on Bluebird as I was making the turn.

Following a quick right down the hill at the first stop sign, I turned left at the next street. A pair of headlights had turned down the hill behind me but I had no idea if it was the Russians. Not taking any chances, I started zigzagging through the maze of backstreets, one block west and one block south.

At Moss Street, I ran out of options. Either I jumped onto Coast Highway or turned left onto Laurel. I chose Laurel and raced down that darkened street, going airborne every few hundred yards from the speed bumps. With a glance in the rearview mirror, I saw more headlights coming down the road behind me; well back but coming fast.

I turned down Upland and pulled into the alley behind the Casa Lagoon Inn & Spa. The old adobe building hung over a row of parking slots in back. I parked with a van blocking my Impala from view and ran back to make sure it wasn't visible to anyone passing by on Upland. Satisfied, I hurried down to the office entrance on Coast Highway. A short set of steps with ornamental tiles led up to a red paver sidewalk and the sidewalk passed between two halves of the building. The path was shrouded by palms and ferns and banana trees. I walked up to the old wooden door of the office and went in. The Greek who had renovated the hotel in recent years was behind the counter.

"Ah, Mr. Devlin," he said with a smile.

I put a finger to my lips and darkness fell over his face.

I pulled out my money clip and peeled off two, one hundred dollar bills.

"I need a room and if anyone asks, you haven't seen me."

He played with his chin for a moment in thought.

"Are you parked in back?"

I nodded. He reached for a set of keys.

"This room has a door that leads out to the courtyard in back. The courtyard has a path leading up to the parking."

"There's a van parked right next to me. Is it staying?"

"It's mine. I have no plans to go anywhere."

"Thanks, Mikolas."

I started to leave but stopped.

"If you see guns, you tell them where I am. Don't risk your life over this."

He held up his hands. I went back outside and up to the end of the shrouded pathway. The wooden door to my room was at the end. The atmosphere of the room was Mediterranean. Save for the sound of traffic echoing up from Coast Highway, it was as if I had checked into a small hotel on a remote Greek island somewhere.

I lay on the bed with my troubled thoughts. Where was Nacho? Where was Vanderhof? And why had the Russians suddenly reappeared? Was this Audrey playing me for a fool? I was starting to doze off when my phone rang. It was Vanderhof.

"Hey buddy," he said when I answered. "What are you up to? You're not stirring up any trouble for me, are you?"

"Who said I was stirring up any trouble?"

"Okay, you're not."

I lay there, weighing Vanderhof's words.

"Hey, you sound kind of down."

I explained about the foreclosure notice.

"Look, didn't I tell you already? Get onboard and you can quit worrying about all this shit."

"Yeah, yeah. I heard you."

"I mean it, partner. I'll buy you the whole block if it comes to that. Just don't go playing both sides of the street on me, all right? I'm counting on you to cover my back."

"Sure," I said.

"Aw, cheer up. You're on the team. You haven't a thing to worry about for the rest of your life."

"Sure," I said again.

"Don't be so goddamned stubborn, Devlin. We're all here to help each other. Haven't you ever helped someone before?"

"Sure I have."

"So don't be so proud about receiving a little help in return."

"Yeah, sure. You're right."

"Hey, meet me in the bar somewhere and we'll have another drink."

"I can't. I have people on my tail."

"Like who?"

"Like Russians. Got any ideas who that might be."

There was a moment of silence.

"Look, if you've got Russians on your tail, you're playing on the wrong side of the street."

"Yeah?"

"Yeah."

"What happened to 'I take care of you and you take care of me'?"

"Can't help you with those boys. You'd better get clean, whatever it is you're doing, because they don't mess around."

"I guess you'd know."

"I know enough to stay out of their way."

I had a sick smile over that one.

"All right, then. Thanks for nothing."

"Hey, I'll check in with you tomorrow."

"Assuming I'm still alive."

He warned me again to watch my back and the phone went dead. I closed my eyes with the world closing in fast, a grim world where people got locked up for things they hadn't done and you sold your soul for a little taste of the easy life.

27

An hour passed with just me and my conscience. I was beginning to feel more corrupt than good for trying to see justice done in this world, and that was a lousy feeling. If I had one wish, it would be for enough hours to finish what I had started. I wanted the world to think that, for all my flaws, I had been a decent human being. That when all else was lost, I had laid my life down for a friend. They could chisel that onto my gravestone and let everyone shed a tear.

Having dozed off for a spell, I reawakened to the sound of traffic rushing by out on Coast Highway. Self-doubts were quickly gnawing away at my gut again. That look on Audrey's face would not leave me alone.

Oh. So you're not the alpha male.

But Vanderhof could fix all that. All I had to do was sell my soul.

Tired of the feelings, I went in and tried washing them off with a shower. The effort failed. My only virtue appeared to be a penchant for taking risks, a penchant that hardly seemed like a virtue right then. And my best shot at salvation appeared to be going even further off the reservation.

Having toweled off and dressed, I strapped on my .38 and headed downtown. Something had to give, and when it did, I liked my chances better in a crowd.

As usual on a hot summer night, the traffic on Coast Highway was bumper to bumper going in that direction. I used the back streets instead, parked a block over from my office building and slipped quietly in through the back door, pausing beneath the stairs to wait and listen. When I heard the sound of someone moving upstairs, my .38 came out. I waited for the better part of a minute before starting cautiously up the stairs, my ears pricked for the sound of more movement above the din of the crowd out on the street.

When one of wooden stair treads creaked, I stopped again, then started up even more cautiously, pausing every few steps to listen. A few feet down the hallway from my office door, I paused one more time. I had heard something moving up here. I was certain of that, but now there was only the bustle of tourists and traffic outside.

Cautiously reaching out with one hand, I tried the doorknob. It was locked. Still wary, I quietly unlocked the door and stepped back as it opened. Nothing. I peeked inside. The office appeared to be empty but I vaulted out into the open with my .38 ready to fire. Nothing.

Having searched in all directions, I went back out into the hallway to listen. A few moments later, I heard the creaking of a chair. Hell. It was just the kid three doors down who ran a computer repair business.

I took my racing heart and returned to the office. The phone was blinking on my desk. I sat down and listened to the messages. There were several of them but nothing important.

I leaned back in the chair and grew lost in thought. Time passed. I checked my watch. It was a quarter to ten. The plan was to stop by Colby's place around eleven. Chances were, I'd have the neighborhood all to myself by then.

In the meantime, there was Whalen to consider. Having no better glass slipper to bargain with, I grabbed the flash drive out of my desk drawer and headed out the door. Explaining how it had come into my possession was a problem all its own, but I had to give Whalen something, and the flash drive was of no further use to me. I had copied its contents. What the information on it meant, I had no idea.

On foot, I had crossed Beach and was passing alongside a string of rustic, cedar wood storefronts when Dick and Tom appeared between two of the buildings, far down at the end of a long passageway, where it joined an underground parking lot. Tom waved me over. My impulse was to greet them with my gun out, but I decided to be civilized. Dick and Tom weren't displaying theirs, so when in Rome.

That was my first mistake. Once out of plain sight in the parking lot, Tom shoved his pistol into my guts.

"What? Did you have a bad day with the missus?"

Tom smiled while Dick frisked me.

Relieved of my gun, Tom turned me around and used his pistol to guide me towards a small office that faced the parking lot from the back of a gift shop. A young man was visible inside through a small window, working at a bank of computers. When Dick tapped at the door, the young man got up to answer it. Dick quickly had a gun in his chest and just as quickly had him asleep with a blow to the back of his head. While Dick dragged the body out of the way and closed the blinds to the window, Tom nudged me inside and closed the door.

"Consider me disappointed," I said once we were all cozy together.

"Why's that?" Tom said.

"I was promised a black bag over my head at thirty-five thousand feet."

"Don't get cute," Dick said. "Where is it?"

"Who are you two and who are you working for?"

Dick nodded at Tom, who jammed the pistol harder into my back.

"Yeah, so much for Uncle Sam," I said while Dick patted me down again.

When Dick felt the flash drive inside my coat pocket, he pulled it out.

"And here I trusted you like a brother."

In glancing over my shoulder at Tom, I noticed two shadows crossing the closed blinds directly behind him. Dick was too busy making a call to notice.

Then the door flew open and Nacho barged in with one of his pals. Nacho quickly had a Micro-Tavor to the back of Tom's head. Tom let his gun dangle from one finger. Nacho took Tom's gun and kept an eye on Dick while his partner frisked him. That done, the three of us were lined up together.

"Looks like we're all going on a budget vacation," I said to Tom.

"Looks like we are," he said.

"That's right, you fucking gringos. Because now we got the cannons and jou're holding jour fucking huevos."

Nacho nodded and his partner quickly had Dick and Tom's hands tied behind their backs with some industrial grade zip ties. Nacho placed my .38 in the waistband of his Levi's and held up the flash drive.

"What's this all about, gringo? Is this going to be telling me where to find my shit?"

"I don't know. It's in code. Nobody can read it."

Nacho put his cannon up against Dick's head.

"Somebody is going to be singing like a chuparosa or I'm going to splatter some brains all over the walls. Vámonos! Who likes to start talking first?"

While I stood there waiting to see Dick's brains make an omelet on the wall, some cars braked to a halt at the far end of the parking lot. Nacho's partner went to peek around the corner and came back cursing in Spanish. Whatever he had said, it hardly needed a translation. Nacho quickly switched his cannon from Dick's head to mine.

"Fucking gringo. Ju set me up."

"How could I set you up, Nacho? I had no idea we were going to have this party down here tonight. I told you to lay low until I had some answers. Remember?"

Nacho went off in Spanish again, his finger twitching at the trigger. While I worried about having my brains splattered all over the walls, I heard the sound of footsteps slowly approaching from the far end of the parking lot. Nacho's partner had set himself up at the door, ready for a fight.

"No, ¡Vámonos!" Nacho whispered. "Before we have the policía up our asses."

His partner cracked the door. Nacho came up close to my face.

"Get my shit, gringo, or jou're going to be sleeping with los fucking muertos."

"My gun?" I said before Nacho had a chance to leave. Nacho looked down at my gun in his belt and back up at me.

"Ju got balls, gringo."

"I promise not to shoot you in the back."

Nacho pulled out the .38 and weighed it in his hand before giving it back to me. I slipped it back into my holster.

With a final look at me, he whispered "vámonos" to his partner and they slipped out the door. A moment later, I heard tables and glassware flying and assumed it was Nacho and his partner plowing their way through the outdoor patio of the English Cottage.

Boris and three of his pals made their entrance a few moments later. Boris patted Dick on the back with a smile.

"How do you say in your country? Looks like you've got your dick in your hands."

I thought that was worth a smile. Boris seemed pleased to know he had amused me. Otherwise he wasn't all that happy. I received a gentle slap on my face, mafia style.

"A very strange confluence of people we're having tonight," he said.

"The stars must be aligned."

Boris nodded and his big goon placed his Walther to my forehead.

"Like I already told you, you live as long as you're useful to me. Now where is the flash drive?"

"Those cartel boys just ran off with it."

Boris' face turned black. I was preparing for my final rights when more cars came to a halt in the parking lot, only in a screech of tires this time. Car doors flew open, followed by the sound of hard shoes hustling across concrete.

"Looks like you live another day," Boris said with a final slap of my face.

He slipped out the door with his three pals. I heard the back door to the restaurant open and close. Decker and his cavalry raced into the office a moment later with guns drawn.

"It's you again," Decker said to me.

"I've tried to be someone else but it never works."

Decker turned to Dick and Tom.

"How are you boys doing?"

They both wiggled their pinkies behind their backs. Decker nodded and one of his men cut them loose.

"What the hell is going on here? Decker said. "And who's this?" he added with a nod at the kid passed on the ground.

Dick and Tom both glanced my way while rubbing their wrists. I looked from them back to Decker.

"There was a fiesta and this guy ended up being the piñata."

"And who put him out?"

"Those cartel boys from south of the border."

"And what happened to them?"

"They saw the Russian mafia coming and got out of Dodge."

"And where did the Russians go?"

"After the Mexicans."

"And what was this all about?"

"That flash drive."

"Yeah? And did you ever figure out what was on it?"

"No. It's still Greek to me."

"And where is it now?"

"With the Mexicans?"

While we stared, the pop, pop, pop of an assault rifle disrupted the peace of a warm summer evening. This was accompanied by screams. Decker nodded and two of his cavalrymen ran out the door to join the chase. I heard a

320

collective gasp as they crashed through the restaurant patio and headed up the block.

Decker reviewed the three of us again.

"He any trouble to you?" he asked Dick and Tom.

"Nothing we can't sort out among ourselves."

"They any trouble to you?" he asked me.

"It's not been much of a friendship, but no. I have no particular beef."

"All right. You're free to go," he told Dick and Tom. "But watch your step. It's a dangerous world out there tonight."

Both of them looked over their shoulders before slipping out the door.

Decker looked back at me.

"You have a way of attracting trouble."

"We're old pals."

"Funny," he said. "But you'd better have a better explanation for why so many people are chasing around after that flash drive or you're not going home tonight."

"So you've said before."

"Spill it."

"I already told you. Whatever's on that flash drive is Greek to me."

"And where were you going with it?"

"Taking it up to Detective Whalen."

"And then the Mexicans interrupted you."

"That's the way I remember it."

There were the sounds of sirens and more gunshots.

"We'd better get down there," Decker said to his partner. "All right, smart guy. We're done here for now but don't get cute and run off."

"I don't know where I'd go."

"Funny," he said again and started to leave.

"Hey Decker," I said.

"Yeah, what?"

"Maybe I have a question for you."

"Yeah, like what?"

"Like, up in San Pedro you didn't know a thing about Dick and Tom. And now you seem to be on a first name basis."

Decker smirked.

"Call it old friends from the company. Now, if you're done asking questions, I've got a party to attend. And you'd better hope we find flash drive or we'll be back for more fun."

"Yeah, yeah. Everybody's got to be a tough guy these days."

"That's the way it is."

"Yeah, that's the way it is."

Whalen's cruiser screeched to a halt outside and Fowler quickly came running up. Whalen strolled up casually behind him.

"Looks like they'll be taking things from here," Decker said.

"Who are you?" Whalen wanted to know.

Decker showed him his badge.

"What did you want with him?" Whalen said, nodding at me.

"Seems like he had some evidence. Only those boys shooting it up down the street have it now."

"What evidence?" Whalen wanted to know.

"Ask your boy here."

Whalen looked at me. I stared.

"Son of a bitch," he said. "Okay, Devlin, that's it. I'm taking you in."

"For what?"

"For withholding evidence. What do you think? Now let's go."

I went along, finally out of stories to tell him.

"And you, big shot," Whalen said as the Feds were heading back to their cars. "Next time you come around turning my town into the OK corral, clear things with me first, all right?"

"Yeah, sure," Decker said. "Next time we're planning to have a shootout at the OK corral, you'll be the first to know."

Decker nodded and left. Whalen stared after him for a long moment before turning back to me.

"All right, let's go."

To his credit, Whalen skipped the cuffs and perp walk. He hadn't even bothered to frisk me. Fowler was holding open the back door of their squad car and grinning from ear to ear.

"Goddamn it," Whalen said, hearing more gunshots ring out into the summer night.

"Sounds like they're coming from out by the art festivals," Fowler said.

"Yeah."

Whalen looked over the back seat at me.

"We're taking a ride, Devlin and you'd better behave yourself until I lock you up."

He hit his siren and plowed into the downtown traffic as if we were the ones being chased. At the top of the block, he blew through the intersection and left a New York traffic jam in his wake. As we neared the lane merging onto Canyon Road, we heard another round of shots, along with the muffled sound of distant screams.

"The Sawdust," Fowler said.

"Yeah, sounds like it," Whalen said.

The light changed just before he was able to merge, leaving Whalen at the ass end of curb-to-curb traffic. Having heard the siren, everyone reflexively pulled to a stop, making things even worse.

Short of having Fowler climb out to untie the traffic jam, Whalen had one option, jump the curb and navigate a broad stretch of asphalt sidewalk where Forest made the curve onto Canyon Road. He did that with pedestrians flying out of his way. Whalen flattened a traffic sign in the process then bounced back down from the curb opposite the art festival and hit the gas. Given the usual parade of cars and limos in front of the Sawdust, Whalen skipped the access road and double-parked out on Canyon Road. He and Fowler quickly jumped out.

"Damn it, Pat," I said. "Don't leave me here with my dick in my hand. If one of these bastards happens by, he might plug me."

"Just my thought," Whalen said. "Save us both a whole lot of trouble."

"You prick."

He hesitated before opening the back door.

"Stay out of the goddamned way."

He and Fowler dashed across the access road and into the sawdust strewn entrance with guns drawn. I gave them a decent lead and got on their heels. More shots were popping off inside the festival and a crush of people were rushing out towards the street as if they had seen a monster.

I pushed my way through the stampede and saw Whalen and Fowler heading left up the main stairs towards the performance stage. I turned right and headed in the opposite direction. Another round of semi-automatic gunfire went off near the back of the festival.

"Man down!" I heard someone shout. "I need a medic!"

One of Decker's men came down towards the front of the festival with a wounded partner under his arm. The front of the man's shirt was red with blood. Both men had blood splotched all over their hands and clothing.

"There's a bunch people up there shot!" another man said running past me.

I pushed on deeper into the maze of booths and narrow, winding pathways. On a normal evening, it was a bit like being in a house of mirrors. With the panicked crowd rushing all around you and the guns going off, it was veering closer to an unwelcome acid trip.

I glanced back towards the wide entrance. A phalanx of cop cars had gathered out in the street. Several of the cops were rushing in. A sergeant was on his two-way radio, coordinating the operation with Whalen.

Just then, a fire truck pulled up, followed by two ambulances. Amidst the growing circus, I saw the wounded Fed being placed on a stretcher.

Continuing on, I spotted Whalen and Fowler far down an intersecting lane. Whalen spotted me and gestured with his thumb back towards the entrance. I showed him my .38 and he drew a hand across his throat. I ignored him and continued up towards the top. At every intersecting lane, I could see Whalen and Fowler steadily converging with my path.

Near the top of the festival, I turned right and came to the far outside lane. Up ahead, where that lane made a hard left turn and intersected the back row, an old wooden waterwheel was turning round and round.

I had started forward again when Nacho and his partner appeared beneath the waterwheel, backing their way down from the top lane. Nacho had a young blonde in one hand and his Micro-Tavor in the other. He spotted me over his shoulder but appeared too pinned down to do anything about it.

When a shot rang out, Nacho and his partner let loose with a barrage of bullets. Nacho's partner took cover behind a booth and kept exchanging fire. Nacho used the distraction to back down the lane my way with the young woman. I ducked into a furniture booth and crouched behind a slab of redwood. Nacho came by looking this way and that, knowing I was at his back somewhere. I was preparing to take a shot when more gunfire went off and several bullets tore through the booth directly above my head. Nacho let go of the woman and went galloping down towards the entrance. Fowler followed down a parallel lane of the festival in full pursuit.

The woman was sprawled out in the lane, frozen with fear. She recoiled with more fear when I dashed out to grab her. I put a finger to my lips and she seemed to understand.

I got her back to the safety of the booth with more shots going off up by the waterwheel. I peeked out in that direction. Decker and his pals were unloading gunfire into a grove of eucalyptus trees farther up the hill.

A moment later, a blood splashed body cartwheeled back down the hill, gathering dust and brush as it came. In that state, Nacho's partner hit the waterwheel face down. Time seemed to stand still as he traversed over the top and slowly started back down towards earth. As a final insult, the waterwheel dumped his body more or less face up on the sawdust covered ground.

One of Decker's pals quickly went through the pockets.

"Nothing."

"Shit," Decker said.

Whalen ran up.

"Where did that other bastard go?" he asked me.

"Down towards the entrance. Fowler was on his tail."

"And you didn't shoot him because?"

"It's not my job? He wasn't shooting at me? I don't shoot people in the back? All of the above?"

"You're about worthless."

"Thanks."

"Give me that fucking thing."

Whalen took my .38.

"You okay?" he said to the young woman.

Still in shock, she nodded. Several uniformed cops ran up just then.

"Stay with the body," Whalen told them. "All right, let's go," he said to me.

Whalen jogged down towards the entrance with me at his side. Two of Decker's underlings were on our heels. A platoon of uniformed cops was there to meet us at the entrance.

"Did you see him?" Whalen asked everyone in general.

"No one came this way," the lead cop said.

"Damn it. And where's Fowler?"

"He took off on foot towards town."

"Well he's about worthless too. All right, get the paramedics up there. I've got two seriously wounded tourists up by the stage."

Two shots rang out in the direction of the diagonal parking slots at the north end of the festival, accompanied by a woman's scream. A car backed wildly out into the street, the passenger side door flew open and a body tumbled out onto the asphalt.

"There's that son of a bitch!" Whalen said.

Every available firearm was quickly pointed at the car but the woman had kneeled over the wounded man, blocking the line of sight. With Nacho peeling off down the access road, firemen and paramedics ran towards the wounded man.

"Davis!" Whalen shouted. "Call the sheriffs and see if they can block the road at El Toro! And Reynolds, take two squad cars and get on that bastard's tail! Sloan, get up there with that other body! I don't trust these big-league boys as far as I can throw them."

Whalen had a look at the two Feds at the curb and looked back at me.

"All right, bright boy. Time to take you down to the station."

28

Whalen placed me in the back of his cruiser. Not a word was said on our way back down to the station. Whalen played it straight and let me call Jim Harrison. Then he set me down in an interrogation room and started the grilling.

"Okay, killer. What was this all about?"

"A flash drive."

"And who did this flash drive belong to?"

"Colby."

"You son of a bitch. I knew you were out there messing with that corpse that night."

"Come on, Pat. Like you said, Hernandez had already searched him."

"Yeah? So how did happen to come in possession of it?"

"It fell out of the sky."

"Don't get cute with me, Devlin. I've got dead bodies all over this town. Now spill it. Where did you find it?"

"I can't tell you that."

"You're going to be up there with your pal Steve if you don't start talking."

"Look, it doesn't matter how I got it. I got it and was on my way up here tonight to turn it over to you when suddenly I'm surrounded by tough guys."

"Which tough guys?"

"You want them in order?"

"Yeah."

"For starters, the two who roughed me up at the Sea Shanty the other day. Then two Mexicans. Then some Russians. Then Mr. Big Shot FBI Guy."

Whalen shook his head.

"And what was on the flash drive?"

"Nothing that made sense to me."

"And you're really not going to tell me how you found this little gem."

"I don't have to tell you everything I do, Pat. All I'm going to say is, in trying to clear Steve McPherson's name, I've come to believe that there's one person linking together all four of these murders."

"And that person would be?"

"Vanderhof."

Whalen scoffed.

"You don't really believe that shit, do you?"

"What's the matter, Pat? That $100,000 donation to the Policemen's Association make you go blind?"

"Don't you ever fucking question my integrity."

"All right, we'll blame it all on the chief, but there's a big elephant in the room and for some reason, nobody's willing to acknowledge it."

"Look, Devlin. All you've got on Vanderhof is rumor and innuendo."

"I've got a lot more on him than you've got on Steve McPherson."

"I can't believe you still think that son of a bitch is innocent."

"And I can't believe you're still dumb enough to think he's guilty."

"All right, all right. Let's not go back down that road. Tell me what happened tonight. How did this whole thing blow up on you?"

"Hell if I know. I never mentioned the flash drive to anyone but Kenny and my part time secretary and that was only in the privacy of her own home."

329

"So just like that, this flash drive falls out of the sky and everyone magically knows about it and starts chasing you around, ready to put a slug in you."

I shrugged.

"Your story's not adding up, Devlin."

I shrugged again.

"Maybe Decker had bugged Teresa's house. Maybe Dick and Tom too."

"Then how do you explain those narco boys?"

"Just following me around, I assume. They definitely didn't know about it before our rendezvous tonight."

Pat shook his head.

"Look, Pat. All I know is, I was on my way up here to talk with you and all of a sudden I had trouble on my hands."

"And Audrey had nothing to do with this."

"Not a thing."

"And that's it?"

"That's it."

"I don't know exactly what to charge you with yet, Devlin, but you are way more than ass deep on my shit list."

"Look, Pat. You gave me until tomorrow. About midmorning, if memory serves me correctly. So why don't you let me get back to work. I'm close, and if I'm right, and I find out who's behind these murders, I'll hand the whole thing over to you and you can take a victory lap, just like I said."

"And if you're wrong?"

"If I'm wrong, you can lock me up for being a lousy detective."

"All right," Pat said, standing up. "Get out of here. But if you don't come up with some answers by tomorrow, trust me. I'll dream up something to charge you with."

"May I have my gun back?"

He handed it to me with a sour look.

"Thanks."

"Don't thank me. I've got the cowboys and Indians out there shooting up the town, a growing collection of dead bodies, a bunch of tourists who went home instead of spending their money on a summer night and a mayor and city council who will be up my ass first thing in the morning, if not sooner, and all thanks to you, as far as I can tell."

"Go on, get out of here," Pat added when I could not come up with anything clever to say.

I found Jim waiting for me out in the lobby. The cross street in front of the police station was a circus, patrol cars and fire engines scattered all over the intersection and news trucks lined up end to end.

"Hey Devlin!" Bernie called out to me and came up. "Just feeling lonely again tonight?"

"I usually am."

"Tell me something I don't know."

"Two and two is four."

"Yeah, thanks."

"Sorry, Bernie. I'm working on a case and what I know is confidential."

"Shit. See if I ever help you again."

I leaned in closer and whispered so the rest of the vultures out there couldn't hear me.

"If I give you a lead and it gets you somewhere, you promise to check with me before you run with the story?"

"Sure. What have you got?"

"Your word."

"My word."

We bumped fists.

"I think Vanderhof is tied up in all of these murders."

"Holy shit. That would be news. The cops are supposed to be feting him for Citizen of the Year on Saturday night. How do you figure he's involved?"

"If I knew, I wouldn't be asking you. Just check with me first if you get ready to blow the lid off this thing, all right?"

"Will do."

I grabbed Bernie by the arm before he ran off.

"I mean it. You come to me first or I'll let your wife know you've been screwing around with that stripper up at Captain Crème's. With pictures attached."

He smiled. I smiled back and let him go.

"You think that was a wise idea?" Jim said as Bernie ran off.

"I don't know, but I'm not having any luck. Might as well see if Bernie can flush out some rats. If nothing else, maybe another Injun on Vanderhof's trail will get him rattled. When people get rattled, they tend to make mistakes."

I stared up at the helicopter circling around out by the art festivals.

"Pain in the ass. We'll all be lucky to get some sleep tonight."

"I'm heading up to spring Doris," Jim said. "Want to come along?"

"What? They charged her with something?"

"No. Just holding her as a material witness."

"For how long?"

"For as long as it took me to get through to the judge with a writ of habeas corpus…So? You want to come?"

"Sure."

We jumped into Jim's car and headed up the coast.

"They catch Nacho yet?" I asked along the way.

"Not to the best of my knowledge. What do you know?"

I explained everything I had learned since the last time Jim and I talked.

"What do you have planned for an encore?" he asked with a glance my way.

"I don't know, but I'd better come up with something. If this Nacho character gets caught and starts talking, I'm cooked. Whalen's ready to toss me to the sharks already."

At Jamboree Blvd., Jim turned right. A few minutes later, he turned right onto Santa Barbara Dr. and into a parking lot next to the police station. It was a big, drab rectangular building with a heliport on top, in case you needed to invade a sleepy little neighboring beach town on a hot summer night.

I missed the old days, when Newport was its own quaint little beach town. You drove down onto the peninsula to visit the cops and from there could walk a block over to have lunch at the Crab Cooker and take a stroll out on the pier.

Inside, Jim made it clear that his client would not be answering any questions until he had time to consult with her. Did they want to set up an interview? They did, in the morning. Jim explained about the funeral so they arranged a meeting with Doris for the following day. A cop with a bad attitude brought her out from in back five minutes later. She gave me a hug. She looked good. She smelled good. She was greatly relieved to see us.

"This is Jim Harrison."

Doris shook his hand.

"Thank you," she said. "Thank you both."

She looked shaken but ready to suck it up like a trooper.

"Come on," I said. "We'll go have a drink and talk things over."

"Oh god, could I ever use one of those right now."

We found Ciao still open on Marine Avenue and sat at one of the tables outside. It was late, and cool, as summer nights went, with a heavy scent of brine coming up from the canal where Rick had been shot.

Doris ordered a glass of Cabernet. Jim had a Scotch.

"I'll have an Ivanhoe," I told the waiter.

"You're a real riot," Doris said as he left.

"Yeah, everybody thinks I'm a riot these days."

I looked at Jim and back at Doris.

"Are you up to answering a few questions?" I asked her.

"As long as you're gentle with me."

"Sure. We'll be gentle with you."

I gestured for Jim to go first.

"Tell me what was said."

"Per your instructions, not much. A woman in the crowd remembered seeing me. They wanted to know why I went back home when I saw my boyfriend dead. I told them I wanted to talk to my attorney. They asked me, then or now. I said now."

"Did you get the impression that they really thought you were guilty?"

"Maybe. Do you guys?"

Jim shook his head. So did I.

"No," she said. "But I'm sure the police are starting to think so."

I was drumming my fingers while studying Doris. She looked at the fingers and back at me.

What?" she said.

Before I could speak my mind, our drinks arrived and we backed out of the way for the waiter. When he left, I grabbed my glass and held it aloft.

"A benediction seems in order."

No one could think of what to say so we toasted in silence.

"So?" Doris said to me after she had set her drink down.

I kept studying her with a question burning a hole in my head but decided to set that to the side for the moment and moved on to something less confrontational.

"What more can you tell us about the two calls Rick had?"

"Not much."

"Tell me what you do know."

"Well, in the course of the first call, Rick went outside. That was actually the first thing that caught my attention. He was never one to keep his business to himself."

She made a face to emphasize her point. I nodded to commiserate.

"And this would be the call he made, not the one that came in?"

"Yes."

"And you were listening."

"A bit."

"And did this seem to be a person he knew personally? I mean more than a business associate?"

"I'd say so, yes."

"Any ideas who it might have been?"

Doris fidgeted with her drink.

"I don't know. It sounded like someone important."

"Yeah?"

"Yeah."

"And what gave you that impression?"

"Oh, just the fact that Rick wasn't being so bossy. He usually is when he's talking to other people. Instead, it was like he was trying to be all silky and persuasive. It just sounded all out of character."

"And the second call? You think that Rick was talking to the same person?"

Doris nodded and went back to fidgeting with her drink.

"And you never got curious about who it was?"

She shrugged.

"His silence got me curious more than anything. I had heard him talking and then nothing so I went outside to look."

"Think it could have been Vanderhof?" I said.

Doris darted a look at me and returned to fidgeting with her drink.

"I suppose."

I stared at her until she looked back.

"What?" she said.

"We never did discuss why Vanderhof drove down to your place the other day."

"I never said that he did."

"No, you didn't. However, I just happened to overhear the phone call that led him to get all worked up and dash out the door and race off to Balboa Island."

She kept playing with her glass.

"But you have no idea why that was."

She shrugged noncommittedly and drank without answering me. I looked at Jim. Then both of us were staring at Doris.

"There is one other thing I can tell you," she said.

"What's that?" I said.

"My regular attorney called today with news of who took my place in Dan's will."

"And?"

"It was Audrey Black."

Jim and I exchanged glances again. He had a drink of his Scotch.

"Well, don't you find that telling?" Doris said. "I mean, wouldn't that have given her a motive to kill Dan?"

"I suppose so, yeah," I said.

"And if Rick had found out about her killing Dan, wouldn't that have given her a motive to kill Rick, too?"

"Yeah. I suppose the one would follow the other."

"But you don't think any of that's possible."

"I wouldn't rule it out. It's just way too pat for my tastes."

"Well, she's nothing but a little gold digger as far as I'm concerned and I wouldn't put it past her."

"Like I said, I wouldn't rule it out."

The three of us were left staring at each other. I nodded Jim's way.

"We'd better let the counselor here start grooming you for your grilling on Thursday."

My thoughts drifted off while Jim prepped her.

When the waitress came back around, we shook off a second drink. Being gentlemen, Jim and I walked Doris home. She stopped to face us at her front door.

"I guess nobody's going to be there tomorrow to hold my hand."

I looked at Jim.

"I've got my hands full," he said.

I looked back at Doris.

"Same here," I said.

"Oh, it's all right," she said. "I need to start being a big girl about these things. Besides, I'll be surrounded by family and friends."

"You're sure," I said.

"Yeah, I'm sure."

336

She shook both our hands.

"Thanks again for being there."

Jim and I said goodnight and headed back to his car in silence. Some minutes later, we were motoring down the darkened coastline. It was a moonless night and all you could see was the surf bristling white out there against the black sea.

"What was that all about?" Jim asked

I explained following Vanderhof that day in more detail.

"Does that mean he was on his way down to see Doris when I lost him? I don't know but she hasn't come right out to deny it. And all the elements are there for the whole thing to make sense. At least to me."

Jim glanced over at me while driving.

"How so?"

"Well, let's say I'm right and there's a secret in Vanderhof's past that everyone's trying desperately to keep buried. And let's say that Doris foolishly let Rick in on the secret, and that Vanderhof's goons just happen to be tapping Doris' phone. That would explain why Vanderhof raced down there to confront her that day and suggests that he was already thinking to put Rick six feet under when Rick called to put the squeeze on him. I'm not saying Rick was trying to play a heavy hand. By what Doris claims to have overheard, Rick was being slick about it. 'Hey, you scratch my back, I'll scratch yours.' But Vanderhof's not one to leave loose ends, and having established that Rick was at Doris' place, he had his goons drive down to the island, then gave Rick another call and invited him out for a drink to discuss things and, bang, bang, the goons shot him dead."

"Do you believe any of that?" Jim said.

"If my life depended on it? Yeah, I'd say the truth is in there somewhere. Vanderhof's name just keeps popping up in too many places for it to be a coincidence."

"Well, you'd know better than me."

"I know this much. Vanderhof went racing off that day, and he just happened to head down to Balboa Island."

Jim nodded. I yawned, weary right down to my soul. My thoughts were wandering far, far down the coast.

As soon as this is over, I told myself, I'm heading down to Baja. It did not seem that it ever would be, but a man cannot live without hopes.

South on Pacific Coast Highway

29

Three hours after all the excitement had started, Jim dropped me back at my office. As he drove off, I looked up. The Newport Beach police chopper was still buzzing the town. A couple of local cops were parked in the intersection across from the English Cottage, lights on, ready for trouble if it came around. Otherwise, Laurel Lagoon had emptied out; the news trucks, the gawkers, the revelers, all of them gone. It was as if the cops had issued a curfew.

Having left my regular cell phone in the office, I went to grab it and caught the scent of Elfie's perfume on my way up the stairs. She had been there. She had gone. I viewed that fact with mixed emotions. Elfie was such sweet comfort, but her silky beauty had failed to tame my wayward heart. Red hair and pale skin were the only talismans to my devotion. That Audrey might be the reincarnation of Mata Hari was my burden to bear.

The screen on my phone was lit up with a half dozen messages when I walked in. I sat down and quickly scrolled through them. They were all from Vanderhof. Something had him worried. Good. Let him twist in the wind. I had no interest in dealing with his BS at that hour.

Leaning back in my chair, I grew troubled again over Audrey's behavior. The way she had grown cool at the hint of my poverty cut deep. Doris' words of caution troubled me too. Audrey had a motive in at least three of the four murders. She had even pulled a gun on me.

I did not like these pesky little details getting in the way of my dreams. I had adored a woman with all my heart once and wanted to feel that way again. If I was wrong about Audrey, shoot me. Without devotion, my life was like Elliot's wasteland. Little was left between me and six feet of dirt, save for bestial impulses. I took my dearest hopes and dreams and headed downstairs, on my way back over to Colby's old place.

Rather than pull onto Allview Terrace, I parked one street down and followed an arroyo up the undeveloped hillside. At the backside of his house, I paused, wanting to make sure that no one had followed me. The night was alive with insects. The dark slope above me was still giving off the warmth of the summer sun. I sensed the hum of the universe under a starlit sky, the hum of life and things ancient.

When I felt certain I was alone, I tried the door and found it locked. My hair stood on end. Damn it. I had purposefully left it unlocked the last time, so somebody had been here. I assumed someone assigned as a caretaker. It wouldn't make sense for someone to lock the door and wait inside.

Either way, I was unwilling to break the door glass and hiked back down to my car. Five minutes later, I was back with my lock kit. A few minutes after that, I slipped inside with my .38 out, prepared for trouble. I stood there for a long time, listening to the quiet. Failing to hear any sounds, I started up the stairs towards the third story loft. With every few steps, I stopped to listen again.

I arrived to the top floor with no sign of an intruder. It must have been a caretaker, coming around to check on things and noticing the door unlocked. Whoever it was, they were bound to come back, but probably not at this hour. All I needed was for my luck to hold out for another half hour.

Audrey had told me the safe was hidden behind a secret panel in the bookcase. I fumbled around among the books until I found it. That done, I opened the file cabinet and pulled out the folder of poems. There was a twinge of jealousy now as I read through them. Why? What did I care? The man was dead.

And yet a flame burned in my heart as I thumbed through Colby's words of love and devotion.

Having rifled through the entire contents several times, and failing to find the combination, I scanned back through the dates at the bottom of each poem, hoping to see a pattern.

Nothing. I turned and stared out at the lights along the coast, swept away again by the enchanting view. With Vanderhof's money, I could have bought the place on a whim. Maybe selling out to him would be the easier thing to do.

I had been distracted for a minute with that devil's bargain when another thought popped into my head. I grabbed a pencil and used it to push the paper label out of its plastic tab at the top of the folder. Turning the label inside out, I found three numbers.

With label in hand, I turned the tumbler, staring, fixated, my heart beat wildly. Then, with the third number in place, I pulled on the lever and the safe opened. A large, rectangular shaped package sat inside, neatly wrapped in black plastic. I removed it from the safe, placed it on top of Colby's desk, carefully undid the tape and pulled back the wrapping. I was staring at bundles of one hundred-dollar bills. I pulled one bundle free and counted it. Ten thousand dollars. I did a quick count of the bundles. Two hundred of them. Two million dollars. There were a few island getaways you could buy with that kind of money. The only problem being, Audrey and I would be looking over our shoulders for the rest of our lives, which would probably be brief ones, having screwed a cartel.

I rewrapped the money, closed the safe and secret panel, rearranged the books as I had found them and started cautiously downstairs. Hearing a creak, I froze, my heart back to beating wildly. Maybe the ghost of a dead Hollywood starlet had awakened with envy. A minute went by before I was satisfied that it had only been the old wooden house stretching and groaning.

All the way across town, I felt as if I was being tailed. Nacho might be dead, but the people he worked for were very much alive and well and fond of vengeance. Somebody somewhere was thinking about that money. I performed several evasive maneuvers and pulled into the same back street parking slot behind the hotel, reasonably certain that no one had followed me. In the room, I found an attic access panel and hid the money up among the ceiling joists.

That done, I crawled into bed. The down pillows and Egyptian cotton felt like heaven. The crap going around in my head felt like a hostage crisis.

My biggest dilemma now was how to find the right person and cut a deal. I did not dare to try Nacho's number. Even if he was still on the loose, my call would probably go straight to Decker.

Sometime before dawn, I bolted awake from a disturbing dream. It had started out with me trying to meet with an old friend for a drink. The usual frustration had ensued; down winding streets and alleyways, through strange rooms, a seemingly endless string of missed connections.

Then I was walking home along a winding lane by the sea, a lane that quickly morphed into a narrow, treacherous, rocky trail with the sea far below on my right. I came upon two young girls playing among the steep rocks and was about to warn them of the danger when one of the girls slipped and fell. Down, down, down she went, screaming, and against the logic of dreams, hit back first onto the rocks. The last thing I saw before awakening, she was writhing in pain, a hundred feet below me.

I went to empty my bladder and drank a glass of water before crawling back into bed. The image of the little girl went on haunting me. Her agony had been visceral and remained so. I lay there for a long time, wondering what in the world the dream had meant.

Having slept again, I called Audrey first thing upon awakening. When she failed to answer, I called the front desk of her hotel. The receptionist informed me that Ms. Black had already checked out. I hung up and immediately called

Audrey's mobile number again. It rang and rang and finally went to voice mail.

I threw the phone across the room. Son of a bitch. Playing me for a fool. But what did you expect, Devlin? The woman had dollar signs in her eyes and you're a few bucks short of being Sir Lancelot.

But Audrey had trusted me to retrieve the money. Why would she do that if she was playing me for a fool? Unless it was a set up. I had visions now of the Feds beating down my door and this whole mess being dumped in my lap.

Then I remembered how Audrey had kissed me with such tenderness. Yeah, but things went south the minute she got wind of my poverty. But she had told me about the money before she got wind of my poverty. And anyway, we had two million dollars now, so what did that matter?

I sat there brooding for a spell and getting nowhere.

Oh hell. Maybe she's in trouble. I retrieved the phone from across the room and called her number again. When the call went to voice mail, I left a message. It's your fool on the white horse. Give me a call if you can spare a minute.

After a shave and shower, I drove home to change, and from there went down to the office. I had two hours before my gilded carriage turned into a pumpkin. What was I going to tell Whalen?

Deciding it would be best not to face the gallows on an empty stomach, I went down to the street and headed over to Coast Highway with ham and eggs on my mind. As I hit the crosswalk button, I noticed a yellow Ferrari idling up at the next light. It was Vanderhof with the top open. Audrey was sitting in the shotgun seat next to him. I ducked into a corner shop. Vanderhof was just then looking over at Audrey with a smile.

The light changed and the Spider passed by. Audrey was playing with a strand of her long red hair. Vanderhof looked as if he didn't have a care in the world.

343

When the light changed again, I continued over to the café. Half an hour later, I was still pushing the ham and eggs around on my plate.

Well, that answers one question, Devlin. You're definitely a fool. But what else did it mean, Audrey being back with Vanderhof? Probably business had brought them together at some point in the past and that had led to some screwing around. Whatever else could be said about their past, they certainly appeared to be screwing around now.

It was an understandable play on Audrey's part. In one direction was a fool and his dreams, in the other, money, lots and lots of money. When all was said and done, Audrey had simply gravitated in the direction most natural to her.

I stared out at the coast, watching the waves wash up and over my misplaced dreams.

Back at my office, I got back to watching waves break down the coast. The beachgoers were starting to show up with their umbrellas and ice chests. The scent of suntan lotion carried on the salty air. A lot of people would be down there having fun today. I was still stuck with the question of four murders and what to do with two million dollars. I'd deal with my emotions the next time there was an intermission.

I had been watching a little girl at play with her sand pail when my dark dream from the previous night flooded back into my thoughts. And as a physicist might suddenly grasp an insight to our universe, or a chess player might see a set of brilliant moves up ahead, everything about the case suddenly fell into place for me, or so it seemed. At the very least, my new theory could easily explain how all this trouble got started.

Good lord, I thought. I had started to pick up the phone and make a call when I heard footsteps hurrying up the stairs. They were hard shoes, but not boots. It was someone other than my Mexican friends. Just to be safe, I opened the drawer with my Smith & Wesson again.

When shadows appeared outside the door, I prepared for the door to fly open. It did and Decker came in. He had brought along two of his friends. There were worse possible scenarios. There were better ones. I closed the drawer and acknowledged them with a nod.

"I take it you've yet to find Pancho Villa."

"No. But that's not why we're here."

"Okay. I give up. Why are you here?"

"For whatever you found over at Colby's place the other night."

"Some not so half bad poetry, if that helps."

"Cut with the crap, Devlin. Spill it."

"I've got nothing to spill, Decker."

He nodded and his boys promptly set about making a mess of my nice, clean office. It didn't take them long to find the safe hidden in my bookcase.

"Open it," Decker said.

I went over and obliged him. With the door open, Decker's men went quickly made a mess in there, too.

"Satisfied?" I said.

"No," Decker said. "Let's go. We're taking a look at your house next."

"Fine, but you'll be wasting your time over there too."

"Devlin, you're going to be looking at a cold dark cell until you start singing."

"Then we're both going to have a long wait."

He stared.

"Look," I said. "I assume we're working the same side here so why don't we see if we can cut a deal."

Decker kept staring.

"All right, go on."

I offered up my best theory of the case, leaving out my sudden vision. Something told me Decker did not know about that angle yet, and I wasn't about to tell him.

"Al-Hamad?" I concluded. "I have no idea what he was up to. You probably know better than me, but I'm convinced that Colby was planning to divert that shipment of guns down to a cartel in Mexico, which would explain Nacho and his band of

345

banditos running around shooting up things. And Al-Hamad getting screwed in the process would account for the Russians. But you put all that together and something still doesn't add up. It hasn't since the day Cliff Black got himself shot underneath my office windows. Not unless there's another motive at work that I don't yet understand."

"Which would be?"

"I already told you. I don't know. My plan was to set out some bait tonight and see who shows up. Can you stay out of my hair until then?"

I explained enough of what I was thinking to get Decker off my back for a few hours, but not enough to have him in bed with me.

Decker glanced at one of his men. I didn't like the look. They knew something they weren't telling me."

"All right," Decker said, looking back. "I'll cut you some slack until later tonight. If this plays out the way you say, great. If not, we'll get back to tearing up the furniture."

"If it doesn't work out the way I have planned, I'll already be going down for being a lousy detective. You can add on whatever charges you like on top of that."

He and his boys filed out. I waited until they were back down on the street before calling Vanderhof.

"Hey, I've been trying to reach you, old buddy," he said in answering the phone. "What have you been up to? I heard reports of all kinds of fireworks going off the other night."

"Says who?"

"I read the news."

"Yeah? Well I had a couple of bad seeds breathing down my neck. I'm not sure exactly what they wanted but they came to town with guns. The boys from the big leagues showed up next and all of a sudden, I've got the shootout at the OK corral on my hands. The Feds plugged one of the bad seeds and they're still looking for the other one. I guess you know the rest."

"What do you mean, I know the rest?"

"Okay, you don't, but I've got a question for you."

346

"Go ahead, shoot."

"Someone told me you knew Steve and Connie McPherson back in the day."

Vanderhof was silent.

"Is that true?"

"Yeah, I knew them. Not very well, but I knew them."

"Okay, so would you happen to know why someone would want to kill Connie?"

"No. And why do you care?"

"Steve happens to be an old friend of mine."

"No kidding."

"No kidding and I had been trying to clear his name when someone called out of the blue to say they knew how she got killed."

"Yeah? And who is this person?"

"I promised to keep that confidential. But once I hear the story, I'd like to run it by you. Maybe from knowing the McPhersons you can tell me if this intel sounds credible or not."

"Sure, sure. So when are you supposed to meet up?"

"Tonight."

"Tonight, huh?

"Yeah. We're supposed to meet here at my office at eight."

"Well, sure. I'll be happy to give you my two cents, for what it's worth."

"Thanks," I said. "And what about you? Sounds like you've been having a few fireworks of your own."

"Eh, it's nothing. That's why they have attorneys, my friend. That's why they have attorneys."

"Okay. I'll get back to you as soon as I've heard what this person has to say."

"All right," he said. "I'll be around."

I got off and immediately called Jim from a burner phone, explaining to him what was going on.

"I'm worried about Doris. There are tigers out there on the prowl and she's more or less our sacrificial goat right now."

"And?" he said. "You wanted from me?"

"To put her up for the night."

"Sure, if she knows how to keep quiet. I'm busy here working out of the house today."

"I said tonight. Remember, she's at the funeral today."

"Oh, right," he said. "Well, I'll be here. Just have her knock."

"Thanks, Jim. You'll probably be seeing her sometime late this afternoon."

I leaned back in my chair, weighing all that had gone down since the day of Connie's death. Three men murdered, one of whom had been very high on my list of original suspects, until he too got himself shot. Although dying in the interim did not necessarily rule out Rick as a suspect in Dan Colby's death. Given the limitations of time and space as I knew them, I was inclined to rule out Audrey being the one who had killed Rick, but that did not rule out her killing Dan Colby, or her husband. Then there was Doris, though I struggled to see her handling a gun, let alone using it. The only thing that kept me suspicious of Doris was the way she had parsed her words with regard to Dan Colby's murder. When asked if she knew anything about it, she had never said no. She had claimed a lack of involvement and otherwise acted cagey. Something must have happened long ago. Something had left Doris terrified of opening her mouth. I thought I knew what that was now, but I had been wrong many times before.

Finally, there were the Russians and Nacho and Vanderhof to consider, Nacho with an apparent motive to kill both Colby and Rick, the Russians with all their treacherous motives to be involved and Vanderhof with a possible hand in all four murders. I doubted his involvement went as far as pulling the trigger but he was everywhere I looked.

Meanwhile, I had foolishly fallen in love with a dead man's wife, for the simple fact that she had red hair. I had not bargained for her questionable scruples in the process. In Audrey's defense, she had grown up in a society that seemed to value self-aggrandizement above all else. Who was to blame for that? Setting aside her marriage to Cliff, the responsibilities that went with it and her cheap play at me in the hotel the other day, she was as decent as the next person who came down the pike. Had she never married Cliff, or had divorced him at some more appropriate time in the past, I would have been prepared to write off most of her sins. I wasn't sure what to make of the world that had helped to shape her.

It was easy to get distracted, but whether it be one man or two, or several, or a woman, whoever had been committing murders was still on the prowl. I wasn't sure why, given all those loose ends, but I figured by ten o'clock that evening I'd have the whole case neatly wrapped up in a bow and ready to hand it over to someone above my pay grade.

With a glance at the clock, I realized the time had come for my gilded carriage to turn into a pumpkin so I gave Whalen a call.

"This had better be good," he said before I had time for any pleasantries.

"I need another twelve hours."

"You're wearing me out, Devlin."

"I don't know what you're going to charge me with, Pat, but let me come up and explain what I've got on my hands."

"Sure. Knock yourself out, but I can't guarantee you'll be leaving again any time soon."

I walked up the block, laid my predicament out on the table and threw in enough thrills to keep Whalen from putting the screws to me about what he did not know.

"All right," he said when I was through. "You're nothing but trouble, Devlin, and if you ever expect the Laurel Lagoon Police Department to play fair with you again, this had better go down the way you have planned."

"I've heard that warning several times of late."

"Yeah? Well that ought to tell you something."

I went back out the door and down the street, feeling sore. The way I saw it, I was an honest, well-intentioned man. Why the world couldn't see me that way, I struggled to understand.

In the mood for an ahi burger, but knowing there was a good chance I'd run into Pat at the English Cottage, I walked over to the bar at the Laurel Lagoon Hotel instead and ordered a club sandwich. The windows facing the beach were tinted and made everything look like one of the home movies my parents had made before I was born, the sea a blue-green color, the sand almost yellow, the reds brighter than popsicles. I sat there growing lost in the magic of days gone by.

Was it pointless for a man to look backwards in this way? Were memories anything but useless illusions? Was this what happened to everyone as they grew older, always longing for days past and what had been lost? Or was it simply a magical time the world had known in those few fleeting decades right after the war, where everything had conspired to make it a good and decent life and therefore worth resurrecting?

It was hard to find any decency now. That much was clear.

I went back to my office and killed a few hours answering messages and otherwise trying to look responsible. No, I told three jaded husbands in succession. I was no longer in the divorce business. Thank you.

Finally, I gave Doris a call. It was quiet in the background. It sounded as if everyone had offered their final condolences and left for home.

"How did it go?" I asked her.

"All right. Some people never forgive you."

"I know the feeling."

"Do you?"

"Sure."

"Well, Dan's family still holds the divorce against me."

"That's too bad. Bitterness is such a waste of time."

"Yes it is. Well, what's on your mind? I know it's something."

"I think you're in danger, so I want you to drive over to Jim's place. He's working out of his home today and is expecting you."

"Oh god, Michael, please. I'm just getting comfortable here at the house again. Why? What is it this time?"

"I can't tell you, but trust me, okay? I wouldn't be calling unless I thought you were truly in danger."

"Okay," she said wearily. "I'll pack up a bag."

"Jim's a great cook and has a terrific ocean view. Better bring your knitting or whatever you like to do in your spare time."

"Ha," she said.

I gave her the address.

"You'd better get going right now."

She seemed to sigh again.

"I'm serious, Doris. I think I've finally solved this case, but things are moving fast. Bad things, so get out of there as soon as you can. Whoever shot Rick must be planning to shoot you next. I'd stake my life on that one fact if nothing else."

"All right. I'll leave in a minute."

"Good. I'll stop by to say hello later on."

"All right," she said again.

Feeling adrift, I went online and poked around about doing some PI work overseas. An abundance of opportunities quickly popped up in the Middle East, but that wasn't for me; too hot, too dusty, too much madness.

I tried the Caribbean and a lead came up down Curacao way. I Googled some pictures. It looked lovely in winter; turquoise seas, blue skies, beachy bars and white clouds drifting overhead.

Feeling even more adrift now, I had a sudden urge to call Caitlin. I was duly wary of the impulse, but she had such a sweet and melodic voice, like wind chimes on a blustery day, and I very much wanted to hear her voice right then. It had always caused my heart to sail away.

Tomorrow, I told myself. If I'm still around tomorrow, I'll give her a call. My heart raced at the very thought of dialing her number.

30

Having done everything in my powers to set this scheme in motion, I went out the door and down the hallway. Unlike mine, the other doors in the building were still the original five-panel Craftsman type. They hadn't been changed in over a hundred years. They hadn't been painted in nearly thirty.

When I got to Betty and Leonard's office door, I found it uncustomarily closed. I knocked.

"Come in," Leonard called out from the other side.

He looked up from his computer when I entered. Having ditched the Band-Aid, Leonard did a double take at my now scabbed over wound. Butch jumped up on his hind legs and pranced around for some attention.

"Where's Betty?" I asked while petting Butch.

"Went to a casino with some friends."

I walked over to his desk in back and sat down opposite him. There was a picture book of World War II and the '40s on the desk. I picked it up and started browsing through the photos.

"How are you doing?" I said.

"Fine. What can I do for you?"

"Were you there?" I said in reference to the war.

"No, my father was in Italy."

"Must have been a lovely time," I said, still thumbing through the book. "Especially right after the war. Swing music. All the world in front of you. Suppose they knew how special things were, or were they just as screwed up and unhappy about their lives back then?"

"I imagine the war had sharpened everyone's senses. Then there was a big sigh of relief and things got back to normal, as they usually do after a war."

I was heartbroken. A few years of heightened awareness and then everything was back to a routine.

"What can I do for you?" he said again.

I placed the book down.

"Like to play cops and robbers with me tonight for a spell?"

"What did you have in mind?"

"I might need to hide a lady. Around eight or so. Just for a spell."

"I doubt I'll be around," he said.

"That's probably just as well."

"I don't know."

"Okay," I said and started to get up. "It was just a thought."

"I didn't say no."

I sat back down.

"Is this lady in trouble?"

"Probably. Probably both of us will be by eight o'clock tonight. My plan is to get her out of harm's way before things get too dicey."

"I don't want any bullet holes."

"Oh, I don't expect anything like that," I said, lying.

Leonard reached into the top drawer of his desk with an eye still on me. His hand came out with the key.

"I'd like this back in the morning."

"Sure. If I'm here before you, just pop your head in my door, or I'll come by as soon as I get in."

"Ever thought of writing a book?" he said.

"More times than I can say."

I stood up.

"See you in the morning...I hope."

Leonard was staring as I went out.

An hour later, I started up the narrow, winding road to Jim's place. The sheer, sandstone walls of a narrow canyon surrounded me, leaving but a slice of blue sky above that shadowed world.

At the top of the hill, I turned right onto a short lane, and then right again onto a long driveway. The driveway serviced three houses. Jim's house was at the very end, a square box sheeted with rough-sawn plywood, painted a light chocolate-brown. It could not have looked drabber from the outside if you tried. Then the door opened and you almost gasped. The far end was all glass and perched over a cliff, facing the ocean. There was a view of the white water at main beach and from there all the way up to Palos Verdes. As with the third-floor loft of Colby's old place, standing too close to the windows left you feeling queasy.

Jim welcomed me in and followed me downstairs. Doris was lying on the living room couch with a book. Her pose was an affectionate homage to everything feminine, one foot with its painted toe nails up on a pillow, the other foot tucked up under her satin slacks. She made relaxing look erotic. As I entered the room, she placed the book down but otherwise did not move.

"Something to drink?" Jim asked me.

"No, I'm fine, thanks. I just dropped by to see how Doris was doing."

"I'll be in my office," he said.

"Well, Mr. Mysterious," Doris said. "You weren't kidding about the view."

"Ready to move in?" I said quietly.

She smiled coyly. I sat opposite her on the couch and reached for the book. It was something about vampires.

"Have you ever read her books?"

"I'm still working on Hemingway," I said.

"Ha ha."

"Yeah, it's hell being stuck in the previous century."

"Well, something tells me this is more than a social call."

I had been trying all day to come up with a cute way to frame what I needed to say, and not getting very far with a cute way of saying it, so I tried a prologue.

"I honestly remain baffled about this illicit technology business mentioned in the papers. I'm not even sure that Dan was aware of it. That said, I have little doubt he was planning to smuggle some guns down to Mexico, expecting to make a small fortune in the process and somehow that business got all mixed up with the other three murders, Connie McPherson's included. I just couldn't seem to figure out how and why, but I think I know now."

I explained to Doris most of what I had learned and what I had conjectured as the result of last night's dream. Doris sat there chewing on a nail.

"The point of me being here is, I believe you are one of only three living people who can confirm my suspicions, one way or the other."

Tears welled up in Doris' eyes as we sat there. She was biting on her lower lip now instead of her nails.

"Am I right?"

She nodded.

"It's always torn at me knowing the truth, and I always thought I should have gone to the police about it, but I promised Dan. He's the one who told me that he had made a blood oath to keep things quiet."

Doris hung her head and shook it side to side.

"Though what a blood oath was supposed to mean under the circumstances, I'll never understand."

"I'm afraid it's worth a long time behind bars."

Doris wept quietly.

"God. I've been so ashamed. Trying to protect that bastard, and for what? To end up in jail for agreeing to cover up his sins?"

I went to the nearby powder room, returned with a box of tissues and left Doris to her grief.

"So, what do we do now?" she said, once she was down to working on her sniffles.

"Well, first of all, I need you to tell me everything you know, from that point forward to Connie's death."

355

She did. It took a long time.

"So, what do we do now?" she said again.

"I can't make any promises, Doris, but if you'll come by my office tonight around eight, I think it will go a long way towards keeping you out of legal trouble."

I explained about my neighbor's office and what I had planned.

"The idea is to use you as bait. If I'm right about someone wanting to silence you, they'll show up the minute they know you're there, and that should serve as an indictment. And deflect any attention from your role in that murder."

Doris stared without speaking.

"I'm not going to force you," I said, getting up. I pulled a business card out of my coat pocket. "But the address to my office is there. I'll be waiting if you decide to play along."

She took the card reluctantly. I went in to talk with Jim for a minute before leaving. Doris found it hard to look at me as I went out the door. She had every reason to feel torn. I doubted she would show up.

Rather than returning to my office, I drove to the motel. It was late in the afternoon and I needed some time to think. When people were murdered, it always left a pile of loose ends. Where did Rick and Cliff and Colby fit into this mess? Within any given system, things were always becoming more disordered and their deaths had added greatly to the entropy. I had roughly three hours to see if I could reverse the second law of thermodynamics.

At a little past six, I showered and dressed and gave Sylvia the fortune teller a call. She answered after several rings.

"I'm calling out of concern for Audrey."

"She called a few hours ago and said she was home."

"You'd better give me the number. She's in a lot of danger. Probably the only place safe for her right now is in a jail cell."

Sylvia gave it to me.

"A great burden is about to be lifted from you."

"I know. You've said as much, but experience has shown me, you get rid of one burden and another one takes its place."

"No. I saw it in your palm. You are nearing a crossroads. Follow your heart and don't be afraid when the call comes. You'll soon be in a place you really love."

"Thanks for the encouraging words."

I got off and gave Audrey a call. To my surprise, she answered.

"I'm really, really sorry about disappearing again, Michael."

"It's all right. I saw you with Vanderhof this morning."

There was a long silence.

"It's not what you think."

"Yeah? Well maybe someday you'll explain it to me but we don't have time for that right now. We need to figure out what to do with this money."

"It was there?"

"It was there. A lot of it and if we don't play this right, those cartel boys will just send another hit man across the border, and another one and they'll keep sending them until they get what they want, or a lot of people are dead. Probably both."

"What do you suggest we do?"

"I don't know. I haven't even accounted for those Russians yet but I'm working on things. It appeared that I had this train headed in the right direction last night, only Nacho got antsy and came looking for me before things fell into place. You probably heard an abridged version of what transpired from there on the news. We played cops and banditos for an hour or so. Nacho got away and now I don't know how to reach him, and that's assuming he's still alive."

"I'm sorry," Audrey said again.

"Are we talking about the money or Vanderhof?"

"Don't be so cold, Michael."

"Sorry. It comes with the years. Anyway, I already know what you're hiding. I know what your husband was trying to tell me that day he lay dying on the sidewalk below my office windows. 'My wife Audrey, she knows the'."

357

She was silent.

"Yeah, I figured as much. Somehow you learned the reason why Connie was killed, and it's the same reason Dan and Rick were killed and it's why you're next on the list, so you'd better get yourself to some place safe for the night."

"I don't know where I'd go," she said.

"Stop with the helpless bit, Audrey. It really doesn't become you."

"Why are you so angry, Michael?"

"Why? Because I don't like seeing love turned into a business deal. You know, there are actual feelings involved."

"I told you. There's something going on that you just don't understand."

"I know. The same line of crap you gave me out in the desert. Your lips are sealed. You swore a solemn oath. I'll look for an article in the business section of tomorrow's paper to clear things up."

"Michael, please," she said. "I just need your help tonight."

"Doing what?"

"I want you to take the money down to your office."

"Why would I do that?"

"I'm just asking you to trust me."

"Like hell."

"Please, Michael. I trusted you. All I'm asking is for you to do the same in return."

"Not without some sort of explanation."

"If you want me to beg, I will. I'll do anything you ask. I'll go anywhere you want me to go if you'll just do this one thing for me."

"I'd be a fool without knowing what this is all about."

"Please, Michael. I'm on your side. You know that."

"No, I don't."

"Please?"

"No."

I listened to the sound of silence in the receiver.

"All right, it's about Vanderhof," she said. "You think you know what happened with him in the past but you don't know the half of it."

"Okay. I'm all ears. Explain."

"Please, Michael. All I'm asking you to do is take the money down to your office. I'll be there around eight o'clock. Then everything will get sorted out and you and I can run away together if you want. Okay? Please, Michael," she said again when I had failed to answer.

"All right. I don't know why I'm being such a fool for you but I'll be there."

"With the money."

"Yeah, yeah, with the money."

"Okay. I'll see you soon."

"Yeah, I'll see you soon."

"I still love the way you hold me."

"Yeah, sure," I said and hung up, feeling as if I had just arranged for my own funeral.

Once I had gone down to settle up for the extra night with Mikolas, I grabbed the money out of the attic and headed back downtown. I hid the money in my office safe and went down to see if Leonard was gone. He was. I closed his blinds and left his door unlocked.

Seated at my desk, I felt again like I was setting myself up for the fall, and that led to a strange urge to smoke a cigarette. Memories of my days bumming around Europe as a young man followed, and that brought to mind the bifurcated nature of a man's past. A café in Paris, my Gauloises and a paper, those things seemed at once as distant as the stars and so close I could almost reach out and touch them.

Looking the other way, the end seemed nearer than distant now. There were no memories yet of the possibly thirty or forty years I had left to live, but I was fairly certain I would look back from those distant years, feeling the same way about this moment as I did now about the past. Each moment would seem at once far, far away and as if it had happened just yesterday.

Some of those days would have passed by like an eternity. Some would have flown by in the wink of an eye, but either way, I would find myself at the end, thinking, my god, what have I done? What have I done? It went by so quickly. Did I give it all I had? Was I ever there, all of me, in the moment I was living?

I sat there for a long time, a prisoner of that still unfinished script.

Sometime later, I glanced at the clock. It was half past seven. I had been lost for nearly an hour.

With another half hour to kill, I went online to check the news. A story was trending.

Feds Kill One Man, Still Searching For Another Terrorist Plot Thwarted in LA Harbor

The article went on to explain how both the dead man and the one on the run were tied to a Saudi arms dealer, who was himself tied to a rogue FBI agent now chilling out behind bars.

How neat and tidy, I thought, getting to the end of the article, except they were a Mexican cartel, the Russian mafia and three dead bodies shy of a proper denouement. Had I not known any better, I would have bought it too, just like every other fool who was reading this news.

I had been thinking to call someone and set the record straight when the door to the street opened downstairs and the sound of high heels started up the wooden steps. Was it Audrey with a gun? Or Doris? Either way, I knew too much and someone needed to shut me up.

Just to be safe, I got cozy with that Smith & Wesson again and ready for trouble. A moment later, a shadow appeared outside my office door. There was a knock.

"Come in," I said.

The door opened. It was Doris. She did not appear to be packing.

"You came."

"I really don't know why. My conscience, I guess."

"Yeah. They're a pain in the ass, aren't they?"

"Yeah they are."

"Well, come in." I stood up. "Welcome to my kingdom. It's not much but it has a view."

I discreetly made sure that Doris had taken a tour in front of the open blinds.

"Are you ready?" I said.

"For what?"

"I'm going to hide you down in my neighbor's office."

"Why?"

"To keep you out of trouble. If somebody's after you, they already know you're here."

I put a hand to the back of her cashmere sweater and guided her out the door.

There was one light on in the hallway. The inside of Betty and Leonard's office was completely dark.

"Sorry. No lights on in here. There's a sofa. Why don't you lie down and take a nap?"

"Ha," she said.

"Okay. Lie down and think of better days. Are you having a nice time at Jim's place?"

"What? Are we playing matchmaker now?"

"Sorry. It's probably a bit too soon but he's definitely an upgrade from Rick."

Doris stared through a ton of sadness and regrets.

"Jim's a very nice man," she said.

"I never talk about this, but I suppose he's my best friend. I don't have many."

"I guess that would have its pluses and minuses," she said.

"I can assure you it does."

Doris kicked off her high heels and lay down. She was wearing jeans, with no nylons. Her black pumps had left little creases on the insteps of her delicate feet. There was something raw and sensuous about the woman. I felt a twinge of envy towards Jim.

"Will you be all right?" I asked her.

"I just hope this isn't going to take all night."

"I don't think so. A few hours. And don't scream if you hear guns."

"Ha," she said.

"Seriously. Don't make a sound, no matter what."

"I'll do my best."

I touched her shoulder reassuringly and locked the door on my way out. In the hallway, I cracked open the door to the fire escape and left it slightly ajar. I reached up and unscrewed the hallway light.

Back in my office, I sat down at my desk to wait. The bankers lamp was on. The rest of the room was in darkness. Just to be safe, I pulled out the Smith & Wesson and placed it on a hidden shelf under the drawer.

How long would it take, I wondered? Were there even any rats out there nibbling on my bait? The response came sooner than I had anticipated.

I heard the door to the street open. The door to the alley opened and closed a moment later. Then two sets of footsteps started up the stairs and continued down the hallway. Whoever it was paused outside my door before opening it. It was Dick and Tom again.

"What brings you boys around?"

"Unsettled business," Dick said. "Where is she?"

"Where's who?"

"Don't get cute."

Tom came around and looked out the window before looking back at me with his usual smile. Dick nodded and Tom patted me down.

"He's clean."

"Where's the fireworks?" Dick asked me.

"Down in the car."

"And where is she?"

I stared at him, trying to read his mind. Was he looking for Doris? Or Audrey? Not knowing which one for sure, I gave him a generic answer.

"She heard you coming and ran off."

Dick nodded and Tom went out to have a look. He came back in.

"Looks like she may have gone down the fire escape."

"Go out in back and check around."

Dick fished a cell phone out of his coat pocket and made a call. His gun was pointed in the general direction of my guts.

"I have him here," he said when someone answered. "No, she slipped away."

There was a pause.

"All right. See you then."

Dick got off and made another call.

"Anything?" Dick said into the phone. He paused to listen. "All right. We'll find her. Just keep the back of the building staked out for now."

Dick got off.

"What now?" I asked him.

"We wait."

"Well, like most romances, it was kind of fun there at the start."

"And like most romances, someone always gets screwed in the end."

"Like Dan Colby."

Dick ignored me and looked at his watch.

"How much are they paying you, Dick? It must be millions to shit all over your once hard-earned reputation."

Dick kept checking his watch.

"You ever lie in bed at night, wondering where you went wrong?"

"Shut it," Dick said. "You got a problem, you can take it up with the boss."

"Oh, okay. So the president's on his way over."

Dick stared out the window in response. I had never liked him all that much. I liked him even less so now.

31

Moments later, the street door opened again and fresh footsteps started up the stairs; slowly, laboriously. I followed their progress down the hallway until a shadow appeared. Dick opened the door and Vanderhof stepped in. I wasn't surprised.

"Our citizen of the year," I said. Vanderhof smiled his not so pleasant smile. "I guess we can forget about that bailout plan."

He shook his head at me.

"This could have turned out so much differently."

"Just the facts, Vanderhof. You can spare me the dramatics."

"Well, the fact is, you seem to know too much." He nodded at Dick. "Any news?"

"No sign of her yet."

Vanderhof checked his watch.

"Okay. We'll give it a few more minutes."

He glanced at me once like I was an inanimate object and out the window.

"Do I get a last wish?" I said.

Vanderhof looked back.

"Yeah, sure. Why not. What do you want?"

"How about clearing up some of the loose ends for me. I'll sleep much better knowing the truth."

"Okay, but let's do that with a bit of background music."

Vanderhof turned on my CD player and hit the button. I had been listening to Miles Davis the previous evening and the last track picked up where it had left off with *Flamenco Sketches*. I immediately thought of Caitlin. Well, doll, guess we'll have to try this again next time around.

Vanderhof turned up the volume a bit.

"Okay, where did you want to start?"

"How about at the beginning?"

"I don't know where that would be."

"Okay. Here's how I see it. You're young and fresh out of college and life is nothing but fun and games. The whole world is ahead of you. But all of a sudden, you have this little girl on your hands. Cute as a button, but she's a real screamer and it's driving you mad. Your once carefree existence has flown right out the window. So you try shutting her up during one of those middle of the night crying sessions and lose control. And next thing you know, you've got a dead little girl on your hands."

Vanderhof looked down. I was staring at him in the silence. Dick was staring at him in the silence.

After some moments, Vanderhof looked up.

"Am I getting warm, Dirk?"

"Look," he said. "You're bringing up some very sad memories and I want you to know right now, it still hurts me. I really loved that little girl and would never have done a thing to hurt her."

"But you did."

He shook his head, but without much conviction, the willingness to lie seemingly kicked right out of him.

"Anyway, the way I figure it, Elfie must have been out of town. Something, because she never knew the truth. But her absence gave you a chance to cook up a story, and that's when you went to see your partner, Colby, who liked you and needed you enough to help you cover up your crime. A crime that literally remained buried through the years, the truth of it rotting away inside of you, with never a word said to anyone, not even Elfie. But then you ran into Connie McPherson one day. She's getting a divorce and you've always had a thing for her and next thing you know you're lying in her arms late one night, confessing your sins. For going on fifteen years, you've

366

been dying to get this thing off your chest. Only, the next morning, you realize what you've done and Connie has to go. And she goes. And lucky for you, Steve McPherson has been out stalking his wife and looks all dressed up to be your fall guy."

"Sounds like a great Netflix series, there, partner."

"Could be, huh?"

"Sure…" Vanderhof checked his watch. "You about done?"

"Oh, not by a long shot. But what the hell. It's my last hurrah, right?"

"Yeah, sure. Knock yourself out."

"About this arms shipment. I admit to being baffled by the backstory, but as best as I can figure, what Colby knew about your past somehow got mixed up in the deal. How or why? I have no idea. You'd have to explain that one to me."

"The fact is, Devlin, there are some things in this world that people like you aren't supposed to know or understand."

"Is that how it is?"

"That's how it is." Vanderhof smiled in a way that spoke of treachery more than mirth. "That said, I never entirely understood Colby's gamble, either."

"How do you mean?"

"Well, Colby had been around the block a few times. He knew how these things played out. The company asks you to help facilitate a transaction, so you go along and everyone comes out smelling like a rose. Why be a fool and go off the reservation for one big pay day?"

"The company. As in, *the* company?"

Vanderhof nodded. I glanced over at Dick. He was keeping an eye on things out on the street. A busy summer night was in full swing down below us. I looked back at Vanderhof.

"You were saying. About Colby and one big pay day."

"Yeah. I still don't know exactly what got him motivated but some serious interests were crisscrossing through that shipping container up in the harbor. Colby knew I had been called in to help things play out smoothly and all he had to do was play along with us. He knew there would be some serious perks for keeping his mouth shut and staying in line."

"And he didn't, so he had to go."

Vanderhof shrugged.

"It was probably a smart move," I said.

"And why do you say that?"

"Because Colby was in love with Audrey, and once he got wind of you playing around with her too? It wouldn't have taken him long to think of pointing a gun at you."

"He was in love with Audrey? Wow. I knew Colby had been hanging around with her a bit, but love? How did you know that? And how did you know I had been fooling around with her?"

I raised my eyebrows.

"Oh right. You're a private detective. So tell me about Colby."

"It was in his will. He had it changed. Audrey in, Doris out."

"Wow," Vanderhof said.

"Yeah. There were poems too."

"Poems, huh?"

"Yeah. Jack found them on the company computer and told Doris about it. On the sly. That said, there was no mention of who Colby's love interest was, so Doris didn't know the answer to that until probate."

"Tough break for Doris," Vanderhof said.

"Yeah, tough break."

Vanderhof had another look at his watch.

"Where the hell is she?" he said to Dick.

Dick shook his head.

"All right. We'll give her another minute."

Vanderhof looked back at me.

"Nice song, by the way," he said.

"A lovely way to go, isn't it?"

He smiled.

"You're all right, Devlin."

"Well, I thought I was doing okay there for a bit...but those are the breaks."

"Those are the breaks. Don't worry, pal. We'll make it easy on you."

"Thanks. You want me to play the song again?"

"I was kind of hoping we were done with this little fairytale of yours."

I hit the button and the song started again.

"No, not by a long shot. See, as best as I can figure it, Colby must have been worried enough about being next in line that he started to put his affairs in order, which included this Audrey in, Doris out of his will business. Meanwhile, you must have gotten worried, knowing that Colby was one of only three people in this world who knew about your little girl. I'm guessing here, but with this shipment deal going sideways, there was always a chance of someone putting the screws to Colby and Colby shooting off his mouth. To save his own ass."

Vanderhof smirked.

"I have to hand it to you, Devlin. You have a colorful imagination."

"Yeah, so I've been told. Anyway, that's the way I figure it. I know this much. Colby saved something onto that flash drive, something he thought would keep you from putting a slug in him, though I never did figure out what that was. Maybe a grid for where your girl is buried?"

Vanderhof started drumming his fingers on my desk, looking agitated.

"Getting warm, am I?" I said.

He looked back at me.

"Sure, sure. Whatever you say, Sherlock. Let me know when you're done."

I nodded.

"Oh, I admit. My theory has a few holes in it. Like why didn't whatever Colby had placed on that flash drive stop you from putting a slug in his chest."

"That's a pretty big hole."

"It is. But the way I figure it, you were starting to feel squeezed from several directions. It was only natural that you'd start to get careless."

"Yeah? That's the way you figure it, huh?"

"That's the way I figure it. See, at the time, knowing about the poems, but not about Audrey, or the will, Doris had Jack put a gentle squeeze on Colby, just to find out where she stood, not imagining in her wildest dreams the kind of hornet's nest she'd be stirring up, or that you might get involved. Then there was Rick. Doris never told him about your daughter, but she let slip with her suspicions about Connie. And Rick, caught somewhere between being a fool and his Napoleonic complex, tried to play a hand on you, so you had Dick add him to your collection of dead bodies."

Vanderhof was looking evermore impatient and shook his head.

"You know, Devlin. I actually like you. If you could have just minded your own business. I saw us building our own little beachy bar down there on the coast. Throw up a couple of nice shacks for getaway places. Make some money together. Fly down there every few months. Do some fishing. Get our feet in the sand. It would have been the life."

"You'd have found a reason to put a slug in me too. Sooner or later."

Vanderhof eyed me for a moment and nodded at Dick, who made a call. Vanderhof was staring out the window while he did.

"No answer," Dick said.

Vanderhof frowned and made a call of his own.

"Shit," he said, hanging up. "I wonder where she is?"

"You looking for Doris?"

"Don't think you're so smart, Devlin."

We all stood there exchanging glances.

"All right," Vanderhof said. "The bedtime stories are over."

He nodded at Dick.

"Once you get him tied up in your van, have Tom come back up and wait, in case she finally shows up."

Dick walked around behind me. The last bars of Flamenco Sketches came to an end. Dick turned off the CD player and nudged me with his gun.

"Mind if I turn out the light?" I said. "I like to do my bit for global warming."

Vanderhof nodded. I pulled the chain on the banker's lamp as he opened the door. In that split second of darkness, I deflected Dick's gun hand, gave him an elbow to the throat and broke his right arm with a twist. Vanderhof, hearing Dick yelp, disappeared out into the hallway. I reached under my drawer for the Smith & Wesson and started to step over Dick. He was reaching for his gun with the left hand so I gave him a good rap on the head. He went still with a groan.

I had started around my desk when Vanderhof reappeared at my door, backing up with his hands in the air. Audrey appeared in the doorway a moment later with her Pink Lady .38 pointed at Vanderhof's guts, the two of them etched in moonlight while playing out their little drama.

"You don't want to be doing this, doll," Vanderhof said.

"Don't tell me what I do and don't want to be doing, Dirk."

"Hey, come on. We were just talking about going away together this morning."

"That was your plan, not mine."

"Come on, doll. Anywhere you want in the world, remember?"

He made an affectionate move towards Audrey but she jabbed at him with the .38 in response, like she really meant business.

"Don't even try it," she said.

"All right, doll," he said, half chuckling to himself and backing further into my office.

"And quit calling me doll. I am so tired of you calling me doll."

Audrey glanced at me with both of her hands on the gun, albeit a bit unsteadily.

"You wanted to know what this was all about, Michael?"

"Yes, but you have to trust me. This is not the time and place to be explaining it."

"Yeah, you'd better try and talk some sense into her," Vanderhof said. "In fact, you'd both better take a long, hard look at what you're doing, because if one of us goes down, we're all going down together."

"You bastard," she said. "I'm so tired of your threats hanging over my head. I'm so tired of your bullying and lies."

It's all right, Audrey," I told her. "Everything's going to be straightened out here in short order. Now please give me the gun before you do something stupid."

I went to reach for it but she brushed me away.

"No, we're going to get everything out in the open right now. Starting with how Dirk obtained his rights to that online gambling website in China."

Audrey glanced from Vanderhof to me and back at Vanderhof.

"You see, he traded illicit technology to the Chinese as part of his deal. And had me set up a dummy corporation to cover his tracks."

"You made a lot of money on that transaction, doll."

"I said quit calling me doll!"

"Audrey," I said. "I'm telling you again. Don't do this right now."

"No, you're going to hear me out. You see, Dirk never told me up front what he was doing. So, by the time I found out, I was up to my neck in his crimes and he had something to hang over my head every time he needed it. If he went down, I was going down with him. The last straw was when Dan Colby told me about the little girl. Somehow Dirk figured that out and he's been making my life a living hell ever since. I'm sure he thought that I had told Cliff and that's why he had Cliff killed."

"Okay Audrey," I said. "You have a witness. It's all out in the open now. Just give me the gun and let me take care of the rest."

Audrey moved my way with the gun still pointed at Vanderhof.

"You forgot to tell Devlin about one little thing, doll. The little baby we were going to have. You know, I'm still really, really hurt that you decided to have an abortion."

"You bastard! I hate you! You ruin everything you touch!"

The .38 went off and a bullet smashed into the plaster wall behind Vanderhof's head. While I snatched the gun from Audrey's hand, Vanderhof tried to deck me but I ducked and put him down with a knee in his groin. In that instant, the front and back doors of the building both flew open and footsteps stormed up the stairs. As they raced down the hallway, I dragged Audrey behind the desk with me. She recoiled at the sight of Dick lying there looking dead. Vanderhof was on his knees in the middle of the room, groaning. The shadows of several men appeared out in the hallway and the parted door opened slowly the rest of the way. Three of Decker's men came in with guns drawn, followed by Decker.

"What the hell?" he said, seeing Vanderhof on the floor.

Vanderhof was still groaning. Decker peered into the darkness.

"Are you in there, Devlin?"

"Yeah, I'm here.

"And Audrey?"

"She's in here with me."

"I heard shots. Did somebody get plugged?"

Dick was just coming to and groaned behind me.

"No, but I gave this one a nice souvenir…We're standing up now."

I positioned Audrey behind me and hit the banker's lamp. Decker's men helped Vanderhof up. Decker came over and had a look at Dick.

"Jesus Christ," he said with a look back at Vanderhof. "Do you always have to make my life so goddamned difficult?"

Vanderhof tried to smile but it came off poorly.

"Okay," Decker said to Audrey. "Where's this money?"

I looked at Audrey.

"What did you do?"

"I made a deal with him."

"What kind of deal?"

"He told me if I gave him the money, he'd clear my name and get Dirk off my back."

I looked from Audrey to Decker and back at Audrey.

"Aw, kid, you don't know what you've done here."

"All right, all right," Decker said. "If everyone wants to go home tonight, the only way we're going to make a neat little package out of this mess is with that money, so where is it?"

Decker waved his gun back and forth. Reluctantly, I went over to the safe and opened it. Once the package had been placed on my desk, one of Decker's men stepped over and pulled back the plastic wrapping.

"Is that all of it?" Decker said to me.

"That's all I found."

"All right. Get him out of here," Decker said with a nod at Vanderhof. "And take Dick here with you."

Two men hoisted Dick to his feet and dragged him towards the door. Vanderhof glanced back once with a slightly better smile. Decker pointed his gun back at Audrey and me.

"You two are under arrest for selling firearms to the Sinaloa cartel."

"What?!" Audrey screamed.

She tried to take a swipe at Decker but I caught her arm and pulled her back to my chest.

"You lying bastard! You lying bastard!"

She had completely fallen apart. I looked back at Decker.

"What's the matter, Decker? We know too much? Afraid we'll put a hitch in the 'show and tell' you had planned for the press corps?"

"Don't think you're so smart, Devlin."

"I'm smart enough to know that Vanderhof's been blackmailing her, and I'm guessing you know that too."

"I don't get involved personal squabbles."

"Bullshit. The man's a walking felony."

"And like he said, Devlin. There are some things in this world that people like you aren't supposed to know or understand."

"Go to hell."

"Yeah? Well, that's the way it is."

"Then you'd better put a bullet in me, because that's not the way the story's going to go down when I start talking."

He nodded and two of his men came around to start cuffing me.

"You know what really makes me sick, Decker?"

"Yeah? What's that?"

"Seeing people like you, so caught up in your backroom board game, you don't realize that you've become worse than the problem."

"And if you haven't noticed, Devlin, most people are pretty happy with the arrangement. We keep the bad guys away from the good guys and everyone gets to have their Sunday afternoon football."

"Yeah. It's all black and white out here on the front side, right? While you get to slink around in that gray, murky world of yours."

"All right, enough with the storytelling," he said.

Just as Decker's men were leading me away with Audrey, several cars screeched to a halt down in front. Decker had a look out the window.

"What the hell?"

I looked too and saw Whalen and seven other cops rushing into the building. They had shotguns cocked and loaded. Two other cops stayed behind, one of them with a shotgun at his hip. The other one was rolling out some caution tape. The folks over at Mark's Bistro were choking on their linguini.

A few seconds later, Whalen and his gang barged in, ready for a shootout.

"Did you get it?" he asked me.

"More or less."

"What? Either he confessed or he didn't?"

I glanced at Audrey and back.

"You've got enough to indict him…and then some."

Whalen pulled the pen out of the penholder on my desk. Two of Pat's men were leading Vanderhof back into the room. Pat turned to face him and waved the pen.

"You ever seen one of these? Records just about anything you want. Meaning, you're under arrest for the murder of Zoe Vanderhof."

"Now wait a damned minute," Decker said. "We're running the show around here."

"Yeah?" Whalen said. "Well, you were running the show around here, until we showed up. And now we've got more guns than you do."

Decker had a look at the posse of shotguns pointed in his direction. Vanderhof looked at Decker. It was hard to tell if Vanderhof was truly concerned, or just irritated. Probably a little of both.

"Don't get yourself all worked up," Decker said to him. "We'll have this all straightened out by tomorrow morning."

"Yeah," Whalen said. "You'll come around pulling strings, but by then Vanderhof will be in the hands of a Superior Court judge and grand jury. Of course, if you think we can divide him up into pieces, I'll be happy to loan you the part I don't need."

Whalen nodded at me.

"Is that the money?"

"Yeah."

Whalen nodded at his boys to gather it up.

"Uncuff him," he told Decker.

When Decker's men appeared to reach for their guns, the shotguns came up.

"Careful," Whalen said.

One of Decker's man undid my cuffs.

"You two had better come with me," Whalen said. "Hanging around with this crowd doesn't look to be good for your health. Price and Stafford, you stay here with Langston. I'll send Burrell right over to take care of any forensics. Make sure these boys don't get their mitts on anything else in the meantime."

Whalen and the rest of his men started backing us out of the office. They had shotguns pointed in all directions. I couldn't help myself from taking a shot at Decker as we went by.

"You were saying, Decker? About all the things in this world that people like me aren't supposed to know or understand."

"Come on," Whalen said, grabbing me by the arm. "This is no time for fucking around."

I joined Audrey out in the hallway. Whalen and his men backed us down the stairs with their shotguns pointed front and back.

Once they had Vanderhof cuffed and sitting in the back of a squad car, I squatted down by his door. The last light of day was lingering over the rooftops. A solitary crow was cawing away in the Ficus tree above our heads.

"Sorry about…you know…what happened back there."

"I wouldn't worry yourself, Devlin. About any of it."

I looked down in the general direction of his handcuffs. He nodded.

"Like I said, I wouldn't worry yourself. I've got enough money to buy whatever I need in this world, including justice."

"Yeah. Is there enough in there to buy yourself a clean conscience?"

One of Whalen's men got behind the wheel and gave me a nod. Realizing it was a waste of time, I stood up.

"I'll be thinking of you, Vanderhof. Next time I'm down there sipping a cold one at that beachy bar."

Vanderhof looked forward. I closed the door and tried to imagine the dark road out there ahead of him. As usual, it was hard to tell how much this state of affairs had him worried and how much he viewed it as just one more pain in the ass problem for his stable of attorneys. Either way, the search was back on for that citizen of the year award.

32

Up at the station, Whalen took my statement first. Audrey was offered a chance to call an attorney but declined.

"I just want the truth out," she said with a look at me.

Whalen glanced my way. I shrugged. If that's the way she wanted it, fine. There was no hope of a happy ending between the two of us until she came clean.

While Whalen worked her over, I walked back down to my office. The alley in back was lined with news trucks from end to end. The street in front was a carnival of cops and cop cars. From the shadows moving around in my office, I knew the forensics folks were still busy poking around. Bernie hustled down the stairs from my office building while I stood out in the street waiting.

"What did you find out?" I asked him

"Nothing on Vanderhof yet. I'm still looking for a scoop."

"All right, Bernie. My ass is in a sling here but I'll tell you what you would have found out, if you were any kind of reporter."

"Screw you."

"Yeah, well, just remember, I'm going to get my ass grilled at some point tomorrow by the chief and the DA, so I have to hold a few cards back, and you didn't get this from me."

"Anonymous sources," he said.

"That's the way it's got to be. And you owe me one."

Over the next fifteen minutes, I provided Bernie with a Reader's Digest version of what had gone down, covering my own ass as much as necessary and leaving Audrey out of things as much as I could, Doris too.

By the time Bernie ran off, the forensics people were done upstairs. All but a few of the cops had melted away into the night. I walked up to free Doris from captivity.

"I have to pee," she said the minute I had opened the door to Betty and Leonard's office.

I shrugged apologetically. I had failed to consider that angle.

I waited at my office door while Doris used the bathroom down at the end of the hall.

"Come in," I said when she was done. "Have a seat."

She did. I closed the door and went around to my side of the desk.

"So now what?" she said.

I explained everything that had happened in her absence. We were left staring at each other.

"So?" she said.

"I don't know, Doris. That's really up to you."

"You're not going to turn me in?"

I scoffed

"Why would I do that? Whatever happened is between you and your own conscience. And whatever gods you happen to believe in."

She hung her head in tears. I watched and waited.

Finally, she looked up.

"I feel like I should go and confess."

"Why don't you give it some time. Go talk to Jim. He's a good shoulder to lean on. Our society's big on extracting its pound of flesh but I prefer to look at the bigger picture. You had nothing to do with that poor little girl's death, and I know you truly regret the part you played. What's the point of sending you to prison? Nothing's going to bring her back."

Doris wiped at fresh tears.

"God, I wish I could somehow. She was such a sweet little thing."

I got up and went around to comfort her. She looked up at me after a spell.

"Just do like I said, okay? Go talk to Jim. Is your stuff still up there?"

She nodded.

"Is he expecting you?"

"I don't know, with the hour and all."

"Oh, I'm sure he'll be happy to see you."

I called Jim while Doris watched. He answered groggily.

"I'm sending the troops back up the hill."

"Fine. Tell her I'll be at the door whenever she knocks."

"He's waiting for you," I said when I got off. "Come on, I'll walk you down to your car."

Doris got up and followed me down to the street. We stopped to face each other at the door of her car.

"Don't be too hard on yourself," I repeated.

Doris nodded.

"Nothing would have brought her back."

Doris threw herself at my chest before climbing into her car. I waited until she had driven off before heading back up to the station. It was late when Whalen finally let Audrey go. As part of the deal I had made with him, if she came out clean about the murders, he'd ignore any white-collar crimes and leave that to the Feds.

Before they brought Audrey out, Whalen sat down to level with me.

"You know what that was all about?" I asked him. "I mean, the deal she was trying to make with Decker and Vanderhof and the money."

"I've got her side of it. Hell if I can figure out the rest. I don't think she shot anybody, and I don't think her hands are dirty in either the Al-Hamad or Colby scheme, but that's not saying she's clean."

"Clean enough to go home tonight?"

"Clean enough for me. I can't vouch for what the Feds will want to do with her, but unless something else comes up, she's out of my gun sights."

"Okay. Thanks. Are you done with me?"

"Probably not. I'll go to bat for you as much as I can, but you'll have to face the DA and the chief no matter what."

"I know. Is she coming out?"

"I'll send her out in a minute. I'd be careful if I were you."

"Thanks. I already had my guard up."

He disappeared in back. I stood up when Audrey appeared in the lobby a minute later. She gave me a hug and we walked back out to the street.

"Thanks for being here."

"Sure. Where's your car."

"Over on Mermaid."

"Come on. I'll walk you down."

She took hold of my arm and shook me.

"You seem like you're a million miles away now."

"Yeah?"

"Yeah."

"Well that's just the way it feels, Audrey. Call me confused."

"Confused about what?"

"About everything, I suppose. Come on, I'll walk you back to your car."

As we walked, Audrey related the gist of her grilling by Whalen. We arrived to her car. She hit the wireless lock and leaned against the door.

"Do you really think he's done with me?"

"He said he was but neither one of us are completely out of the woods yet. Me with Whalen, you with the Feds, both of us with that cartel."

We stared at each other under the moonlight.

"Tell me what that was all about. With Decker."

"He came to question me and I assumed I could make a deal with him. I thought he would want to take Vanderhof down."

I shook my head.

"What?"

"Oh, nothing. I suppose a few days ago, I would have thought the same thing. The cavalry comes riding in and all that."

"You think I was a fool."

"Like I said, a few days ago, I would have thought the same thing…If you had come to me first, I probably could have saved us both a lot of grief…A little bit, anyway."

"So where do we stand, Michael?"

"I'm not sure. They'll be grilling me tomorrow and I suspect the Feds aren't done with you yet."

"I'm not talking about that. I'm talking about us."

"I don't know about that either."

"Take me home with you," she said, pressing her body against mine.

"No. That's not going to happen. Not tonight."

"Please."

"No."

"Oh Michael. Why are you doing this?"

"I just need some time to think, that's all. I'm heading down to my place in Baja for a week or so. Maybe things will seem clearer to me when I get back."

"You're still mad because you saw me with Dirk."

Hearing her refer to Vanderhof by first name was just another knife in my heart. Suddenly, all their little intimacies were imaginable to me.

"I just need some time," I said again.

"Okay, Michael. Maybe we both need some time."

I kissed her. I kissed her good, like it was for forever and a day, and waited there at the curb while she drove away, weighed down by my own failures as much as hers. In any case, I had no stomach for talking through what Audrey and I would have to talk through to make things right. At least not on that night.

In the morning, I called to make sure Jim would be there for my ass chewing. He said he would. Jim was being more reticent than usual. I sensed Doris was still hanging around the house. I got off without prying.

The bout up at the police station was scheduled for two. Whalen had a ringside seat. I was to bring along my homework; a report on every little lie I had told and every little law I had fudged and every little secret I had failed to disclose. I spent several hours at my desk, trying to draw up a version of things that made some sense without cooking my own ass.

The mood was grim when I walked into Chief Daly's office. People had been murdered and someone had to answer for it.

The cops had already determined that the hairs on Connie McPherson's dress were a match with Vanderhof. And using a call she had made from her cell phone, they were able to place Connie and Vanderhof in the same general vicinity on the day of her murder. Also, earlier in the morning, they had dug up the remains of Vanderhof's daughter at Colby's shipyard. My suspicion about those curious numbers on the flash drive had been correct. Foreseeing that Vanderhof might one day turn on him, Colby had made a grid for where the body was buried and had placed that grid on the flash drive once Vanderhof started playing rough with him. Worried about my own ass, I had saved the information onto a CD.

Of course, Vanderhof denied it all and that's why they had attorneys. With enough money and lawyerly parsing, you could turn what seemed plain and simple to the average person into something complicated beyond your wildest dreams. And I imagined Vanderhof's attorneys were busy working to that end that very second.

I handed my homework over to the chief and sat down to take my licking. A stenographer was there to chronicle the event. Jim was there in case anyone thought I wasn't being honest.

The chief nodded at our arrival and offered me a pained smile.

"I appreciate you coming in, Mr. Devlin."

"Glad to help."

384

Thirty seconds and we had already told two more lies.

The chief quickly scanned through my homework and glanced around the room. He was a transplant from an east coast city; older, urbane looking. This was Chief Daly's swan song of sorts. The city of Laurel Lagoon had imported him a few years back, in the wake of a police scandal. Next stop was retirement. Whatever else you could say about Chief Daly, he did not look like your typical west coast cop.

He nodded at Jim.

"I suppose we can start by informing counsel that the murder charges will be dropped against Steve McPherson. All agreed?"

Whalen nodded. The DA did too, however reluctantly.

The chief looked back at Jim.

"I believe we can arrange for you to pick Steve up tomorrow morning."

Jim nodded. The chief looked at me.

"The general consensus on you, Mr. Devlin is that you ought to be drawn and quartered. Disturbing a crime scene..."

"Objection," Jim said.

"All right, all right," the chief said. "Having no proof of the fact, we'll pretend that flash drive materialized out of thin air, but at some point over the past week, we arrive at a juncture where Mr. Devlin is clearly withholding evidence and giving false testimony."

"Objection."

"All right, counsel. We're mincing words here. My point is, your client has been telling something less than the truth and I'd like to know why. Care to elaborate, Mr. Devlin?"

He held up the front page of that morning's LA Times.

"For instance, we have an article here, cataloguing what the FBI claims to have found in a shipping container up in LA harbor. Some small arms, ammunition for the small arms and..."

The chief pulled the newspaper back around and read from the article.

"Spare helicopter parts destined for a repair facility in Liberia'...when apparently they don't even have a helicopter repair facility in Liberia."

"Here," he said, handing me the paper.

I took it and stared at the article while Chief Daly continued his scolding.

"Am I to believe that some gun store grade armaments are what led to my town being shot up two nights running?"

I looked up from the paper.

"I was told there are things that folks like me aren't supposed to know or understand."

"Who told you that?"

"Decker. Vanderhof. Dick and Tom."

"Who on earth are Dick and Tom?"

I looked at Whalen. So did the chief.

"The two operatives working for Vanderhof," Whalen said. "Well, we believe they were working for Vanderhof but they're not talking, neither is Vanderhof and we're being stonewalled by Decker and the boys higher up."

"Humph," the chief said. "So, you were saying, Mr. Devlin?"

"About what?"

"About this article in The Times and all the stuff that folks like you aren't supposed to know or understand. And let us not forget about this two million dollars sitting here on my desk."

Everyone glanced at the stack of money.

"Where would you like me to start, sir?"

"How about with the article."

"I would take it with a grain of salt."

"Why's that?"

"As you've already said, it's hard to explain shooting up Laurel Lagoon two nights running over some small arms and spare helicopter parts."

"Then what do you think was actually going on?"

"I'm not sure."

"Would you care to hazard a wild guess?"

"Off the record?"

The stenographer glanced up at me and the chief as she worked. He remained staring at me.

"I'm afraid this is all being written down for posterity, Mr. Devlin. But in this one instance, I promise not to use it against you."

I looked around the room and back at Chief Daly.

"Then here's my take. There were three agendas mixed up in this mess. Colby's, this business with Al-Hamad and his FBI pal and whatever Decker and his pals were cooking up. And of course the Russians. I guess that's four. Anyway, things were bound to get a bit complicated, given the conflicting interests."

"Let's start with Colby. What do you know about him and his motives?"

I explained what I knew for sure and asked if they had found Nacho yet.

The chief and DA and Whalen all shared a look. The chief looked back at me.

"It would seem that he has slipped from our grasp. For the moment."

"Then short of his return and a complete confession, you've heard my best theory. Colby was trying to divert that arms shipment down to Mexico, all in an effort to buy Audrey a million-dollar yacht and a lifetime of sunsets."

"And I understand you don't think she was culpable in any way."

"That's right."

"Not in the least?"

"Her ethics may be suspect, but hopefully none of us here are on trial for our ethics."

The chief looked at Whalen and back at me.

"I can understand you being rather fond of her, Mr. Devlin."

"I've been known to make poor decisions when it comes to women, sir, and I'll probably do it again, but I don't think she's guilty in any of this, other than by association."

"Humph. Well, I have to admit. Things seem to have gotten rather complicated. Shall I assume you have a theory to explain the rest of it?"

"I only know what I've heard in the news, and what I've surmised by reading between the lines."

"I'm all ears."

I shrugged.

"My guess is, Al-Hamad and his bad seed in the FBI had placed, or had intended to place, some sort of top-secret technology into that shipping container bound for Liberia."

"Why Liberia?"

"I suspect Liberia was merely a transit point. As to what kind of technology and its ultimate destination? Who knows? Perhaps some drone blueprints destined for Iran? Or Russia? Or both? Again, I'm only guessing. I really have no idea."

"And that's it?"

"Well, making another educated guess, let's say the Feds had become aware of the plot and decided to let things play out, just to see where it would lead them. So they substitute bogus blueprints or whatever and put Vanderhof up as a front man, expecting they could make a few careers out of this bust, using Al-Hamad and his FBI pal to catch some bigger fish."

"I'll buy that as a working theory. Go on."

"Then Colby comes along, mucking up the works with his plans to divert the container down to a cartel in Mexico, and Vanderhof, who becomes aware of Colby's plans, starts to lock horns with him. It would be at this point that Colby trots out their dirty laundry and I imagine you can figure the rest of it from there."

"And do you believe any of that?"

"I don't have enough facts to go on, but I think Colby's infatuation with Audrey and that two million dollars are enough to explain his motives. I'm guessing there was another eight million or so on the other end of the transaction, once the guns had been delivered. Nacho was definitely looking for his shit — if you'll excuse my use of the street parlance — and was ready to kill to get it. As for the Feds, the Russians and Vanderhof, I presume all of them in their own way had learned about the existence of the flash drive, Vanderhof worrying that Colby might have saved their secrets onto it, the Russians, thinking it would lead them to their stuff and the Feds, justifiably concerned that someone, somewhere might learn what they were actually up to. According to an article I read in the Times last week, nuclear arms technology was involved so who knows what was really going on. I suppose we again come to the place where folks like me aren't supposed to know or understand. Anyway, I'd bet my house that the truth is somewhere in what I've just described."

"And our murders? Who do you think was behind all of that?"

"I'm convinced that Vanderhof killed Connie. Did he kill Colby too? Or, more precisely, did he have Dick and Tom do it for him? Without the ballistics, I'm at a disadvantage but it's hard for me to imagine Nacho and his pals killing Colby in the way that it went down. You would have found his body out in the desert somewhere, with signs of torture. They wanted what they had paid for, or their money back, and you don't go about killing people before you get those answers."

"And Mr. Black?"

"I suspect that once Colby had threatened Vanderhof with their long-held secret, Vanderhof saw danger everywhere he turned. It was bad enough that Colby and Doris and Audrey already knew the truth. All Vanderhof needed was for Audrey to spill the beans to Cliff. Certainly, if Dick and Tom had been listening in on my phone calls with Cliff, they would have suspected he knew about the little girl."

"Do you think he did?" the chief said, interrupting me.

"He knew something. Audrey had scribbled a note on her desk calendar. Something that was alarming enough for Cliff to have called and hired me."

"Did you ever ask Audrey what that was?"

"Yes. When I first cornered her out in the desert but she seemed sincerely puzzled as to what it might be."

"And you believed her?"

I shrugged again.

"I'd take everything she says with a grain of salt, but in this case, I think she was being truthful. As she said, she scribbled dozens of idle thoughts on her calendar over the course of a month. The point is, Vanderhof feared that Cliff knew the truth, so when he heard that Cliff was planning to stop by my office, he had Dick and Tom get rid of him. All that would explain why Dick and Tom were chasing Audrey around."

"And Rick Duncan? Do you think he was killed for the same reason?"

"As far as I know, Rick was clueless about Vanderhof's little girl, but avaricious fellow that he was, when Doris shared her suspicions, that Vanderhof had killed Connie, Rick played a hand, guessing that Vanderhof could be muscled and losing his life for trying."

The chief shook his head.

"Quite a mess, isn't it?"

"Yes. Quite a mess, sir."

"Does any of this ever make you angry, Mr. Devlin?"

"Which? The murders or that someone gets to play a game of monopoly with my life?"

The chief took off his glasses and rubbed his eyes.

"Both, I suppose." He put his glasses back on. "Never mind. I'm not sure why I asked you that question."

"I'll answer it anyway. Sure it makes me angry, but I doubt my feelings matter all that much, because someone will go on playing a game of monopoly with my life, no matter how much it angers me. Anyway, you start down that road, and pretty soon you're sending off mail bombs.

Having grown distracted by the newspaper article again, the chief's eyes snapped back at hearing me speak of mail bombs.

"Well, Mr. Devlin. I suppose that brings us back to you and the laws you've broken."

The chief looked at both Whalen and the DA.

"Gentlemen, either one of you care to say a word?"

"I've already told Michael how I feel," Whalen said with a nod in my direction. "I'd just as soon put him behind bars for some of the shit he pulled. On the other hand, he was right about Vanderhof and in the end I guess we're all on the same side of the playing field in this thing."

"Mr. Giovanni? Your take?"

"I don't know what the hell Pat's thinking here. I've lost count of how many times Devlin ran afoul of the law along the way."

"Well, Mr. Devlin. Anything you have to bargain with in return?"

"I don't know if it's much of a bargaining chip, sir, but I do have one issue of my own to resolve."

"And that would be?"

"That pile of money sitting on your desk. If I don't get some cover, I'm sure to have that Mexican cartel busting down my door any day now. And I'm sure the same can be said of Audrey. I assume you don't want another murder or two on your hands."

"What would you suggest that we do?"

"Parade the money around in front of the press. Say you found it at Colby's place and believe he was into some kind of smuggling scheme. Dream up whatever story you like, just as long as Nacho and his pals are relieved of any notion that I still have their cash. Detective Whalen and Mr. Giovanni can take a victory lap in the process and everyone goes home happy. More or less."

"Like hell," the DA said.

The chief held up a hand.

"Mr. Giovanni, I'm not so sure you have anything that will stick in a court of law when it comes to Mr. Devlin, so unless you're absolutely certain of your hand, I would encourage you to cut a deal here. Clearly Mr. Devlin had nothing to do with this money and he's right. We don't need any more dead bodies on our hands. What do you think?"

Giovanni looked around the room, grousing.

"Yeah, all right," he said. "But just so you know, Devlin. Next time you pull this kind of crap, I'll throw the book at you."

I nodded penitently.

"Well, it appears that you've escaped with your life one more time, Mr. Devlin. You're free to go."

The chief stood up and shook my hand, then Jim's.

"Sorry to take your time, counselor. I suppose there was always a chance your client would need to post bail. Oh, and please hold off making any statements to the press until we've had our turn in front of the microphones."

33

Jim and I nodded and walked out into what was left of the afternoon. The press instantly surrounded us. Jim gave them the usual line, about being unable to comment on an ongoing investigation, and nodded in the direction of the English Cottage. We dashed across the street and slipped in through the front door. As always, the interior was cool and darkened, and mostly empty at four o'clock in the afternoon.

Jim and I held up our drinks when they arrived. His was Scotch. Mine was club soda.

"To broken hearts and fallen soldiers," I said.

We drank.

"You can't help but feel sorry for Cliff Black," Jim said. "No idea he was playing with fire."

"Are we talking about Vanderhof or his wife?"

"Vanderhof," Jim said. "Perhaps both."

"Yeah, I'm inclined to cut Audrey some slack. At least legally speaking. Vanderhof too, for that matter. It did seem that he preferred negotiations to blood. Maybe he was just having a hard time figuring out where to fit Roy Orbison onto his payroll?"

Jim smiled.

"You suspect Vanderhof was offering Audrey the same deal he offered you?"

"I do. It wasn't such a bad deal, if you could dispense with your conscience."

"You think Audrey has one?"

"That I don't know. The romantic in me would like to think so. She did seem truly disturbed to learn that Vanderhof had killed his little girl."

"And you still think that Vanderhof had Colby killed."

"I do."

"And Rick."

"I do. Vanderhof had Dick and Tom following me around. That means they would have seen Rick head down to the shipyard that night. Vanderhof must have known he was getting close to the truth. Or at least feared as much."

"To be a fly on the wall," Jim said.

"Yeah. The truth is, I'm beginning to think that there are some things in this world I *don't* want to know or understand."

We drank and watched the world go by.

"I'll be interested to see what happens to Dick and Tom," Jim said after a spell.

"Yeah. 'They all worked for the company once.' I suppose that one thing pisses me off more than anything. We all knew each other from working for the company. Like that gets you a pass from obeying the law."

Jim had a sip of his Scotch with a wry look my way.

"Yeah yeah, counselor. I've been known to bend the rules along the way, but mine are done for a higher calling."

Jim laughed one of his rare laughs now.

"Well, on that note," he said and tossed back the rest of his Scotch.

"Bastard," I said and followed him outside.

The summer afternoon was hurrying towards dusk. I was going home alone. Jim was going home to Doris. Jim and Doris. That was something to smile about but it probably had a better shot than most love affairs. Doris loved to dote and Jim was really a big, lovable hound dog inside, despite his laconic nature and razor-sharp wit.

"Thanks for all your help," I told him. "All your lawyerly moralizing aside."

He smiled.

394

"Come up for dinner some night."

"Oh yeah, and be a spectator to your newfound domestic bliss."

"Bring Audrey."

"You're getting colder."

"Not to meddle, my friend, but why don't you give it a chance."

"I don't know. I'm broke and at risk of losing my home. I figure I don't look so good when all the guns stop going off."

Jim patted me on the back.

"I have a nice paying job for you when you get back from Baja."

"Thanks. I could use it."

"I guess we'll see you in the morning, then."

"Oh yeah, Steve. Yeah, I'll hang around until you get back with him."

I gave Jim a final fist bump and started down the block towards my office in the now dusky light. What a mess. I could not seem to find justice in it, no matter which way I turned. Ditto enduring love. When it came to romance, my mantra had long been, know your own heart, then pick someone to match those characteristics. There were no guarantees, either way, but at least if you had some of the most basic characteristics in common, the romance had a fighting chance. Without that, it was doomed before you ever pulled anchor.

So, where did that leave me? Everything led me back to a woman who did not want my affections in return. Like most everyone else in this world, I seemed to want something I could not have.

I went home and crawled in bed that night with an old paperback of some early Hemingway stories, before the booze had made him sloppy. Bullfighters, whores and lost souls. It was real, it was sad, it was often funny, and perhaps a great deal more like my own life than I cared to admit. It was some comfort to know that I wasn't the only lost soul on the planet.

I awakened the next morning to find the heat had returned with a vengeance, but dry heat this time. People were always saying that dry heat was better than sultry heat but I died a bit, either way. With the eucalyptus trees out there sounding like rattlesnakes, I had dreams of a brisk day on Baffin Island.

That I was headed south may have seemed paradoxical, but that was one of the joys of the Baja peninsula. It was narrow enough to feel like an island, the sea along that stretch of coastline beyond my trailer turning blustery every afternoon, with white caps and gulls and breaking surf, as far as the eye could see.

I packed for the trip and started down to my office. My plan was to hit the road as soon as Steve was back safe and sound. The idea of heading south was met with both gladness and a touch of anxiety in my heart. I loved heading out on the road all alone, but I knew the ache of loneliness was waiting for me out there too, just a few miles farther down the coast from my solitude.

Either way, I looked forward to the escape from modern society, if only for a spell. Once past all the border crap and the port of Ensenada, you entered a world where people still lived off the land and what they brought home from the sea. They kept time by the sun and the moon and the stars and measured their wealth by the sound of goats and happy children in their yard. The idea of gross median income had never entered their minds.

The phone was ringing when I opened the door to my office. Without any hurry, I went to answer it. Another marital case. Another troubled man looking for help. I told him I was busy and offered up a referral. I was done with other people's broken hearts. I had enough work keeping up with my own.

With a notepad in front of me, I set about making a list of loose ends to resolve before I left. While I did, I heard a knock on the door.

"Come in."

The glassman poked his head in through the partially opened door.

"Sorry for not calling first. The glass came in and I had an emergency repair right down the street. Figured I'd take a chance and see if you were around."

"No problem. Glad to have it done."

While the two of us busied ourselves with our separate tasks, Lars, the landlord, popped in. He had heard the news on his favorite news channel and wanted to get the dirt first hand.

By the way Lars dressed and the car he drove, you would never have taken this tall, Slavic looking fellow to be filthy rich. You would never have taken him to be a cheapskate by his sunny countenance, but he was.

Betty must have heard his voice and marched down the hall, Butch on her heels. Lars did a double take on Butch. Betty ignored that and started in about the crumbling plaster walls and fading carpets.

"Why don't you drop a dime on this place, Lars? It looks like hell."

Cornered, Lars promised to have the hundred-year-old carpets cleaned and someone would be by to look at the walls. I smelled a rent increase but fine. I was headed down to Curacao. Somewhere far, far away. Fifty years old and my heart was still wandering over the next hill.

The mailman came in and joined the party. He too had caught the story on the news.

"Let's hear all the gory details," he said while sorting through the mail.

"Are you familiar with Greek tragedy?" I asked him.

"A bit, why?"

"Oh, just figured I could save myself a lot of hot air."

Seeing that no one was satisfied, I offered up an abbreviated version of the tale. Lars started backing out the door the minute I was done. Betty gave chase. I heard her putting the screws to him as he retreated down the hallway. Betty came back in.

"Cheapskate," she said.

I smiled and reminded my ersatz native with the palm fronds to hold the mail while I was gone. He agreed and headed out the door.

"Well, all done," glassman said.

He handed me an invoice. I wrote him a check.

"Sounds like there's been a lot of excitement around here lately," he said on his way out the door.

"Makes you appreciate the peace and calm all the more."

He did a double take on the check before slipping it into his pocket.

"Thanks."

"Thank you."

"Should I leave it open?"

"Yeah, sure."

He left. Betty and I were alone. She took a seat with Butch in her lap.

"Oh, your key," I said and handed it to her.

"Wonder where that Steve is?" she said.

I glanced at the clock.

"Should be here any minute."

We were still chatting about the excitement of the past few days when the door to the street opened. Footsteps came up the stairs. A moment later, Steve appeared with Jim. Butch leapt out of Betty's lap and fell all over Steve's shoes. I thought the little bugger was going to wiggle right out of his fur.

"Who gave him the haircut?" Steve said, glancing up.

I nodded in Betty's direction.

"He looks cute," she said.

Steve continued his reunion with Butch while shaking his head. I gave Steve a hug when he finally stood up.

"You all right?"

"Oh god, it's such a relief to be out of that place but...you know..."

"I know."

"Oh man. Nothing's ever going to be the same."

"Give it time."

"Yeah, I know. Give it time."

Steve looked down at Butch.

"This is all I have left of her now."

With those words, he broke down and wept.

"Aw, come here," Betty said and gave Steve a big hug.

Butch sat there watching all this with a forlorn look on his face.

"Oh Butchie, come here," Steve said, pulling away.

And like Zen, Butch was all blissful again.

"I've got his bowls and leash down at my office," Betty said and ran off.

While she was gone, Steve pulled out a check and handed it to me. It was for ten grand.

"Steve, you don't need to do this."

"Are you kidding? I would have paid a million dollars to have my name cleared."

He put a hand to my shoulder and shook me.

"Please. I hope you're not mad but Jim told me you were struggling…So will that get you caught up on your mortgage?"

"Yeah. More than caught up."

"Good. Believe me, old friend. I can never repay you, so anything else you need, just ask."

"No, no, this is more than enough, Steve. Thanks."

"Thank you. You know, while I was sitting there in that jail, I kept thinking of all the things we used to do as kids. Remember going up that storm drain on summer days with our torches?"

"Yeah, all the bats. Scared the girls right into our laps."

"God, to go back and do it all over again," Steve said.

"We had a time, didn't we?"

"Yeah we did."

Betty came back in and Butch obediently accepted his harness.

"Well, are you ready?" Steve said to Jim.

Jim nodded.

"We'll see you soon, Michael. And thanks again for going to bat for me."

"You know I did it gladly."

"Thanks. And thanks for looking after Butch, Betty."

"He's a joy, so any time you need a break, you just drop him off with me. Isn't that right, Butchie?"

They had a last little love fest and Steve started out the door with his miniature poodle. Only in Laurel Lagoon.

"Well, back to work," Betty said and trotted off in her Barbie Doll shoes.

I sat back down in my empty office. Remembering the mail, I went through it. A check was there from Jake.

Well, I'll be damned. My ship had come in. It was more like a skiff, but at least I was afloat.

The phone rang, breaking me from my thoughts. I saw it was Kenny and looked out my window at him. He was smiling at me from his window across the street.

"Was there any reward money?" he asked once I had answered.

"Kenny, Kenny." I snapped my fingers several times. "I'm trying to place the name."

He laughed. I waved the two checks at him.

"Far out," he said. "You mean I'll actually get paid."

"Yeah. I'll have to deposit them and let the funds cure overnight. I'll make sure Teresa takes care of everything tomorrow."

"Far out."

"Yeah, thanks for your help, Kenny. Let's see what kind of mischief we can cook up when I get back from Mexico."

"You're heading south, huh?"

"I've been heading south for a long, long time, my friend."

We both had a good long laugh.

"All right," I said once I could catch my breath. "I'll have Teresa take care of you."

I hung up and immediately called her about the checks.

"Oh, and can you remember to water the plants while I'm gone?"

"Of course," she said.

I said goodbye and got off.

That left three items on my check list and while I waited around to resolve one of them, I went online and pulled up a number for that job opportunity down in Curacao. A gentleman in Key West answered my call. He ran a shipping concern. Problems came up from time to time. No, it wasn't a steady position, and yes, he'd be happy to put me on a list for occasional work. Just send him a résumé. I said I would and hung up.

I was down to Caitlin and Elfie and had put off making both of those calls.

In Elfie's case, there had been an impulse to reach out to her the day after Dirk's arrest. Then indecision had set in. Was I welcome in the middle of her grief? Unsure of that answer, I had decided to let her make the first move and that's where things stood, with me waiting one more time for Elfie to reach out before I headed south.

34

I was about to give up when the door downstairs opened again and the sound of high heels started up the stairs. My heart fluttered, with both anticipation and dread. Beauty and romance were on the prowl, but so were my mixed-up emotions. And there was the sad fate of Elfie's little girl.

For my part, I had come to accept that I only loved one woman in this world and every other emotional entanglement came up hard against that wall to die. And how did you admit that to the next woman in line? To do so was to say a love affair was over before it had begun. To keep it inside was to live a lie. I was screwed either way.

And yet Elfie was like silk sheets to a beggar and as soon as I saw her silhouette, I got up to open the door. Elfie looked like she had stepped out of the '40s with a cloche hat draped over her silky blonde hair. I let her in, closed the door and gave her a hug. She wept quietly. When she was done, she looked back up at me. There was a deep sigh.

"I have tried so hard not to think about my little girl, but now I see her everywhere I turn. I feel her last moments of fear and confusion as the very people she had trusted most in this world shook the life out of her."

My eyes filled with tears. Elfie reached up to touch them.

"Oh, you dear sweet man."

"I feel it too."

"Oh, you. Come here."

She hugged me for a long time.

"Do you know what happened?" she said, pulling back to look at me.

I shook my head and kept to myself what I already knew.

"They had buried her little body under a concrete form at Dan's shipping yard. They were already planning to pour a slab a few days after Dirk had killed her and figured no one would ever find the body."

Elfie fought back tears again as she related the story and how they had dug up what remained of her little baby.

"God, I was so conflicted about doing it. A part of me just wanted to leave her in peace."

Elfie looked up at me for answers. I shook my head.

"No?" she said.

"No, it was the right thing to do."

"It was, wasn't it?"

"Of course. You had to give your daughter a proper burial. And the police have to do their job too, as much as it hurts."

Elfie sighed and looked out the window.

"You know, Dirk's got a team of the best lawyers in the country working on this case for him. I'm so afraid he'll walk."

She again looked up at me for answers, and I again shook my head. I didn't think he would, but putting him behind bars would be a long and costly affair, and I wasn't up for telling Elfie as much. The fact was, when you went back to review Vanderhof's confession in my office that night, he hadn't confessed to much of anything, not even to the death of his own daughter. He was going to have a hard time beating that rap, but he stood a 50/50 chance of beating the Connie McPherson charge. Meanwhile, even though the Feds had yet to catch up with Nacho, they were already painting a picture that placed the murders of Rick and Cliff and Colby in his lap. With a team of good lawyers and an insanity plea, Vanderhof might be looking at as little as three years in a low security prison. With good behavior, he could be back on the streets in eighteen months.

"God, I hate being vindictive, but I hope they hang him," Elfie said as she dabbed at her tears.

I gave her another hug, equally reluctant to speak up on the subject of vengeance. Some Christians, we Americans, always an eye for an eye with us, ready to throw the first stone. Draw and quarter folks like we were living by the Old Testament prophets, not by the words of Jesus. Not that I thought Vanderhof deserved much forgiveness or compassion, but all of us had been forgiven more times than we deserved.

Elfie looked up at me again.

"I have this feeling you're going away."

"For a few days."

"They say it will take another week or so for the forensics. Before I can bury her. Will you be there?"

"Sure."

"I'd appreciate that."

"I'll be sure to get back in time."

"Oh God," she said and threw herself in my arms. "Look at us. I can't forget my little girl and you can't seem to forget this other woman."

"It'll be all right."

"No. Nothing will ever be the same again. For either of us."

"Don't talk like that. I'll be back as soon as you need me."

"Will you?"

"Sure."

She pulled away.

"You're going down to your little place in Baja, aren't you?"

"Yes. I think I'll go mad if I don't."

Elfie kissed me. She kissed me good.

"Please call me while you're down there," she said. "I've missed talking with you."

"I will. I've missed you too."

She smiled sadly and went out the door without another word. What was I going to tell the poor woman?

"Nothing will ever be the same again."

I had been thinking to say, don't worry, time heals all wounds, but it had yet to heal mine.

I was about to get up from my desk when Betty paused at my door with Leonard beside her.

"Some doll," Betty said.

Leonard raised his eyebrows.

"That was Mrs. Vanderhof."

"Oh Jesus," Betty said. "If I ever get my hands on her ex, I'll cut his balls off."

I glanced at Leonard and winked. Better watch your step there, buddy. He seemed to get my drift.

"We're going down to lunch," Betty said. "Care to join us?"

"No. I'm heading south here in a minute."

"As in south of the border?"

"Yes."

"Must be pretty down there."

"It is, but not your kind of place. No bingo or slot machines."

That got a smile out of Leonard.

"By the way, if you see anybody breaking in while I'm gone, make sure they take everything."

Leonard smiled again. Wow. A record. Two in one day.

"How long?" Betty said.

"I'll be back in about a week."

"Adios," she said.

Once I heard them go out the front door, I headed out the back. My car was in the alley. My bags were in the trunk. It was getting on towards noon. That was always a good time to head south. You were sure to miss both the morning and evening rush hour traffic around San Diego. With stopping at the border to gas up and exchange a few dollars for pesos, and a few pit stops along the way, I would be pulling into Socorro around six o'clock.

If arriving there at the end of the day was accompanied by too much loneliness, I would stop at the government hotel for one night. The staff would come out to greet me as if we were old friends and it always warmed my heart to see the blue sea breaking out past the open plaza at the center of the hotel, with the miles and miles of white sand dunes rolling down the coast.

The hotel was usually empty save for a handful of gringos heading south or coming back the other way. Given the scarcity of souls, if you dined at the hotel, it was only natural to say hello from your table to theirs. Next thing you knew, folks were pulling up chairs and swapping tall tales. It was enough to keep you from going mad when you returned to your room at night with nothing but a book and the sound of surf breaking off for a hundred miles.

Heading south on Pacific Coast Highway a few minutes later, I put on a Django Reinhardt CD. The old honkytonk piano hit the intro and *Stardust* started to play. I dialed the number and with each ring, my heart beat more wildly. With every interval, I was ready to hang up.

Then I heard the voice. It was magical. It was funny. She always said hello as if she didn't know who it was, when she had a caller ID with font as big as a senior citizen's Bible.

"Guess who?" I said.

"You're under water," she said and we laughed.

It was a stupid gag, about the way a person sounded while driving in their car and talking on a cell phone. And like all our gags, we had been rehashing it for years, and if we rehashed it for a thousand lifetimes, we would never stop getting a kick out of it.

"I'm heading down to my trailer," I said.

"You are?" she said.

"Yeah, but I was thinking of you."

"You were?"

"Yeah. I'm always thinking of you."

I fought back the emotions.

"I can't seem to kick you, doll, and I guess I'll always feel this way. For all the millions and billions of lifetimes to come, I'll still be in love with you."

"That's a lot of lifetimes," she said.

"Yeah it is. It's a long time to love someone so dearly and never even get a chance to hold their hand."

She was silent and I dreaded what I was about to say next, but said it anyway.

"I'd love to see you when I get back."

There was a pause before she finally said, "Sure."

"Sure, Caitlin? You'd like to grab a bite to eat with me and say hello?"

"Sure," she said.

I laughed, at which point, she thought I was laughing at her and that was enough to get her nose tweaked all over again. And given the reasons for my laughter, I was not at liberty to explain myself. She seemed to view me the way I viewed Elfie and Audrey, and every other woman in this world.

Yeah, sure. Whatever. She could take it or leave it.

If only she would tell me what she really thought, but she never would. I assumed she just hated being made vulnerable. Maybe she already felt vulnerable and just hated admitting to that fact. It was a wonderful bit of theater, either way.

"I don't know what to think anymore, Caitlin. I've tried to forget you but I can't. You're always in my heart. You're everywhere I look."

"Well, I'll never understand how it gets to this point."

"To what point?"

"That we can't just pick up the phone to talk."

"Because, if I don't call you, you never call me. Because you won't see me anymore. You won't let me back into your life, the way it used to be."

There was silence.

"Just call me when you get back, okay Michael?"

"Fine," I said with mock petulance and she laughed.

"You're really starting to sound underwater now. Where are you?"

"Just driving by the fortune teller's place right now. I could stop by and give you a kiss before leaving."

"You can't."

"Sure I can."

"You can't. I've got too much stuff to do."

"It's summer, Caitlin."

"Oh boy, here we go."

"What?"

"Whenever you call me Caitlin, I know you're getting mad."

"Must you always reduce my emotions to a singularity, dear? You know, I have more than one of them."

"Okay, I've got to go," she said.

I was about to explain my side of things a bit further when I heard, "goodbye, goodbye" and the phone went dead. I threw it on the floor.

Good god, the grief. It knew no bounds. Any attempt to express a contrary point of view with the woman and she hung up on you. Not that there had ever been any real hope. It was clear to me now that things would never change. Some sort of spiritual bliss existed between our two souls, but that bliss was never to be realized on this earth, at least not in this lifetime. Upon my return, Caitlin would have this or that crisis come up — her work, her dog, her birds, her aging mother — all of them entirely legitimate, separately or collectively, but somehow she would never quite find time to see me and the senselessness of it would drive me mad. Two people, who loved each other so dearly, but not one moment shared together.

Stardust came to an end and I played it again. A few bars later, I slammed my fist against the steering wheel.

Why? Why did it have to be this way? The woman made a saint of me. I knew eternity at the sound of her voice. Why am I left here with these dear, dear dreams, forever beyond my reach?

The coastline south of Doheny came into view around the next bend. Such beauty and all the grief of the past few years came pouring out of me at the sight of it, my emotions as ephemeral as the waves breaking down that open stretch of coastline looking south.

About The Author

The product of an Irish/Italian family, Mr. Corcoran was transplanted as a boy from the clapboard New England of his youth to the stucco subdivisions that steadily displaced the old ranches and orange groves south of Los Angeles during the 1960s. True to his rebellious nature and the folk music/coffee house idealism that helped shape his early worldview, Mr. Corcoran chose to resist the Vietnam War, was a man without a country for several years and can count incarceration in a Mexican prison as one of his many colorful experiences from that era.

Having pursued a love of reading and writing in various forms all his life, Mr. Corcoran finally took that passion seriously around the turn of the millennium and has dedicated the remainder of his days to authorship. The author recently returned to the New England of his youth and currently resides on the coast of Rhode Island.

www.ingramcontent.com/pod-product-compliance
Lightning Source LLC
Chambersburg PA
CBHW051057030726
47504CB00006B/1674